DEVIL'S BREED

TRACKDOWN VI

MICHAEL A. BLACK

ROUGH
EDGES
PRESS

**ROUGH
EDGES
PRESS**

Devil's Breed

Paperback Edition
Copyright © 2022 Michael A. Black

Rough Edges Press
An Imprint of Wolfpack Publishing
9850 S. Maryland Parkway, Suite A-5 #323
Las Vegas, Nevada 89183

roughedgespress.com

Paperback ISBN 978-1-68549-172-7
eBook ISBN 978-1-68549-171-0
LCCN 2022945851

DEVIL'S BREED

DEDICATION

To our brave service members, and to those who were killed on August 26, 2021 at Hamid Kazarl International Airport in Kabul, Afghanistan.

They gave their all for our country. Let us never forget their courage and heroism.

Lance Cpl. David L. Espinoza, Marines
Sgt. Nicole Gee, Marines
Staff Sgt. Darin T. Hoover, Marines
Staff Sgt. Ryan C. Knauss, Army
Cpl. Hunter Lopez, Marines
Lance Cpl. Rylee J. McCollum, Marines
Lance Cpl. Dylan R. Merola, Marines
Lance Cpl. Kareem M. Nikoui, Marines
Cpl. Daegan W. Page, Marines
Sgt. Johanny Rosario Pichardo, Marines
Cpl. Humberto A. Sanchez, Marines
Lance Cpl. Jared M. Schmitz, Marines
Hospital Corpsman 2nd Class Maxton W. Soviak, Navy

We few, we happy few, we band of brothers,
For he today that sheds his blood with me
Shall be my brother.

Henry V
Act IV, Scene 3
William Shakespeare

CHAPTER 1

MIXED MARTIAL ARTS FIGHTING ACADEMY
PHOENIX, ARIZONA

The focus mitt hung in the air for a split-second before Wolf smashed a hard left hook into the padded surface. Georgie Patton, his assistant trainer, grinned as his arm went flying off to the side. Wolf followed up with a right hand that snapped into the focus mitt on the other hand.

"That's what I like to see," Reno Garth yelled from the side of the gym's octagon. "Combinations. Now you're looking good. Pick up the pace."

Georgie skipped to the left like a black wraith and held the pad on his right hand up again.

Wolf feinted with his left and then sent a straight right into the pad. He then moved in, and since his trainer was wearing thick padding, delivered a series of alternating hooks to the body.

Kill the body and the head will die, he thought, replaying the old boxing adage in his mind. Truer words have never been spoken.

Droplets of sweat cascaded off his face and bare forearms. The matted floor now had numerous standing puddles and Wolf felt his foot slide a little as he stepped in one of them. This sent him off balance slightly, but he recovered in an instant.

"Good, good," Georgie said. "Keep your balance."

Balance was the key, or rather never being off balance, even if you missed a punch.

"Hey, Steve, you all right?" Reno yelled in a semi-mocking tone. "You're looking a bit shaky all of a sudden."

Wolf didn't answer or even glance toward the other man. He knew it was only part of the drill... Reno's way to reinforce the habit of remaining completely focused on your opponent, even in a training session like this one. Reno often threw in a diversionary comment or question trying to get Wolf drop his guard, to lose his concentration.

After another minute or so, Reno banged his palm on the solid, black cyclone fencing barrier surrounding the matted surface and yelled, "Time."

Wolf now was able to lower his arms. Each felt like it weighed 500 pounds. His breathing was ragged, even with his mouth fully open now. The mouthpiece was still fixed in place, and Wolf reached up to remove it.

The air, stale as it was in the crowded gym, tasted sweet and fresh.

The images of the few people who had gathered outside the octagon to watch the training session gradually came into Wolf's focus. When he was inside, whether it was in training or for real, everything outside became virtually invisible. Silent, too, except for the sound of Reno's voice. It somehow always managed to filter in above the noise of the crowd, sort of like the strange filtering sounds of gunfire in a fire fight. Wolf had been in plenty of those.

He was clad in his fighting garb, his fingerless padded gloves, a pair of tight-fitting black compression shorts, and nothing more. His feet were bare. It was getting too close to fight night to train any other way now, and he wanted to once again become accustomed to the near-nudeness in which he'd be fighting. It was all about preparation and planning and peaking at the right moment. At this point in the training, he was feeling pretty close to perfect, but was dreading telling Reno about tomorrow. The fight was only four days away—Saturday night in Vegas.

Training was like a trek up the mountain, and he felt that he was almost at the top.

Georgie had slipped off the mitts and picked up a towel. He blotted Wolf's face first, and then began wiping his shoulders, arms and chest. Wolf took in a few deep breaths and struggled to get his breathing back to normal.

"Reno, this guy Shultz is known for switching stances," Georgie said. "We need to do some more work on that."

"Yeah, yeah," Reno answered. "But my main man here's not gonna have any trouble knocking old Schultzy out, are you, Steve?"

"I'll give it my best shot," Wolf said.

The rough, textured material of the towel felt stimulating against his skin.

"Forty seconds," Reno said, holding up his stopwatch. "Forty-five… Fifty… Get ready."

Stepping back, Georgie slapped the towel over the top of the cyclone barrier, bent down, grabbed the two focus mitts and slipped them back on.

"Time," Reno shouted.

Wolf lifted his weary arms into guard position and began the circling movements again as Georgie moved to Wolf's left with a dancer's grace. Concentrating on an intercepting course, Wolf slammed a solid combination into the pads once more. Reno told Georgie to switch to southpaw, and the nimble black man adjusted his stance so that his right arm was in the foremost position. Wolf immediately stared circling back to the other man's right side, taking care to keep his advanced left foot on the outside of Georgie's right foot, dotting the perpendicular focus mitt with a double jab.

"Let's see you mix in some leg kicks," Reno said.

Wolf obliged, slamming his lead left foot against Georgie's padded right thigh.

Georgie did a slight stutter-step and Wolf brought his right leg up with a front kick to his trainer's copiously padded abdomen. The kick was so powerful that it caused Georgie to grunt emphatically as the air rushed out of him. He scurried straight back and as Wolf advanced to follow up with some punches Georgie crossed his arms and muttered, "Time out."

Wolf immediately halted.

"Come on, man," Reno said. "It's no time to take a break."

Georgie was still bent over, holding up his hand.

"Damn, that last one felt like a sledgehammer," he said, grinning. "How's about you give this old man a rest and get in here yourself?"

Reno laughed. "Fat chance. Now let's go. We got way too much time on the clock to be lollygagging."

Georgie took in a deep breath and nodded. "Okay."

He brought the pads up again and Wolf went to work, smacking each one with alternating punches, but held back this time, not putting his full force behind the blows.

Reno bellowed, "You playing patty-cake, or what?"

Mixing in a few kicks, Wolf continued his circular movement to the left, shooting out a series of jabs and straight rights, as well as alternating the punches with some kicks. Georgie held the right focus pad out at head level and Wolf snapped a roundhouse kick upward. His instep made a smacking sound, like the crack of a whip, as it collided with the pad.

"Okay," Reno said. "Time."

Wolf knew this round must have been way over the regulation five minutes, but he wasn't complaining. The harder you worked in training, the better off you'd be once the bell rang for real. He walked over to the side and leaned against the fence, pulled out his mouthpiece again, and continued to drip perspiration onto the mat. Once again, he gradually become aware the small audience and the plethora of ambient sounds: the cacophony of weights clanging and thumping as they were lifted and then dropped to the floor, the staccato rhythm of the speed-bags bouncing against the backboards, and the sharp exhalations of the gym's other participants smacking punch after punch into the heavy-bags. Instead of the usual heavy rock, rap, or country music that was alternately played every day, today Barbie had put on a CD of Christmas songs.

Burl Ives was urging everyone to have "A Holly-Jolly Christmas."

Well, Wolf thought. *It is December after all, albeit early in the month.*

But there was no fragrance of evergreen or mistletoe in the air. Instead, it was a mixture of masculine odors—sharp testosterone-laced perspiration and foul breath, composing the classic training gym's smell.

Reno was on the other side of the other side of the octagonal cage now, his face only inches from Wolf's.

"What the hell were you doing?" Reno asked.

Wolf didn't reply, still trying to catch his breath, but it was getting easier.

"You were phoning it in the last half of the round," Reno continued. "You couldn't have knocked out my grandmother with them punches."

"She looking for work as a sparring partner?"

"Don't get smart. This is all about getting ready, about peaking at the right time." Reno paused and snorted. "Hell, the damn fight's only a couple of days away, and we took it on short notice. Again."

"Saturday night in Vegas," Wolf said.

"Right," Reno said. "And today's Wednesday. You're almost there, but not quite on the razor's edge like you gotta be."

"I'll be ready."

"You'd better be," Reno said. "Remember, you're the champ. You've got the belt. Schultz is gonna be looking to take it from you. He ain't gonna be holding back. All he's gonna be thinking about is trying to separate your head from your shoulders."

Wolf nodded, but in truth he felt he was ready. His body was there, and he hadn't missed doing his roadwork since getting back from North Carolina... Over ninety days. The cut he'd sustained back in the summer during his last match was completely healed now, and he felt he was topping out in close-to-perfect condition. Even his urine was practically colorless, which was always a good sign.

"So what the hell else is bothering you?" Reno asked.

What else? Wolf reviewed the question in his mind. There was a whole bunch of stuff. His lawyer, the Great Oz, was getting ready to contest Wolf's original court martial conviction before the Military Board of Appeals. Wolf had temporarily ended his romance with Yolanda, his lady-love in Vegas, due to his ex-con status and her new job on the police department. At least he hoped it was temporary. His younger brother, Jimmy, was struggling with jump school at Fort Benning, and his mentor, Big Jim McNamara, was still doing some dangerous and unauthorized policing down on the border. Wolf was back living in the apartment above Mac's garage in Phoenix, where he'd started over again after getting out of prison, and his bank account had taken some significant hits in the past few months, mostly due to helping out his mother and uncle back home. While he'd originally looked upon this MMA career as only a temporary job, it had recently taken on a greater significance. At this point in his life, he needed the money, especially to pay off those mounting legal bills the lawyer was running up on this appeal process.

But if Oz can clear my name, Wolf thought. *It'll all be worth it.*

He recalled the incident in Iraq, the missing eight

minutes in his memory where three Iraqi nationals had been brutally killed along with one of his squad members. Another had lost a leg. And Wolf had lost everything...then served four years in Leavenworth.

"Your defense attorney didn't do you any favors," Wolf's present lawyer had told him. "But at least he had you plead under an Alford plea. We'll have that going for us in the appeal."

An Alford plea... Pleading guilty while still maintaining your innocence, feeling that the prosecution had enough evidence to find you guilty. A lot of it had to do with those missing eight minutes. In the original investigation Wolf hadn't been able to offer any explanation as to what had happened.

Head wounds will sometimes do that to you, he thought. But he'd subsequently recovered what he hoped would be the exculpatory evidence that would exonerate him. At least Oz was optimistic about that, but he always concluded with, "Of course, nothing in this business is a sure thing."

Sort of like stepping into the octagon, Wolf thought. You never know what's going to happen.

"You listening to what I'm saying?" Reno asked. "You look like you're a million miles away."

Not a million, Wolf answered in his mind. Only a few hundred. The Great Oz was based in Las Vegas.

"I'm not going to be able to make morning workout tomorrow," Wolf blurted out.

"Huh?" Reno's voice was a cross between surprise

and outrage. "Why the hell not?"

Wolf took in a deep breath and was mildly pleased to note that his respiration had pretty much returned to normal.

Tip-top condition, he told himself.

He turned to face Reno.

"I've got to help teach a class out at Best in the West," he said. "But I'll be done by late afternoon. Then I'll come by."

Looking through the metallic latticework, Reno's face twisted in confusion and concern. When he spoke his voice sounded almost like a whine.

"The fight's only three days away. And remember, we took it on short notice."

"I know," Wolf said. "You already said that."

"Well, obviously I didn't say it enough. What kind of bullshit is this, you skipping out on training?"

Wolf sighed and looked at his feet. "I'm not skipping out. I'll be here tomorrow night for sure. And you always say that it's best not to overdo it the last week or so, right?"

Reno didn't answer. Wolf knew that in some ways the fight meant more to Reno than to him. His friend was trying to vicariously regain his former MMA glory days through him. The big block letters painted in red, white, and blue on the front window of the gym still proclaimed: *RENO GARTH, MMA CHAMPION, TRAINS HERE.*

Reno had been a champion, all right, but then in

Mexico that dream had dissolved, but it had also forged an unexpected and unlikely friendship

The irony of the evolution of their relationship struck Wolf once more.

Ironic… That was the word for it, all right.

When they'd first met, Wolf and Reno were the bitterest of enemies, poised to go toe-to-toe on the street at any moment. And then the incident south of the border happened. Reno's leg was shattered by a 7.62 mm bullet, along with his aspirations of regaining his lost MMA title. His good friend was killed. And Wolf and Mac had saved Reno's life. Now he was managing Wolf's own fighting career and had steered him into the USA MMA light-heavyweight title.

For he today that sheds his blood with me shall be my brother, Wolf thought, recalling the line from Shakespeare.

"Well, hell," Reno said, his frown deepening. "Work on the damn speed bag then while I go rustle up a sparring partner for you. We've got to work on some ground techniques, too."

Wolf went to the door of the cage and stepped out. His gym shoes were by the opening and he slipped them on. Although his feet were tough and going barefoot wouldn't have bothered him, he had to take care not to step on anything that might cause a cut. That could throw his fight game off.

One of the speedbag stations was empty and Wolf positioned himself in front of it. It was one of the things he truly enjoyed. Mac had installed a speedbag in the workout section of the garage, and Wolf often used it when he was contemplating things. Just as the refrain of "Grandma Got Run Over By a Reindeer" began to play, Wolf began punching with the familiar rhythm.

In the bond of friendship that had formed, Reno had kept his end up by never divulging what had actually happened down in Mexico, even when being questioned by the FBI. CRS—can't remember shit, had been his reply through repeated interview sessions. The inquiry by the feds seemed to have run its course, with Wolf, Mac, and Reno escaping further scrutiny, until a few months ago when another interested party had dropped by the gym. Just as before, Reno had divulged nothing, and even used his contact at Phoenix PD to find out who was asking the questions. And not so coincidentally, Bill Franker, Kasey's husband, had also reported a guy named Bray filing a FOIA request on the Belize incident, allegedly for a life insurance report

Robert Bray Investigations.

Who the hell were they and why had they been nosing around asking questions at both Reno's and the FBI?

The name Bray meant nothing to Wolf, and Bray's FBI inquiry had actually been about another shooting incident farther down the line in Central America. But enough time had passed with that one that

Wolf's concern about it had all but vanished. Still, it remained a small piece of one of those niggling items that continued to bother him, however slightly.

Like having a rock in your shoe, he thought as he used alternating hands to pound the leather bag. Not really painful, but just irritating enough to throw off your stride.

And with the fight only three-and-a-half days away, Wolf knew he couldn't afford any distractions.

***

THE HUDSON MEN'S CLUB STEAM ROOM
LONG ISLAND, NEW YORK

The air was so hot that Robert Bray kept on having to take those constant, shallow breaths. Even filtered through the cloth mask, it felt like he was inhaling fire. Steam kept emanating from the metallic boiler off to the side and swirls of gossamer-like vapor hovered before him. He took a minute amount of solace in seeing that the damn lawyer was not enjoying this conference much either. In fact, Jason Abraham appeared even more uncomfortable than Bray felt.

Good, the private detective thought. *Serves him right.* Who the hell would agree to meet a client in a god damn steam room anyway? And force us to wear these stupid face coverings to boot.

Who indeed?

But that depended on the client, and this one was a doozey: Edgar Von Tillberg, the Third.

The heat seemed not to be bothering the diminutive little twerp at all; of course, he was the only one not wearing a mask. It sent a clear message: To hell with everybody else's health and comfort. He was on the uppermost tiled ledge, leaning back against the slick white tiles of the wall behind him. Bray wondered if he had assumed that position because it allowed him to gaze down upon him and Abraham like some damn king, or something. The twerp had barely said two words to them when they'd been ushered into the locker room at the private health spa. He'd been standing there naked, with a thick white towel wrapped around his waist, and told them to put their clothes and belongings in the lockers and they'd get underway once they all were inside the steam room. Even Bray's comment that he was armed didn't seem to faze the rich man.

"No need to fret," he said. "My men are always armed and they'll be standing by until we've finished."

When they'd all stripped down and walked inside, Von Tillberg was noticeably the shortest of the quartet despite his thick-soled clogs. Now the little shit had usurped the high ground and was looking at Bray and Abraham from a position of dominance. Not a bad tactic to remind everyone who was in charge.

And the presence of the massive bodyguard didn't hurt the intimidation factor, either. The big, black son of a bitch was the only one of them who wasn't completely nude under the waist-wrap towels. The guy was about the size of like a defensive lineman and wore a nylon fanny-pack that Bray knew contained a Glock 19. Instead of stripping down all the way, the big brute had only removed his shirt and pants, revealing a pair of short, black tights covering his ass and privates. The fanny-pack rested in front by the man's well-stuffed groin area, and he'd kept his designer gym shoes on was well. Abraham had explained to Bray that Von Tillberg was a fanatic about security, always fearing someone might be surreptitiously recording him. The only place he'd consent to a meeting about sensitive topics, besides one of his own offices, where people were routinely scanned and searched several times a day, was a steam room where everybody was practically naked.

But from what Abraham had said, the guy was rich enough to dictate whatever terms he wanted. Small in stature, but large in power.

Little big man, Bray thought, remembering the title of an old movie he'd seen on some streaming network while he was conducting one of the surveillances.

But it was okay. He'd jump through a few hoops for what Von Tillberg was now paying them for this gig. Bray was actually hoping to ride it into a fat bank account. He and Abraham were being paid top dollar by this exclusive client, and so far hadn't had to do shit except monitor the comings and goings of a two people, James McNamara and Steve Wolf. Observe and report, and Bray's two assistants were doing the majority of that. For once, it was like Fat City.

Von Tillberg coughed slightly.

The bodyguard's head turned.

"Some water, sir?" he asked. There were traces of some kind of foreign accent in his words, but Bray couldn't place it.

Von Tillberg nodded and the bodyguard pushed open the door and stepped out of the hot box. Through the pebbled glass of the door, Bray saw the first behemoth, the black one, mutter something to the second guard, who was standing just outside the door. That one was white, fully clothed, and almost like a twin, size-wise, of the black one. The second guard vanished and the first one stepped back inside.

"Now," Von Tillberg said. "Where was I?"

"You were asking about the details about your uncle's demise," Abraham said.

"Yes. Do go on."

"He was," the lawyer continued, "down at his estate in Belize. My associate, Marco Fallotti, was with him. Mr. Von Dien was in a contentious negotiation for an antiquated Middle Eastern artifact."

Von Tillberg made a noise that sort of sounded like

a bird squawking. Bray had to suppress his amusement.

"I know all about my uncle's rather reckless proclivities regarding the stolen artifacts. As a result, the FBI has frozen all of his Stateside assets, pending an investigation." He paused and took a deep breath. "As his principal heir, I'm not all that desperate for it to be settled, but I would like it to simply go away."

He compressed his lips as he sat in silence, his gaze fixed on the opposite wall.

Bray and Abraham exchanged looks. The lawyer had already mentioned that Von Tillberg had privately expressed his dissatisfaction with the "governmental intrusion upon the finances" at the reading of the will.

"Let's cut to the chase, shall we?" Von Tillberg ran his hands over his forehead and flicked the residual sweat outward with a flip of his hand. Bray felt some of the droplets strike him and it disgusted him. "When we spoke last you mentioned you were maintaining surveillance on the two men who'd killed him."

Bray watched as Abraham squirmed a little.

"Right. Jim McNamara and Steve Wolf. My associate, Mr. Bray, has had them under surveillance for some time, as you directed."

"Tell me again what happened," Von Tillberg said.

He wiped his brow with his fingers and again flung the moisture away with careless abandon.

"Your uncle had kidnap—" Abraham broke off in mid-sentence, and then corrected, "I mean had been *holding* McNamara's daughter at his place in Belize. She was to be his... guest until he and Wolf returned the precious artifact."

"The one that had been in the Mexican statue?" Von Tillberg said.

"Right," Abraham said. "The Lion Attacking the Nubian. It was—"

"Spare me," Von Tillberg said, rolling his eyes. "As I told you, I'm very well aware of my late uncle's idiosyncratic proclivities."

"Both Wolf and McNamara have extensive military experience." Abraham paused to swallow.

Despite the uncomfortable heat, Bray was enjoying watching the lawyer squirm as he laid on the euphemisms and tried to downplay the criminal aspects.

"They went down there with a bunch of men and forcibly took her back," Abraham said. "When your uncle and my late partner tried to flee, they shot down his helicopter with some kind of military weapon."

Von Tillberg flung away another handful of his sweat.

Bray once again felt the spray of droplets but noticed that some of them also struck the black behemoth. If he felt them, he didn't show it.

"And this was how the FBI gained possession of all the stolen artifacts?" Von Tillberg said. "And why all of his stateside assets then became frozen."

"Exactly," Abraham said.

The second bodyguard could be seen approaching through the opaque glass of the door. He pulled it open and handed a frosty plastic bottle to the black one. After using the corner of his towel to cover the cap while he twisted, the guard then handed the bottle to Von Tillberg. He removed the cap, tossed it down onto the floor, brought the bottle to his lips, and took a long, leisurely drink. The big bodyguard bent down and picked the cap up, closing it in his huge hand. When his boss lowered the bottle he looked directly at Bray.

"And where might they be now?" Von Tillberg asked. "These soldiers of fortune, McNamara and Wolf."

Bray's throat felt parched and he longed for a bit of water himself, but he knew better than to ask.

"Wolf was living in Las Vegas but has now moved back to the Phoenix area," he said. "He's training for an MMA fight that's coming up this weekend."

Von Tillberg's eyebrows jerked in unison with a slight nod of his head.

"McNamara's still down in Texas by the border. He and some friends are doing some unauthorized border security work for some private ranchers."

"Unauthorized border security work?" Von Tillberg's face took on an expression of amusement. "He's arresting illegals?"

"Yes," Bray said. "Those that they can't frighten back across the border, they turn over to the authorities."

After another long pull on the water bottle, Von Tillberg licked his lips and asked, "I imagine that's not too popular with the cartels."

"It's not. But McNamara's a former green beret. He's got extensive military training, and he's joined up with some other ex-military types. Basically, they're discouraging the cross-overs from coming across at certain locations. They've been so effective that a lot of the coyotes have simply moved to other areas to cross."

"What parts of the border?" Von Tillberg asked.

Bray told him.

The space between the diminutive man's brows furrowed slightly.

"Do you know which cartel's controlling that area?"

"Not really," Bray said. "I've heard that it might be the Cortez group."

A slight smile flickered on the rich man's lips. "Esteban Cortez?"

"You know of him?" Abraham asked.

"I've dealt with him a few times. He's not a man to be trifled with."

This didn't surprise Bray that much. He'd heard

that Von Tillberg was purported to have connections in the human trafficking world, specializing in young, nubile girls. The rich man was purported to have his own pleasure palace on some island in the Caribbean. And Cortez, one of the hot shots down in Mexico, dealt in drugs and flesh peddling.

"From what I've heard," Bray said, trying to sound nonchalant, "he most certainly is not."

"Perhaps Esteban will take care of this problem for us," Von Tillberg said. "Although I definitely don't want to ask him at this point. I really don't want to owe that man a favor."

Abraham cleared his throat and reinserted himself back into the conversation. "What action do you want us to take?"

Instead of answering, Von Tillberg took another long pull on the bottle, draining it. He then tossed it to the big black man. The bodyguard snatched in midair, showing impressive reflexes.

Big and fast, Bray thought. *I wouldn't want to tangle with that dude.*

"For the moment," Von Tillberg said, "just continue to maintain surveillances on them. At some point, I'd like to eliminate them from the equation since the FBI seems to be pursuing the entanglements my uncle was involved in with his artistic pursuits. Their testimony might provide a linkage that could prove embarrassing to me."

"As I mentioned, Wolf's got military experience, too," Bray said. "And I think you should know, he and McNamara have proved very formidable in the past. Your uncle—"

"My uncle was a pathetic old fool," Von Tillberg said. "He squandered a fortune trying to obtain antiquated pieces of onyx and granite. He had no appreciation of the finer, softer things in life."

The trace of a smile flickered on his thin lips.

Bray was unsure on what to say so he glanced at Abraham.

"Maintaining surveillance," the lawyer said. "We can do that. Anything else you'd like us to do?"

"Andre," Von Tillberg said. "Get me another water."

The black giant's head made a fractional nodding motion and he slipped through the door again to speak to the white behemoth.

"Just maintain the surveillances until I decide what to do," Von Tillberg said. "I'd like to have these two potential loose ends taken care of eventually, but I can't afford to bring any undue attention onto myself."

"We understand," Abraham said.

Bray glanced at him. This current situation was becoming way too much like the one he and Abraham had just gotten out of with the mafia don—another rich, powerful man using them as flunkies in a plan involving two murders.

And not so much the lawyer as me, Bray thought.

He had no doubt who would be left holding the bag when the smoke cleared.

"As you suggested," Abraham continued, "maybe we can work it out so that the cartel takes care of them."

The bodyguard returned with a second bottle of water, uncapped it, and handed it to Von Tillberg. He smiled and nodded as he accepted it and then glanced down at the two of them.

"Oh, how boorish of me," the rich man said. "Would either of you care for anything? If not, Andre will show you to your shower facilities."

We're being dismissed by the king, Bray thought. *He's making sure we know our place.*

But at least the job was easy so far and the money was good. And hopefully, he wouldn't have to get his hands dirty neutralizing Wolf and McNamara.

At least not just yet.

***

CASA DEL ESTE DE ESTEBAN CORTEZ
YUCATAN, MEXICO

Alfredo Carlos Rivera, also known as *El Tigre*, stood on the uppermost layer of the cement platform as he flicked the wheel of his gold-plated lighter and held the flame to the tip of the long, narrow cigar that his boss, Esteban Cortez, held between his fingers. Cortez, *El Jefe*, made a grunting acknowledgement as he rotated the tobacco-laced cylinder between his thick fingers and puffed. The bright jewels of the ring on his pinky sparkled in the sunlight. Two beautiful women, one Mexican and one Anglo wearing diaphanous gowns that left little to the imagination, sat on either side of the tall-backed wicker chair upon which Cortez was seated. He was clad in a white shirt with ruffles, a black leather vest, and light tan pants. A gold medallion, the size of a trio of American silver dollars rested at the base of his neck amongst the bushy crop of black hair visible at the shirt's open collar. The man's enormous girth, along with his outfit and the expertly trimmed black hair and full beard, gave him almost an ursine-like look. He had, in his younger days, gone by the nickname, *el oso grande*—the big bear, and had made a name for himself with his prodigious strength and ruthlessness. Now, however, time had softened him substantially, at least physically, and Rivera thought the big man now looked more like a panda.

Rivera himself was a well muscled two hundred pounds and with his free hand stroked the exquisitely coiffed mustache and beard on his broad face as he contemplated what was about to ensue. He was called *El Tigre* chiefly because of his auburn hair, which, along with his fair skin, gave him a distinct, non-Mexican appearance. People often compared his looks to that of middleweight boxer Saul "Canelo" Alvarez, but Rivera was much bigger. He stood about six-two. Those who were familiar with him, the members of the Cortez Cartel, and any others who had been unfortunate enough to challenge him, knew the *El Tigre* nickname had less to do with his looks than with his incredibly fast reflexes and tremendous strength. It was said in hushed circles that if he had indeed pursued a boxing career, like Canelo Alvarez, *El Tigre* would have been the champion of champions. As it was, he had once been a top amateur contender for the Mexican Olympic boxing team. But that was before Esteban Cortez had discovered him. It hadn't taken much to steal the young Rivera away from the hot, smelly gym in the slums of *La Ciudad de Mexico* and into the organization. He'd started out small, as a petty collector and enforcer, and quickly worked his way up the ladder. His Anglo appearance, his physical prowess, and the fact that Rivera's mother, a gringo, had taught him English, made him an invaluable asset.

So did his loyalty. Or so it seemed.

He snapped the lid of the lighter closed after Cortez winked and nodded.

Two bodyguards, both armed with Glock 19 pistols with extended magazines flanked them, and to his right, on the next level down on the cement platform, Esteban Cortez, *El Jefe's* favorite son, sat in a similar looking wicker chair just beneath that of his father. He was smoking as well, but his vice of choice was a cigarette.

Rivera smirked. He eschewed all forms of tobacco and watched as the younger Cortez eyed the exquisitely shaped bare leg of the Anglo girl rubbing his father's thigh. The tip of the son's tongue flicked over his lips in lizard-like fashion.

He wants her, Rivera thought, *but she is currently his father's favorite. I doubt he will give her to him, at least not until he tires of her. Until then, he covets with unrequited lust.*

But such was the way of life, Rivera knew. One always wanted what one could not have. Just like this hacienda. It was an enormous three-storied structure with twenty bedrooms and gold fixtures on the sinks and toilets.

The yard where they were now was around thirty yards square and the middle of the lush, grassy ground was partially paved with decorative stones, each shaped like a half circle. They radiated out from a circular center stone and led to a glistening swimming pool. A statuesque fountain featuring Poseidon riding a dolphin accompanied by two mermaids poured a continuous stream of recycling water into the clear water of the pool. The sea-king's helmet and armor were trimmed in gold which glistened in the bright sunlight. A ten-foot-high cement wall surrounded the courtyard, and swaths of bougainvillea crept upward on the side toward the top ledge. Three strands of barbed wire crept along the flat edge of the very top.

"*Alfredo,*" Cortez Sr. said. "*Diga me de la situación del borde.*"

"*Los americanos todovia nos digan algunas problemas,*" Rivera said, telling his boss of the troublesome gringos impeding the trafficking operations up north.

"*¿De donde?*"

"*Cerca de Piedras Negras.*"

Cortez frowned and puffed on his cigar before switching to English.

"*Son los mismos*—the same ones that you told me about before?"

"Yes," Rivera answered in English as well, figuring *el jefe* did not want the others privy to this part of the conversation. The knowledge of English by both him and *su hijo* was fairly good. That of the others was mostly limited to a few words like body parts, some standard broken sentences, and the barest of essentials. The Anglo girl was Russian, and although conversant in both Spanish and English, was no doubt too stoned to be paying much attention, much less something in a foreign language.

"The big guns did not frighten them?"

"No. We even shot the fifty caliber machine gun over their heads."

Cortez Sr. emitted a harsh sounding laugh and moved the Anglo girl's hand up to his crotch.

"And that did not do the trick?" he asked.

"It did not. They shot back at us."

Cortez raised an eyebrow. "They shot back… They were *la migra*? Border Patrol?"

"No. More like a private army."

Rivera shook his head as he watched the girl's probative fingers with disapproval.

¿Qué pasa? he wondered. *¿Quiere una puñeta aqui?*

The sight repulsed him. *El Jefe* was *un pelado…* Totally without dignity. And the fact that he was so ostentatiously pushing his favorite son to take over made the *el oso grande* even more despicable.

The job, the top position, should go to me, Rivera thought. *It is I who have earned it, not* el hijo gandalia.

But he said nothing.

"And tell me, what have you done about this?"

"I felt it better not to get into a fire fight with them. It would bring too much attention to us. As we discussed, I think it best if we go with the plan to move things a few thousand kilometers west."

"West." The big man's head moved up and down with a slight jerking motion. "Where did we decide?"

"Around Sasabe."

El Jefe drew on his cigar, blew out some smoke, and licked his lips.

"*Es bueno.* I never liked dealing with those *pendejos* in Coahuila. They are *chingados todos*, eh?"

Rivera didn't answer. Was the old man merely *baracho*, or was he losing it? They had discussed this all before, and it was all but decided. Now it was like having to explain it all over again. And Rivera was also getting progressively more disgusted by his boss's blatant lack of modesty and circumspection.

Suddenly, *El Jefe* emitted a low guttural noise and then brushed the girl's hand away from his groin.

"*Bastante bien*," he said to her. "*Más tarde.*"

Her hand moved down to his knee and resumed the massage there.

"*Bueno*," Cortez said. "*Nogales está cerda de...* closer to *mi fuerte* in Caborca. *Pero ahora* we must complete this new arrangement with *Los Merodeadores* y los otros *americanos... Como se dicelos?*

"*Las razas del diablo*," Rivera said. "The Devil's Breed."

Cortez smiled as he exhaled twin plumes of the heavy, gray smoke though his nostrils.

"Ah, *sí.* The Devil's Breed."

The tip of his cigar glowed red once more.

"This new pipeline should work better for us," he said. "When are you meeting with them?"

"Soon," Rivera said. "I'm waiting for *Los Mero-*

deadores to get back to me on that."

Los Merodeadores—The Marauders. The Mexican/American motorcycle gang that was the connection to the American gang.

"*Muy bien.*" Cortez flicked his fingers down toward his son. "I want you to take Esteban with you on your next trip. I want him to learn how to do everything."

This hit Rivera like a punch he didn't see coming. It was bad enough that this *cipote gordo* was going to hand over everything to his pathetic offspring, but now would be tagging along to complicate things.

The heir apparent… *El consanguineo chingado*— the fucking bloodline. It was like *rozando su cara en un montón de mierda.*

But Rivera once again said nothing.

My time will come, he thought. *And sooner than this* pendejo *expects.*

"*Por supuesto,*" he said. Of course.

Cortez stroked his facial hair absentmindedly. "And there is the matter of that new crossing. The tunnel we want to make. Is it not the one where that rancher—*¿Como se llama?*

"Pierce," Rivera said. "Rolando Pierce."

"Rolando? *¿Es mexicano?*"

"*Media.* His mother was Peruvian."

Frowning, Cortez muttered, "*Un hijo de puta.* He is being… difficult?"

"*Sí, jefe.* He said he was not interested. Would not

even discuss the matter with me."

"And you offered him the money?"

"*Sí.*"

"Then he must be made more cooperative, if we are to set up this new location."

Rivera nodded. "What do you wish me to do, *jefe?*"

Cortez brought his hand up and rubbed his index finger and thumb together.

"Offer him a little more money, but not a lot."

"And if that does not do the trick?"

El Jefe considered this question for a moment, gazed down at one of his girls, and then smiled. "He has a beautiful daughter, *¿verdad?*"

"I believe he does."

"Then that is the key. Find her, take her, and make it clear to him that the arrangement must be made."

"It will be done."

"But not until this other matter has been completed."

"*¿Qué? Algunas testarulos nuevos?*"

"*Sí. Tienes que ir el norte pronto,*" Cortez said. "*Triagan trece mas.*"

Thirteen more drug mules—testarudos, *were being readied for a crossing*, Rivera thought. An unlucky number, thirteen. At least that was what the Americans say. But hopefully not an unlucky one for us.

"*Y no te olvidas de los Merodeadores.* Do not forget them. You must find out if they have met with *los otros. Los americanos. ¿Como se dice?"*

"The Devil's Breed. *Y no he olvidado,*" Rivera said. I will not forget.

"*Bueno, bueno.*" *El Jefe* sat in his padded wicker chair and puffed on the last remnants of his huge Cuban-made cigar. It was now a short stub. His lips curled back in disgust and he exhaled loudly.

"*Ahora,*" he called out. "*Tráelos.*" Bring them.

The two disgraced coyotes were escorted into the open courtyard by the trio of armed guards, two of whom carried M4 rifles. The third guard, Oscar Buenaventura, was the leader and had a Glock 21 in a leather holster on his right hip.

The two hapless looking men were marched in front of Esteban Cortez and made to kneel.

El Jefe glared down at them, drew deeply on the cigar, and blew out a thin stream of smoke.

"*Mátalos, papa,*" Cortez Jr. said. "Let me do it."

The elder Cortez held up his hand in a silencing gesture. Accordingly, no one spoke.

Mátalos, papa, Rivera thought silently distorting the son's high-pitched tone. *El Jefe* is grooming his worthless son to step into the top position, but it will not work. *Son grandes zapatos para llenar...* Big shoes to fill.

Rivera glanced at the boss man's highly polished boots and then to those of *el hijo.* The son was wearing sandals.

Pathetic.

Perhaps thirty seconds of silence settled over the scene. The only sound was the flow of water from the fountain into the pool.

The sea god is taking a piss, Rivera thought with amusement, but his face betrayed nothing.

He was waiting to see what the old man was going to order, or rather, who he was going to have do the deed. The two coyotes had committed the ultimate sin. They'd gotten caught skimming some of the profits from their latest trek north. They'd also unnecessarily murdered three of the women they were charged with smuggling across the border. All three of them had been stuffed with the little balloons filled with fentanyl. It was sheer profit wasted.

"*¿Qué tienen que decir?*" Cortez asked. "What have you got to say?"

Neither man replied. They both knew what was coming. They were hard and tough.

Cortez tossed the stub of his cigar at one of them, hitting him in the face.

Still no response.

Hombres duro, Rivera thought.

"Esteban," Cortez said to his son. "*¿Quieres darles un abrazo de oso?*"

Rivera kept his face impassive, but internally he was laughing. The old, fat fool was trying to get his indolent son to administer a bear-hug that would crush the life out of the two *traidores*, but these two were tough, hard men. Rivera knew them both. They would not go down easily, not from the *abrazo de oso* of this soft *gordo*.

Nevertheless, *el hijo* stood, tossing away his cigarette. He lumbered down the elongated steps of the cement platform and stood in front of the two kneeling men. Bringing his arm back, he swung an effete blow at one of them. The man's head hardly moved. *El hijo* drew his arm back once again, but this time the would-be recipient sprang upward, seizing the younger Esteban by the throat, squeezing with both hands.

"Alfredo," *El Jefe* yelled.

El Tigre was already darting down the elongated stairs, his right hand pulling the folded raptor knife from his pants pocket. He could have used his Glock 19 to end it faster. But risking a shot with *el hijo* being so close, even with the attached laser light, wasn't something he wanted to risk. Besides, *la garra del tigre*—the talon of the tiger, was easier and more personal. He much preferred to use it. His movements were fluid and fast, but the truth be told, he wasn't moving at his top speed. No, he was taking secret delight at the sight of the younger Cortez's porcine face turning blue, his tongue lolling out of his mouth.

I should slow down more and enjoy it, he thought.

Still, this was not the time.

The other man was rising from his kneeling position now as well.

Dos compañeros, El Tigre thought. Ready to go down fighting.

He did a jumping kick to this rising man's groin and his upper body folded forward. Reaching out with his right hand, *El Tigre* then made a slashing motion with the raptor knife to the arm of the one doing the choking. The knife's curved blade made a swishing sound as it swept through flesh and tendons. Bringing the blade back in an upsweep, he raked the point across the left side of the assailant's neck, slicing through the left carotid. Blood sprayed outward in an arc as *El Tigre* pivoted and delivered a straight left to the other man's face just as he was just straightening up. This second man twisted downward, his knees jutting in one direction, his upper body in the other.

The first man still had a one-handed grip on the neck of *el hijo.* The fat *cerote* squealed.

El Tigre almost wanted to let the *hombre duro* maintain the partial strangulation, but he knew *El Jefe* was bound to notice. Besides, these two had *valor,* in their own sort of way. They deserved a quick death.

He brought the raptor blade downward once more, cutting across the other side of the choking man's neck. More blood spurted forth dappling *el hijo* and his ruffled white shirt. The man's grip loosened and he dropped to the ground.

El Tigre then turned and grabbed the hair of the other one, slitting his throat with smooth and decisive motion. That one's head made a plopping sound as it smacked down against one of the decorative stones. The crimson flow turned the rocks bright red as it surged over the rough surface and began to seep down into the cracks between the layered stones.

"*Papa,*" *el hijo* cried out, coughing and sounding more like a woman than a man. "*Mira. Mi camaisa está ruina.*"

Tears rolled down his fat cheeks, which was only now returning to a normal complexion.

The face of the senior Cortez was set in a deep frown. He glared first at his son, then to the two fallen *hombres*, and then to *El Tigre*.

"You should have done it slower," Cortez said in English. "It was too quick."

El Tigre merely nodded in acknowledgement, but his unspoken reply was terse and to the point: *Chinga tu madre, pendejo viajo.*

CHAPTER 2

THE MCNAMARA RANCH

PHOENIX, ARIZONA

As Wolf pulled onto the road leading up to Mac's ranch, he felt the afterglow of earned exhaustion. Once he'd mentioned about having to help teach the class tomorrow, Reno had taken the workout to the next level. He'd brought in three fresh sparring partners and had each one go two five-minute rounds with Wolf. That was one more than he'd have to go on Saturday night. He'd done pretty well, spending almost one full round on the mat doing ground techniques. At the end of it he was tired, but knew he still had something left in the tank, albeit not very much. Reno clapped him on the shoulder and told him he was ready. Whether Reno really felt that way or not was something Wolf wondered about, but when stepped on the scale he was gratified to see it register 205. This was the weight he had to come in at twenty-four hours before the fight at the weigh-in. Wolf figured he'd lost between eight and ten pounds of water-weight during today's all-day workout session, and this one was supposed to be his final, really hard workout. He was on track for a moderate workout tomorrow, and then another light one once they got to Vegas on Friday. A session in the steam room right before the weigh-in and he should be right on the money. Friday into Saturday would give him time to rehydrate. At fight time he'd hopefully be a rough and ready 215. An image of Adam "Commando" Shultz standing across the octagon flashed in Wolf's mind, but only for a moment. Shultz was purported to be a tough customer. He'd won six of his ten fights by submission and the other four by knockout. Wolf and Reno had watched them all, and Wolf had been impressed. Although Schultz had a background as a wrestler, he obviously had studied some striking techniques.

As Wolf made the left turn onto the driveway he smiled as he realized how preoccupied he was becoming about the fight.

The nerves are starting, he thought.

It usually happened about this time and got steadily worse the closer it got to fight-time.

A couple more days and he'd either be basking in the glory of another win, or lamenting having to hand over his belt. At least Chad had the original one. Wolf had given it to the kid for a show-and-tell session in school about his honorary uncle's MMA career. When Wolf left for Vegas all those months ago, he'd told Mac to let the little guy keep it because he liked it so much. Kasey had been less than pleased, but what the hell. The kid had gone through so much—his parent's divorce, abduction by his father, and then seeing his old man get shot right in front of him. Add to that the attempt on all their lives by that group of mercenaries who'd shown up to kill Wolf and gain possession of the Mexican bandito statue.

The bandito... Wolf hadn't thought about that thing, which still adored a place on his mantel, albeit several pounds lighter now that the stolen Iraqi artifact had been removed.

But the little guy looks good after surgery, he joked to himself.

Kasey had tried to throw the bandito away when it had first rested on Mac's fireplace shelf. He'd rescued it from the garbage and asked Wolf to take it. That was before they knew that the plaster statue held a significant piece of the puzzle of why so many people had been after them. They'd both been glad to close that chapter, even if it did require them shooting down a helicopter with their covert enemies in it.

Wolf saw Kasey's car parked in front of the house and wondered why she was still there. As of late, with Mac gone, she'd just been coming by in the mornings to work on the books and review any inquires for Trackdown Inc. In truth, since he'd moved back to the garage from Vegas, he'd appreciated that she wasn't around as much as in the old days when she and her son had lived in the house. Her most recent marriage to Bill Franker had changed that. Not that he disliked her, but there had been a constant tension between her and Wolf when Mac had brought him to live there after Leavenworth. She'd never readily accepted Wolf, and blamed him for the fiasco down in Mexico when her father had gotten wounded. Her stance softened quite a bit after they'd rescued her from Von Dien and company down in Belize, and then she'd married Franker and moved in with him. Mac had said they were in the process of buying a house, but that had been about six months ago—back when Wolf was still living in Vegas. Whatever they were going to do, he wished them well. At least she was out of his hair.

He pulled his Jeep up by the garage, picked up the bag containing his supper, and got out. Pausing to open it, the odor of the broiled chicken and peas made his mouth water. One of the good things about being back in Phoenix and training at Reno's was that Barbie took her job as training chef very seriously. Besides being a knockout, she could cook, too. Glancing back toward the house, he saw the lights were still on. Mac had most of the rooms on timers, but there were more on than usual. After unlocking the door, he headed over to the stairway and his upstairs apartment.

The story of my life, he thought. *I keep shuffling from one small compartment to another.* A vision of the monthly apartment he'd had in Vegas flashed in his memory as he ascended the stairs. Still, both of them were a lot better than the barracks or tents from his army days, and certainly better than the 8x12 cell where he'd spent four years.

That thought reminded him that he still had to call the Great Oz to get an update on the appeal. Just as he got to the top of the stairway, he heard the knocking on the side door.

His inbred caution made him go to the upstairs window and gaze downward to see who it was. There had been too many attempts on his life during the past year or so for him not to do so.

Kasey stood below. She knocked again, a bit harder this time.

A bit perplexed and wondering what she wanted, Wolf turned and descended the stairs. When he opened the door he saw she was holding his MMA Light-heavyweight Championship Belt.

Wolf opened the door, said hi, and stepped aside allowing her entry.

She didn't move, but her cheeks twitched with a quick smile.

"I saw that you were working later than usual," he said. "What's up?"

"I was waiting for you to get home."

At least she'd used the word "home." That made Wolf feel a bit more relaxed, but he was still convinced that she thought of him as a freeloader, even though he'd insisted on paying Mac rent this time around.

"Reno kept me a bit longer than usual at the gym," he said. "I was just going to fix myself something to eat. I can put on some coffee if you'd like to—"

"No," she said quickly, and then added, "thanks anyway."

A few more seconds of awkward silence passed between them, and then she thrust the belt toward him so rapidly that collided with his abdomen.

"Here," she said.

Gripping the belt, he raised an eyebrow and asked, "What's this?"

"It belongs to you."

"But I…" Wolf tried to read her, but as usual, found her pretty much inscrutable. "I told your dad to give it to Chad. He liked it so much."

"I know, and I appreciate it." The corners of her mouth turned upward displaying a lips-only smile. "But it's best that he not get too attached to something that isn't his."

Wolf recalled the little boy's ecstatic expression when Wolf had first brought the belt home after winning the championship. The kid had asked if he could take his "uncle's belt" to school for show and tell. Wolf suddenly wondered if her new marriage to FBI agent Franker had anything to do with this. Maybe the new roles of husband and step-father was putting good old Bill through the wringer.

But what about Chad?

The picture of his disappointed little face hung in Wolf's mind's eye.

It wasn't fair, but then again, life seldom was, and she was the kid's mother.

He slung the belt over his shoulder and nodded.

"Okay, but tell him he can have it back anytime he wants."

"I will." She dug in her purse, apparently for her car keys. "And thanks for understanding."

Wolf didn't feel good about it, but didn't know what else to say. Struggling, he asked, "Heard from your dad lately?"

"As a matter of fact," she said, her eyes still evading his, "I have." She was hurrying around his Jeep and heading to her car now and spoke over her shoulder. "He should be calling you tonight."

He stood in the open doorway until she gotten into her car, fired it up, and then drove off. Wolf waved, but the tinted windows kept him from knowing if she reciprocated, not that it mattered.

Trudging up the stairs again, with a bit less verve than the last time, he set the belt down on the table and glanced over to see the plaster statue of the Mexican bandito on the top of the bookcase. It stared at him with that same, imagined malevolence as always.

Wolf placed Barbie's pre-cooked meal in the microwave. After getting himself a bottle of water, he checked the timer and saw that it still had four minutes to go—almost the same as a round in the octagon.

He grabbed a knife, fork, and spoon from the tray of washed dishes by the sink and tore a paper towel from the rack. The microwave finished its cycling and he took out the plate and sat down opposite the championship belt.

Looks like it's just you and me, buddy, he told himself.

Then the thought of possibly losing it next Saturday hit him with a delayed reaction. An image of the official handing the belt—his belt, to Schultz was like a bolo punch to the liver. Although this octagon exchange was purely symbolic and for the cameras, at least this way they wouldn't have to take the extra belt Reno had purchased and kept in the display case at the gym. They could just hand over the original.

He resolved not to let that happen.

At least not if he could help it.

But what if he couldn't?

Schultz was supposed to be pretty tough. Although both of them were undefeated, Wolf had a draw on his record, while Schultz had all wins. Wolf tried to tell himself that records meant little by comparison. It was all in how ready you were when you showed up to fight that night.

Regardless, Wolf thought. *Somebody's O is gonna go.*

Wolf stared at the belt for a solid half-minute until the microwave alarm sounded.

His cell phone rang just as he'd taken his first mouthful of food. Glancing at the screen, he saw it was Mac. Hoping everything was all right, Wolf pressed the button to put him on speaker and answered with a muffled, "Hello."

"Sounds like you've got a mouthful of something," McNamara said.

Wolf managed to shift the food mostly to his cheek. "You just caught me. I do."

"How'd that dirty little cadence ditty go?" Mac asked, and then sang out the old refrain. "A Ranger and his girl laying up in the grass, a mouth full of pussy and a handful of ass."

"Not applicable in this case," Wolf said. "I'm eating supper."

He heard McNamara's low chuckle. "Well, as long as we're not talking about a mouth full of shit, I guess it's all right."

Wolf felt like laughing, too, but finished chewing instead. He recalled some of the ditties he'd recited while running, but not that one. "Don't recall that particular cadence song."

"Probably before your time." Mac laughed. "Yeah, you couldn't get away with it nowadays in this man's army, but I remember, back in the day, being down at Benning my first time in jump school. The drill sergeant was leading us in a double-time across the base using that same refrain, and we passed by this one butter-bean lieutenant ninety-day wonder asshole son of a bitch. He had a female officer with him, probably some gal he was jocking, and they overheard it. The little son of a bitch stopped us and made the poor drill sergeant write down all the words and marched us all over to stand in front of the orderly room before the company commander. The CO was a combat vet who'd worked his way up as an enlisted man before going to OCS and becoming an officer. He listened to the lieutenant saying this was done in the presence of a female officer. The old man raised his eyebrows, gave everybody a stern look, and then told the LT that the word 'pussy' referred only to him, and him alone, and told us to fall out."

"Yeah," Wolf said. "Things change."

McNamara laughed. "And not always for the better. I hate to think what's gonna happen the next time we get in a real shooting war. But I guess we'll win the latrine diversity contest."

"Your comedy routine is going to make me choke," Wolf said. "How's things down Texas way?"

"Getting worse all the time. The governor's talking about deploying the National Guard. It's still catch and release, though. Only difference is the number of hoops they're making everybody jump through. Plus, we're catching some flak from both the federal G and the Texas AG about use of force. Our only authority is the citizen's arrest statute, and it's vague at best. Our main thrust has always been preventing them from crossing here, and now we're turning anybody we do catch over to local law enforcement instead of the Border Patrol."

"What are they doing with them?" Wolf shoveled in another mouthful.

"They're charging them with trespassing." Wolf heard Mac click his tongue. "Then they eventually turn them over to the feds, so they can give 'em a notice to appear in court and turn 'em loose. It ain't much of a deterrent, but like I said, it's making them think twice about crossing our little section of U.S. soil. We nicknamed it God's Little Acre."

"Erskine Caldwell already used that title," Wolf said.

"Erskine who?" Mac laughed again. "Now there you go, getting all literary on me. Next thing you know, you'll be quoting Shakespeare, or something."

Wolf struggled for an appropriate Shakespearian comeback quote, but couldn't think of one.

"The bad guys still shooting at you? Last time you said something about a fifty caliber."

"It sure sounded like one." Mac laughed again. "Old Ron was flying that chopper and it shook him up. He had a flashback to the Nam. That's one sound you never forget."

Wolf had heard his own share of rounds being fired at him in anger. "Damn, I feel like I should be down there with you."

"You got more important things to worry about," Mac said. "And besides, it's like I told you, they didn't hit nothing."

"Just the same, it sounds like things are getting a little above your pay grade." Wolf was liking the sound of this less and less. After his return from North Carolina, he'd rendezvoused with Mac and the Best in the West team in Vegas for their R and R. He'd offered to join then at the border, but Mac instead convinced him to move back to Phoenix to keep an eye on the ranch and help do some teaching at Buck's Best in the West Training Academy. Ready for a move out of Sin City, Wolf agreed mainly because Reno had set up another MMA match for him. Teaching and training for the upcoming fight prevented him from doing any border work.

"And," Wolf said, "you could probably use somebody who could speak a little Spanish, right?"

"Well, Buck's got a good working knowledge of it, Miss Dolly and Brenda have taught me a couple of words."

"I'll bet they have." Wolf laughed. "But not the kind of words you want to be using."

Mac laughed, too, then added, "I'm getting by, but actually, we're finding a lot more than just Mexicans and people from Central America coming across now.

There's Haitians, Russians, Ukrainians, Africans, and a whole bunch from the Middle East."

"So you're putting that Arabic and Pashto you learned to good use."

"Sometime," Mac said. "How's your training going? You ready?"

"Pretty much."

"Pretty much?" Mac snorted. "You know I'm thinking about coming up to Vegas this Saturday to see you kick that fucker's ass, don't ya?"

This filled Wolf with more apprehension. He knew he'd never want to perform poorly or lose in front of Mac.

"I'll do my best," he said.

"You damn well better. I already called Miss Dolly and Brenda and told them we're taking you and your lady love out for a victory dinner afterward. How is Yolanda, anyway?"

"She's good, I guess." Wolf knew there was a sound of hesitancy in his voice and hoped Mac wouldn't ask about it.

McNamara was silent for a moment, and then asked "You and her making out okay?"

"Well, we're sort of in a mutual trial separation," Wolf said. "At least until she finishes her police department probation, or I clear my name."

"And how's that quest going?"

"The Great Oz is taking it to the Military Court of Appeals next week."

"Outstanding. I'm sure he'll kick ass. Now all you got to worry about is kicking this other guy's on Saturday. What's he call himself again?"

"Schultz," Wolf said. "Adam Commando Schultz."

"Commando?" McNamara said. "He a veteran?"

"I don't know."

"Hell he better be, using a moniker like that. But then again, commando's a British term. He a Brit?"

"I don't think so."

Mac laughed. "Hell, I like your chances better already. Anybody borrowing a half-assed nickname like that can't be too tough."

Wolf realized his food had gotten cold.

"I guess we'll find out Saturday," he said.

***

THE ALGONQUIN HOTEL
MANHATTAN, NEW YORK CITY

Bray was still feeling dehydrated after the lengthy session in the steam room despite having drunk two bottles of water on the way back to the hotel. The meeting had done little more than reaffirm his and Abraham's current position, which was little more than an ongoing holding pattern of dual surveillances, and Bray couldn't shake that growing feeling of uneasiness. The lawyer had looked particularly drained after the steam session and Bray thought the man was foolish to be ordering an alcoholic drink now. He told him so.

"Alcohol's a diuretic, you know," Bray said. "After being damn neat parboiled in that meeting, you'd better be careful."

"Good point." Abraham snapped his fingers and the waitress reappeared. "Get me a glass of water in addition to that martini, will you."

"Make it a pitcher," Bray added.

The girl's eyes narrowed slightly above her face mask as she nodded and then departed.

"So what did you think of him?" Bray asked.

Abraham shrugged. "I'd met him before. At the reading of the will, but this was the first chance I've had to really converse directly with him. Up until today, instructions were given through an intermediary."

Bray resisted the temptation to say that he thought their new employer was kind of strange. Instead, he merely said, "He seems like an interesting character."

The waitress returned with the pitcher and two glasses. Bray took charge of it right away and poured a glass for Abraham and one for himself.

The lawyer ripped off his mask and took a drink.

"Ah," he said. "Much better. You were right."

"I've been right about a lot of things." Bray took off his mask as well. "Now where do we stand on all this?"

Abraham finished off the water and then poured himself another glass full.

"Wasn't that made clear? We're just to continue surveillance monitoring and periodically report."

Bray drank some water as well.

"Any idea where all this is leading?"

"Well, our client is a very cautious man. He doesn't want to call undue attention to himself."

"Obviously."

"And his main concern is the federal investigation into his late uncle's activities. He wants to avoid being drawn into that."

Bray polished off his glass and was starting to feel better now.

"So we're sort of in the same situation we were the last time with the Don, aren't we?"

Abraham cocked his head and smiled.

"More or less. But luckily for us, our current client is a good deal more circumspect. So, as I just said, for the moment, we just continue our observation and report."

Bray felt that the lawyer was being patronizing. "Doesn't it bother you in the least that if the feds are investigating this other matter with the uncle's shady art dealings, that we might eventually be drawn into it?"

"He's officially hired me as legal counsel. We're covered by attorney-client privilege."

"Not if we get tangled up in some illegal acts."

Abraham frowned. "What illegal acts? We're simply maintaining a surveillance on certain parties who may or may not be involved in a potential legal matter."

Bray felt like saying, "Whaddya mean, 'We?'" But the waitress came with their drinks and set them down.

"Would you like to order something from the kitchen?" she asked.

"Yes, let us see the menus," Abraham said.

After she'd gone Bray glanced around and leaned partially over the table.

"I already told you before," he said in a low voice. "I'm not getting involved in any murders Not without some layers of insulation."

"Neither am I." Abraham's lips twitched slightly after he took a sip of his drink. "So in the meantime, just maintain your surveillances, and perhaps you'll think something."

Bray couldn't help but notice that the lawyer had switched from using the plural pronoun, "we," to the singular "you."

A good indication of who the patsy's going to be, he thought.

"I'm flying back to Phoenix first thing in the morning," Bray said. "And in the meantime, I've got my operatives on both of them."

"Beautiful." Abraham took a sip of his martini. "Like I said, we need to stay on top of things."

I'm glad it's back to "we" now, Bray thought.

***

YUCATAN, MEXICO

The headlights of the big Dodge Ram pickup truck cut through the darkness as it bounced over the uneven ground and drove past the asymmetrical rows of mesquite and stunted trees along the back road. Alfredo Rivera, *El Tigre*, sat in the front passenger seat. One of his most trusted associates, Juan Garcia, was driving. In the backseat section Luis Menendez sat on the right side, and Esteban Cortez *hijo* was on the left.

"Take my son with you to dispose of the bodies," *El Jefe* had told Rivera. "I want him to learn how to do things... How to be a man. You will teach him this, ¿ *verdad?*"

Teach him what he needs to know, Rivera thought. Have me raise your son, so you can continue to play with your bitches. School him so that he can assume the position that should be mine—the one that I have earned. He reflected with a bit more bitterness that *el hijo* was only few years younger than he was.

The heir apparent. *El consanguineo*—the bloodline.

But his answer betrayed none of this bitter animosity.

"*Por supuesto, el jefe.*"

Perhaps it was time to consider another course of action… A coup? Rivera knew he commanded the respect of the majority of the men, but Cortez had a small contingent of bodyguards who remained fiercely loyal to him. And these days he seldom left the safety of his *hacienda fuerte.*

Pero, Rivera thought, *mi tiempo llegará.* My time is coming. And sooner than *el jefe* thinks.

"How much farther?" Cortez Jr. asked. "I have to piss."

Rivera made no reply, but fantasized about stopping the truck and letting the fat pig get out, and then just driving off. It would be a good lesson for *esa chingadera,* but he would no doubt go whining to his papa about it.

"Drive over there," Rivera said, pointing to the right.

The ground was flat and didn't have many trees. It would do.

Juan steered off the roadway. The younger Cortez grunted and repeated his need to urinate.

"*Un momento, Esteban,*" Rivera said.

They continued over the rough terrain for perhaps forty seconds more before Rivera gave the signal to stop. Juan left the engine running and the headlights on for the moment. The lights gave the surrounding terrain an eerie glow. The four of them got out and started surveying the immediate area for a suitable place, or at least three of them did. Esteban Cortez was busy unzipping his pants and digging to free his penis. Rivera saw a low spot in the ground clear of brush that looked like it would contain few stones and be easy digging. He told Juan and Luis to get everything.

El Hijo was finishing up his task, shaking his *chorizo*, and stuffing it back into his pants. When he'd finished he began walking back to the truck. Juan had removed four shovels and a rake, and Luis was pulling the long tarp with the two bodies out from under the truck bed's canopy. Esteban opened the door and started to get into the back seat again.

"What are you doing?" Rivera said.

"I'm tired," Cortez said. "I want to rest. Let me know when you're done."

Rivera caught an almost imperceptible snort of derision from Juan.

"Give us a hand first," Rivera said. "We must bury them."

"What the hell for?" Cortez's face wrinkled up in obvious disgust. It looked somewhat like a prune. "Just dump them on the ground and leave them."

Rivera had thought about doing just that, but decided against it. The two dead men were traitors, but they had been good *hombres* overall. They deserved a burial. Even old man Cortez understood that. Word of their deaths would certainly get around, but it was also best that their bodies never be found.

"It is what your father directed me to do," Rivera said. "It will go faster if we all work together."

El Hijo gave his own derisive snort, pulled open the door, and started to shift his substantial bulk up into the cab.

"No way." He started to close the door, but Rivera grabbed and held it.

The other man's eyes widened in shock.

"Have you forgotten? We have to go to the border *mañana*," Rivera said. "Your father said I should take you with. To show you the ropes."

"I know the damn ropes," Cortez said. The corners of his mouth twisted downward into a scowl. "Now let go of that fucking door or I will tell *mi padre*."

Rivera held it open for several more seconds, his nostrils flaring in anger. He wanted more than anything to pull this fat fucker out of the truck, drag him over to the arroyo, and make him dig the two graves with his fucking hands.

"Your father wants me to show you things," he said. "So how are you going to learn if you do nothing?"

"I am no *empleado*. You do not tell me what to do." He tried to pull the door closed, but Rivera held it motionless. Cortez's face twisted into a scowl. "Let go, or I'll tell my father."

Rivera kept his hand on the door a few moments more, and then released it.

"*Hace buen siesta*," he said and turned away.

Luis was already dragging the heavy tarp over the ground and Juan was carrying the tools. Rivera reached down and grabbed the other end of the tarp and picked it up.

"*Vago*," Juan muttered under his breath.

"*Sí*," Luis reaffirmed. "*¿Tenemous que llevarlo con nosotras esta noche?*"

"It is what *el jefe* wishes," Rivera said.

"*Lastima*," Luis said.

Rivera smiled. Dissention among the ranks was sometimes a good thing. He knew he could count of these two being on his side once he decided to make his move.

"*No te preocupes, amigo*," Rivera said. "*Nuestro tiempo se acerca.*"

"*Creo que sí*," Luis said with an accompanying grunt.

"*Estamos contigo*," Juan added. He glanced over at Rivera as they carried the burden and grinned. "*Diganos cuando.*"

Rivera grinned as well and nodded.

I will tell you soon, he thought. *But not now. It will be at a time and a place of my choosing.*

CHAPTER 3

BEST IN THE WEST—TACTICAL TRAINING
INSTITUTE
MESA, ARIZONA

The boots of the twelve men scraped hard against the asphalt of the roadway, making a stomping, skidding sound with each step. Twenty-three soles colliding with the pavement. Pete Thornton wore only one boot, and his left pant-leg ballooned out with each step over the hook-shaped titanium prosthesis on his leg. He was a slender, waspish man who moved with a slight awkwardness of gait, but his fierce pride, that of a former marine, drove him with an indomitable fury.

Once a marine, always a marine, Wolf thought as he monitored Pete's pace and condition.

It was Wolf's second run of the morning, but

this one hardly counted. The midmorning sun was beating down on them, but the temperature was only in the mid-sixties and hardly uncomfortable at all. Plus, the pace was only a typical military-style double-time—one hundred-eighty steps per minute. Wolf hadn't even broken a sweat on this one. The same could not be said for the eleven others. Pete Thornton was leading the formation with his un-gainly running stride. Despite having a prosthetic on the nub of his left leg, he was holding up fine. He'd lost he lower portion of his leg in Afghanistan, but kept himself in peak condition. The other ten were a conglomeration of law enforcement types, federal, county, and municipal, who'd signed up, or had been signed up, to take this one-day movement and tactics qualification course. Most of them didn't look used to the physical training aspect, plus they had the added burden of running with their rifles in hand.

Wolf didn't.

One of the bennies of being an instructor, he thought with a grin.

They'd almost completed their first lap. The road-way wound around the five buildings, two of which were pre-fab and one was cinderblock.

Pete glanced back over his shoulder to make sure they hadn't lost anyone as then headed toward the main roadway and the series of man-made berms that formed the five consecutive rows of gun ranges. They passed the first ones, which were designed primarily as rifle ranges, and Pete held up his fist to signal a halt. The twenty-four feet stopped with a one-two stomping precision. This one had half a dozen old cars parked at spaced distances between two berms. The targets, six in all, were spaced along the far end.

"Form up," Pete bellowed, motioning with his hand for the group to get into a line.

The group spread out into a line, each man standing at attention and holding his rifle at port arms.

Not bad for a half-assed training run, Wolf thought. On his earlier jaunt that morning, at zero-six hundred, had taken him down the road next to McNamara's house and half-way up the nearby mountain, as usual. He'd also been wearing one of Mac's pistols, a Glock 19, in a nylon shoulder rig under his loose-fitting sweat shirt. As an ex-con, he was prohibited from owning a weapon, and couldn't qualify for a concealed carry permit, even for his bail enforcement work with Trackdown, Inc. But that hadn't stopped him from carrying one of Mac's guns on his solitary runs. There had been way too many attempts on his life since Leavenworth, and while he believed that he'd put the man responsible for them, Dexter Von Dien, in the ground, Wolf still couldn't shake that uneasy feeling. So, at Mac's urging, when Wolf had returned to Phoenix to stay at the ranch, he'd taken to surreptitiously carrying the Glock on his morning runs. As long as he didn't get caught, he figured he'd be all right. And the possibility of unexpectedly finding himself in a situation where he needed a gun and didn't have one firmly outweighed the legal consequences. The Great Oz had been adamantly opposed to it, having warned Wolf that getting arrested for anything, especially an illegal weapon charge, would adversely affect his appeal. Wolf had complied when he was living in Vegas. But the reappearance of that private investigation firm, Robert Bray and Associates, back here in Phoenix, had unnerved Wolf a bit. There'd been no trace of them in Vegas, but the fact that they'd been here and nosing around was a red flag. No way was he going to get caught flat-footed ever again. Thus, he was wearing the weapon in a hard polymer pancake holster now, with an extra magazine also on his belt. The Best in the West facility was private property. It was surrounded by a twelve-foot cyclone fence with three strands of barbed wire running along the top. The front gate was also secured with a chain and padlock. The austerity of the set up almost reminded him of some of the base camps he'd served at in Afghanistan and Iraq. But this was no combat zone.

Pete strolled along in front of the line of men, bellowing instructions in his gruff voice.

"It goes without saying that maintaining top physical condition goes hand-in-hand with being able to stay alive in a combat situation. That's why we include the morning run in these training sessions. Yesterday was the lecture portion on tactics, and today will be the live fire exercises." He paused and then yelled out, "Do you understand?"

"Yes, sir," the ten men replied in loud unison.

Once a marine, always a marine.

He liked Pete and didn't mind the military-style discipline and instruction. Pete had handled everything by himself the previous day, but today, with the live firing, it was essential to have someone assisting.

Even if it pissed Reno off, Wolf added mentally.

"All right," Pete continued, his voice still elevated. "We will be taking a short, fifteen minute break, after which you will report back here and draw your ammo. Any questions?"

Again the group belted out the appropriate negative response.

Pete called them to attention, and then dismissed them.

He turned to Wolf as the group was making its way toward the row of port-o-potties lining the side of the road. Grinning as he looked at Wolf, Pete said, "And thanks again for coming today, Steve. I don't think I could have handled it today without you."

"No problem."

"I know you're training for that fight on Saturday. Hope this ain't gonna mess up your training too much."

That makes two of us, Wolf thought, but he said, "It shouldn't. I'll go in tonight for a workout, but I'm pretty much ready."

The two of them walked toward the flagpole alongside the roadway. Thornton pulled a ring of keys from his pocket and unlocked the metal box on the base of the pole. He pulled out a small, red flag and affixed it to the line.

"I'll go get the truck with the ammo," Wolf said.

Thornton was about to answer when his head swiveled toward the road leading to the main gate.

"Looks like we've got company," he said.

Wolf could see what appeared to be a tan colored sedan on the access road.

"I'm expecting a reporter to come by this morning," Thornton said.

"A reporter?"

"Yeah, from *Razor's Edge Tactical Training* magazine. Just called a little while ago. Wants to do a feature article on Best in the West. Lord knows we could use the publicity."

"Every little bit helps."

"You know it," Thornton said. "I wonder if that's her?"

Her?

The female pronoun surprised Wolf a bit. There weren't a lot of women working for those types of publications. Or were there? He realized he was out of touch and ignorant of such things. The approaching car, however, didn't look like a reporter's vehicle. Instead, it had an almost governmental aspect to it: utilitarian, blasé, uninspiring.

Since the main gate was locked and at least a hundred yards or so away, Wolf figured it would be a long trek for Pete with his missing leg. Although the man never complained, Wolf had, on past occasions, seen Thornton in severe discomfort at the end of a long day's training. The guy was tough—former marine tough.

"I'll run over there and see," Wolf said. "If it's anybody else, want me to tell them they'll have to make an appointment?"

Thornton grinned. "Not hardly, if they look like they might be a paying customer. They'll be free to watch for a little bit, too."

Wolf smiled and took off at a trot. At least he was getting a bit of exercise in, and he still had a workout to look forward to this evening. Reno would see to that.

He got to the gate just as the sedan was pulling to a stop on the other side. Wolf saw another car, this one a red Honda, turning onto the access road as well.

Now that one had more of a look of a reporter. Plus, the sedan had government license plates.

It was then that Wolf heard Pete's pickup truck

rolling up behind him.

It came to a stop and Thornton got out.

"I forgot to give you the keys," he said with a smirk.

Wolf felt a bit foolish, and then was even more stunned when the driver's door of the sedan opened up and a big guy in a gray suit got out. The man was wearing sunglasses and had a well-trimmed mustache and goatee. His blond hair was long and pulled back into a small ponytail. There was something familiar about him, and as he straightened up to his full height, Wolf realized who he was.

"Hiya, Wolf," Lucien Pike said. "Small world, ain't it?"

***

LAGUARDIA INTERNATIONAL AIRPORT
NEW YORK, NEW YORK

Bray sat in the restaurant/bar closest to the gate. His flight didn't start boarding for another forty minutes and the thought of sitting there with a damn mask on gave him immense discomfort. He thought little of the precaution, and to exacerbate his irritation, the former director of the CDC had now issued a statement saying that cloth masks offered virtually no protection against any airborne virus. This wasn't news to Bray. He'd suspected it all the time. The masks were nothing more than a symbol of compliance for the masses. Still, it was his job to not make waves and fly under the radar. His main concern was keeping tabs on McNamara and Wolf and not being noticed. That was essential once the inevitable kill order was given by the rich, young sociopath, Von Tillberg.

And Bray harbored no doubts about his and Abraham's wealthy employer's motives or lack of compunction. His obvious lack of any concern for either Abraham or him in that hotter-than-hell steam room proved that.

The guy's an asshole, Bray thought. Sitting there guzzling water the whole time, while me and the lawyer were parched.

Just as he was taking a sip of his drink, a perfect Manhattan, his cell phone jangled.

It was Maureen.

He took a swallow before answering and felt the sharp astringency of the alcohol slid down his esophagus.

"What's up?"

"I've followed Wolf out to that Best of the West place," she said. "In Mesa."

"Mesa? I thought he was busy training for the fight Saturday. What's he doing there?"

"I figured I'd find out."

"What?"

"As soon as I tracked him there, I checked the place

out on the Internet. It's some kind of training facility, and Wolf helps out there sometimes as an instructor."

"He didn't see you following, did he?"

"Relax," she said. "I told you I put that tracker on his Jeep, didn't I?"

Bray took another sip of the drink.

"So I figured I'd go in for a closer look," she said. "I'm posing as a reporter for *Razor's Edge Tactical Training* magazine."

A sudden tightening apprehension joined the booze in the pit of Bray's stomach.

"Letting Wolf get a close look at you is not a good idea. You should know better."

Her laugh tinkled over the phone.

"Again, you need to relax, big guy. I'm wearing one of my famous disguises. A black wig, my brown contacts, lots of make-up, and a pair of big, oval glasses. They're Versace's, no less, and to top it off, I'm wearing a thin, low cut top and no bra. My headlights are standing out about a quarter-inch."

Bray felt a jolt to his groin as he thought about that.

She laughed again. "So take a guess what he'll be looking at, and I guarantee it won't be my face."

It sounded sufficiently precautionary, and Wolf had never seen her up close, nor would he again in the most likely surveillance scenarios. Plus, it would be good to get a fuller glimpse of what old Stevie boy had planned. Maybe he was pulling out of the fight to join McNamara down on the border.

"*Razor's Edge Tactical Training* magazine?" He took another sip from the glass. "Is that a legitimate publication?"

"It is. I read it all the time. I've submitted articles to them, too. Got a press card and everything." She laughed again. "Under my pen name, of course."

She had pluck and initiative, all right. This he knew, and appreciated.

"All right, but play it cool. See if you can find out what his plans are, but do not make him suspicious. Understand?"

He heard her musical laugh again.

"Don't worry yourself, lover," she said, lowering her voice to a velvety tone. "I'm really good at playing Mata Hari, remember?"

The not-so-distant memory of one of their bedroom, pre-sexual games came rushing back to him. The thought of her was electrifying.

"All right," he said. "Let me know how it goes. I'm about to fly back now. I'll call you when I land."

"Mmm," she said, the sultriness still imbued in her tone. "I can't wait for you to get here."

Neither could he.

"Okay," she said. "I'm pulling up there now. Gotta go. Bye."

Bray terminated the call and then downed the remainder of his drink.

Maybe this ongoing surveillance operation wasn't such a bad gig after all, as long as he maintained his overall distance and anonymity.

Insulation, he thought. *That's the key.*

He glanced at his watch, saw that he still had twenty minutes or so, and signaled the bartender to give him another.

***

BEST IN THE WEST—TACTICAL TRAINING INSTITUTE
MESA, ARIZONA

"Pike?" Wolf said. "What the hell are you doing here?"

The big man's grin was still wide on his face. "Actually, I was in the area and thought I'd stop by. Always like to look up old friends. Like I said, small world, ain't it?"

"Not that small." Wolf glanced at the approaching red Honda. It was about thirty yards away now, and had California plates, which probably meant that it was a rental. He could see a dark-haired woman behind the wheel who appeared to be the lone occupant.

He turned back to Pike, unsure as to how to introduce him to Thornton. The last time they'd crossed paths, back in North Carolina, the federal agent had been working undercover.

"This is... a friend of mine," Wolf said, the hesitation evident in his tone. He locked eyes with Pike and then cocked a thumb toward Thornton. "And this is Pete Thornton. He's one of the owner/instructors here at Best in the West."

The big man extended his hand. "Lucien Pike. Glad to meet you."

Thornton shook the other man's hand, gazed down at the front license plate, and raised an eyebrow.

"Yeah," Pike said. "I'm a fed. DEA."

"Pike here was working undercover back in North Carolina," Wolf said. "He ended up helping out my little brother, for which I'm eternally grateful."

"I also saved your life," Pike said. "Don't forget that."

It was no exaggeration, but their past association had been based on exigency and a need to rescue Wolf's brother from a malicious drug baron. In the resulting shootout, one in which they'd been outgunned, Pike had saved Wolf's life. It wasn't something he was about to forget.

Wolf smiled. "Why do I have the feeling you're not about to let me do that?"

Pike laughed and gave a quick glance at the Honda, which had stopped behind his government vehicle.

"Looks like you've got company," he said.

"Most likely a magazine reporter," Thornton said.

The door of the Honda shoved open and a pair

of elegant looking calves and black, high-heeled shoe appeared beneath the lower rim of the open door. Then the woman leaned forward and stood up. She was tall, maybe five-seven or eight, or was that because of the heels? The sleeveless, light green dress clung to her body like a leather glove, and it had a low cut in front that showed more than just a little cleavage. A large purse, which appeared to be a genuine Louis Vuitton, dangled on a strap on her left forearm. As she walked toward them Pike emitted a low whistle.

Wolf concurred with that assessment. The lady was a knockout.

"I hope I'm in the right place," she said. "I'm Ms. Tonya Knight, Razor's Edge Tactical Magazine."

"You're in the right place, all right," Thornton answered. He identified himself as the person she had talked to earlier on the phone. "My associate, Steve Wolf, and Mr. Lucien Pike. He's—"

"Just an old army buddy," Pike interjected.

Thornton smiled. "Except that I was in the marines."

Pike laughed. "We don't hold that against you, right, Steve?"

"Same side, different team," Wolf said. He figured Pike didn't want his federal status revealed to this female reporter, but the plates on his car spelled F-E-D. Still, that could mean anything from a special agent to an OSHA inspector. His U/C status was most likely safe and secure.

Ms. Knight's dark eyes, behind large, oval lenses, moved from each of them, and then settled on Wolf.

"Steve Wolf," she said. "Now why does that name sound so familiar?"

"He's a famous mixed martial arts fighter," Thornton said. "And a part-time instructor here, as well."

Ms. Knight's full lips formed an O-shape.

"Wow, you're *that* Steve Wolf? I'm a big fan. I thought you looked familiar, but you're a lot handsomer in person." She turned to Pike. "And what about you? You a fighter, too?"

"Hardly," he said. "I'm more of a lover."

She laughed. "Good choice. You here to take a course?"

"Something like that," Pike said. He brought his hand to his face and rubbed his fingers over his moustache. His eyes, were glued on Ms. Knight's rather substantial décolletage, Wolf noted, as were the eyes of Pete and himself.

"Hey, guys," she said, tapping her index finger against the frame of her glasses. "My eyes are up here."

Embarrassed, Wolf forced himself to look at the woman's face, which was almost as fetching.

"Say, Steve," Pike said, looking away from the girl's chest and focusing on Wolf. "I got to run something by you, but now doesn't seem like such a good time."

Wolf turned his attention to Pike.

"I'll be here until five, and then over at Reno's gym tonight. Training."

Pike nodded. "Yeah, well, I know you've got the fight on Saturday, right?"

Before Wolf could answer Ms. Knight jumped into the conversation.

"Oooh, that's right. I did hear about that. It's in Vegas, isn't it?"

Perhaps she was a fan after all, Wolf thought. *Good to know I've got some following.*

"Yeah," he said. "It's at the MGM Grand."

"Wow," she said. "Now who is it you're fighting?"

"A guy name Adam Schultz."

"It's for the United States light-heavyweight title, no less," Pete chimed in. "Steve's the champ, and he's gonna knock the other guy out."

"Awfully confident," she said, smiling demurely. "Aren't you?"

Wolf felt himself blush.

"Steve'll win," Pete said. "He wouldn't dare lose. Me and the rest of our gang's gonna be up there rooting for him. Besides, he's the best."

Ms. Knight sauntered forward and squeezed Wolf's upper right arm. He caught a whiff of some fancy perfume.

"Mmm," she said. "I'll bet he is."

She dug in her expensive looking purse and came out with a smart phone.

"Got time for a picture?"

Before Wolf could answer, she sidled up next to him, held up the phone, and snapped a selfie. The flash triggered a second time, then she turned the phone toward the other two and snapped one of them as well.

Pike had swiveled his head to the side and then held a big open palm in front of the lens.

"I'd rather not have my picture taken, Miss," he said.

"Oh, pooh," she retorted. "Don't be a spoil sport. Come on. I'll put you in the article."

"Thanks anyway." Pike kept his large hand in front of his face and turned to Wolf. "Your cell's still the same, right?"

Wolf gave a quick nod.

"I'll call you later then," Pike said, and walked toward his car.

Ms. Knight held up her phone and started to snap another picture but Wolf's hand shot up to block it. She turned and stared at him, both eyebrows raised in surprise.

"He's real camera shy," Wolf said.

Ms. Knight giggled and lowered her phone. It made several clicking sounds and Wolf wondered if she'd just taken a surreptitious series of shots of Pike or his car or both. It clicked again, and he figured she had.

"Oh, goodness," she said. "I'm always doing that since I got this new phone." She brought it up and moved her finger over the screen. "There. I've deleted them."

But did she?

He thought about asking to see her phone so he could verify, but decided that would only create suspicion. Besides, if Pike was that worried about his undercover federal status being in jeopardy, he should have taken better precautions.

The big man was already backing his sedan around her Honda. He swiveled the vehicle in a half-circle, stopped, and then drove off down the road. Wolf was wondering how in the hell Pike had found him out here.

"So aren't you going to show me around?" Ms. Knight asked. "I'd really like to get a feel for what you're doing out here for the article."

"I'd be glad to," Pete said. "If you'll just follow me over to the orderly room I'll give you the grand tour."

"Fine." She stepped over to him, and then stopped and raised a highly polished red nail to the corner of her mouth. Her lipstick matched her polish. "Oh, I guess I'd better move my car, huh?"

Without hesitation she pivoted and marched back toward the Honda. Both of them watch the alluring sway of her lyre-shaped hips in the tight dress.

"Man, she's gorgeous," Pete said in a hushed whisper. "But she's kind of scatterbrained, too, ain't she?"

"Maybe," Wolf said. "Or maybe not."

There was something about Ms. Knight that bothered him. Something didn't quite fit, although it certainly wasn't that dress. He wasn't sure what it was, but he continued to appreciate her beguiling saunter.

But one thing was for sure: she had a set of very dangerous curves.

***

NEAR THE MEXICAN/AMERICAN BORDER
PIEDRAS NEGRAS, MEXICO

Slanted beams of the fading afternoon sunlight continued to filter in through the filthy windows, the dirty spots dappling the floor and tables in the large room of the old, abandoned house with amorphous shadows. The room stank with the pervasive body odor of the unwashed, coupled with a tangy sweat-smell of lingering fear. Rivera watched as three of the four coyotes, Paco, Fernando, and Roberto went about their tasks. Fernando, always the joker, still had his black *BIDEN LET US IN* t-shirt on that he used for recruiting people who wanted to cross illegally.

He walked up and down the aisles pouring water into the cups for *los testarudos*. Six men, six women, and one young boy. He was not really a boy—perhaps thirteen, but not yet a man either. Paco reached over and slapped the kid's head. He still had over half of the balloons, tightly wrapped condoms, to go. Each one of them had to swallow thirty or so of them. Whatever they couldn't fit into their body cavities, had to go down their gullets. The women had an added advantage in that respect, being able to stuff their *conchas* and *cachas* with the wrapped balloons. In another eight to twelve hours or so they'd be getting shuttled across, and then the messy part, the retrieval, would begin. If all of them made it across, and if none of the internalized balloons ruptured, then the laxatives would be administered. It was a laborious and dirty process, but it offered the safest way to ensure the transport. And it was the cheapest as well. Each mule had paid handsomely to be escorted across the border. The women had given themselves up numerous times along the way as well. The boy had, too, no doubt. He had that look, that loss of innocence in the eyes. And Paco's proclivities along those lines were no secret.

This would be the final crossing at this point on the border and Alfredo Rivera, *El Tigre*, was glad of it. The Del Rio area across the way was getting too heavily policed on the other side, especially with the enhanced security measures taken by the Americans. And on this side of the border the *Piedras Negras* had become hostile territory of late, as the tenuously arbitrated arrangement with the Gutierrez clan continued to deteriorate. There had been too many apprehensions and failed crossings, too much lost product of late. It was better that they were going to be shifting things west, to Senora.

"*Más agua por favor*," one of the women said.

Her voice sounded distorted, her mouth full of the little, tied-off rubber bundles. She wasn't bad looking, but at this point in the journey she was also filthy and smelly. Rivera wondered how many times she'd been used and abused at every step along her journey to get to *el norte*. He wondered where she was from and where she was going. Perhaps she had people in *los Estados Unidos*. Relatives who would take her in. There was no better time that he could remember for skipping across the border, and he knew it wouldn't last forever. Once they eventually started cracking down, things would get more difficult again. But until then, they rode the crest of the wave.

Rivera glanced over at Esteban Cortez Jr., who was looking at the woman, too. When they'd arrived, the fat *pendejo* had settled himself into the only padded chair in the house, farting and picking his nose, a sour expression twisting his features. The *pendejo* was upset because there was no cell phone service out here. He was watching the woman performing her rhythmic regime of picking up one of the wrapped condoms, placing it into her mouth, and bringing the cup to her lips. Her eyes had the same lost innocence as the boy's.

Cortez Jr. pursed his lips and made a kissing sound as he looked at her, and then he laughed.

"*Quiero a darta algo más para trager, puta*," he said.

The woman inserted another condom into her mouth and looked away.

Rivera was disgusted by the comment. He had little sympathy for these wayward illegals—he couldn't afford any compassion in his position, but neither did he despise them. This was strictly business, and they were little more than vessels, to be used and discarded. But you didn't unnecessarily mistreat your pack animals on a journey through the mountains. Not if you wanted to finish it optimally.

Strictly business.

Cortez Jr. started to get up and muttered something more to woman.

"Leave her alone," Rivera said. "*Ella tiene mucho más para tragar.*"

Cortez Jr. turned his gaze toward him and spat out a profanity, followed by, "I do as I please, with whoever I please."

Rivera stood glaring at him, saying nothing, but not looking away or moving either.

If only the old man hadn't insisted that I bring him along, he thought.

He let his anger simmer, fantasizing about giving *el hijo* a pair of latex gloves and having him sift through the *mierda* and stick his fingers up the assholes of the men, extracting the balloons jammed in there. Grinning, Rivera smirked and winked at him. It was meticulous work, and Rivera had a suspicion that *el pendejo gordo* would be good at it.

"What are you smiling about?" *El Hijo* asked. "I'm bored watching all this shit."

"It is your father's wish that you learn how to do all this," Rivera said. "First hand. And it is my responsibility to teach you."

Cortez Jr. blew out a derisive snort.

"I've seen enough," he said. "And smelled enough, too. When do we get out of here?"

"Soon," Rivera said. "Very soon."

Cortez Jr. got up from his chair with a ponderous effort. He glared at Rivera, and then to the woman he'd been ogling. She had finished downing the remainder of the wrapped condoms before her.

"*Venga, puta*," Cortez Jr. said. "*Tengo algo que quiero que hagas.*"

The expression on the woman's face grew tight, worrisome. Slowly, she started to get up.

"Forget that," Rivera said. "Let her rest for the journey tonight."

"You dare to defy my wishes?" Cortez Jr. glared at him. "Have you forgotten your place?"

Rivera hadn't forgotten. Nor was he overly concerned about the woman. It wasn't about defending her. He simply didn't want to vary the delicate balance of the time table.

Cortez Jr. stared at him a moment more, then a smile stretched over his lips. He strode over and grabbed the woman's upper arm and began pulling her toward the door. "Now, I want some action."

Rivera thought again how much he was going to enjoy cutting the throat of this *pendejo gordo*.

When the time comes, he told himself. But only when the time is right.

A sudden noise emanated from the door. A scuffing sound and it burst open. Martín burst in, his face covered with droplets of sweat.

"*Viene un camion,*" he said, his breath coming in gasps. "*Creo que son los hombres de Gutiérrez.*"

"*¿Cuantos?*"

Martín shrugged, his mouth twisting to one side. "*No sé. Están muchos. Tal vezdiez.*"

Ten men. And most likely ten hard men.

Rivera noted with amusement the expression of alarm that was spreading over the visage of Esteban Cortez Jr. He released his grip on the woman's arm as the fear was almost visible on his fat face now. He'd insisted on wearing a big Walter Q4 Steel Frame

Vintage pistol with fancy gold inlay engraving— the most expensive gun his father could buy. Now it was time to see if he had *los cajones* to use it.

At last, some work for a man, Rivera thought as he withdrew his Glock 19 and smacked the bottom of the magazine to ensure it was properly seated. He glanced over at *el hijo gordo* and smiled.

"*¿Quieres algo de acción?*" he said. "*Esta aquí. Vamos.*"

***

BEST IN THE WEST—TACTICAL TRAINING INSTITUTE
MESA, ARIZONA

Even after the attractive but distractive Ms. Knight had long been gone, the day had continued to be one of problematic interruptions. Besides her insistence of wanting to take numerous photos with her cell phone and pose hold a couple of the weapons, she'd insisted on getting both Pete and Wolf's cell phone numbers in case she had any further questions regarding the article because of a pending deadline.

"I'll let you two know when it's coming out," she said. "I promise."

Wolf had subsequently gotten two phone calls that broke the flow of the training sequence. One of the calls had been from his attorney. The other had been from McNamara.

"Get ready," the Great Oz had said. "We're set to make our appeal bright and early on Monday morning."

His tone was imbued with optimism, and Wolf wondered just whose spirits he was trying to buoy up, Wolf's or his own.

"Great," Wolf said, hoping he wouldn't be sporting any black eyes or a swollen face. "Where's it at?"

"Washington D.C., of course," Oz said. "It's the Military Court of Appeals."

The thought of hopping on a plane on Sunday, the day after the fight, hit Wolf like a gut punch.

"We got to be in D.C.?"

The Great Oz emitted a short laugh.

"No, sorry. Didn't mean to shake you up, or anything. In this age of COVID, everything's done remotely. We'll be on Zoom."

Wolf felt foolish not having assumed that.

"So you'll need me there?"

"Yeah. It'll look better that way." He laughed again. "And you've got that fight on Saturday night, right? Try not to get hit too many times in the face."

"I wasn't planning on it, but you never know."

The Great Oz laughed again. "Not to worry. My administrative assistant is great at applying makeup."

Wolf thought about the lawyer's gorgeous secretary, or administrative assistant, as she was called in these politically correct times.

"I'll try to keep my guard up," he said. "So what do you think our chances are?"

He heard Ozmand chuckle.

"I think we've got a decent chance, especially in view of the new evidence we can introduce. But..."

There's always a "but," Wolf thought.

He waited for the other shoe to drop. When it didn't, he interceded.

"But what?"

He heard Ozmand's heavy sigh.

"Like I told you before, Steve, that damn JAG lawyer you had before was pretty much incompetent. He didn't mount that good of a defense, but of course, you having your temporary amnesia about the incident didn't help any. The transcript reads like you're guilty. And the Alford plea was a double-edged sword."

The Alford plea, which Wolf's JAG lawyer had advised him to do, stipulated that he was maintaining his innocence while acknowledging that the government had enough evidence to prove him guilty.

"However," the Great Oz continued, "like I said, we've got that potentially exculpatory recording admitting you were set up. Proving the authenticity is paramount. As is getting them to accept it. But don't worry." He emitted another chuckle. "I'm ready to go to mat for you, Steve."

After the lawyer had hung up Wolf was feeling like he had back-to-back fights coming up. One of them had his title hanging in the balance, and the other one his whole future.

No sooner had he finished talking to Ozmand than his phone rang again. This call was from McNamara.

"You and Pete taking those boys through their paces at Best in the West?" Mac asked.

"We're doing our best," Wolf said, relieved to hear from his friend. "How's things down Texas way?"

"Not too good. We're getting ready to pull out of here."

"Oh?' And then he remembered Mac's promise to attend the fight on Saturday. But there seemed to be something more. "What's wrong?"

"Things are starting to go to hell in handbasket," Mac said. "When we first got down here, it was easy money and sorta like a game, laying a bunch of non-lethal booby traps and shooting inflatable rafts. It was like tossing darts at a balloon board at the carnival."

"You starting to worry about the people on those rafts too much?"

McNamara didn't answer right away, then said, "We always tried to pop them before they started across, but the damn river was mostly so shallow they could just walk across in a lot of places. Up until last week, that is."

Wolf could hear the hesitation in his friend's voice. "Up until last week?"

"Yeah. We got some rains and the depth and current picked up. Some little girl and her mother were crossing with the mother holding her... The little girl slipped out of her arms. Drowned."

"That's too bad," Wolf said.

"Yeah, it brought back a lot of bad memories. You know, the kind you'd tried your best to forget."

Wolf knew exactly what Mac was talking about.

"Way too many of those for all of us," he said.

"Damn straight. It wasn't near where we were, but it hit us hard just the same." McNamara was silent for a good five seconds. "Anyway, that's pretty much why we decided to get the hell out of here. Buck's got to stick around and settle up to get the rest of our pay. Then we're going to switch to southern Arizona. No more Texas. No more Rio Grande." A few more seconds passed, and then Mac added, "Besides, like I told you I'm coming up to Vegas to see your fight on Saturday anyway to see you kick some ass."

"I hope I'll be able to live up to your expectations."

"Hell, me, too. Buck's talking about putting some of our hard-earned money on you to win by knock-out."

Wolf laughed. "You'd better check the odds first."

"Will do."

"You said you were going to Arizona after that?"

"That's the plan." McNamara laughed. "The Yuma area. Used to be the most secure place along the border. Don't know what it's like now."

"I guess you'll be finding out."

"I will." McNamara laughed. "*After* I take Miss Dolly and Brenda out on the town, of course. And, as always, you're welcome to join us, if you want. The local ranchers and farmers are hiring their own security to keep the illegals from messing up their crops and properties. The pay's supposed to be good, and we shouldn't have to worry about no fifty calibers."

"Sounds good, but I have to stay in Vegas for a court session on Monday." He explained about the phone call from his lawyer.

"The appeal's gonna be in Sin City?" Mac asked.

"No," Wolf said. "It's going to be a Zoom thing in Ozmand's office."

"The Great Oz, huh? He doing you any good?"

"I guess I'll find that out Monday."

"Damn." Mac snorted. "Sounds like you've got two fights coming up then. Good luck with both of them."

The two conversations had clung to Wolf like a weighted vest for the rest of the day and his case of the nerves continued to escalate. Now, as he finally neared the end of the day's training, he tried to eliminate all the extraneous doubts and pending anxiety to concentrate on the last training session of the day.

Wolf carried the timer once again as he ran alongside the last of the shooters. The man took cover behind the first barricade, a three-foot-high wooden box, aimed his pistol, and fired down-range twice. He jumped up and they both rushed across the width of the lane to the second barricade. This one was a metal replication of an old mailbox.

The shooter crouched beside it and leaned around the side, trying to expose as little of himself as possible, but unintentionally exposing the top of his head over the curvature. He fired three more rounds.

Both he and Wolf then sprinted to the next station, an old Buick Regal. This time the shooter knelt by the front tire, using the engine block area as cover. He reared up and fired three more rounds. That made a total of eight. His Sig Sauer 219 had one more round left in the magazine and the shooter was supposed to do a combat reload from behind cover. Instead, apparently being overly concerned about the clock, he rose and ran downrange toward the final station, the ten-yard line, where he had to engage the array of the three stationary targets and double tap each one.

He fired and the slide locked back. Realizing he needed a reload, he dropped the mag, slammed a fresh one into place, pulled back on the slide, and completed the firing sequence.

Wolf pressed the button to stop the clock.

The shooter shook his head, holstered his weapon, and grinned.

"How'd I do?"

"One minute twenty-five seconds," Wolf said. "Not bad, except you forgot to do your combat-reload behind cover."

"Yeah, I know."

Wolf clapped the man on the shoulder and they

headed back toward the starting point where Pete was waiting for them.

Wolf held up the timer clock and showed him the red numerals. Pete nodded and scribbled the numbers down on the tally sheet.

"Did Steve tell you about the combat reload mistake?" he asked.

"Yeah," the shooter said. "I know I screwed up."

Pete grinned. "Well, if you're going to screw up, this is the place for it—in practice. You make the mistake in a real fire fight, you pay the price, right Steve?"

"Can't argue with that," Wolf said, but his mind was on the training session tonight and the upcoming fight. He hoped he wouldn't make any mistakes in the latter.

But I won't know until the time comes, he thought.

***

NEAR THE MEXICAN/AMERICAN BORDER
PIEDRAS NEGRAS, MEXICO

The Gutierrez truck was roaring up the dirt roadway toward the old house as Rivera barked out orders for Paco and Roberto to stay with the mules. Since they'd all finished swallowing the drugs, they were valuable commodities now and must be protected.

It is time, Rivera thought. Time for *El Tigre*.

"Get all of them on the floor." He looked at Fernando and Martín. "You two come with me."

Esteban Cortez Jr. stood there, the fat on his distended belly quivering, his right hand gripping the fancy semi-automatic holstered on his right side.

"Why don't we use the truck to get away?" he asked. "Or our car?"

Fernando and Martín stared at him in disbelief. Or was it disgust?

"No time," *El Tigre* said. "And we are men. We do not run."

"Maybe we can talk to them," he said.

El Tigre smirked and shook his head.

"You do not talk to men like that."

"But if they know who I am," Cortez Jr. said, "they won't dare to hurt us. My father would never stand for it. It would start another war."

Another war? *Qué idiota.* What did this pathetic *cerote* know about wars?

El Tigre smirked again and then glanced at Martín. He wore a trace of a smile as well.

For a brief moment *El Tigre* took time to revel in the incipient terror building in *el segundo Cortez.* But he also knew it wouldn't bode well with *El Jefe* if his fat son got killed while in Rivera's care.

"No," he said. "If they find you are the son of Esteban Cortez, they will take you for ransom and kill the rest of us. You would be the ultimate bargaining chip for Gutierrez."

Cortez Jr. swallowed hard. The sweat was already pouring down the sides of his corpulent face.

"Then what should we do?" he asked.

The tremor in his voice made him sound like *un maricón.*

Now it was "we," *El Tigre* reflected. He was going to take great pleasure in slitting this fat pig's throat when the time came. But for now, the situation dictated that he safeguard *el hijo gordo.* Gutierrez was evidently pissed off that *El Jefe* was reneging on their payment agreement to use the border crossing point in Gutierrez's territory. Cortez Sr. had obviously miscalculated; otherwise he would never have sent his son along on this one. Now the bill had come due and *El Tigre* was sure it would be paid in blood.

But whose blood?

That was the question.

Martín had an AR-15 with a thirty-round magazine as did Fernando. They carried no spares. Paco and Roberto each carried Glocks as well. *El Tigre* had his Glock 19 and one fully loaded spare mag. That left him with thirty-seven rounds in a possible total of around one hundred thirty-five or so.

"*Van allí y allá,*" *El Tigre* said, directing Martín and Fernando to go to each sides of the house. The shrubbery had been cleared away leaving little or no cover or concealment.

"But what about me?" Cortez Jr. asked.

His voice sounded brittle.

"*Quédate aquí,*" El Tigre said. "*Dentro de la casa. Y dame tu pistola.*"

The fat son's eyes widened for a moment.

"*¿Mi pistola? ¿Porque?*"

"Because I may need it." *El Tigre's* voice was harsh, guttural. "*Dámela, ahora.*"

Cortez Jr. fingered the fancy, textured grip of the Vintage Walter for a few moments more and then pulled it out of his holster and handed it over. The gun was all metal and had more heft than the polymer Glock. *El Tigre* pointed to the other man's fat belly.

"*¿Alguna magazinas más?*" he asked.

"*¿Qué?*"

"*Las magazinas. ¿Tienes algún?*"

El Hijo shook his head.

Pendejo, El Tigre thought. Carrying a fancy gun but no presence of mind to also bring an extra magazine.

He heard the truck getting closer. It would be here in seconds.

"Get your fat ass on the floor and stay down until I come for you."

El Tigre watched *el hijo gordo* scurry back inside the house and flop down on the floor, the door sung closed behind him. Glancing at the road, he saw that the truck was less than fifty feet away now and he told the others not to open fire until he did.

He debated what to do. Their two vehicles, a van and a Jeep, were parked in back of the house and out of sight, for the moment. He could take cover behind the well and hope that those in the truck didn't see the movement. But that would also potentially alert them to impending trouble.

No, he thought. El Tigre *does not hide in the bushes. Let them come.*

Instead of taking cover himself, he strode to the center of the roadway and waited. It was starting to get dark now and that would give him the advantage if he could move fast enough. About thirty feet off to his left he saw the old well. The base of it was made of stones, and it had an old crank and wooden crossbar. It would provide enough cover once the shooting started. Turning slightly to his left, *El Tigre* assumed a boxer's stance which not only concealed his Glock down by his leg, but also made him into a narrower target. He pushed his mane of red hair back away from his face, and then he bent down and rubbed his fingers in the dirt. Bringing the soiled digits up to his face, he swiped them over each cheek.

Now he had dark stripes to match his red hair... Now the tiger was ready. Now he was *El Tigre.*

The truck sped toward him, then abruptly jerked to a halt.

Three men were in the cab, seven more in the rear portion, all holding rifles. As the truck stopped, one of the men in the back on the driver's side twisted and pointed an AK-47 at him through the windshield. A second one leveled an AR-15. At least he hoped it was an AR and not its fully automatic cousin, an M4 or M16. Either way, it was bad.

El Tigre estimated who he'd have to shoot first and did a subtle shift to his left, putting himself squarely in front of the truck's grill and thus out of the field of fire of the two *hombres* inside the truck who had been pointing their guns at him.

Diez hombres duros. Ten hard men.

"*¿Qué quiéren?*" he shouted.

The man on the front passenger side stuck his head out the window and bellowed, "*Hola, amigo. ¿Quién es?*"

Three of the men in the rear of the truck stood up now and slammed their rifles onto the top of the cab.

"*Voy a la frontera,*" *El Tigre* lied, feigning ignorance. "*Quiéro a ir a los estados un indos. ¿Está cerca de aquí?*"

The man leaning out of the window barked a gravelly sounding laugh.

"*¿Crees que somos estúpidas, cabrón?*" His face twisted into a scowl.

Before the man could say anything more *El Tigre* pretended to shrug and emit a nonchalant laugh, but at the same time he was bringing his Glock up and acquiring a sight picture. He squeezed off three rounds, letting the trigger slide back ever so slightly each time until it reset, thus decreasing the trigger pull, and put one round into each of the heads of the standing riflemen. As the three heads jerked spasmodically in the halos of a crimson mist, *El Tigre* lowered his Glock and shot through the windshield, taking out the driver first, and then the other three men in the cab.

Although his ears were ringing, he was able to hear the volleys start from the rifles of Martín and Fernando as he sprinted to the cover of the well. The men in the back of the truck were sending a fusillade of rifle fire in all directions, the muzzle flashes becoming visible in the dusky air. *El Tigre* did a rolling dive, landed on the other side of the stone well, rolled to a prone position, and extended his Glock toward the truck. The men in the bed of the truck all danced and jerked as the rounds tore through them. *El Tigre* began squeezing off rounds until the slide locked back on his Glock. Instead of reloading, he pulled out the Walther and squeezed the trigger.

Nothing happened.

After racking back the slide, he tried again and this time it fired.

Qué idiota, he thought. The fat *pendejo* hadn't even kept a round in the chamber.

El Tigre laughed as he fired off the remaining rounds, then dropped the empty weapon into the dirt as the slide locked back.

Let gordo worry about cleaning his pretty gun, he thought.

He then picked his Glock back up, ejected the empty magazine, and slammed a fresh one into the grip.

All was quiet.

Fernando yelled to him asking if he wanted them to check the truck.

"*Sí*," *El Tigre* yelled back, and got to a crouching position by the rounded network of stones. There was no movement from the truck now. From his position he could see the feet of Martín and Fernando as they approached the truck. He rose also and advanced, his pistol held at combat ready.

None of the ten men moved.

As he got closer it became apparent that they were all most probably dead. He ripped one of the rifles, an AR-15, away from a pair of slack hands and methodically pumped a round into the heads of each of *los hombres duros*.

It was best to make sure.

He set the rifle on SAFE and slung it over his shoulder. At least they'd gotten some new weapons.

Both Martín and Fernando were staring at him, their eyes filled with awe.

"*El Tigre es grande*," Fernando muttered.

"*Muy grande*," Martín added.

I now have two more supporters for my eventual

coup, El Tigre thought.

He grinned and looked at both of them.

"*Son grandes también, compadres.*"

Pay them a compliment to ensure their unending fidelity. He glanced over at the house. The windows facing this side were all shattered and the wooden framework was riddled with bullet holes in zigzagging patterns. The rounds from the rifles had no doubt pierced the walls. Hopefully, the injuries inside were slight.

"*Dentros en el casa,*" he yelled. "*¿Están bien?*"

He then heard Paco yell back to him from inside the house.

"*Sí, pero una de las mujueres...*"

One of the mules, a woman, had been hit.

"*¿Está ella muerta?*" El Tigre asked.

"*Sí, está muerta.,*" came the reply.

"*Y Esteban,*" he shouted. "*¿Está bien, tambien?*"

"*Sí. Está bien.*"

One woman dead. That meant one less body to do the smuggling. They would have to make an adjustment. At least his pathetic charge was unharmed. That much had gone right, although the *pendejo* had probably shit his pants. Now they had their work cut out for them. Burying these ten *hombres duros* in a shallow grave would take some time, but it would be better not to leave them where they could be easily found. The truck was still drivable, and they could be left it far away, when it came time to leave. But first they would have to cut the drug-filled condoms out of the dead woman's gullet, and other places.

El Tigre smiled at the thought of this, and knew who he'd assign to that task.

El hijo gordo is going to get his hands dirty after all, *El Tigre* told himself with a smile. He wanted a taste of a woman. Now he will get one.

Paco came out of the house and walked slowly toward the bullet-riddled truck, his jaw gaping.

"*Madre de dios*," he said, glancing from the carnage to the three men standing there. "*¿Quien hizo esto?*"

"*Era El Tigre*," Martín said. "*Todos.*"

"*El Tigre es magnifico*," Fernando agreed. "*El es un campeón grande.*"

El Tigre smiled and nodded at both of them.

Two more converts for my side, he thought. *Un campeón grande...* A great champion.

He rather liked the sound of that, imagining, for a moment, that he was inside an auditorium on an Olympic platform having the gold medal placed around his neck.

CHAPTER 4

MIXED MARTIAL ARTS ACADEMY
LAS VEGAS, NEVADA

Wolf continued his easy jog inside the steam room as the wispy vapors swirled around him. The sweatpants and gym shoes were totally sodden and felt like they held more than the six pounds of sweat he was trying to lose. It was Friday afternoon and the weigh-in was in a little over two hours and he wondered how many pounds he had to go. The five hour ride up from Phoenix had been uneventful, but had left him only about three and a half hours to hit the gym for the final workout, traditionally not a strenuous one, and then start the dehydration routine. He was well into the last hour now. He had to get down to the limit, 206, and he figured he had a few more pounds to go.

Georgie Patton opened the door, stuck his head

inside, and grinned.

"How you doing, brother?"

Wolf grinned back, as best he could. "I could use a couple of ice cubes."

Georgie shook his head. "Ain't gonna happen. Not till after we hit that scale. Pick up the pace little a bit." He was an ex-boxer and did a fluttering series of rapid punches. The old shoeshine. "And mix it up a little bit, too."

Before Wolf could ask how much longer Georgie shut the door, leaving Wolf to breathe in more of the superhot air. He wondered if Schultz was having this much trouble making weight. It would be good to get a look at his opponent up close at the weigh-in. It would be the first time they'd actually see each other face-to-face.

He danced around in the narrow confines of the tiled room and threw about fifteen quick punches, and finished off with a little shoeshine of his own before resuming his jog. Quickening his pace, he inhaled more of the hot air and then tried to take his mind off the immediate task of dropping the water weight by reflecting on Reno's admonishments from the drive.

"I know you got your pretty gal in Vegas," Reno had said. "But remember you ain't getting laid until *after* the fight."

Wolf smirked at the memory of his felicitous reply. "But if I wait till afterwards, I'll be too tired."

"You better not." Reno's brow creased. "Women

weaken legs. Just think about how tired you'll be once you start dancing inside the Octagon. That damn Schultz has probably been living like a monk up in the mountains training for this."

"If he has, I'll bet I know what his mind's going to be on."

"It'll be on taking your head off and stealing your belt, that's what."

Reno touched the bag that contained Wolf's championship belt, the one that Kasey had given back to him. He would hate to lose it. it hadn't occurred to him how much it meant until he gave it to Reno that morning and told him they would be taking this belt to the match.

"Damn, I just thought of something." Wolf was making the most of the continuing fun. "If what you're saying is true about this guy's abstinence, what if he turns out to be gay?"

"Huh?" Reno looked perplexed.

"I mean, that could add a whole new dimension to the clinches and ground game."

Barbie, who was driving, burst out in laughter.

"That's a good one, Steve," she said.

Wolf had kept the faux debate going just for fun, until Reno, sounding on the edge of desperation, threatened to spend the night in Wolf's room if he had to.

"Now that would really make people talk," Wolf said.

He let Reno fume for a few more moments, and

then chuckled and added, "Relax, I'm not in the mood anyway."

Barbie laughed again.

Wolf let the topic drop and thought about Yolanda. Since they'd agreed to separate, and he wasn't even living in Vegas anymore, she probably wouldn't even show up. Chances were good that he wouldn't even see her at all on this trip.

One less reason not to stay in Vegas this time any longer than I have to, he thought, and began ruminating about what the Great Oz had said on the phone yesterday.

One thing was certain he had a lot more than just the fight riding over the next couple of days, but for the moment all of his demons were lurking just over the horizon. A sudden cramp bit into his left calf and he knew he was nearing that total dehydration state, and he estimated that he must be getting close to the desired limit.

Soon it would be time to start confronting the demons.

***

MCCARRAN INTERNATIONAL AIRPORT
LAS VEGAS, NEVADA

Robert Bray watched and waited for the damn luggage carousel to begin turning, but it was frozen.

More people from the plane were beginning to get there so he didn't think it would take much longer. At least he hoped not.

The lighted sign posted the information that the luggage from their flight was coming next, but the oval conveyor belt didn't move.

Bray looked around again.

Roll with the flow, he told himself.

He saw Maureen walking toward him now, holding her cell phone out in front of her as she walked and fiddled with her hair. They'd flown to Vegas together and still had to get the progress report from Jack Powers, who had been assigned to follow Jim McNamara and his old army buddies down in Texas. From what Powers had said on the phone, the last time Bray had heard from him before the plane took off, McNamara was several hours into a non-stop drive back toward Phoenix, Arizona. The rest of his cohorts were still in Texas, but appeared to be closing up shop. Regardless, they were in separate vehicles anyway, with McNamara driving that big, armored Hummer. Bray knew the beast belonged to Reno Garth, and McNamara was apparently going back to Phoenix to return it to him.

But Garth was traveling to Vegas with Wolf. It was about a twelve or thirteen hour jaunt from Del Rio to Phoenix, and then another four and a half or five from there to Vegas. It was a lot of driving, but

McNamara had supposedly said he'd be at Wolf's fight. Bray knew that he was taking a chance having Powers tail them by car, but he did seem pretty adept at doing that. Plus, he said he'd been able to plant a GPS tracker on the Hummer one night when McNamara and his friends were out playing "pretend border patrol."

It should be safe enough, Bray thought. Allow him to follow at an extended, safe distance.

In a way it was too bad that McNamara and company hadn't tangled with the Mexican cartel. It would have most likely taken him out of the equation permanently. But that might not be such a good thing, either. With one-half of their surveillance assignment eliminated, this sweet gig would be significantly curtailed. Bray was feeling better about things now. His and Abraham's new employer, Von Tillberg, seemed a lot more circumspect then their previous one, a mafia don, had been. The rich pervert merely wanted all of the possible loose ends regarding his late uncle's sordid affairs tidied up. He wasn't out for revenge, which was all the better. If anything, the rich man had a reptilian-like core that made him virtually devoid of emotions. That made the pressure, and the possibility of Abraham and him getting drawn into some double-murder investigation seem less likely. For now, anyway, it was just watch, record, and report.

Maureen was next to him now and she smiled.

They'd spent an intimate night together in Phoenix before getting up early to tag Wolf going from his garage apartment at McNamara's ranch to the gym where he met up with his cadre of trainers. The group then proceeded to I-93 and were no doubt driving here to Vegas. Wolf's fight was tomorrow, the weigh-in tonight, so there was no need to keep him under constant surveillance.

Just as she got there the buzzer sounded, the yellow light began whirling, and the first of the suitcases crept up the ramp and onto the rotating metallic belt.

"I hope we can grab something to eat after we check in," she said. "I'm starving. I haven't had anything to eat since we left Phoenix."

Bray grinned. "You had some snacks on the plane, didn't you?"

"Ugh. Pretzels and lousy crackers. I sure wish they still served peanuts."

"How about I take you to In-N-Out as soon as we get our car."

Maureen frowned. "How about the Peppermill instead? I really like that place a lot better."

"Wherever you want," he said. "All we have to do is pick up our tickets for the fight tomorrow night. Then we'll wait for him to come to us."

She started to say something but his cell phone rang. It was the burner, which meant that it was either Abraham or Powers. He glanced at the screen and saw that it was the lawyer.

"What's the situation?" Abraham's voice asked.

"We're in the airport now. Getting our luggage."

"The airport? In Vegas?"

Bray was beginning to get irritated with the other man, and almost answered that he'd already told him that when they'd talked earlier, but instead answered, "Correct."

"Is our boy there?"

"No," Bray said. "He's driving."

Abraham was silent for a moment, and then asked, "What about the other?"

Even though they were on burner phones, Bray appreciated the lawyer's due diligence to protocol: never use a proper name on the phone when an obscure reference will do.

"He's on the road, too. Heading home."

"You got somebody on him?"

The worried tone had returned to Abraham's voice.

"I do, but relax," Bray said, doing his best not to sound irritated. After all, technically the lawyer was his boss, or at least the one okaying the expenses. "If what was overheard today at BITW, he'll be here tomorrow night as well. All our eggs will be in one basket for a change."

"BITW?"

"Best in the West."

"The training facility? You were there?"

"Not me," Bray said. "My female associate."

"Her?" Abraham sounded alarmed. "She didn't tip our hand, did she?"

His voice was so loud that Maureen apparently caught that snippet of the conversation. She frowned, raised the middle finger of her left hand, and flashed it at Bray's cell phone.

"Of course not," Bray said, smiling and winking at her. "She's a pro. I would be employing her if she wasn't. She merely overheard a conversation that the one in Texas was pulling up stakes to come up to see Wolf's fight."

He heard the lawyer blow out a long breath.

"Okay. And then what?" Abraham asked.

"And then we see where they lead us from there."

Another loud breath and then the lawyer said, "Sounds good. Keep me posted."

With that he hung up.

Bray slipped the burner phone back into his pocket.

"What an asshole," Maureen said. "Does he think I'm a neophyte, or what?"

Before Bray could reply, her head twisted and she walked toward the spout where the suitcases were being ejected. He followed.

Maureen was at the edge of the carousel now pulling one of their suitcases over the rim. It appeared to be his.

He watched with appreciation as the taunt muscles of her ass danced under the thin fabric of her pants.

Yeah, he thought. *She's a pro, a pretty good operative, all right, and she does have her uses.*

He glanced at his watch and calculated how much time taking her to dinner would take. It wouldn't do to expect her to make love on an empty stomach, much less his. But of course, she'd probably want to change clothes it they were going to the Peppermill. Maybe room service would be better.

She studied his face as she wheeled the suitcase in front of him.

"What are you thinking?" she asked.

"Oh, nothing," he said, and then winked.

She frowned and turned away, apparently picking up on his innuendo.

Grinning to himself, he hoped this gig would continue on for a while longer.

***

SAN ANTONIO INTERNATIONAL AIRPORT
INTERNATIONAL GATE
LAS VEGAS, NEVADA

Alfredo Rivera, *El Tigre*, tapped Esteban Cortez Jr. on the shoulder and motioned him forward toward the Custom's official.

"Get your passport ready," Rivera whispered in Spanish. "And don't forget to use the right name. And act natural."

Cortez Jr. appeared perplexed. "*Pero—*"

"Shhh." He raised an extended index finger to cross perpendicularly over his lips.

El hijo gordo stopped protesting.

Rivera had made the trip to the U.S. many times using the expertly forged passports. It was imperative that you acted natural and innocuous. Just a couple of *turistas* eager to see *los Estados Unidos*. That this *stupido* had to be schooled on everything was a constant source of irritation. He held up his real passport and the official tourist visa.

"*Haga simpatico,*" he repeated.

The young Cortez frowned and mumbled something unintelligible under his breath as he poked through his *veliz*.

Rivera felt the irritation building within him but pushed it away.

The time will come, he thought. And *su arrogancia* will make it even sweeter.

When they had returned from *Piedras Negras* the older Cortez had been totally taken in by the exaggerated description of the encounter with the Gutierrez band. Both taken in and impressed. So impressed was he that he instructed Rivera to take *el hijo* with him to *los esados unidos*, despite the protestations *el pendejo gordo*. Rivera had thought that fishing though the dead mule's slithery innards the day before would have been enough for Cortez Jr. to implore his father to delay the next phase of his education.

"*Lo qué pasó en Piedras Negras fue muy duro,*" *El Hijo* had said. "*No me gusta.*"

"*Tonterías,*" the older Cortez shot back. "As I have told you, it is good for you to see how our operation works. How I built it from the ground up. And Alfredo is the best of teachers."

The younger Cortez frowned.

"*Pero antes, durante la batalla—*"

"*Cállate,*" Cortez Sr. barked. "Alfredo has already told me all about it. And he said that you performed well under fire."

The younger one's eyebrows arched ever so slightly in what had to have been surprise. Then his dark eyes shot a glance toward Rivera, who stood there smiling.

The image of finding Cortez Jr. lying on the floor in a puddle of piss, sobbing hysterically, floated back to him. And afterward, when they split open the woman's belly to retrieve the stuffed condoms, the younger man had turned away and puked as her guts spilled out. The recollection of all this made the smile broaden as he stared at *el hijo*.

That is correct, Rivera thought. *I lied to your father, making you into the hero that you are certainly not. But make no mistake, pendejo gordo, when the time comes, I will enjoy watching you piss your pants again and beg for your life.*

They moved forward in the Custom's line and stepped to the table together. The gringo sitting there had a bored, disinterested look on his face.

"Passport and visa, please."

Rivera handed the requested items to the official and stood motionless. His eyes, however, scanned the room looking for cameras. He saw several. This was why they had to enter using their own, correct identification. The facial recognition software now was thorough and comprehensive, but he hoped the masks would obscure them. Should any hint of deception be suspected, like using a false name, it could throw the entire operation into jeopardy. They had to get through this entry without arousing suspicion, and then the race to tag up with the others would begin.

The custom official glanced at the picture and nation of origin on the passport, then up to the face of Rivera and asked him to lower his mask. The space between the official's eyebrows creased into two parallel wrinkles and he then said in Spanish, "*¿Es usted mexicano?*"

"*Sí,*" Rivera said, flashing a grin. "But I no look it, eh?"

The official glanced back and forth, between the passport and the man standing before him, then shone an ultraviolet light device on the passport.

"Actually, you kind of look like that Mexican boxer," the official said. "What's his name? *Canelo?*"

"*Sí, Canelo,*" Rivera said. "That means cinnamon. His name is actually Saul Alverez. I have seen him fight, but he is no relation."

"You sure do look like him. With the red hair and all."

"Many people have told me that, *señor.*" He allowed his head to loll back as he emitted a brief laugh. "I only wish I had his money, no?"

"You and me both."

Engage him, Rivera thought. Be *señor simpatico.*

"In truth," Rivera continued, fitting the mask back over his face. "My mother was an *americano*. But I was born and raised in Mexico. Monterrey. My father met my mother when she was visiting. He met her in Monterrey, you know, like the old song by Frank Sinatra. Only it was reversed. My mother met my father there, instead of the other way around."

"Interesting," the official said. "And what is the

purpose of your visit?"

"Visiting family." He turned and gestured toward Cortez Jr. "And this is my cousin, Esteban. He has never met the relatives of my mother. It is his first time in your country. Show him your passport, *primo*."

Cortez Jr. handed over his passport and visa as well.

Good, thought Rivera. *He is keeping his mouth shut, just like I told him*.

The official's eyes moved to *el hijo*, and then back to the forms. He stamped them, handed them back, and then asked if they had anything to declare.

"*Nada*," Rivera said. "Nothing. As I told you, *señor*, we are here to see family."

"You can pick up your luggage over there," the official said. "Enjoy your time in the United States."

And so we will, Rivera thought. *And so we will*.

As they walked over to get their luggage, Cortez Jr. whispered, "I am tired of playing these stupid games. What is the purpose of all this and why is my father making me do this?"

¿Los estúpidos juegos? Stupid games? Rivera suppressed his irritation once again.

"Listen," he said. "And learn. Your father has assigned me to educate you. So you do what you have to do. *Siempre...* Always."

The other man made no reply, but his nostrils flared in an indication of disgust and rage as he slipped his mask back up in place.

Siempre, Rivera thought. *Tu siempre seras la estúpida idiota. El pendejo gordo.*

***

MEN'S LOCKER ROOM
MGM GRAND GYMNASIUM
LAS VEGAS, NEVADA

Six-tenths of a pound, Wolf thought as he sat naked on the wooden bench in the sauna and continued to drip sweat. His head was killing him… A dehydration headache, no doubt… A bad one, too.

All for little over half a fucking pound.

That was what the scale had said, but he still didn't believe it. He already could feel the cramps creeping up his legs. Now he would have a little less than twenty-four hours to rehydrate, provided he could make weight after the one hour extension.

He still didn't believe it.

The scale at the gym had shown him to be 205, which was one pound under the limit. There was no way he could have gained the extra pound-and-a-half in the short time it took to drive to the weigh-in. Maybe the platform had been slanted, or something.

The cramps edged up farther. He couldn't wait to grab some water… Maybe a nice, ice-cold Gatorade…

What flavor did he want?

Icy Blue would be nice. But so would the green, traditional kind.

Whatever, he thought. As long as it's liquid and cold.

Visions of shaved ice floated in his mind's eye.

More sweat dripped onto the cement floor.

That damn scale had to be off.

Schultz had weighed at 204 and ¾. Plus, he looked ripped. He'd flexed his biceps for the cameras and tensed up his abs. His stomach looked like a washboard, his arms massive and ropy veined. And he was probably already started on his rehydration.

But this wasn't going to be a bodybuilding pose-down contest.

Wolf had planned on doing the same once he stepped off that scale, only to be told he was over the limit.

Reno had stormed over to protest, and got into a yelling match with the official.

Never a good thing to do.

The final face-off was filmed really fast, with Wolf and Schultz standing nose-to-nose and glaring at each other. Once they separated, the officials told them Wolf had one hour to make weight, or he'd be fined, and it wouldn't go down as a proper title defense. Schultz made some wild gesticulations and his handlers began yelling, but Wolf knew it was all just bullshit and hype.

Schultz dropped the pretense once the cameras stopped rolling and wished Wolf good luck in dropping the weight. It was a classy thing to do, but he could afford to be magnanimous. He was probably already slugging down his bottles of Gatorade and water. And now he had an extra hour to rehydrate that had been stolen from Wolf... All because of that damn erroneous scale.

As Wolf was once again debating which flavor he was going start off with, Georgie and Reno appeared on the other side of the long glass window in the door. Reno rapped his knuckles on it.

"How you feeling?" he yelled.

Wolf figured they didn't want to open the door to let any of the super-hot air out.

"Like a damn prune that went through a clothes wringer." Wolf shouted back.

"You doing okay?"

"I'm feeling like shit."

Wolf saw Georgie turn and say something inaudible because of the glass barrier.

Fuck the fine, Wolf thought. *Who cares if it's less money? Just let me out of here.*

He was about to say that when Reno knocked on the glass again.

"Steve, we got about five minutes left. Get ready to slip outside and let Georgie dry you off real good."

"I need a shower," Wolf said.

Reno raised his open palms and shook his head.

"Not yet. Too dangerous. You might swallow some water."

Just the mention of that made Wolf's body ache more.

He stood up and felt woozy.

"Can you take me over there in a wheelchair?" he asked.

"You need one?" Reno's voice was full of alarm.

Wolf managed a half-hearted grin. "If I don't get out of here and get something to drink pretty damn soon I will."

Georgie pulled open the door and held out a big, fluffy towel. He had a second one draped over his arm. The air in the locker room felt suddenly cold, and then the towel's texture felt like sandpaper as it rubbed over him.

Reno held up some compression shorts that looked brand new in one hand and a terrycloth robe in the other.

"Let's see where you're at on the scale," he said, "and then you can figure out if you want to put these on or not."

Georgie was smoothing the towel over Wolf's back and then his legs. It still felt like sandpaper. He stopped and handed a second towel up to Wolf.

"Dry off your hair real good," Georgie said. "And then your privates."

Wolf took the towel and began drying his hair. It was feeling less chilly now.

"Come on," Reno said. "Use this scale over here."

After finishing up the last of the wipe-down, Georgie grabbed the towel away and Wolf moved forward with short, hesitant steps. He stepped onto the white plastic top of the digital scale and exhaled.

Both Reno and Georgie were leaning over, not touching him. Their bodies blocked the view of the reading, but Wolf didn't want to look anyway.

"Looks like he's right on the money," Georgie said.

"But that's what we thought before," Reno said. "That damn, fucking scale they got over there has got to be off."

All Wolf could think about was getting something—anything, to drink.

"Tell you what," Reno said. "Just wear the robe with nothing on underneath. You can step on the scale naked."

"And show off my shortcomings?" Wolf said.

Reno smirked. "Me and Georgie'll hold the towel

front of you."

Between the escalating cramps and the pounding headache, Wolf was ready to agree to anything.

"Whatever works," he said, and silently prayed that he'd left that six-tenths of a pound in the puddle on the floor of the sauna. "You do what you have to do."

CHAPTER 5

**A HALF-MILE FROM THE INTERNATIONAL BRIDGE
DEL RIO, TEXAS**

Alfredo Rivera, *El Tigre*, squatted next to a section of
small trees in the darkness and studied the half-moon
suspended against the velvet sky, appreciating his
second night in America. A myriad of stars twinkled
overhead, but down here, in this expanse of empty
field, it was it was totally dark... No lights at all...
Like someone had dropped a huge, ebony cloak over
everything beyond his immediate area. It was quiet,
too, except for the ubiquitous chirping of the insects.
He was surprised that they were still active, with the
less than hospitable temperatures of late, even down
here near the border. There had been a couple of
frosts farther north, killing their brethren. But these
were the survivors, and they, too, served a purpose.

When the chirping stopped, it meant someone was near. Nature's alarm system. And in the absence of any appreciable moonlight was a unique camouflage, too. You could barely see ten feet in front of your face. Fortunately, he had a bit of augmentation to provide some technological advantage in that department. He flipped the night-vision goggles down in place and the blackness was transformed into a new, green-tinctured world, as clear day. Rotating his head, he did a quick survey of the area.

There was nothing but patches of mesquite, stunted and gnarled trees, and waist-high grass cast in various shade of green... He knew that beyond this point, further into the darkness, lay the *Rio Grande*. Hopefully, his coyotes were ferrying the mules across.

Rivera appreciated the silence once again. The insects had resumed, but their constant trilling melted into the placidity of the new green world.

"*¿Ver cualquier cosa?*" one of Europa's gang asked. The guy was good-sized and tough looking. Probably the enforcer of the group.

And at least this one spoke Spanish.

"*Nada,*" Rivera said. "*¿Donde esta tu jefe?*"

"*Por ahí.*"

"Tell him I want to talk to him," Rivera said, switching to English.

"Okay," the man said, and started to move away.

"Hey," Rivera said.

The other man stopped.

Rivera flipped up the goggles and studied him for a moment. He was sure he could take him if and when the time came. And, in Rivera's right front pants pocket there was the comfortable feel of his raptor knife, which had survived unmolested inside his luggage.

"*¿Como te llamas?*"

The guy's face registered a little surprise.

"Julio," he said. "*Pero ellos me llaman martillo.*"

Rivera flashed a quick grin.

"*El martillo.* I like that," he said. "The Hammer."

Julio walked away with a dumb grin on his face.

And it was good to know. This one was big and strong and dumb. He could be easily manipulated if and when the time came. What was a hammer when compared to a tiger?

Flipping down the goggles again Rivera did another sweep of the area.

Still nothing was stirring.

After pushing the goggles up once more, he stared at the darkness, and then checked his watch. The signal would come. Soon he'd see the quick, solitary flash of the red-colored light in the darkness, followed by another. Until then, they would wait.

No complaints, he thought.

After all, thus far everything had gone like clockwork. They'd rented the van in San Antonio with one of his false driver's licenses portraying him as an American with the Irish-sounding name of James

Joyce, he and Cortez Jr. had driven down to the Del Rio area. Along the way they'd stopped at several pharmacies and a Walmart to pick up a couple of boxes of latex gloves, several cases of bottled water, saline solution, laxatives, and twenty enemas. There was no trouble finding the meeting spot, a lonely diner on some non-descript highway. Eight motorcycles were parked out in front. Inside they'd made contact with *Los Merodeadores*—or, in English, The Marauders, the Mexican/American motorcycle gang that Cortez Sr. had been using for distribution here in the U.S. Their leader, Enrique Europa, was a skinny little shit who wore his dark hair clipped short on the sides but long on top. So long that he kept the excess wound into a top knot about the size of a tennis ball. The punk wasn't that fluent in Spanish either, and couldn't even read the language. Rivera had never been very impressed with him. In addition to being a skinny little shit, he was purportedly an American product of some tough barrio here in Texas. He did appear to be somewhat smarter than the rest of them, and that most likely explained his status as the leader. A lot of these gang leaders in *los Estados Unidos* were little shits, small in stature, but able to project authority, to take command because they were a little bit smarter than the rest of them. His chief source of status, however, was that he had an older brother, Jesus, a former gang-banger and leader of *Los Merodeadores*, who was now serving time—a life sentence no less, in a federal prison in the U.S. The brother had been a major player in the drug trafficking business and had killed a DEA agent. That gave him immediate stature, and this stature, by association, subsequently transferred to his younger brother, Enrique. None of this mattered much to Rivera, anymore than did the family relationship of Esteban Cortez Senior and Junior.

Dos pendejos grandes.

He exhaled a long breath.

No, he thought, *it does not matter.*

As long as Europa served his purpose here and provided the right connection to get the product to the right dispensers, everything was good. The gang was mediocre, as tough motorcycle gangs went. Certainly nothing like *los duros de mexico*, but they had a good, solid footprint here in this locality of Texas and a little bit beyond. Lots of Mexican-Americans, and even more illegals were here now. They blended in quite well, but once things expanded to the new receiving area, the one in Arizona, they were going to have to merge with that bigger American motorcycle gang now. And Cortez Sr. had already set this merger up. It would only take an introduction.

The Devil's Breed, he thought. Their tentacles purportedly stretched in all directions, to each coast and even up to Canada. They were the key to expanding things, and Cortez Sr. knew this.

El Tigre hadn't liked the idea of change, but the *el*

jefe had taken numerous pains to set things up. The younger Cortez had sat in virtual silent repose in the passenger seat, and Rivera knew the *el pendejo gordo* had to be feeling overwhelmed with the complexity of the operation. He was still in the van, sitting silently, and maybe even asleep. The *pendejo* hadn't said one word in over an hour. This suited Rivera just fine. He smirked. In the fat boy's heart, he had to know that he was not ready to take over the operation, as his father wanted. He would never be ready, nor would he get the chance

Still, the picture would become clearer once he met with the new gang. It was planned for next week in Arizona when the coyotes would be bringing the next wave across. Yuma was supposed to be even easier now than here in Del Rio. And they were getting higher paying clients from all sorts of countries from all over the world—Russia, Ukraine, Africa, the Middle East... No longer was it just *los pobres de mexico y sus hermanos de america central y suda america*. This international clientele made the communication a bit more challenging, which is where Rivera's fluency in English made him so indispensable. He smiled. His *gringo madre* had taught him well, even if her whoring ways had led to him and his brothers and sisters growing up in squalor.

An education from the streets... From Monterrey to *la Ciudad de Mexico*, it had been hard and tough.

He had learned it all, and learned it well.

Soon, he would put it all to good use.

Soon he would be taking over the entire operation.

"What's up, Alfie?" Europa asked, walking up. "Hammer says you wanted to see me."

Alfie?

Rivera merely gazed at him without speaking.

He had the big punk with him. In the previous times they'd met on these night border crossing meetings, Europa had always made it a point not to call him Alfredo or *El Tigre*, which he preferred. It was always "Alfie" to this little shit. He would be made to pay for his disrespect.

One day soon I will have to rectify it, El Tigre thought.

"Did you get a hold of Griggas?" he asked.

"Yeah, the older one's sending his brother and a couple of his boys with the money. I'm supposed to call them to come in once we've got the stuff all washed and ready for transport."

"Good. We'll be taking the money with us back across the border tonight. Once we finish extracting."

Europa smirked. "Ain't that gonna depend on how quick we can get them to shit it all out of them?"

"Once we get everything inserted, it shouldn't take that long."

Europa laughed. "Yeah, well, we'll see about that, won't we?"

A red light flashed in the darkness about a hundred yards away.

"Look," Europa said. "That them?"

Rivera waited.

Another red flash.

Taking out his burner phone, Rivera hit the button to dial the number. Martín answered on the first ring.

"*Hola.*"

"*Tráelos,*" Rivera said. Bring them.

"*Hay una problema,*" Martín said.

"*¿Qué?*"

"*Uno de los testarudos está enfermo.*"

"*¿Como?*"

"*Dentro de su cuerpo,*" Martín said. "*Creo que hubo una ruptura.*"

"*Mierda,*" Rivera said. "*¿Puede caminar?*"

"*No.*"

"*Llevarlo. Apurarse.*" He disconnected.

"What's going on?" Europa asked.

"One of the mules," Rivera said. "It sounds like the fucking condoms broke inside him. He's overdosing. They're carrying him in now."

"Shit," Europa said. "We gonna have to cut it out of him then?"

Rivera merely nodded. It had happened before, the price of doing business. They would lose whatever packages had broken open, but hopefully, if they were careful, they could salvage the rest. At least, judging from what Martín had said, it was recent, so they didn't have to carry him very far. It should just be a simple matter of slitting him open and removing whatever was left of the in-tact condoms while the rest of them were downing the laxatives. It would be best if the others did not see too much of the gruesome details. Having one OD and the corresponding extraction could cause the rest of them to panic. He had taken care to keep the others away from the previous mishap with the woman who'd been shot while they were still in Mexico. Her packages had all been recovered unharmed. Luckily, the stray bullet had struck her in the top of the head as she lay on the floor. Those condoms had then been re-distributed between the rest of *los testarudos*... A bit of an overload for some of them. Perhaps that was why this one had died—like the old saying, putting five pounds of shit in a four pound bag. But it was inconsequential. The only thing that did matter was to keep moving forward without any unseemly delays. If the others saw the disemboweling, it could cause some of them to scatter into the darkness. It could be tricky and time consuming to track them down.

That could present problems, especially with Griggas's people on the way with the money for the exchange.

He flipped down the night-vision goggles again and saw the green-tinted group of them pushing their way through the waist-high grass. Two of the men were carrying a twitching body between them. That had to be the one who was overdosing.

Europa had his goggles down as well.

"They're almost here," he said. "How do you want to handle this?"

El Tigre glanced back toward the van as he fingered the angular metal of the raptor knife. Cortez Jr. was still sitting in the passenger seat. He appeared to be smoking a joint now.

Pendejo, *El Tigre* thought. Mellowing out, he called it. But we will see how mellow he is after make him reach into the dead mule's guts to extract the product.

It was time for the son of a bitch to get his hands dirty.

***

THE FIGHTER'S LOCKER ROOM
THE MGM GRAND HOTEL AND CASINO
LAS VEGAS, NEVADA

Wolf lay on the table, trying as best he could to relax, but that was next to impossible. Across the room Barbie sat transfixed in front of the TV watching one of the preliminary bouts. Reno was now back and sitting next to her, but he kept looking over toward Wolf. It had been over thirty minutes since the officials and one of Schultz's handlers had come in to watch Georgie wrap Wolf's hands. Reno had gone to Schultz's dressing room to watch the same procedure in there. It was a standard regulation to prevent any illegal tactics, like sprinkling plaster of Paris on the fighter's bandaged hands that would turn hard as concrete once the match, and the sweating, began. Georgie had taken his time and done it right, down to periodically checking the tautness of each wrap and then adjusting the gauze padding under the watchful eyes. When he was done, he slipped each of Wolf's hands into the regulation, padded-leather MMA gloves. Then the blue tape was wrapped around each wrist fastening, and the official initialed them. Schultz's man slipped out and they waited for Reno to return. When he did the ref, a tall, burly white guy who was a retired cop, was with him and went over the rules and asked if Wolf understood them.

"Yes, sir," he said, falling back into his habitual military courtesy.

"He's the champ," Reno chimed in. "This ain't exactly our first rodeo. You just make sure that the other guy fights fair."

The ref raised an eyebrow.

"That's my job," he said.

"Yeah," Reno said, scrunching up the right side of his face to form a half-squint. "I know it is. But I heard through the grapevine that him and his corner are known for dealing from the bottom of the deck sometimes."

"Where'd you hear that?" the ref asked.

"Around," Reno said. "I'd appreciate it if you kept your eye on them, just in case."

After the ref left Wolf asked Reno what he'd heard.

"Nothing." Reno grinned. "Just planting the seed. That fucker hits you low, or something, the ref's gonna remember and ream his ass really good."

Wolf smiled.

Vicarious achievements, he thought. *Reno has more riding on this than I do.*

Now, about twenty-five minutes later, the waiting game continued. One of the prelims was in progress on a large flatscreen monitor in the far side of the room, but Wolf couldn't watch it. He was concentrating on two things now: trying to get whatever relaxation he could in these last few minutes and trying to put aside the escalating case of the nerves that always came before a match.

Relax, he told himself as he breathed in and out.

That plan ended sooner than he expected when Georgie Patton appeared next to him and slipped on a pair of focus mitts. He slapped them together.

"You ready, champ? Time to start warming up."

Wolf tossed off the blanket he'd had covering him and followed Georgie over to the area that was clear of any benches or obstructions. He still had his sweat shirt on, the one with the sleeves cut off, and he slipped that over his head.

Georgie slapped the mitt together again, and Reno came ambling over.

Wolf raised his hands and delivered a quick

one-two combination to the outstretched pads. He
practiced moving a bit and repeated the combination
a few more times. His timing was there, the dehydration cramps had all vanished, and he was feeling
good, but not great.

So was he ready?

I guess I'll find out soon enough, he told himself,
and threw another set of combinations.

***

A HALF-MILE FROM THE INTERNATIONAL BRIDGE
DEL RIO, TEXAS

The first thing Rivera did was to tell all of them to
strip off all of their clothes. The naked bodies now
stood before him in the enveloping darkness all high-
lighted in green by the enhancement of his night-vision goggles. The males stood there unabashed and
unconcerned, while the females crossed their arms
in front of their breasts, or demurely kept a palm
flattened over their pubic areas. That these *mujueres*
still retained a trace of dignity amused him. He saw
Cortez Jr. eying the women. Only three of the them
were worth looking at, and those not very enticing in
their present filthy condition. Five men, five women,
and with the boy, made it eleven.

A lucky number, or so *los americanos* said. The

group had gone from unlucky thirteen to the now lucky eleven.

Or had they?

It still remained to be seen if their luck would hold out.

Martín and Fernando carried the sixth man, now unconscious, to the other side of the van.

"*¿Será bien?*" one of the women asked, cocking her chin toward the departing figures.

"*No tenga cuidado a el,*" Rivera said. He kept his voice low and firm as he added that it was prudent for her just to be concerned about herself. The young boy moved closer to one of the women and she placed a protective arm around his shoulders. Perhaps he would live to see a new day here in *el norte...* Or perhaps not.

Rivera told Roberto and Paco to check the clothes of the mules and then put them on their hands and knees for the treatments. He turned to Europa and saw that the skimpy leader had a grin plastered on his face.

"Something funny?" Rivera asked.

"You gonna start with the enemas now?"

"We are, and my men will need some help sifting through the shit later."

Europa pursed his lips and blew out a derisive breath.

"Good luck with that."

Rivera didn't have time for this skinny little shit's fastidiousness, but he felt it best, for the moment anyway, to keep on schedule by having things run smoothly. "Have your men set up a perimeter. You have some goggles, right?"

"Yeah, me and Julio do," Europa said. He nodded to *El Martillo*, who began shouting orders. The rest of the gang began moving toward their motorcycles.

Rivera then clapped Cortez Jr. on the shoulder and motioned toward the van.

"*Vamos.*"

The younger Cortez followed, his feet dragging almost reluctantly. When they got to the other side of the van, Martín was holding his hand over the dying man's mouth and nose. The mule's legs were still twitching, but only a little bit now.

Rivera estimated that it had been about twenty-four hours since the ingestions. Depending on the speed of the man's digestive cycle, the condoms should be somewhere in the digestive tract. But with the rupture, it was going to be tricky. He pulled out a packet of disposable black latex gloves and tore it open. After taking out a pair for himself, he gave another pair to Cortez Jr. and then tossed the package to Fernando.

"*No más,*" he said to Martín.

It was taking too long, and they had a lot of work to do. Reaching into his pocket, Rivera withdrew his hooked, raptor knife and used his thumb to flick open the blade.

Martín glanced up at him and withdrew his hand.

The dying man's breathing resumed with several snorting gasps.

Rivera looked down at Martín.

"*¿Tienes un cuchillo? Quítate la camisa a el.*"

Martín nodded and pulled his knife out of his pants pocket, flipped it open, and began cutting away the man's shirt.

Cortez Jr. held up the black gloves. "What do I need these things for?"

"Don't you want to earn your stripes now?" Rivera jiggled the knife and looked at him.

The other man's mouth twisted into a frown.

"What do you want me to do?" he asked. "Cut his throat?"

He was speaking in English now, apparently knowing that neither Martín nor Fernando had much understanding of that language.

"Among other things." Rivera smiled. "We have to do another extraction. Just like in *Piedras Negras.*"

"No way. I ain't doing that."

"You will do as I tell you to do. That is what your father ordered."

Cortez Jr. swallowed hard, and then shook his head.

"I said no. And you can't make me."

The man was sweating rather profusely now and Rivera wondered if *el pendejo gordo* had been doing more than just marijuana when he'd been sitting in the van. But where could he have gotten it? He had been talking to that little piss ant, Europa. He must have given it to him. Maybe he'd slipped him some coke, or something.

"That is not what your father wanted," Rivera said. He was enjoying the game too much to easily capitulate.

"I don't care." Cortez Jr. pursed his lips, looked at Martín and Fernando, and then leaned close to Rivera.

"Please, I cannot do it. The blood, the smell… It makes me sick."

Rivera stood in silence, a lips-only smile gracing his mouth. Then, finally, he spoke.

"Do you remember how I lied for you before? I told your father you were brave and strong."

The younger man said nothing.

"I do not like to lie to your father," Rivera said. "He is my *patron*. My *jefe*."

"Please." His voice was barely a squeak.

After extracting a few extra beats of silence, Rivera clapped the younger Cortez on the shoulder and grinned.

"*No importa*," he said, knowing that he owned the fat prick now, and this would come in handy down the road. "Watch me and I will show you how it's done. *Tenga cuidado de la sangre.*"

Martín moved back out of the way, wary of any blood spray as Rivera knelt and grabbed the convulsing man's hair. He pulled the unconscious man's head back, exposing the throat, and then used the raptor knife to slit the neck area from ear to ear.

***

THE BUBBLE
MGM GRAND HOTEL AND CASINO
LAS VEGAS, NEVADA

Robert Bray and company sat about three rows up from McNamara and the group who was with him. Maureen sat on one side of Bray, and Jack Powers on the other although not exceptionally close. Powers was drinking a beer and looked exhausted. He'd said following McNamara back to Phoenix and taken a solid fifteen hours. Luckily, the GPS he'd slipped on the Hummer down in Del Rio worked like a charm, allowing him to trail the man at a discreet distance. Then things got a little bit trickier as McNamara drove to Mesa and picked up another guy. They dropped the Hummer off at Reno Garth's gym. After that, they then drove together in McNamara's Escalade up to Vegas. Luckily, they hadn't done the drive to Sin City until Saturday, so he had some down time in between. As it stood, however, Powers said he hadn't been able to change clothes or shower for two days.

From the smell of him, Bray believed that was about right.

Maureen, on the other hand, smelled fresh and clean and was wearing her favorite enchanting perfume.

La Fem Fatale, she'd told him.

Whatever it was called, it sure beat smelling Powers' pervasive B.O. Bray hoped it wouldn't make him more noticeable, but hell, they were in a sports arena. There should be enough competing odors to go around, and who the hell would be paying any attention anyway?

He leaned closer to Maureen, putting his arm around her, and whispered in her ear. For all appearances, they were just a couple at the fights.

"Use these binoculars," he said. "I've got a zoom on my camera."

She took the mini-binoculars and snapped them open. Bray lifted the camera to his face and zeroed in on the group three rows down from them. It was on auto focus and as hit pressed the button for the zoom lens, the people below became clearer.

"Okay, down three rows we have McNamara," he said. The red headed woman on his right is Dolly Kline, and the Hispanic one on his left is Brenda Carrerra. They're both bounty hunters. Call themselves the P Patrol. Or at least they used to. The black chick next to Brenda is Wolf's girlfriend, or maybe his ex now, since he's moved back to Phoenix. Her name's Yolanda Moore. Watch out for her because she's now a cop. Las Vegas Metro."

"She's gorgeous," Maureen said. "In fact, all three of them are."

"Yeah," Bray said. "Now it's your turn. What about the guy with them? Anybody look familiar."

Maureen adjusted the binoculars focus ring.

"Yeah," she said after a few seconds. "The slender guy to the left of the black bitch. He's Pete Thornton. Wolf was teaching that class with him at Best in the West last Thursday."

That fit with what Powers had reported. McNamara had stopped off in Mesa and picked somebody up there before driving to his ranch house, and then on to Vegas.

"He's a veteran," Maureen continued. "Marines. Has an artificial left leg."

Again, this was something that Bray already knew, but he let her continue.

"Hey, wait a minute," she said and adjusted her view a bit. "See that big guy with the blond hair sitting close to Thornton?"

Bray shifted his own viewfinder and focused on the subject.

Blond male, mid-thirties, longish hair, tied in a small ponytail. Large shoulders. Looked to be good-sized.

Was he another MMA fighter?

"What about him?" Bray asked.

"He looks familiar," she said, adjusting the focus some more. "Yeah, it's him. all right. He was at Best in the West, too. When I, or rather when Ms. Tonya Knight, magazine reporter, was there."

"Taking the class?"

"Huh-un," she said. "He was just visiting. His name's... Let me think." After a brief pause, she said, "Lucien Pike." She paused and smiled. "I remember thinking he was kind of cute. In a rough-cut sort of way."

Bray felt a quick twinge of jealousy, but it passed quickly. What did he care if she occasionally looked at another man? He'd own her body tonight.

"Let's stick to business," he said. "You recall anything else about him?"

Maureen giggled. "Yeah. Well, Wolf made some kind of bullshit up about him being an old army buddy, or something. but he's the one I told you about. He's some kind of fed. He was driving that car with government plates."

Bray blew out a long breath. He suddenly hoped he hadn't made a fatal mistake bringing her in this close to watch McNamara, especially with this federal agent now tagging along. Plus, McNamara's son-in-law, William Franker, was an FBI agent. He did a quick scan to check for any signs of him, but saw none. Still, a federal agent… Not good.

"A fed," he said slowly. "You know what kind?"

"No," she said, rolling her head to make it look like she was delivering a sexy tidbit. "Like I said, his car had G-plates."

Bray compressed his lips, lowered his ocular camera, and reevaluated the current surveillance. He had expected that Thornton would be here, but not some damn fed. He wondered what agency the guy worked for. Glancing around again, he mulled over the prospect of terminating things for tonight. "Maybe we should abort."

Maureen lowered the binoculars and snuggled against him, and he felt the soft pressing of her breast into his side.

"Aw, come on," she said. "I want to see the rest of the fights. Or at least Wolf's. We're far enough away that they won't notice us."

"I don't know," Bray said. "I don't want to take the chance on one of them recognizing you."

Maureen laughed. "Will you relax? I told you, I was in disguise—glasses, contacts, dark wig. And the only thing they were looking at were my boobs."

She snuggled even closer to him.

He was glad her attributes were undercover tonight. She'd worn a baggy, Golden Knights sweatshirt for this evening's surveillance, and had her hair, which was back to her natural blonde hair color, pulled back into a ponytail. She looked almost unremarkable, but still pretty. However, it was still no time to take chances at this stage in the game. They had little left to learn tonight anyway.

Powers took a swig of his beer and tapped Bray on the shoulder.

"Hey, I'm gonna go get myself another beer," he said. "You want anything?"

"No," Bray said. "And we're here to work, remember? So take it easy and don't get sloppy."

Powers got what appeared to be a wounded expression on his face.

"Hey, I been on the job pretty much for the last forty-eight hours non-stop," he said. "Seems to me I earned a little break."

"You have," Bray said. "But not quite yet. After you get your beer, move to a different spot.

Powers's face wrinkled. "Huh? What for?"

"Because I want you to get closer to our target. See what you can hear. We're too far away up here."

Powers cocked his head slight and frowned.

"But, boss, I'm really bushed. Can't Maureen do it?"

Bray just stared at him to let his air of authority sink in, and then shook his head. "There's too great a chance she might be recognized."

"Recognized?"

"She was up close and personal with Wolf and two other guys, one of whom is apparently a federal agent, on Thursday."

Powers got the message and rose to his feet. As he

started to move away Bray added, "And like I said, take it easy on the beer."

Powers gave a curt nod, but didn't look back.

"Isn't he the poop," Maureen said.

"Stinks like it, too."

Maybe it was time to get rid of bad smells and dead weight, Bray thought. *But he's still useful fodder. There may come a time when someone has to take a beating or a bullet and it ain't gonna be me.*

"Look," Maureen said. "Wolf's coming in now."

Bray decided to let the Powers matter ride for the moment. After all, it always made good sense to keep a couple of expendables around.

***

Wolf had to do the walk down the catwalk alone and as always felt that it had to be the longest walk in the world. The lights in the surrounding auditorium had been subdued and he knew the TV cameras were focusing on him. He wore the red satin gown that Barbie had given him, the one that Reno used to wear, and under it he wore only his standard black compression shorts, which were more like a slightly enlarged speedo swimsuit, with the cup supporter in place. As the defending champion, he got to enter the octagon second although it mattered little to him. Reno had insisted he delay it for several minutes to allow the tension and nerves to eat at his opponent.

"Let him feel the pressure standing in there waiting for the champ," Reno told him. "It's psychology."

The psychology pronouncement struck Wolf as both funny and ironic. Didn't it stand to reason that the waiting would adversely affect Wolf as well as his opponent? Both of them were anxious to get it on. It was also "psychologically obvious" that Reno wanted this win more than Wolf did. Before they'd left the dressing room, Reno had placed both hands on Wolf's shoulders, leaned close to him, and whispered to him.

"I know you can do this, Steve." His tone was soft, almost bordering on intimacy. "You're as ready as can be, and you can take this guy. Now I wasn't gonna tell you this until after the fight, but I just got the word that we got a shot at the world title if you win this one."

Wolf saw the gleam in Reno's eyes. It was his chance at redemption, his chance to regain the title that had slipped away from him after he'd been shot down in Mexico.

"So you gotta win," Reno said, his head bowed almost in the manner of a supplicant. "You gotta."

"I'll do my best," Wolf said.

And here he was.

His quick glance around confirmed that the auditorium was filled to the new, socially distanced restrictions. A bunch of the spectators applauded as he walked and Wolf cast a quick glance around. He could distinguish bodies, but not faces, and wondered just who was sitting up there in the stands watching. Suddenly a man, sitting amongst a group of males and females, waved.

Was it Mac?

Wolf wasn't able to make out any details due to the dimness of the lighting, but he was certain it had been. And the women... Was one of them her?

He took in a deep breath.

Most likely Mac was up there. He'd said he was coming, although Wolf hadn't heard from him. And Miss Dolly, too. Maybe Brenda, the second member of Miss Dolly's team, but who else" Maybe Pete? Or Buck, Joe, and Ron?

No, they were probably getting things set up for the next gig down at the border. Pete might be there, if he'd made the trek up from Phoenix, maybe with Mac.

But the real question in his mind was whether Yolanda, his lady love, was up there. Even though they'd mutually agreed to each take a step back, Vegas was her home town, and she had to know about the fight. Did he really hope she was up there, or not? At this point, he wasn't sure.

He got to the edge of the octagon and stopped. Schultz was already inside the cage, bouncing around on the balls of his feet and throwing punches. He looked as impressive as he had yesterday at the weigh-in.

Wolf slipped out of the robe and tossed it to Reno, who was standing off to the side with Wolf's championship belt slung over his shoulder.

The gold inlays of the belt gleamed under the bright lights and Wolf suddenly felt a twinge of regret that he'd brought this one along, instead of using Reno's copy from the gym display.

I sure don't want to lose it, he thought. *So get your mind back in the game.*

He cast one more look at the belt, and then waited for one of the officials to do the body-grease inspection and mouthpiece verification. No ointments on the fighter's body were allowed before or during the match due to those types of substances made it harder for an opponent to grip a limb or apply a lock for a submission hold during the match. Once the sweating started, of course, those applications would become more difficult to effect. Reno, Georgie, and Clancy, the cut man, meandered over as the ref was applying the thin layer of Vaseline to Wolf's face. After he finished, he looked at Reno and asked, "Second mouthpiece?"

Georgie held up the plastic case with the alternate mouthpiece inside. It was a requirement of the rules in case the one Wolf was currently wearing became damaged during the fight.

Delays for safety violations were always kept to a

minimum.

"Okay," the ref said and then asked, "Any questions." Wolf shook his head and the ref stepped back, allowing Reno, Georgie, and Clancy to give him the ceremonial hugs and good luck wishes. Beyond them, Wolf caught another glimpse of Schultz over in his corner bouncing around.

"Kick his ass," Reno said.

"You the champ," Georgie added.

"Remember that." Reno's voice was firm. "We got a lot riding on this one."

Clancy was his usual taciturn self, saying nothing, but holding his kit. Wolf knew if he got cut there was no one better to address it.

Wolf went up the steps and stepped through the gate and into the octagon and Reno and Georgie accompanied him. Pacing around, Wolf tried to get the soles of his bare feet used to the somewhat abrasive texture of the mat. Schultz was barely fifteen feet away now with his manager and trainer. This was the closest the two of them had been since yesterday's weigh-in. Across the open expanse his opponent was strutting around now, the expression on his face broadcasting total confidence. His body had several tattoos, which he'd seen yesterday at the weigh-in, but failed to scrutinize. There was a jungle cat, a panther, on his left pectoral muscle, and a leopard on his left. Both arms had some kind of

Chinese characters running from the deltoid to the wrist, and as he turned Wolf saw that the man's back had a colorful dragon twisting up from the base by his waist to the stretch over his broad shoulders with its enormous black, red, and blue head displaying a gleaming yellow eye bisected by a dark slash to represent a reptilian pupil. The skin was stretched taut over a network of well-defined muscles. Schultz appeared to be in really good shape.

But this isn't a pose-down, Wolf reminded himself. It's a fight.

Wolf's only tattoos were the set of jump wings on his right forearm, which he'd gotten after graduation at Fort Benning, and the word *RANGER* outlined in black on his left shoulder. As he looked at Schultz's decorated body, Wolf was glad he hadn't gotten any more.

I wonder if he's feeling as anxious as I am, Wolf thought.

"Okay, seconds out," the ref yelled.

Reno winked at him and again said, "Kick his ass."

Georgie gave him a fist bump.

Everyone left through the gate leaving only Wolf, Schultz, and the ref.

The cyclone fencing of the eight-sided ring was jet black and had the standard padded black barrier running along the top. Sixteen perpendicular, padded posts secured the fencing in place.

The octagon announcer, a dapper man with gray hair and clad in a tailored black tuxedo, entered through the gate, microphone in hand. He strutted to the center and went into his standard spiel, saying this was to be five, five-minute rounds in the light-heavyweight division with the United States Light-heavyweight Championship on the line. The continued building the hype first introducing the challenger, "Fighting out of Boca Raton, Florida, and standing at six feet-two inches, weighing in at a rock solid two hundred-five and three quarter pounds, the challenger, Adam 'Commando' Schultz."

Boca Raton, thought Wolf. He'd passed through there once.

Schultz raised his arms and did a quick little dancing rotation.

The applause sounded obligatory.

This close, Schultz's body looked just as "rock solid" as it had yesterday and Wolf wondered how hard it had been for his opponent to make the weight.

"And in the blue corner his opponent," the announcer continued in his exaggerated tone of voice. "A man who needs no introduction here in the octagon or in Las Vegas…"

The litany went on and on, as he erroneously listed Wolf as being "from Fayetteville, North Carolina, by way of Las Vegas…"

Neither was correct. It was New Lumberton,

which, for the moment, had been changed to Spencerland. And his Vegas residency was just a fleeting memory now.

"The reigning United States light-heavyweight champion, Steve 'Ranger' Wolf."

The applause sounded much more substantial this time, but Wolf wasn't sure if that was due to his popularity or if it was coming from Reno and company standing just outside the cyclone fencing.

The thought made him smile and he raised his arms in acknowledgment.

The announcer made a few more pronouncements that Wolf paid little attention to and he smacked his fingerless gloves together to check the tight fit.

As the announcer moved from the center of the octagon and slipped out the gate, the burly ref took his place in the center. His face was dead serious. He raised his arm and held it straight out, pointing to the red corner.

"Are you ready here?" he asked Schultz.

He nodded.

The ref turned to Wolf.

"Are you ready here?"

It was Wolf's turn to nod, but was he?

He asked himself that question, and then made a conscious effort to push any negative thoughts from his mind.

"Then let's get it on!" the ref shouted, dropped his

arm, and darted away from the center of the mat.

Both fighters moved forward and Schultz extended his left arm in a show of respect.

Wolf did the same and they touched gloves.

It was time to rumble.

***

A HALF-MILE FROM THE INTERNATIONAL BRIDGE
DEL RIO, TEXAS

Rivera pulled off his shirt, hung it on the side mirror of the truck, and glanced down to check how the draining of the man's blood was going. The night-vision goggles were upright on his head, but he didn't need them to see the dark fluid was seeping into the sandy earth at a steady rate. He also noticed Cortez Jr. casting a sideways glance at him. Rivera's arms were large, his body powerful with rippling muscles and an artful design of tattoos. A row of thick black bands decorated his back and chest, mimicking the stripes of his namesake.

Cortez Jr. held his head askance... his eyes were still on *El Tigre.*

The surreptitious glance made Rivera wonder if *el hijo* was secretly gay. He constantly professed a desire for women, but maybe that was an act.

El Tigre laughed out loud at the supposition. What did it matter anyway?

What did matter is that now he had seen the fear in the other man's eyes?

Fernando was standing and holding the dead man's legs, allowing the flow to be assisted by gravity. Martín told him that the blood was almost gone now.

"*Bueno*," *El Tigre* said, and turned to Cortez Jr. "Now, just like before. We must carefully remove the packets from his intestines."

Cortez Jr. started to say something and then stopped abruptly. The corners of his mouth twisted downward and he strode several steps away. After bending over, he began puking.

Both Martín and Fernando looked at him and suppressed their laughter as they grinned up at *El Tigre*. He grinned back at them.

The loud vomiting cut into the pervasive silence of the night.

El hijo del jefe es muy débil, he thought. The boss's son is very weak.

But for the moment, he decided to leave it alone. He raised his finger to his lips in a gesture designating silence and was about to speak when a scream pierced the night. *El Tigre* backpedaled and saw that one of the women and the boy had ventured away from the group and had seen the vacant stare of the dead man.

"*Lo están matando*," the boy screamed. "*Ellos lo mataron.*"

He broke away from the woman, who was trying to shield his eyes, and he sprinted toward the high grass. The woman started to run as well, then a couple of the men fled, their naked butts quivering with each stride.

"*Mierda*," El Tigre said. Another fucking delay, and if he did not catch them quickly, it could be costly.

He told Fernando to go get the woman and Martín to get the boy. He shouldn't be able to get too far.

El Tigre then pulled the raptor knife—*la garra del tigre*, back out of his pants pocket and ran off after the two fleeing men.

The fools. Where did they think they could go?

His lungs drank in some of the cool night air as he ran through the high grass in the direction they'd gone and he felt the customary thrill and exhilaration of the pursuit.

It was time for the tiger to hunt again.

***

THE BUBBLE
MGM GRAND HOTEL AND CASINO
LAS VEGAS, NEVADA

The first round had been nothing short of a war and Wolf practically collapsed onto the stool. Both Reno and Georgie grabbed him to keep him from falling off. It flashed through Wolf's mind that it hadn't looked good him slipping like that. He hoped that no one from Schultz's camp was watching close enough to see it. But hell, they had their hands full treating their own fighter.

Clancy stood off to the side with his kit which Wolf took to mean that he didn't have any cuts. The wet flow he could feel cascading down his face was apparently sweat. About the only other thing he was cognizant of was his breathing—rapid breathing echoing in his ears.

Georgie pulled out Wolf's mouthpiece, sprayed some water inside his mouth, and then held up the spit-bucket.

Wolf spat into it. The water was mixed with blood.

Georgie set the bucket down and wiped Wolf's face with a towel as Reno massaged him.

Breathe, Wolf told himself. Get it under control.

"That one was pretty much even," Reno said. "How you feeling?"

"I'm okay," Wolf said.

About twenty-five seconds had passed and he suddenly became aware of the growing pain in his legs. Schultz's kicks had given Wolf's left leg, his lead leg, quite a pounding. It was starting to ache. Or was it the dehydration he'd gone through yesterday coming back?

Either way, it felt like somebody was squeezing his thigh with a giant nutcracker.

Then he looked down and saw that it was Reno's massaging.

"Gimme some water," Wolf said.

"You sure?" Georgie said.

He was pressing a flat, metal end-swell against Wolf's right cheek. Schultz had tagged him there twice, both with left hooks. The guy could deal. But Wolf had given as good as he'd gotten, delivering some hard hooks to the body himself, and catching Schultz with a straight right.

"Water," Wolf repeated.

Reno snapped his fingers at Clancy, who handed over a plastic bottle.

"Just a swallow," Reno said. "Not too much."

Wolf felt a teaspoon's worth pass over his tongue and down his throat.

"Steve," Reno said as he ripped back the bottle and spilled some of the water down Wolf's chest. "Listen to me. He's catching you with that rear leg kick as you're circling because you're too far out. Move it in closer when he starts to throw it. He's telegraphing his kick, shifting his shoulder before each one. You got to start timing his moves better. You just missed connecting hard with that straight right. Understand?

Wolf nodded. The pain in his leg was starting to subside. Or was it just feeling numb?

The ten second buzzer sounded and Reno said, "Mouthpiece."

Georgie sprayed some water on Wolf's mouth guard and slipped it back into his mouth. Reno was smearing some of the Vaseline from the big glob on the back of his hand onto Wolf's face.

"Keep on your toes," Reno said. "Move. Stick and move, just like practiced. You can beat this guy. Watch his shoulders for the tell."

As was their practiced custom Reno and Georgie helped lift Wolf up off the stool. For a split second he wished they hadn't done that. It might make him look weak.

Schultz sprang off his stool glowing with confidence. His well-muscled body glistened with sweat, the black lines of his tattoos gleaming like an oil painting, his muscles looking like a statue in bas relief.

The air-horn's blast signaled the start of Round 2.

They met in the center of the octagon and Schultz once more extended his left glove for the tap. Wolf slapped it and then began circling, trying to remember what Reno had told him.

Watch his shoulders for the tell.

Schultz sent out a quick jab. Wolf danced out of the way. Another left jab, and another shuffle step. Then Schultz's left shoulder twitched back ever-so-slightly and the rear leg kick shot out, smacking against Wolf's right thigh once again.

Wolf came back with a kick of his own, catching Schultz on the inner thigh as he brought his kicking leg down. They each exchanged a few arm punches and then Wolf grabbed Schultz, twisted, and threw him down. He hit the mat with a thumping sound.

Wolf tried to follow up on the takedown but Schultz nimbly rolled to his feet before he could be mounted. He swung roundhouse punch with his right hand which caught Wolf in the left side and as he backed away it felt like someone had fashioned a steel lasso around his chest. Trying not to show how much it hurt him, Wolf danced away and grinned.

Schultz grinned, too. He was apparently not buying the ruse, sensing that he'd struck paydirt. Moving forward, he pressed his momentary advantage and sent another front kick to Wolf's leg.

If it had hit higher, Wolf thought, *I might've gone down.* The pain from the punch was now in full effect, having most likely caught him on the liver. Legs ceased to move, breathing was impaired, and then came Schultz crashing into him, arms encircling his chest, twisting, and throwing him down.

The flat surface of the mat came up suddenly to slap against the side of Wolf's face. His head bounced and then Schultz was on top of him.

I can't let him mount me, Wolf thought. In another second he'll be raining down punches.

Forcing himself to reach out, Wolf seized Schultz around the waist and held on with both hands.

Have to get my legs back, he thought.

As it was, he didn't want to stay on the ground any

longer than absolutely necessary. Schultz was strong, and an accomplished wrestler. But Wolf knew trying to stand up on shaky legs would be the worst thing he could do.

As it was, he still was having a hard time trying to hold on. Schultz delivered a few hammer-like punches to the top of Wolf's head and some to his shoulders, but Wolf managed to hold on. They struggled together like ungainly lovers, the pungency of his opponent's sweat assailing Wolf's nostrils as he was wedged between smooth, sweat-soaked surface of the mat against his back, and Schultz's equally smooth, sweat-soaked body on top of him.

A few more punches thudded against his head and shoulders, but he hardly felt them.

He suddenly distinguished Reno's voice amongst the omnipresent cacophony of muffled yells and other sounds.

"Get out from under him, Steve."

Easier said than done, Wolf thought, but the strength was returning to his body. He could feel it. It still hurt to breathe, but he forced the air in, then, gritting his teeth.

More punches, but this time, as Schultz twisted slightly to pound down a blow with his right fist, Wolf jerked his body to his left, managing to shift out from under the other man's chest. Schultz immediately encircled Wolf's head in a locking hold while trying to move his right leg over Wolf's hips to secure him on the mat. They remained frozen for a few seconds more, and then Wolf slipped his head free and pushed his body outward managing to change his position by a few inches.

It brought back a memory flash of going door-to-door in Baghdad looking for a hidden sniper. Every door you kicked down brought you one step closer, but with each one there was a whole new set of problems.

Another minute shift, another tightening of the leg.

"Let me see some action or I'll break you," the ref said.

A reprieve, thought Wolf.

It was the ref's prerogative to call a halt and separate the fighters if there was a sufficient stall in the action and neither one was pursuing an advantage.

If he could just hold on…

More straining grunts from Schultz, more gasping breaths from Wolf.

After what seemed more like an eternity later, the ref ordered them to stop and said he was putting them both on their feet.

Protestations emanated from Schultz's corner, but the ref ignored them. Both fighters were upright now and the ref motioned for them to continue. Just as they started to advance, the air-horn sounded again, signaling the end of the second round. As Wolf dropped his hands he felt a wave of exhaustion sweep over him and saw what he interpreted as an expression of determination on his opponent's face.

He can't be as hurt and tired as I am, Wolf thought.

Reno and Georgie were scrambling toward him now, Georgie holding the bucket and sponge and Reno with the towel. Clancy followed along behind, but his face was mostly placid.

Still no cuts, Wolf told himself.

He managed to sit this time without impairment and concentrated on taking deep breaths. Georgie pulled out Wolf's mouthpiece and sprayed some water into his mouth.

Georgie held the bucket under Wolf's chin. "Spit."

Wolf did, and it was once again tinctured with crimson.

Two five-minute rounds in the books, eleven minutes total. Only seventeen more minutes to go.

But he didn't think this one was going to go the distance. Not after Reno told him that he'd just heard informally that they'd lost the first two rounds big time.

"We did?" Wolf said.

Reno's face was solemn. He nodded.

"You got to turn things around, Steve," he said. "He wins this one, he can coast it out and he's got the decision. He'll be taking your belt."

"Ain't gonna happen," Georgie said, pressing the end-swell against Wolf's cheek again. "You can take this boy, Steve. You just gotta start settling down on your punches."

Wolf knew he was right. He just hadn't been able to connect with anything solid.

"Gimme some water," Wolf said.

"No way," Reno said, and then relented, unsnapping the top from the plastic bottle and bringing it to Wolf's mouth again. "Well, just a swallow. No more."

Wolf felt the grateful joy of another teaspoon of water sliding over his tongue and down his throat.

"Steve," Reno said, pulling the bottle away. "I noticed something. He's dropping his hands a little when he goes to throw a high kick. Time him and step in and throw one of your dynamite rights."

Wolf inhaled two quick breaths. A dynamite right… Could he pull one of them out of his hat?

"Anything else?" he asked.

"Yeah," Reno said, taking a moment to apply more Vaseline onto Wolf's eyebrows and cheekbones. "We gotta knock his god damn ass out. Remember, you look good and we got us a world title shot next."

He grinned.

What do you mean "we?" Wolf thought and almost managed a grin of his own.

All he could muster was a quick nod. The last thing he was thinking of was the match beyond this one.

"You're the champ," Reno said, and clapped him on the shoulder. "Never forget it."

The ten second timer sounded and Georgie rinsed off the mouthpiece and jammed it in. This time a tiny bit of residual water had clung to the plastic, feeling like nectar from heaven as he sucked it down.

Wolf once again noticed that Schultz seemed to spring off his stool.

Didn't this guy ever get tired?

The air-horn blast signaled the start of Round 3 and the two men moved to the center of the octagon and tapped gloves again.

Schultz threw a quick combination, most of which Wolf caught with his gloves and arms, but one right hand did sneak through and rung his bell a bit. The inside of his lower lip felt raw and he tasted blood. He retaliated and tossed a combination flurry of his own. A shoeshine.

That turned out to be a mistake because Schultz managed to seize his right arm and pivoted, flipped Wolf down onto his back with a plop.

Two takedowns, Wolf thought, as he tried to scramble away. But somehow Schultz had landed on the bottom, with his chest against Wolf's back. They were right by the fencing. Wolf could feel the metal webbing against his lower-left leg. Am arm encircled Wolf's neck like a slithering python.

A rear naked choke, Wolf thought. A submission

tap would be seconds away if he could lock it in.

But Wolf wasn't about to let that happen.

He jammed his head downward, his chin tucked, exposing as little of his neck as possible.

I've trained for this, he told himself. In the gym... Just like in the gym.

Schultz's arm felt like a closing vise, but Wolf was still able to safeguard his neck. He pushed up on the other man's arm and managed to get it to slide over his Vaseline covered face. With that he bounced his body and managed to run his feet up the cyclone fencing like he was walking up the side of a building.

"You can't use the fence, Wolf," the ref shouted.

Wolf knew this, but kept on doing it anyway.

Let him stop me if he wants, he thought.

The worst that could happen is the ref would halt things and do a repositioning, maybe even stand them both back upright. That was where he needed to be.

He continued to work his feet and in another second he was using the height and inertia from his fence position to kick forward while flipping his legs in the opposite direction. His body rotated out of Schultz's grasp and suddenly it was Wolf who was on his knees on the side of a supine Schultz. His cornerman on the other side of the fence was screaming. On the other side of the gate, so was Reno.

"Mount him and ground and pound," Reno shouted.

Although he didn't like to strike a downed opponent, Wolf nonetheless brought a couple of chopping
hammer-fist blows crashing onto Schultz's face. The
second one sent a spray of blood shooting from his
nostrils.

Schultz's corner was screaming something unintelligible at their man.

Before Wolf could deliver another blow, Schultz
rolled, grabbed the fence, and pulled himself erect.
Not wanting to be on his knees in front of a standing
opponent, Wolf scrambled to his feet, too.

Both men squared off as a cascade of red flowed
from Schultz's nose. The river of red ran down his
chest and sent splashes of crimson to dapple the mat.

Wolf shot out a jab and caught Schultz in the left
eyebrow. The punch landed with just the right precision and a half-inch slit opened up as Wolf drew his
fist back. Schultz raised his right hand to his eyebrow,
wiped it, and paused to glance at the blood on his
glove.

The second set of jabs, a double this time, smacked
into Schultz's forehead and then his nose, his head
jerking back with each blow. More blood droplets
burst forth in an arc landing on Wolf's forearm and
mixing with his own sweat. In retaliation, Schultz
lumbered forward throwing a lead right. Wolf sidestepped to his own right, slipped the punch, and

countered with a crisp right hooking punch that caught Schultz squarely on the jaw.

Schultz's body stiffened for an instant and jerked, like he'd just touched a live wire and received an immense electrical shock. Then his body was collapsing in a heap at Wolf's feet, the mouthpiece bouncing on the mat, the whole sequence seeming to shift into slow motion.

With his peripheral vision Wolf could see the ref running toward them.

Reno's voice came through as if it were projected by a megaphone: "Mount him! Ground and pound! Don't give him a chance to get up."

Wolf glanced down and saw there was no need for that. Schultz's eyes were half-closed slits, his mouth agape, his body unmoving. He wasn't getting up. The man was out cold, and the bright yellow eye of the dragon tattoo was staring up at him in disbelief.

It was over. There was no need for any more damage to be done.

CHAPTER 6

**A HALF-MILE FROM THE INTERNATIONAL BRIDGE
DEL RIO, TEXAS**

"Those are rather messy, don't you think?"

Michael Griggas looked at the blood covered array of wrapped condoms on the three sets of plastic garbage bags that had been spread out on the ground. "I thought you weren't going to call us until you had it all washed and ready.

The man seemed totally unconcerned that the bodies of eleven people five men, five women, and one young boy, lay gutted in a row about ten feet away.

Rivera didn't feel that much concern either. Although he had hoped to release all of them into the night to pursue their dreams in *el norte* once they were through shitting out all of the stuffed condoms. But it wasn't meant to be. They were no more than *los ganado*—cattle, used for a single purpose and then discarded, or in this case, disposed of. Still, he had felt a twinge of regret when he'd killed the boy, but the little *hijo de puta* wouldn't stop running.

Griggas glanced at his watch.

A man in a hurry... Always checking the time.

Rivera had met him on three prior occasions and each time he had been the same—a tall, slender white guy who was perfunctory and officious. *Piensa que su mierda no tiene un mal odor.* He was the younger brother who did most of the legwork for his older sibling, Lawrence, who was supposed to be the honcho, or "the big guy," as they all called him.

The big guy. Rivera wondered what he looked like. This one was a tall, thin anglo with pale blue eyes. Just for the sake of amusement, Rivera imagined the older brother as short and obese. Sort of an anglo version of Esteban Cortez Sr.

Esteban Cortez Jr. stood nearby, watching but not saying anything. He had not distinguished himself at all during the chase and search for *los ganado*.

El hijo gordo must be worried, Rivera thought. *Probably wondering if I'll lie to his father again and say he was a hero.*

He chuckled a bit and then looked back at Griggas.

"*Ya está listo, ¿no?*" Rivera answered.

"Yes, it's ready now," Griggas said, his tone pedantic. "But we're also behind schedule."

Rivera frowned and shrugged. "It could not be helped.

"There were some complications." Europa stood next to them. He glanced at *Rivera* nervously and the new respect in his eyes was evident. Respect and something more. Fear.

Feeling a sense of satisfaction swell within him, *El Tigre* then smiled. There would be no more "Alfie" bullshit now.

Griggas's head jerked toward Europa. "What kind of complications?"

El Tigre glared at the diminutive punk. It had not been his intention to mentioning either of the ruptured packets lest this stingy bastard, Griggas, maybe hold back some of the money claiming some of the product was damaged or tainted. *El Jefe* Cortez would not like that. *El Tigre* felt like slapping the little piece of shit, and Europa must have sensed this because he kept his mouth shut.

"I asked you what kind of—"

"*Nada importante,*" *El Tigre* interceded quickly. "Do not worry. A couple of them ran away, that is all. We had to chase them down, catch them. And it cut into our time. And I did not want to keep you waiting any longer than necessary. So we performed an extraction to recover the merchandise." He flipped his hand toward the bodies with a carefree gesture.

Griggas raised an eyebrow and stared at him for a

few second. "I appreciate that, but now these bodies are going to attract some unwanted attention."

"Which is a good thing, no?" *El Tigre* paused and flashed what he intended to be a beatific smile. "This is the last time we will be using this crossing point, and the authorities will be looking here."

Griggas raised his eyebrows and rocked his head in a slight, up and down motion.

"That's true, I suppose."

"And we saved *all* of the product for you, *señor.*" He shot an intimidating glance at Europa, implying that the little son of a bitch should keep his fucking mouth shut. "And this way you don't have to deal with a bunch of stuff that smells like shit, eh? *No mal olor.*"

Griggas glanced down at the three separate stacks and frowned.

"It smells almost as bad this way." He turned to Europa. "You have any water left?"

Europa looked to *El Tigre,* who nodded.

"Then I suggest you have some of your people wash it off a bit more before you divided it up for your bike transport," Griggas said. "You don't want to attract any attention during our trip to the warehouse, do we?"

Europa scampered over, grabbed the guy named Julio, and gave him some instructions.

Griggas watched him for a moment and then turned back to Rivera.

"I assume you'll take proper precautions and dispose of the bodies?" he asked.

Rivera shrugged at that.

"Does it matter, *este?*" he said. "*No usaremos esta ubicación después de esta noche, ¿verdad?*"

Griggas, whom he knew spoke fluent Spanish even though he was a Lithuanian, cast him a disapproving glance.

"No," Griggas replied in English. "It's true we will no longer going to be using this location, but I'd rather not attract the untoward attention of the authorities either. I suggest you bury them discreetly."

Rivera said nothing, but his thoughts were the opposite.

Piss on that. He didn't want to take the chance on staying here any longer than he had to, especially burying bodies. You never knew who would be coming along, plus there was always the danger of the border patrol maybe using a helicopter or drone with an infrared camera attachment.

Europa came strolling back to them and stood there looking effete and stupid.

"Me and my people need to get back across the border," Rivera said. "Tonight. And we need to count the money before we leave. You want them buried, have him and his boys do it."

Europa's mouth twisted down at each end, but he said nothing. Having watched *El Tigre* dispatch and butcher eleven of *los testarulos* no doubt gave him pause as far as offering any objection.

"I don't know," Europa said. "Like he says, we been here a long time already. Maybe just leave them."

Griggas took a deep breath and then gave a quick nod after glancing at his watch. It was a fancy looking thing with a luminous dial. The illuminated digital numerals showed in bright red that it was 10:40 pm. He then took out a cell phone, punched in a number, and held it to his ear.

"Bring it," he said a moment later.

Perhaps a hundred feet away a pair of headlights snapped on, the twin beams sending a bright translucence through the high grass. Rivera watched its progress as it wound its way around the parked motorcycles and toward their position. As the big Dodge Ram drew closer the driver cut the lights off. It stopped about fifteen feet away and both the driver and passenger doors popped open. Two men got out, both wearing holstered pistols. Glocks, with extended magazines, from the look of the grips. The one from the passenger's side was carrying a briefcase.

Time to count the money and get the hell back across the border, Rivera thought.

It would be good to get back to *México lindo.* He glanced one more time at the line of bodies, *ganado,* and thought for a fleeting moment about the boy.

Triste, pero inevitable. Sad, but unavoidable.

Such was life… And death.

He turned and motioned to Cortez Jr.

"Come over here and help count your father's money," he said.

El hijo gordo began shuffling forward with pathetic, little, uncertain steps.

Rivera smiled. He was going to have to tell some more lies to the old man about this one to keep things going on track.

Triste, pero inevitable.

***

THE TRIAGE ROOM
THE MGM GRAND HOTEL AND CASINO
LAS VEGAS, NEVADA

After the post-fight interview, during which Wolf made a point to praise his opponent's toughness and predict that he would be a future champ, Wolf, Georgie, and Clancy went immediately to the triage center for treatment. Reno stayed behind to talk with the promoters about the next one, and Wolf was just as glad that he wasn't involved in that.

Maybe there won't be another one, he thought.

But he knew as quickly as the words came to him that there most likely would be. It was a question of economics. With his legal fees mounting, Wolf could hardly afford to lose the one lucrative venture that he had going, and that was fighting. He certainly wasn't making it as a bounty hunter anymore, especially in this cash bond-abolishing legal climate, and he doubted he could swing a full-time teaching job at Best in the West. The prospects for an ex-con were always pretty bleak, and coupled with a dishonorable discharge, he couldn't even collect his GI benefits. Everything was riding on the Great Oz clearing Wolf's name.

But would he?

He talked a good game, mostly about how hard he was working. As far as results, Wolf hadn't seen much.

Maybe Monday will tell the tale, he thought. But for the better or for the worse?

With Georgie and Clancy standing off to one side, Wolf took in a deep breath and gazed at the intricate gold pattern design on the tan walls. The walls appeared to be moveable sections inside a much larger room. But at least he was isolated from the public and any inquisitive reporters for the moment, anyway. Their interest in the two depleted gladiators had dissipated as they moved on to the next two who would be squaring off shortly.

Our blood was now just dried splotches on the surface of the mat, he thought as he settled himself onto the table-like recliner.

The security guard let Schultz, along with his trainer and manager, through the door. He looked over and nodded to Wolf. He returned the nod but said nothing. They'd said all they had to say with their performance in the octagon. Now, all hostilities were forgotten, and they were just damaged goods trying to piece themselves back together.

The triage nurse walked over and did the perfunctory duties—temperature check, blood pressure, eye examination, and general perusal of his bumps and bruises. She was a pretty Hispanic woman who reminded Wolf of Brenda, and then he started wondering if she and Miss Dolly and Mac had made it. He was certain he'd seen Mac waving to him, but before and during the fight his attention was mostly diverted. Afterward, the lights were dimmed over the audience once more to focus on the post-fight interview. They might have been up there somewhere. Mostly he was wondering about Yolanda. He'd already accepted that, in all probability, she hadn't made it.

I've got to face the fact that I've lost her, he thought.

His whole body was starting to ache.

The nurse moved to Schultz, who was sitting on the table opposite looking even more dejected than he looked beaten up. The bridge of his nose had swollen up like a mini balloon and the cut on his left eyebrow was open and ugly. The doctor, a pretty woman with red hair whom Wolf had seen at just about every fight here in Las Vegas, came over and greeted him.

"How are you feeling?" she asked as she slipped on a pair of latex gloves and held a penlight up to Wolf's face.

"Like a *penjata* at a birthday party," he said, and noticed the Hispanic nurse smile a bit.

"Any double vision?" the doctor asked.

The light waved in front of his right eye, and then his left.

"No, ma'am," he said.

This time the doctor's lips parted in a partial smile. Wolf had been resorting to his default, military courtesy, but now hoped he hadn't offended her by implying that she was old enough to be at the "ma'am stage."

Her gloved fingers traced over the planes of his face, causing bits of sharp pain as she pressed here and there.

"Bend forward a bit," she said, and ran her fingertips over his scalp and neck.

After telling him to lie down on his back, she checked his hands, and then did more pressing on his chest cavity and abdomen. Wolf had never been in a post-fight examination this thorough and wondered if she was going to do a short-arm inspection next.

But she didn't, muttering that everything seemed normal.

Wolf tried to think of a snappy comeback but nothing came to him. He swung his legs off the recliner and was about to jump down onto the floor when Georgie appeared and knelt in front of him.

"Here, champ," he said, holding a pair of Wolf's gym shoes. "Put these on."

After sliding his feet into the shoes, Wolf jumped down and saw that Schultz was lying supine on the table. The doctor was slipping on a new pair of latex gloves.

Wolf walked by and held his fist out to Schultz.

"Good fight, man," he said. "You hit like a damn mule."

Schultz gave a weak tap to Wolf's extended fist.

"Thanks, champ," he said. "You do, too."

Wolf felt good to hear the word champ and saw that Georgie was holding up the belt as they headed out the door.

"Want me to put it on you?" Georgie asked.

Wolf grinned. It hurt. He shook his head.

"You carry it for me, okay?" he said. "I just want to get under the hot water.'

Georgie's smile was wide as he made a show of holding the belt up above his head as they walked.

I'm glad I didn't lose it, Wolf thought as he went

out into the hall and headed for his dressing room.

His body was aching with each step, but it felt good to win one for a change.

**

THE BUBBLE

MGM GRAND HOTEL AND CASINO

LAS VEGAS, NEVADA

Bray watched as McNamara, Pete Thornton, the three women, and the big guy, the federal agent, all left their seats and edged down to the main aisle. The main event, the world championship match, was about to start, and almost everybody was moving in the opposite direction after having come back from the restrooms and the concession stands.

They must be going to Wolf's dressing room, Bray thought, and debated what to do next. He turned to Powers.

"Were you able to get tracker on the Escalade?" Bray asked.

Powers nodded.

"Followed them all the way to the hotel from Phoenix, didn't I?" He snorted. "And they're checked in here, too."

There was a little irritating lilt to the tone of his voice. Obviously he was miffed that Bray had made him move closer to McNamara and the others during the fight. But what did he expect? This was work. But the son of a bitch had been working the surveillance and the tail pretty much nonstop for the better part of twenty-four hours. Bray debated the wisdom of making him continue. Most likely Wolf would be too depleted to do a lot of partying. He'd taken a lot of punishment in that fight. And McNamara was a senior citizen, albeit one that was tough as hell, so his late-night partying was most likely not going to be too extensive either.

He was just about to tell Powers and Maureen that it was a wrap for tonight when his burner phone buzzed with a vibrating tell. After withdrawing it from his pocket, he saw that it was a text from Abraham.

Call me as soon as you get this.

Christ, he thought. *Now what?* It had to be one in the morning in New York.

There was no way he'd be able to hear much of anything in this place with all the racket. He stood up and motioned for Maureen and Powers to do the same.

The lights flickered and down below the first of the two fighters was making his way toward the octagon.

"Where we going?" Powers asked. "I kind of wanted to see this main event."

"Me, too," Maureen said. She pressed her breasts

against him and tried to pull him back down.

Bray frowned and held up his phone.

"This is work," he said. "Remember? Let's go."

With that, the three of them began to make their way toward the main aisle.

***

THE FIGHTER'S DRESSING ROOM
MGM GRAND HOTEL AND CASINO
LAS VEGAS, NEVADA

Wolf stood naked under the showerhead and let the water rush over his body. He kept it hot—as hot as he could stand it. The sensory overload caused by the elevated temperature of the water reduced the incremental aches and pains that he was feeling, and it was a given that more were on the way. And one thing was for sure: he knew he was going to be sore as hell tomorrow.

Placing his palms on the small, greenish tiles, he leaned his head back and let the water enter his mouth, which felt lumpy and raw. He'd spit out a lot of blood during the fight, but as he explored the inside of his cheeks and lips he felt no severe lacerations. His mouth was probably just abraded, but that was good in its own way. It meant no cuts inside.

Somebody pounded on the door and he heard

Georgie yell, "You okay in there, champ?"

"Just ducky," Wolf yelled back.

"Okay," Georgie said. "Just checking. You gots some people out here waiting to congratulate you."

Wolf figured that meant Mac had made his way down from the stands.

"And one of us is just itching to come in and scrub your back, darling."

It was a feminine voice... Miss Dolly.

That meant that Brenda was probably out there, too.

But... Yolanda?

"I can handle it," Wolf said. "So tell Mac to restrain himself."

A chorus of laughter followed, with McNamara bellowing, "That'll be the day."

Wolf was glad to hear Mac's voice. It had been a while and he would be glad to finally see him. It had been even longer since he'd seen Miss Dolly and Brenda, too. and he was looking forward to seeing them as well.

But he was still hoping against hope that Yolanda would somehow be out there, too.

Better put that out of your mind, he thought.

The water continued to beat down on him. He grabbed the faucet and twisted the handle to change the water temperature to cold, hoping it would spark an end to his sweating once he got out of the shower.

And he was starting to feel the dehydration effects coming on again. Reno had given him a bottle of water on the way back to triage, but he'd hardly drunk any of it as he walked down the aisle between the stands. There had been too many extending arms with hands needing to be touched or slapped. He'd then downed the entire bottle in a series of long, extended gulps after the medical check. It went right through him in that he was starting to feel the pressure in his bladder now.

The cold water flow was making him pant now, so he adjusted it back to a tepid temperature.

Damn, his body hurt.

What was that old saying? Rode hard and put away wet… He'd been ridden hard, that was for sure.

And now he was wet and ready to be put away. His energy level was at zero.

Grinning, and eager to see Mac and the others, and still holding out a faint hope about Yolanda waiting for him on the other side of that door, he cut the water off, thrust back the curtain, and grabbed a towel. As he was drying off, he realized his gym bag, with his underwear and change of clothes, was in the other room.

First things first, he thought, and stepped over to the commode. As he urinated, he was relatively pleased to see that the stream was a pale yellow rather than red.

Not urinating blood, he thought. So things could be worse.

Moving to the door, he opened it a crack.

"Georgie, hand me my bag, would you?"

As his trainer shuffled over to the locker where his bag was stored, McNamara moved forward with Miss Dolly on one side and Brenda on the other. All three had wide grins.

"Aww, hell," Mac said. "Come on and get your ass outta there. You ain't got nothing we ain't seen before."

"Especially since we just saw you wearing nothing but a modified jockstrap," Miss Dolly said.

Brenda giggled a bit and stared at what was visible through the open crack in the door.

Wolf waited for Georgie, but all the while kept looking out, trying to scan the rest of the room. Mac and company had moved so close that they were blocking most of his view, and Wolf didn't want to ask if Yolanda was there.

Reno was holding a beer in one hand and had his other arm around Barbie.

"That world championship match is all yours for the taking, Steve," he said, and lifted his beer bottle in a mock toast. "Just as soon as we want it."

"Yeah, well give me a day or two," Wolf said, smiling.

He caught sight of Pete Thornton there, too, but

still no Yolanda. His heart sank a bit more.

Georgie was at the door now and handed over Wolf's bag. As he opened the door wider he caught sight of another body, this one big, tall, and familiar looking.

Lucien Pike.

What the hell was he doing here?

***

THE HALLWAY OUTSIDE THE BUBBLE
MGM GRAND HOTEL AND CASINO
LAS VEGAS, NEVADA

Bray waited until he had cleared the actual hotel and was out in the parking garage before he hit the button to call Abraham. The temperature had dropped a bit and it was a bit chilly, but still mild compared to what it must be in New York. Abraham answered after the first ring.

"Took you long enough," he said.

"I'm on the job," Bray answered. "Working around the clock. And in case you're interested, Wolf just won his fight. McNamara's here in Vegas, too."

Abraham was silent, like he was letting all that sink in. Finally, after a delay of maybe five seconds, he said, "All right. Good. Glad you're staying on top of things."

"So, what's so all-fired important that it has you calling me on a Saturday night?"

He heard the lawyer sigh.

"You got enough personnel who can keep tabs on both of them for a couple of days?"

"Yeah. Why?"

"Our employer," Abraham said. "He wants another steam room session. I'll need you in to meet me in Florida tomorrow night. The meeting's scheduled for Monday morning."

"Florida?"

"Yeah, West Palm Beach. He's got a resort there. I've already made reservations for us."

Bray considered this. At least the climate would be more hospitable than the last meeting in New York.

"Let me see if I can book a flight," Bray said. "It's kind of short notice."

"It's already been done. I'll email you the information."

All this was a bit troubling to Bray because he not only preferred to make his own travel arrangements, but it also was creating a paper trail directly back to Abraham and ultimately this Von Tillberg fellow. Should any federal investigation about this subsequently emerge down the road, all the feds would have to do would be to connect the dots. And they always went after the lowest ones on the totem pole first.

"Any idea what this one's about?" Bray asked.

"I'm not sure. But we'll find out Monday."

"Okay. What time's my flight?"

"Ten-thirty. That'll put you there around five or six. I'll have someone standing by at the airport to pick you up. We can eat dinner and discuss things then."

"Sounds good. I'll be looking for that email."

"Already sent," Abraham said. "See you tomorrow."

With that the lawyer terminated the call.

Bray slipped his phone back into his pocket and considered this new wrinkle. Trying to speculate why Von Tillberg was demanding another meeting so soon was fruitless. It could be something as simple as wanting a detailed update… Or it could be something more.

Again, he told himself, there's no way to speculate.

He saw Maureen and Powers standing off to the side by the entrance doors where he'd left them. He'd put her on Wolf and assign Powers to keep shadowing McNamara. And at least he'd be able to spend tonight partaking in and enjoying Maureen's sweet charms. He wondered, once he left, if she'd be fucking Powers in his absence?

Probably not, he thought with a smile. Unless he takes a thorough shower first.

Not that it mattered.

But he doubted it would happen. It was one thing

to fuck the boss, and another to get into bed with the hired help. The girl had a definite preference for climbing up the organizational ladder.

As he walked toward the doors, he mulled over once again the immediate task before them. Wolf and McNamara weren't going anywhere. The trail wouldn't be cold tomorrow.

And as for now, the staff of Robert Bray Investigations might as well take the rest of the night off and enjoy themselves a bit.

They could pick up the surveillance tomorrow.

***

THE FIGHTER'S DRESSING ROOM
MGM GRAND HOTEL AND CASINO
LAS VEGAS, NEVADA

After slipping on his underwear, jeans and gym shoes, Wolf fished a T-shirt out of his bag and pulled it over his head. He was in no mood for greeting his friends and supporters, much less for partying. All he could think about was settling into an easy chair or bed with a bottle of Gatorade. After a deep breath, he pulled open the bathroom door and stepped out to meet everybody.

"It took you long enough," McNamara shouted. He was holding an empty glass and Barbie was pouring more champagne into it. An empty bottle sat on the floor by the waste can, next to a bucket of ice. Mac, and everybody else, had obviously already had a more than just a couple, but this was, after all, a victory celebration. "We were about ready to send in a recon party."

Before Wolf could reply, McNamara moved forward and embraced him, giving his back a couple of slaps with his free hand. Some of the champagne sloshed out of the glass and onto Wolf's back and arm.

Wolf, who had never cared for the exaggerated display of affection of a male on male embrace, stiffened.

"Watch yourself, darlin'," Miss Dolly said. She sounded a bit tipsy, too, as she stepped in and joined Mac. She planted a kiss on Wolf's cheek and he wondered if it left a smear of her ultra-red lipstick.

Brenda hugged him, too, which was quick and light comparatively, and then it was Barbie and Reno's turn. He, too, was obviously feeling the exhilaration of both the win and the booze.

"I'm proud of you, Steve," Reno said. "You done good."

Wolf couldn't wait to extricate himself from them. When he did, he stepped back and smiled. "I couldn't have done it without your help. And Georgie's, too."

The black man grinned widely and winked, holding up his palm for a high-five.

After Wolf gave it a slap. He noticed Lucien Pike

was standing off to the side grinning. He had what appeared to be a full glass of champagne in his left hand, but he didn't look at all drunk.

"And the next one's gonna be as good as gold, too." Reno suppressed a belch. "I got a meeting with the promoters tomorrow. On a Sunday, no less. That's how much they want us. We're not only talking big, big money, but a world title as well." He pointed to Wolf's championship belt, which was sitting on the counter next. "But that's tomorrow. Tonight, we party till dawn."

"Maybe you will," Wolf said. "Me, I've got a date with a nice soft bed."

"But we got reservations," Mac said. "You ain't gonna crap out on us, are you?"

"Brother," Wolf said. "I'm afraid so. As they say, the spirit is willing, but the flesh is weak."

Mac's face contorted with an exaggerated "hurt" expression.

"Now there you go getting all literary on my again," he said. "But there's something you don't kn—"

Miss Dolly put her hand over his mouth and said, "Shh."

Miss Dolly and McNamara exchanged a glance. She started punching in a number on her cell phone.

Let them party the night away, Wolf thought. The aches were stating to return to his whole body.

"Aw, come on," Miss Dolly said. "You ain't gonna

be a party-pooper, are ya, darlin'?"

"I'm afraid so," Wolf said. He shook hands with Pete Thornton, who stood there grinning.

"You looked awesome in there," he said.

Wolf clapped him on the shoulder and looked over at Pike, who was still standing off to the side.

Barbie shoved a glass in Wolf's hand and filled it to the brim. He had no intention of drinking it. He didn't even like the smell of champagne. Luckily, Mac called to her and said Miss Dolly's glass needed refreshing. As Barbie moved away Wolf frowned at the drink. The thought of any alcohol burning his tender stomach at this point was anathema. He set the glass down on the counter next to the belt. He ran his fingers over the fine, red leather, inset jewels and gold inlay.

Damn glad I didn't lose you, he thought, and then felt stupid anthropomorphizing something so inanimate.

"Impressive performance," Pike said, walking over and extending his hand. "You made it look easy."

"Yeah? What fight were you watching?" Wolf said, punctuating it with a laugh.

They shook and Pike set his untouched glass on the counter next to Wolf's.

"I take it you're surprised to see me," Pike said.

Wolf flashed a quick grin that he hoped captured a bit of irony.

"Yeah, I wasn't expecting it," he said. "You're showing up more often than the losing card in a Three Card Monte game."

Pike said nothing.

"So how the hell did you find me?" Wolf asked.

"Hell, I been following your MMA career. Wouldn't have missed it."

"No," Wolf said. "I mean the other day. Out at Best in the West."

Pike smirked then lowered his voice. "I'm a federal agent, remember? I specialize in finding people."

"Me, too," Wolf said. "Once upon a time."

"So I heard."

Wolf looked at him askance. "So you looked me up just to get my autograph?"

Pike snorted a quick laugh. "Not hardly. I got something I wanted to talk to you about."

"What's that?"

Just then McNamara came over and draped his arm around Wolf's shoulders.

"Steve, you just gotta come with us. We got everything all set for you."

"Mac, I just don't feel up to it. I've got bruises in places I don't even want to talk about. I feel like jumping into a tub of Ben Gay."

McNamara's head rocked in a nodding motion, and then he glanced back at Miss Dolly and Brenda. Miss Dolly was still on her cell phone. She then held up her free hand, making an O with her thumb and forefinger.

"Who's this here fella?" McNamara asked. "You a friend of Pete's?"

Pike introduced himself and extended his hand.

"He's the guy who helped me back in North Carolina," Wolf said. "With Jimmy's problem."

"Helped him?" Pike said with a jerking motion of his massive upper body. "Hell, I saved his damn life."

It was Wolf's turn to remain silent, although the claim was true. Pike have saved him from taking a bullet from a violent drug lord.

He clapped Wolf on the shoulder. "But he saved my bacon, too. One thing I've learned, when the chips are down, you can always count on another airborne trooper."

"Shit," McNamara said. "You got that right. You airborne?"

"Damn straight," Pike said. "Hundred and First?"

"Oh yeah?" McNamara said. "How far?"

Pike grinned. "All the way, sir."

"Hey, troop, don't call me sir," McNamara said. "I always worked for a living. Special Forces."

"There's none better than that," Pike said.

"I like this guy already." McNamara smiled and gave the bigger man a light punch on the arm. He turned back to Wolf and said, "I got to talk to Miss Dolly for a minute."

Wolf watched Mac move off and then Pike asked him why he wasn't going with the rest of the victory team.

"Not in the cards for me tonight," Wolf said. "I'm too beat."

"Yeah, that was a pretty rough fight." His eyes narrowed a bit as he stared at Wolf. "Say, you gonna be in Vegas through Monday, right?"

Wolf was surprised at this. How the hell would he know what my plans were? Was it possible he knew about the appointment with Oz? Obviously there was more to Special Agent Pike's agenda than met the eye. A lot more.

"Yeah," Wolf said slowly. "How'd you know that?"

Pike shrugged. "Just a lucky guess."

"You're pretty good at being lucky, aren't you?"

"I have my moments." He grinned. "And this is Vegas."

Wolf just stared at the other man, then he said, "And you're also lucky at finding people. How did you track me down the other day? And, more importantly, why?"

Pike said nothing, then the easy grin worked its way back onto his face.

"You gave me your cell number back in North Carolina, remember? I tracked you through that." Pike stopped, took a breath, and then added, "And as far as the why, I wanted to ask you something."

"What's that?"

Pike squinted again, his head canted slightly, looking Wolf up and down as if considering something.

"Can you ride a motorcycle?" he asked.

Wolf was totally perplexed by the question.

"What?"

After waiting a beat, Pike repeated the question.

"What the hell?" Wolf said. "Why you asking me that?"

The big man shrugged. "Just curious. Thought we might go riding sometime. So can ya?"

Wolf shook his head. He wasn't liking this runaround one bit. "Yeah, but it's been a while. A long while."

"Good," Pike said. "I'll be in town here for a couple more days, too. I'll give you a call on Monday after you take care of whatever business you have to do with your lawyer. Maybe we can rent a couple of Harleys, or something."

This confused Wolf even more. How in the hell did Pike know about his Monday appointment with Ozmand?

"Steve, darlin'," Miss Dolly said, hustling over and suddenly interceding and grabbing Wolf's arm. "Comere. I gotta show you something. Something important."

She pulled him toward the door.

Wolf went along, still wondering what Pike's game

was.

Miss Dolly halted by the door, positioned Wolf off to the side, smiled, and then opened it with a flourish.

Yolanda stood there in the most beautiful low cut red party dress he'd ever seen. Her ebony hair hung to her shoulders like a raven's wing, her bare shoulders looked luscious, her skin a smooth mahogany, and her scarlet lipstick matched the color of the dress as she smiled.

"Hey, boo," she said. "What's this I hear you ain't coming to the party I got all set up for you?"

Wolf was too stunned to speak. Everybody was silent behind him and he assumed they were also all probably staring at him, but he didn't care. His eyes were on her, and the only thing he cared about was standing right in front of him now looking deliciously gorgeous. He wanted to say something but was afraid it would just come out in a stutter.

Yolanda moved close, put her arms around him, and kissed him softly on the lips.

"You looked great in that fight," she said.

"I didn't know you were here," Wolf said, feeling overjoyed.

She smiled again and hugged him closer.

"I thought you might need a little TLC afterwards," she whispered to him. "And listen, we don't have to go to no party if you don't want to. We can just go straight up to your room."

Wolf felt his pulse quicken and suddenly all his fatigue was vanishing.

He managed to swallow and then whispered back, "That sounds like it would be the best thing to happen to me all day."

CHAPTER 7

PREFERENTIAL SUITE
MGM GRAND
LAS VEGAS, NEVADA

Wolf quickly finished knotting his tie so he could watch her put the finishing touches on getting dressed. Yolanda adjusted her elegant breasts into the black sport bra that she'd already fastened, and then slipped the white T-shirt over her head. They'd set the alarm for four-fifteen am sharp, ostensibly so they could both shower and she could fix her hair, but had ended up making love one last time before she had to get ready for work and he had to go to his appointment with the Great Oz. They'd spent both Saturday night and all day Sunday together, and almost all of it in bed, with a couple of time outs to meet Mac, Miss Dolly, and Brenda for lunch. The rest of it had been spent between the sheets.

Thank God for room service, he thought.

He'd been pleased their passion for one another hadn't cooled since his departure from Vegas for Phoenix, but now he found himself once more counting regrets. It had been a beautiful reunion, but ultimately a short one, and with the air of finality. Wolf wondered if he was ever going to see her again after this.

He sat down on the bed to watch her more closely.

The vest went on next and he was a bit concerned when he saw how little it covered compared to the body armor he'd worn on his combat tours. Of course, this Kevlar vest was a lot lighter and infinitely more comfortable. And hopefully she wouldn't have to worry too much about it having to stop something like a 7.62 mm. She slipped into the tan uniform shirt next, and then she stepped into the brown pants. The badge on the shirt gleamed as she bent over to tie her shoes and the early morning sunshine began to filter through the window. Across the street the mock Statue of Liberty and rollercoaster of New York New York was visible.

A roller coaster, he thought. *A good metaphor for my life lately.*

More thoughts of the past thirty-two hours or so filled him with delight. It had been sweet... Delightfully sweet.

Thirty-two hours… Had it only been that long?

Way too short, but now it was coming to an end.

Like all good things…

Yolanda smoothed the Velcro pistol-belt in place and posed for him.

"How do I look?" she asked, cocking her head slightly.

"Way too pretty to be chasing bad guys," he said.

She frowned and rolled her eyes.

"And way to proper and official to be associating with an ex-con," he added.

Her frown deepened.

"Will you stop," she said. "You have your appeal coming up today. Think positive."

Wolf glanced at the clock. It was five-fifty-nine.

"Yeah," he said. "Nine-thirty East Coast time, which means it'll be six-thirty here."

"Which means we gotta go so I can drop you off over there and still get to work in time for roll call. Come on."

Wolf felt like he did when it had been time to ship out in the military: a sense of foreboding and dread, of not knowing where you were headed exactly and what you'd have to face.

But this is nothing compared to what I've been through, he told himself. If only I didn't have to say goodbye to her.

She leaned over and kissed him on the lips.

Her hand lingered on his cheek and she said, "Let's get going, boo."

She slipped a windbreaker over her uniform and pistol. She'd twisted her hair into a ponytail-bun so it was close to her head.

He stood and looked around the room. His check-out time was noon. Plenty of time to come back here and pack after the zoom session with Oz. He'd thought about extending his stay here for a couple of days, but decided against it. She was going back to work after her regular days off, and him sticking around could only mean potential problems. Better to just check out and then rent a car to drive back to Phoenix.

But what was next after that?

Mac, who'd left last night with Pete, had extended an invitation for Wolf to join him and the team down in the Yuma area.

Ersatz border patrol.

Playing the Little Dutch Boy at the dyke. That was how Mac had described it. Building a sand castle on the beach with the tide coming in.

Still, what other prospects did he have, at least until he saw how this appeal might go?

He had a lot riding on this. Hopefully, the Great

Oz could do more than talk a good game.

And keep turning in those billable hours sheets.

They walked out together.

Time to face the music, he told himself. For better or for worse.

***

EXECUTIVE'S ONLY LOCKER ROOM
PINK FLAMINGO RESORT
WEST PALM BEACH, FLORIDA

Bray stood in the locker room, naked except for the towel secured around his waist, and checked the text message on the burner phone again.

On the move.

This one was from Maureen. Powers had checked in earlier with a similar message saying that Mc-Namara was leaving Phoenix and heading south.

Bray had texted him to stay on it, and was surprised to hear from Maureen saying that Wolf was going somewhere now, too. It was still pretty early in Vegas—around seven o'clock. Maybe he was heading back to Phoenix, as well. The air-conditioning in the place must have been set on high and the tile floor felt cold under his bare feet and he stepped into the plastic sandals that one of Von Tillberg's bodyguards had provided him. The big, black fucker had stood there watching as Bray undressed. That guy, Von

Tillberg, was such a fanatic about security and being recorded. At least the place didn't smell like a typical locker room, but then again, he, Abraham, and Von Tillberg were the only three people in it. Except for the trio of bodyguards, of course. They appeared to be the same ones he'd had back in New York for the first meeting.

Another city, another state, another steam room, he thought and dialed Maureen's burner phone.

"What's up?" he asked when she answered.

"I'm not sure," she said. "I got a beep earlier when Wolf and his girlfriend were leaving their room. The mini-cam showed the both of them fully dressed and heading for the elevators. Luckily, I was in my sweats so I high-tailed it to the elevators on my floor and managed to catch them."

Bray felt a surge of panic. "You got in the same elevator car?"

"Yeah. Lucky, huh?"

"Not if he recognized you."

"Relax," she said. "Like I told you, I was wearing a mask, I'm in my sweats, and not fixed up at all. My hair's a mess and no makeup. Plus, I was carrying my gym bag. They probably thought I was going down to the fitness center to catch an early morning workout. And they were all lovie-dovie. They were all into each other, and stuff, gazing into each other's eyes. The chick kept looking at her watch. Wolf seemed kind of nervous, too."

Bray said nothing. He didn't like the sound of it. She shouldn't have gotten so damn close, but what other choice did she have. He decided to let it ride.

"And then what?"

"Well, he was dressed in a sport jacket and tie, and she had a windbreaker on over her police uniform. So I guess she was going to work."

"A sport coat and tie... I wonder where he's going?"

"I'm getting to that," she said, her voice taking on a tone of irritation. "I followed along and saw they were headed for the parking garage, but they stopped to get some coffee and a Danish, so I hustled on past them, got to my rental, and managed to tag them." She made huffing sound. "She drives a Lexus RX Three-Fifty. Really nice car. That chick's got taste."

He found himself getting irritated. When he spoke, he put some authority into his voice. "You find out where they were going?"

"I think so. She dropped him off at an office building near Freemont. They both got out, she hugged him, they kissed, she got back into her car and left, and he watched her go. Then he turned and looked at his watch and went into the building. It took me a couple of minutes to find a parking spot and then I went in."

Another panic surge swept over him.

"He didn't see you, did he?"

She made a tsking sound, and then said, "I'm a professional, remember? And *no*, he didn't *see* me.

So I checked the legend and there was this security guard standing there so I asked him if my boyfriend had just come in. He told me that he did, and I made up some bullshit excuse about not remembering the name of the guy we were supposed to see."

Maureen paused to giggle, but this made Bray even more anxious.

"I'm not in the mood for histrionics," he said. "I've got a meeting in a few minutes here."

"Okaaay." She drew out the pronunciation of the word. "Anyway, the security guy said it had to be Mr. Ozmand's office, because he was the only building occupant who'd come in early this morning."

"Ozmand?"

"Attorney at law," she said. "Funny that he's seeing him at this hour. It's only a little after seven out here."

Bray murmured a response and told her to stay on him, but to be extra careful that Wolf didn't see her.

"I will and I won't," she said, and giggled again.

"And text me with any updates." Bray terminated the call and noticed the big bodyguard standing at the end of the row of lockers. He slipped the burner into the pocket of his pants in the open locker, slammed the door, and took the key. It had a large safety pin attached and he pinned it to his towel.

"Don't worry, sir," the bodyguard said. "No one else is allowed in here when Mr. Von Tillberg is in session."

In session?

Christ, Bray thought. *This guy is some kind of egomaniac.*

"And Mr. Von Tillberg's waiting for you," the bodyguard said, holding his hand out toward the steam room.

Bray nodded and began walking.

He'd have to assume that Maureen hadn't been noticed by Wolf. From the sound of it, he was distracted. And at least the mini-cams that Powers had set up outside Wolf's and McNamara's rooms had worked like a charm. He'd have to remember to tell Maureen to grab them if Wolf checked out. He also wondered what merited such an early conference with the lawyer?

Strange, but perhaps the reason would become clearer as time progressed.

The bodyguard reached out and pulled open the door. The hot, swirling tendrils swirled in the air like an anxious octopus.

***

CASA DEL ESTE DE ESTEBAN CORTEZ
YUCATAN, MEXICO

Alfredo Rivera awoke and stretched, feeling the fine texture of the maroon satin sheets against his naked body. The glowing red numerals of the digital clock on the stand next to the bed showed that it was only seven-forty. The trek back across the border, this time coming back to Mexico from *el norte*, had been uneventful, but it had also been exhausting. They'd taken their time, knowing that the Gutierrez's men they'd killed would probably be missed by now. Not only did they have the money to safeguard, but Rivera also had the added encumbrance of making sure that *el hijo gordo* made it back safely. And when they'd finally arrived, the old man had been eager to hear about how well his son had done. After he'd counted his money, that is. Cortez Jr. had glanced at Rivera with wary eyes as he, Rivera, once again related a completely distorted version of the events making *el hijo gordo* sound like the big hero he wasn't during the fracas. Rivera could almost see the relief on the face of the *pendejo*. They all stank from the exertion and the rough journey, but Cortez Jr. had the stench of fear mingled with his body sweat. Rivera had smelled it before, many times, and each time it gave him the feeling of victory being close.

Soon, he would end it for both Cortez Sr. and his pathetic son.

But not today.

The early rays of the morning sun were peeking through the partially drawn curtains of the bedroom. Today he was just Alfredo Rivera, not *El Tigre*. He was just a man enjoying the fruits of his labors, but that didn't mean he could be lax. He'd spent the night fucking the two women with him, two European girls from the private stock of Cortez Sr. The interludes had been a pleasant diversion from the rigors of the journey through *la selva*, and did a lot to obliterate the memory of the terror he saw flash in the boy's eyes right before he died. It was a hard one to shake, perhaps because he saw in the boy a similarity to his own youth.

Still, it could not be helped.

You would do better than to become bogged down with trifles, he told himself with a rhetorical irony.

And it was time to hone his physical edge once more.

One of the women stirred as he sat up, tossed off the sheet, and slid over the still slumbering naked body of the female on his left.

"*¿Otra vez?*" she murmured, sounding half-asleep.

He patted her on the ass and grinned. It was impressive that she was picking up so much Spanish, which was not her native language.

"*No,*" he said and slid off of the bed. "*Vuelve a dormir.*"

He leaned down and kissed her lightly on the shoulder, catching the slightly tangy smell of the dried sweat on her body. The odor aroused him, but he knew another sexual dalliance would impinge upon his morning training, and that was something he could not afford. Not if he wanted to maintain his razor's edge, his stamina, and his mastery of the techniques.

It was time for *El Tigre* to prowl once again.

He got all the way out of the bed and as the soles of his feet met the coldness of the tiled floor he felt the chill. Rivera reached down, grabbed his underwear and pants, and pulled them on, leaving the leather belt unfastened. The tactical boots that he'd worn on the operation were caked with mud but he slipped them on anyway. His dress clothes, which included a brand new pair of expensive gym shoes, were in the closet, but he would put those on after his training session.

It was early enough that he felt it would be safe enough to run into the town, but with a possible war brewing between Gutierrez and Cortez Sr., he wasn't about to take any chances. He pulled open the drawer of the nightstand next to the bed and pressed his index finger onto the photo-electric cell on the gun locker. The lid released with a soft click and he pulled out his holstered Glock 19. With the practiced ease of many, many dressings, he looped the belt through the slots of the holster and pulled the belt tight before securing it. Then he fitted the magazine carrier to the other side of the belt, with the lip-like base facing outward. That would facilitate an easy and speedy withdraw should he need to reload. The final touch was a dirty sweat shirt with a hood but no sleeves. Although he hated to cover his tiger stripe tattoos and his red hair, he knew it would be prudent for this venture of the outside run. The legend of *El Tigre* and the dispatching of *los hombres duros* had no doubt made the rounds in the lower echelons of the Cortez organization, and he expected that there could conceivably be a leak back to Gutierrez. He could remove the sweat shirt once he returned to the safety of the compound for the martial arts part of his training session.

He whirled and did a series of spinning and jumping kicks, snapping each one with such precision that clumps of mud sprang from his shoes each time.

Something for the maid to clean up, he thought and headed for the door. After unlocking it, stepping into the hallway, and then re-securing the door, he placed the key in his pocket. One of the guards had been sitting in a chair at the end of the hallway and didn't hear his approach. He jumped to his feet with his hand on his gun and then smiled when he saw it was Rivera.

"*El Tigre*," the guard said, snapping to attention. "*Buenos dias*."

Rivera grinned and nodded as he walked past him. The man's deference was another source of gratification.

My legend is spreading, he thought, continuing down the hallway toward the staircase leading to the outside. *Soon my fame will eclipse that of Esteban Cortez and his pathetic son, if it has not done so already.*

Then it will be time for *El Tigre* to shine, to emerge and make his final moves to take over.

Soon, he thought. *Very soon.*

***

LAS VEGAS BOULEVARD AND TROPICANA AVENUE
LAS VEGAS, NEVADA

Wolf pushed through the main doors of the MGM Grand and saw that despite the busy flow of traffic on Las Vegas Boulevard, the sidewalks of the Strip were still pretty much empty. Hotel custodians and sidewalk vendors were busy sweeping and hosing down the sidewalk and preparing for another day of hustling, which would probably get started in a few hours. Before he started his run, he glanced at his watch and figured he still had plenty of time to make the last run here, go shower in his room, and make the final check out. He also wanted to send Yolanda a text telling her what happened.

Struck out. My case wasn't even on the docket.

He paced around the entrance waiting and hoping that maybe she'd call or text him back.

No such luck.

After waiting about ten minutes, he decided she must be busy and slipped the phone into his fanny pack. It was time to get started on his run.

As he shuffled forward, the words of the Great Oz hung in his memory, and they still stung.

"Ya gotta believe," the lawyer had said with a fatuous grin.

"What the hell's that supposed to mean?" Wolf had asked.

"Tommy Lasorda." Oz had said. "One of the greats in baseball. That's what he used to say. You gotta believe."

"Yeah, I know," Wolf said. "But where does this leave me. Or should I say, us?

The Great Oz chuckled and clapped Wolf on the shoulder.

"Look, Steve, these kind of things happen. You gotta roll with the punches, just like the ring."

Wolf didn't correct him that it was an octagon and not a ring. Instead he repeated his question, this time using the plural pronoun.

"But I thought you said we were on the docket this morning? That's why I stayed in Vegas and busted my ass to get here extra early."

Oz canted his head to the side and shrugged his shoulders.

"I thought we were, too. They assured me we were. But sometimes things get twisted around in courts, especially with this pandemic."

Wolf was tired of excuses, and this guy was full of them.

"So where does it leave us now?"

Oz cleared his throat and slipped on his mask, indicating for Wolf to do the same.

Wolf left it lying on the fine mahogany table which still held the expansive laptop they'd set up for the zoom meeting for the appeal that didn't happen.

A fat lot of good those things did anyway, he thought.

"We reapply and wait to get on the docket again," Oz said.

"And when's that going to be?"

"If I knew that, I wouldn't be here." The lawyer flashed a quick smile, exposing his expensive veneers. "I'd be downtown playing the tables."

Wolf said nothing.

The lawyer apparently sensed his client's dissatisfaction.

"Look, Steve, it'll be soon," he said. "I hope."

You hope?"

Seeming to sense that his answer had further irritated his client, the lawyer quickly added, "I give you my word that I'll diligently keep working on it."

And keep billing me for more of your work hours, Wolf thought.

They sat in silence for a several seconds, and then Wolf spoke.

"What if we lose this next one, too?"

"Too? We haven't even been to bat yet."

The baseball metaphors were starting to irritate Wolf even more than being removed from the docket.

"You didn't answer my question," he said. "What if we lose this appeal?"

"Then we've still got the Supreme Court."

Wolf didn't want to even imagine what the expense of doing that might be.

"What are the chances of winning there?"

The lawyer canted his head. "Like I said, you gotta believe."

"Will you stop with the damn baseball stuff? I got the whole rest of my life riding on this."

The Great Oz blew out a long breath causing his mask to puff outward.

"Look, Steve, these things happen in the legal arena. Your appeal was originally scheduled, and then subsequently placed on hold due to the unanticipated full docket and the holidays approaching, which is typical sometimes. We'll get our at-bat next time for sure."

There he goes with the damn baseball comparisons again, Wolf thought. *Words. Just empty words.*

Ozmand went on, trying to assure Wolf that things are going pretty much as expected, and not to be despondent.

The more the lawyer talked, the more pointless the conversation seemed. Wolf stood up and Ozmand stopped talking.

"I guess I was counting on it too much," Wolf said.

This brought another round of fruitless assurances and promises. Wolf was barely listening and began moving toward the inner-office door. Ozmand rose and followed him.

"I gotta go check out of my hotel," he said. "Call me if anything breaks or if they set up a new date."

"Will do," Ozmand said, slapping Wolf on the back. "You're going back to Phoenix?"

Wolf answered that he was, but he was actually thinking of calling McNamara and telling him he'd be joining him at the border. He needed to make some quick dough, at least until he got his check from this last MMA match.

Now, he'd just gone a few steps toward the sidewalk that ran parallel to the boulevard when his phone rang and he stopped, hoping it was Yolanda calling him back. It wasn't.

"Just checking in to see how it went," McNamara said.

"It didn't." Wolf stepped back next to the building and gave a quick rundown of the failed morning venture.

"Aw shit," Mac said. "I was hoping for a better result."

"So was I."

He heard Mac's heavy sigh.

"Well, I'm on my way down to Yuma to tag up with Buck and the boys."

"They're out of Texas now?" Wolf asked.

"Yep. Heading out as we speak. And none too soon, either. Right before they left there was a report that the authorities found eleven illegals dead.

"Damn, that sounds bad."

"It does," Mac said. "Five women and a young kid. All murdered."

"Murdered?"

"Yeah, and not just killed… Butchered. Cut open, from what I heard, it was most likely drug smugglers."

It reminded Wolf of the stories that Mac had related about his time in the Nam—innocent villagers caught between the American troops and the brutal Viet Cong… And also the horror he'd seen and heard about in Afghanistan—Taliban stuff… The kinds of things they'd done before the U.S. went in there and kicked their asses out… And the kind of stuff they were no doubt doing again now that we'd so ignominiously retreated.

He found himself wondering if we'd go back in someday.

Or maybe we should concentrate on our own damn border, he thought.

McNamara's words brought him out of his light reverie. "Like I told you before, you're welcome to join us down Yuma-way. We can always use a good man, and the money's supposed to be damn good. There's a rich man rancher down there who's willing to pay top dollar to make sure his property's protected."

Wolf was on the verge of telling Mac he'd be on the way there tomorrow when his cell phone vibrated with a new call.

He saw it was Yolanda.

"I'll let you know on that, Mac," he said quickly. "I got to go. Another call coming in."

He heard McNamara's low chuckle.

"Well, tell your lady-love I said hello."

Wolf said he would and answered the call.

"About time you answered." Her voice was haughty and full of what Wolf took to be mock irritation. At least he hoped it was. "I was just about to hang up. You know I don't do voice mails."

"Heaven forbid," he said. It felt great to hear her voice again. "I was hoping you'd call. I texted you earlier."

"I know, but this is the first chance I've had to call you back. I'm working, remember?"

Wolf remembered, all right.

"I was talking to Mac, and if it makes you feel any better, I cut it short to answer your call. He says hi."

"Hi back," she said. "And I only got a quick minute. I'm in the washroom. Now what happened?"

Wolf repeated the same run-down he'd given Mc-Namara, and she reacted much the same way.

"Shit."

"My sentiments exactly," he said.

He heard her sigh.

"So, you going back to Phoenix now?"

"I'm doing a run on the Strip, or I'm about to. Then I'm going back to Phoenix after I rent a car."

The silence on the line lasted for several seconds, then she said, "When you coming back?"

Wolf wasn't sure how to answer.

"You there?" she asked. "I told you, I only got a minute."

In the early morning hours of the previous night, they'd cuddled and talked after making love, and agreed not to discuss any more plans for the moment until they found out how the appeal would go.

"Let's wait and see," he said. "Oz is going to try to get it rescheduled, and I'm thinking about joining Mac and his buddies down at the border to pick up some extra cash."

"You need money already? What about your fighter's purse?"

"Hasn't been deposited yet. And besides, it sounds like Mac needs some help and a guy like me is always looking for a buck, and opportunities for an ex-con with a DD come around about as often as Haley's Comet."

She started to say something when he heard the squawk of a police radio asking if she was still 10-6.

"Negative," she said. "On my way."

Another brief silence, another loud sigh, and then, "I gotta go. And we agreed not to talk about negative stuff, remember?"

"Roger that," he said, and added with a grin, "Don't

forget to wash your hands."

That got a laugh and quick good-bye.

He once again slipped the phone into his fanny pack, glanced at his watch, and figured he still had enough time to do the run, take a shower, and check out.

He was looking forward to running this part of the Strip again. It had been a long time.

Wolf took one more look at the MGM's huge golden lion sitting on the white platform which was surrounded by the bright green walls of the massive hotel, and then glanced across the street at the ersatz Statue of Liberty in front of New York New York, the roller coaster, and the mock Brooklyn Bridge. He'd never seen the real ones.

Maybe someday, he thought, then realized he didn't even know when he'd be back to see these ersatz ones again. He figured he might as well take the scenic route. Just as he'd stepped out to the sidewalk, appreciating that it was still early enough that the sidewalks were mostly clear, he heard someone call out to him.

"Hey, Wolf. Wait up."

CHAPTER 8

NEAR THE CASA DEL ESTE DE ESTEBAN CORTEZ
YUCATAN, MEXICO

Rivera allowed himself a certain amount of rumination on his run back toward the guarded gate of the Cortez compound. The round trip on the paved roadway leading to the town and back from the gates of the Cortez compound was perhaps only seven or eight kilometers, but the pace he maintained allowed him the pleasure of breaking a sweat. Why the big man wanted to live so close to the squalor of the village was beyond Rivera's comprehension. Perhaps it gave him the feeling of superiority—that of a feudal lord and master presiding over *los campesinos*. He'd taken some time to cut through some of the back alleys as he angled toward the main road and back to the compound. Men were congregating about at various check points waiting for someone to take them to work in the fields, while others hustled toward their jobs in the shops and restaurants. Women were busy with their chores as well, some of them washing clothes or naked children in large plastic tubs. Theirs was a simple life and it reminded Rivera of his early days. Struggling to scratch out an existence, training for the Mexican boxing team, fighting pick-up matches in grungy back allies and bars, until finally getting noticed for his prowess by one of members of the cartel.

It was a life he would never return to, no matter what.

The guards at the gate saw him returning and hurried to push open the gates. Both of them nodding and flashing nervous smiles.

El Tigre has returned, Rivera thought, slipping off the sweatshirt. He knew the eyes of the guards reflected admiration and envy at his now sweat-covered body with its tiger stripes and rippling muscles. Just like the looks he'd received from the coyote crew on the last mission. His prowess was well known among the minions of the Cortez cartel—the legend of *El Tigre*.

After entering the estate, he stopped in the circular courtyard where a few days before he'd disposed of the men who'd betrayed Esteban Cortez Sr. All traces of their spilled blood had been meticulously scrubbed from the cobblestones. *El Tigre* began going through some of the karate forms that he'd been practicing of late. The forms, which he regarded as little more than demonstrative acrobatics, served a dual purpose. Not only did they provide the opportunity of honing the combinations of his kicking and punching techniques, but he was within the view of several of the compound's guards and word of his prowess, his skill, his invincibility, would continue to spread.

He crouched, threw a series of punches, and then leaped in the air to deliver a perfectly executed reverse spin kick.

As he landed, with cat-like precision and balance, he saw Oscar Buenaventura, one of the main bodyguards of Cortez Sr., approaching. *El Tigre* knew he was being summoned by *El Jefe*. The big bodyguard's mouth was turned downward on each end with a scowl.

He is still angry over the other night, El Tigre thought. *Still miffed that Cortez Sr. had immediately called out to me when his son was being choked.*

It was a reminder to Buenaventura that *El Jefe* knew who the most proficient man was... he knew who was *numero uno*.

Smiling, *El Tigre* continued his form nonetheless, finishing with another leaping spin kick, and landing a few feet in front of the bodyguard. Buenaventura's head jerked back slightly due to the sudden movement, and then his frown deepened. His loyalty to Cortez Sr. was beyond reproach.

"*El jefe quiere verte,*" Buenaventura said. "*Inmediatamente.*"

El Tigre stood a few feet away and made no reply.

"*Inmediatamente,*" the bodyguard repeated. "*Vamos.*"

After waiting a few seconds more, *El Tigre* nodded.

"*Un momento mas,*" *El Tigre* said, before pivoting and doing a final series of kicks and punches to complete the form.

The chief bodyguard stood there doing an obvious slow burn.

After once again landing with flawless grace, *El Tigre* nodded and said, "*Vaminos, mi amigo.*"

He was tempted to address Buenaventura as "*El Segundo,*" The Second, but didn't. After all, he already knew his place, and he was totally loyal to Cortez Sr.

The bodyguard turned and walked back toward the big *hacienda.*

One thing was clear, however.

When the time came to take over, Buenaventura would become *el primero*—the first that *El Tigre* would have to kill.

***

LAS VEGAS BOULEVARD AT TROPICANA AVENUE
LAS VEGAS, NEVADA

The big man trotted up next to him. He had on a camouflaged bandana wrapped around his head covering his long hair, and a black sweat shirt with

the sleeves lopped off, displaying his massive looking arms. They had more tattoos on them than Wolf
remembered. The insignia on the sweatshirt had the
Harley Davidson insignia on it in white. He wore a
pair of yellow tights down below that appeared to be
a bit out of character, but showed off his well-muscled
legs. The tights were tucked into what appeared to be
a brand new set of expensive looking running shoes.

"Pike?" Wolf said. "What the hell?"

The big fed grinned. "Thought you might want
some company? Plus, I want to break these shoes in."

"Yellow tights?"

Pike snorted a laugh. "Yeah, they're something,
ain't they? But my blue Superman ones are in the
wash."

They started going side-by-side down the sidewalk, with various people glancing at them and
hurriedly darting out of their way.

Wolf was mystified. This was the third time in
about a week that Pike had appeared out of the blue.
What the hell was going on?

And Wolf wondered how the hell had he found
him today?

He asked Pike that question.

"Shucks." The big fed shrugged his huge shoulders.
"I stayed over a couple of days, just like I told you I
was gonna do the other night after the fight. And this

morning I got up to do a run and seen you. Coincidence, huh?"

"I don't believe in coincidences."

Pike grinned. "You know, neither do I. But who else, besides two ex-airborne rangers, would be stupid enough to be up at this hour of the morning running down the Strip in Las Vegas?"

Just as he posed that question a pretty female runner going the opposite direction shot past them. They both turned to follow her progress for a moment.

"Think she mighta been airborne, too?" Pike asked.

"Come on. What gives?"

"Well..." Pike was breathing heavier now. "We are in Sin City, and..." He jerked a thumb toward the receding female jogger. "I like to keep *abreast* of things."

Wolf wasn't having any of it. Things didn't add up. There was something too coincidental about the other man's repetitive appearances. Wolf quickened his pace as they passed by Planet Hollywood.

"Hey," Pike said. "You're breaking formation."

Wolf continued to pull away.

"I ain't got time for riddles or smart asses."

"Slow down, will ya," Pike muttered, struggling to match Wolf's pace. "I'm carrying about forty more pounds than you."

Wolf ran at the accelerated pace, almost turning

it into a near sprint, as Pike tried, and failed, to keep up. Glancing over his shoulder, Wolf saw that his running partner was now almost fifteen yards behind him, and losing ground fast. After another few strides, he slowed appreciably as he approached Harmon Avenue and let Pike catch up.

If he wanted answers, he wouldn't get them by leaving the other man in the dust.

"More like fifty or sixty pounds," Wolf said. "And that doesn't even begin to count the bullshit you're spewing off. You gonna tell me how and why you keep turning up like a persistent case of jock itch?"

Pike laughed as they fell into a more moderate pace. They continued in silence for about ten strides and then caught the light. It took the big fed the better part of a minute to catch his breath. Leaning over, hands on knees, Pike said, "All right, Steve. I'll level with you."

Wolf waited. Pike continued to take in deep breaths.

The light changed to green and Wolf slapped the other man on the shoulder and resumed his run. Pike followed and they ran another ten paces in silence. He was fighting to get his breathing under control. Then, after he had it leveled out a bit more, he managed to ask, "Whaddaya want to know?"

"First," Wolf said. "How you been tracking me?"

"Like I told you before." Pike said. "I'm a fed. I specialize in finding and tracking people."

Wolf increased his pace some more.

"Bye," he said.

"No, wait." Pike took in another deep breath, exhaled, and then added, "Through your cell phone. We got the telemetry to pinpoint you down to a couple of feet."

Wolf tried to process this. Was that true? He remembered some of the pinpoint accuracy he'd seen used in the army, the telemetry they used to zero in on the location of a terrorist trying to use a cell phone to command detonate an IED. He'd taken out a number of them in Iraq. It brought back the memory of one enemy combatant on a dusty back street in Baghdad straightening up with a maniacal expression on his face pressing the button as the cell phone frequency jammer did its work. But as far as the sophisticated equipment the army used, and the mechanics behind the process, Wolf actually knew little about how it worked. Mac's daughter Kasey had been pretty good at employing some tracking techniques and had located numerous fugitives through their cell phones. But she did it through a bunch of her off-the-record contacts and it was far from being quick or precise. The G no doubt had infinitely more sophisticated tracking abilities.

"Okay." Wolf slowed his pace a bit more. "Second question: Why?"

Pike was sweating profusely, despite the cool temperatures. Wolf had yet to break a full sweat.

The big fed seemed to be mulling over his reply.

"You proved to be a pretty good back-up in North Carolina," Pike finally answered. "So I got a little proposition for you. How'd you like to help me with another of my latest assignment?"

"Assignment?"

"Yeah," Pike said, between gulps of air. "Just like back in North Carolina."

Wolf felt stunned. The only reason he'd gotten involved before was to save his brother.

"You must have me mixed up with somebody else. Like somebody with an official badge."

Pike barked out a laugh.

"You won't need a badge. And I'll even pay you."

"Pay me?"

"Sure." Pike's breathing was ragged now. "I'll put you on as a CI. Confidential informant."

"Informant? But I don't know anything."

"You know more than you think."

They were coming up on Paris-Paris now and the pink and yellow balloon by the front entrance was almost visible. Across the boulevard, beyond the median strip with the towering assortment of palm trees, he knew the fountains at the Bellagio would be inactive at this early hour. It had always been such an enjoyable thrill when he and Yolanda had gone up to the observation platform on the Eiffel Tower to watch them perform the musical accompaniments.

But back to reality, he thought as they came to Bally's.

"What kind of help could I be?"

They caught another red light at Flamingo Road and had to stop. Pike seemed grateful for the rest. He once again bent over, hands on his knees, and kept taking in copious breaths.

"How far you figure on going?" he asked between intakes of air.

Wolf glanced at his watch.

"At the rate we're going, not much longer. I was planning on going down to Treasure Island and then turning around, but I'll have to head back so I can shower and then check out of my hotel."

"Yeah, too bad you stuck around here in Vegas for nothing, huh?"

For nothing?

This was another stunner to Wolf.

Was Pike talking about the appeal? And if so, how did he know about it?

The light changed to green and Pike straightened up and started across, this time leaving Wolf behind. He sprinted past The Cromwell and on to the Flamingo catching up to Pike and then grabbed the bigger man's arm as they got to the sidewalk area in front of the main entrance.

"What the hell did you mean by that?" Wolf said.

"About what?"

"About me sticking around here for nothing."

Pike flashed one of his broad grins.

"I was referring to your appeal," he said. "Heard it got knocked off the docket somehow."

That hit Wolf like another metaphorical gut punch.

Still holding Pike's arm, Wolf steered him over to a wall by the glass entrance of the Flamingo and balled up his fist.

"I'm tired of your fucking riddles and runaround bullshit. Either you be straight with me or I'm gonna start feeding you some right hands."

Pike's grin remained in place and he held up his open palms.

"Hey, I seen you punch, so I don't want that, and neither do you. A charge of assaulting a federal agent wouldn't look good the next time your case comes up at the Military Court of Appeals."

Wolf hesitated and Pike suddenly raised his right hand and waved to someone behind Wolf. He half-turned and glanced over his shoulder, but saw no one.

"Who the hell was that for?" he asked, his fist doubling around the front of Pike's sweat shirt.

"Just signaling the okay to my partner. He's shadowing me, running cover."

Wolf suddenly wondered if he was being videotaped. He released his hold on Pike's sweatshirt, stepped back, and surveyed the sidewalk and street behind him. The sidewalk was practically empty and no one was carrying anything that looked like a recording device. But those things could be exceedingly tiny with today's technology. Beyond the railing, some cars continued to creep along on Las Vegas Boulevard as well.

"Hey, it's nothing personal," Pike said. "We always operate in pairs, whenever possible."

"Pairs? Why wasn't that the case back in New Lumberton?" Wolf asked. "As I remember it, you were pleading for me and Pax to go back you up at the shopping mall."

"Yeah, but that was during a hurricane, brother." Pike smirked. "Plus, I figured you'd want to save your brother's ass. I heard he's doing well in jump school, too. Nothing like having another airborne ranger in the family, huh?"

"Leave him out of this."

"Sure. But just remember that I helped grease the wheels for him, too." Pike's head twisted from side to side, looking around. Then he pointed over to a deserted section on the expansive sidewalk.

"If you remember," he said in a low voice, "back in N.C. I was involved in a little undercover operation."

Wolf stared at him, saying nothing.

"Well," Pike continued. "That little venture, which I had been involved in for quite a while, stemmed from my deep cover U/C assignment in Atlanta. The pipeline's handled by a motorcycle gang calling themselves the Devil's Breed. I infiltrated them and was doing good when it got interrupted by Batton and his boys getting killed like they did." He paused and snorted. "I'm sure you can appreciate that, since you were a part of it."

Wolf was feeling incredibly frustrated, but nodded.

"This pipeline stretches all the way from the East Coast through the Midwest, to out this-a-way. We've invested a lot of time and effort, not to mention man hours by yours truly, working this thing, infiltrating the gang, and all that jazz."

"So what does that have to do with me?"

"I getting to that. Word is a big cartel boss down in Mexico, a dude named Esteban Cortez, is looking to expand his influence along the dope-line corridor to the eastern seaboard. And to do that, he's looking for a bigger biker delivery system."

Again, Wolf stayed silent, but his mind was racing.

He was still trying to figure out how he fit into this.

"When I infiltrated the Breed," Pike continued, "I cultivated a real good snitch. Well, maybe that's a poor choice of words. A confidential informant who had an axe to grind with one of the Breed's leaders. Her name was Joyce Randal. Her boyfriend was named Popely, and he was not what you'd call faithful, so she got pissed. Long story short, she introduced me to him, and I took it from there. It was all arranged that him and me were supposed to head out here and establish contact with Cortez's people. Except…"

Wolf waited.

Pike blew out a heavy sigh. "The dumb son of a bitch ended up wrapping himself around the wrong end of a semi. And he was supposed to be coming out here to be my introduction to a Mexican-American motorcycle gang called the Marauders. In Spanish they call themselves—"

"*Los Merodeadores*," Wolf cut in. "I speak a little Spanish."

One of Pike's eyebrows arched.

"Oh yeah, that's right. You do, don't you?"

"You seem to know a hell of a lot about me."

Pike used his big right hand to clap Wolf on the shoulder.

"Hey, we're both ex-airborne rangers, right? And before, when I was working that thing in North Carolina that your brother was involved in... Well, I was researching him, and your name cropped up. I like to be thorough, so I read your file. That's how I knew I could count on you."

The bigger picture was starting to come into focus for Wolf now. He remembered how Pike had known so much about him when they met back in North Carolina a few months ago. Know so much that he'd ended up recruiting him in desperation to assist in closing the book on Alonzo Batton. It had involved saving Jimmy, so Wolf had had little choice.

"In my opinion, the army tossed you under the bus," Pike said. "You shoulda never been court martialed for that bullshit stuff. And now, with the recovered spy pen video, you've got a definite shot at redemption. If you can get your damn case heard in front of the Military Court of Appeals."

Something clicked into place now for Wolf. Pike, the federal agent, knew way too much about all this, especially about this morning's failure to get the case heard. Could the big fed have had a hand in gumming things up?

"So like I mentioned before," Pike said. "Popely was supposed to be introducing me to the Mexican-American cycle gang that Cortez and, a couple of guys named Griggas, have been using out this way. But now he can't, 'cause he's dead." He flashed the wide grin again. "And I don't feel like waiting around for the zombie apocalypse."

"What can I do about it?" Wolf asked.

"You," Pike said, "can add legitimacy."

"Legitimacy?"

"Yeah. Does the name Alejandro Europa mean anything to you?"

Wolf thought about it and then shook his head.

"Think harder." Pike said.

The name did sound vaguely familiar. Then it hit him. He'd served time with a guy named Europa, but he didn't recall the guy's first name. Wolf had saved Europa from getting gang-raped in the showers by some of the Aryan Nation inmates with a grudge back in Leavenworth, which put him in good standing with the Hispanic gang, and in good standing with the blacks. And because he was half Indian and half white, he was given some sort of outsider immune status. That, and the fact that he was also the heavyweight boxing champion of the prison during his stay. It was what brought Wolf under that protective umbrella, where he pretty much stayed until his release. Prison was all about alliances and survival.

"You saved Alejandro's bacon back in the joint, right?" Pike asked.

Wolf was beginning to think that this guy knew everything about him right down to his shoe size.

He nodded.

"That gives you a level of credibility with the gang."

"Huh? How so?"

"Alejandro's little brother is named Enrique Europa. Having a big brother, who he idolizes, on the inside gave him the chops to become the leader of the pack. Of the Marauders."

"*Los Merodeadores*," Wolf corrected.

"Right. And because you knew his shit-bird brother in the joint, it gives you credibility by association. We both show up on motorcycles claiming to be part of the Breed, and we're in like Flynn, as they used to say back in my great granddaddy's day."

"I don't know," Wolf said. "What makes you think that I have any influence with them?"

"We show up and you mention your association with his brother in Leavenworth. We then sit back while Enrique checks this out, and as soon as he calls Alejandro, who will verify, because it's true, we'll be in like—"

"Yeah, I get it," Wolf said.

"So all you have to do then…" Pike smiled again. "Is to give me an introduction to Enrique, and then slip out of the picture—family problem or some shit like that, and let me take over from there."

"That's all I have to do, eh?"

Pike nodded. "Yep. Simple as one, two, three."

"And what do I get out of it?" Wolf asked.

"You get the satisfaction that you did your part in serving your country and government by helping to stop the flow of drugs, mainly fentanyl, into this country."

Wolf was silent. The chance to help make a difference in the war on drugs was mildly tempting, but also kind of out of his league. Besides, he had enough to worry about—his appeal, his commitment to join Mac and the boys... Not to mention that he'd be undertaking a very dangerous mission without any type of coverage or benefits or reward besides the satisfaction of doing his part and serving his country.

And the government, he thought. The same government that sent me up the river and now doesn't want to hear the legitimate evidence that would clear me.

"I don't know," he said. "I'd like to help, but—"

"Oh," Pike interrupted. "You haven't heard the best part."

Wolf stared at him. "The best part."

"You help me out, and I'll grease the wheels for your appeal."

"You can do that?"

"Listen, I got friends in high places," Pike said. "And a lot of low ones, too. All it'll take is a little inner-agency cooperation."

Wolf mulled over the decision.

Did Pike have that kind of influence, or was he just blowing smoke?

He also wondered once again if Pike could have had something to do with his appeal being removed from the Military Court of Appeals docket this morning. Ozmand had seemed mystified at first, before blowing it off as "something that happens all the time." Wolf thought that was bullshit then, and he was even more convinced now.

"Okay," Wolf said. "Let me think it over and I'll let you know."

"Steve, what's to think about?" Pike said. "You were a damn good back-up before, I'm telling you I can grease those wheels for you. And don't forget, I did save your life."

"I was wondering how long it was going to take you to pull that card out of the deck."

"Shit, it's true, ain't it?"

Wolf had to agree that Pike had, in all probability, saved him from taking a bullet.

"I don't know," he said. "That asshole Batton didn't seem like a real good shot."

"Whaddaya mean? He was right on top of you. If it wasn't for my superb marksmanship abilities, you'd pushing up daisies."

Wolf grinned. In spite of the possibility that Pike

might have had something to do with the appeal delay, Wolf liked the guy.

"Marksman?" he said. "Is that what you qualified as in the army?"

Pike snorted. "Hell no. Expert with every weapon. And I got the medals to prove it."

"Come on," Wolf said. "Let's head back."

He turned and started running. They crossed Flamingo on a steady green.

Pike was next to him now and asked, "Well, what about it, brother?"

Brother. He was really laying it on thick.

Wolf didn't answer immediately, assessing the situation and Pike's request as he ran. Then he said, "You bullshitting me about being able to help with my appeal?"

"Me? Never. It's not in my DNA, and you have to know that I'd never bullshit another airborne ranger."

Wolf glanced over at the big cement crosswalk that led over to Caesar's Palace and then back south toward Paris-Paris and the Eiffel Tower.

Pleasant memories, or a sign of a place to be revisited? With Yolanda.

And if he did help Pike, what were the chances the big fed could or would do what he promised?

Wolf remembered the earlier meeting with the Great Oz.

Should he contact him and see what he said?

Heading back, they caught another green at Harmon. Pike was breathing even more heavily now, and Wolf wondered if the man was going to fall out. He looked over at him.

"You gonna make it. Pike?"

"Shit," the big fed gasped. "I don't know. It'd help if we slowed down a little."

"Come on. You can make it."

"I don't know."

It was Wolf's turn to grin.

"You know," he said, "Sometimes you just gotta believe."

But as he took off running again, Wolf couldn't shake the feeling that he was on some kind of collision course, but with what he wasn't sure.

Another bout with destiny maybe?

***

CASA DEL ESTE DE ESTEBAN CORTEZ
YUCATAN, MEXICO

Rivera saw Esteban Cortez Sr. sitting outside on the veranda at the huge table that was shaded by a large awning. The table top had numerous smaller dishes and cups and glasses. Two pretty Mexican girls, dressed in black maid's uniforms, stood on either side of him. One held a stainless steel carafe of coffee and the other a glass one containing orange juice. On either side of the girls were two more of the ubiquitous bodyguards. Neither was as formidable looking as Buenaventura, but they had an aura of competency just the same. *El Jefe* was shoveling massive amounts of *huevos y frijoles* into his mouth, and alternating each mouth full with a swig from his coffee cup or glass of fruit juice. A second plate of bacon and toast sat off to his right along with several smaller bowls with fruits, butter, and jellies. His lips parted in a smile as he noticed the approach of his bodyguard and Rivera. The remnants of the masticated eggs and beans clung to his front teeth.

"Alfredo," Cortez Sr. said, waving him closer with his left hand. "*Siéntate. ¿Quieres desayuno?*"

His cheeks were still stuffed and numerous particles of partially chewed food sprayed forth with each word.

Without waiting for a response, Cortez Sr. shouted for the servants to bring a second plate from the kitchen. Another girl appeared, smiling and with a cup of steaming coffee in one hand and a glass of juice in the other. She set them down in front of Rivera as he sat down next to Cortez Sr.

El Jefe is up early this morning, Rivera thought. *I wonder what he has in mind besides stuffing his fat face?*

Cortez Sr. finally finished chewing and swallowing, and then, after gulping down some juice from the glass in front of him, cast a glance at Rivera and smiled.

"Alfredo, it is good that you are up early," Cortez Sr. said, switching to English. "I wish my son was more like you. He is still in the bed with his two *mujeres*." Pausing, he shook his head, and then grinned. The residual food was still stuck along his gum-line. "He has much to learn, that one, and I know you are the one who can continue to teach him. Show him the right way, the strong way."

Another girl appeared with a plate full of scrambled eggs and fried beans. She placed it before Rivera and handed him a spoon and a fork.

He acknowledged the proclamation by Cortez Sr. with a curt nod and picked up the utensils.

"*Coma, coma*," Cortez Sr. said.

The eggs had been prepared to exquisite perfection and he appreciated the delicious smell of the cooked bacon.

Glancing about and seeing the two bodyguards still standing close by, as well as the two *señoritas*, none of whom spoke English, Rivera figured Cortez Sr. had summoned him here to deliver something of a personal nature.

After he finished chewing, he asked, "What is it you want of me, *jefe?*"

Cortez Sr. heaved a sigh and pushed his plate away from him. One of the maids immediately reached out and removed it. His lips flickered with a smile.

"As I have told you before…" Cortez Sr. reached into his pocket and removed a long, thin cigar. He bit off the end, spat it to the side, and waited while one of the bodyguards produced a lighter and lit it for him. After puffing on it several times to get the burn going, Cortez Sr. removed the cigar from his mouth and leaned forward over the table.

"Griggas called me last night," he said. "The man is nervous about setting up this new pipeline in Arizona."

Rivera tore off a piece of toast, placed it into his mouth, and took his time chewing before answering.

"How so?"

Cortez Sr. took another long drag on the cigar and when he next spoke his words came out laced with smoke. "He and his brother want to expand the operation. He is concerned that we are not going to be using *Los Merodeadores* for transportation of the product from Yuma. And Europa says that the man he knew from the new connection to the Devil's Breed is now dead. They are supposed to be sending *un hombre nueva*. This has Griggas a bit, how you say… *nervioso*. *Adicionalmente*, He has concerns that this rancher, Pierce, has not yet been made to cooperate. He says his sources say that the *americanos* have increased their security in the area. Not only with los *agentes del gobierno*, but with private security as well."

Rivera continued to listen without talking. This was nothing that he did not already know from his conversations with Griggas and Europa a few nights ago.

"You wish me to go there to talk with him again? The rancher?"

Cortez Sr. drew on the cigar as he nodded. He expelled smoke from his nostrils this time.

"Offer him more money. If this doesn't not work, take his daughter. Bring her here for a little…" His smile grew malevolent. "*Una vacación exendida.* Explain that we will be continuing her education for a time."

Rivera nodded. He wondered what the girl looked like, and if she was pretty, how he was going to keep *el hijo gordo* away from her. A bargaining chip was not to be mishandled, as long as it had value.

"It will be done as you wish."

Cortez Sr. grunted an acknowledgement, and then spoke again, still continuing in English. "Martín and the others are busy. I have them gathering more *ganados* for the crossing. Twice as many as before, which means that the shipment will be twice as large. I must be certain that this new group, the Devil's Breed, *es cupable*—capable of handling things."

"And you want me to go see to that as well." He didn't phrase it was a question.

Cortex Sr. parted his lips in a smile, letting the gray smoke drift through his teeth.

"*Sí, sí exactamente.* And take Esteban with you. Let him do the more of the talking this time. Make it clear that he is the one that will be taking over someday. Someday soon." Cortez Sr. paused, drew more smoke into his mouth, and expelled it with an accompanying beatific smile. "After all, I want to begin to enjoy life a bit more. And what is a son for, if not to one day step into the shoes of his father?"

Rivera smiled as well, but for a completely different reason.

Someday soon, he thought. *It is coming sooner than you may think.*

***

EXECUTIVE'S ONLY STEAM ROOM
FLAMINGO RESORT
WEST PALM BEACH, FLORIDA

The setup was virtually the same as it had been in New York except that the tiles in this steam room were pale yellow, whereas the ones in the other steam room had been a light blue. The temperature felt just as hot, and the wispy steam circulated about making deep breathing uncomfortable. Bray, Abraham, and Von Tillberg all sat on the segmented sections, with the rich man mounted on the highest portion, and his bodyguard, the black guy, standing by with the short, black tights covering his groin and ass, and the designer gym shoes on his feet. Of course, he also had on the weighted down fanny-pack that rested in front of the chiseled abdomen no doubt containing that semi-automatic handgun.

The big, black son of a bitch was all chiseled muscle and Bray knew he didn't want to do anything that would get on the wrong side of him, or his rich, eccentric, security-fanatical employer.

The little pipsqueak sat on the uppermost shelf looking down at them and occasionally sipping from a frosty bottle of cool water. Once again, Von Tillberg hadn't asked if either Bray or Abraham wanted one.

"So you say they were both in Las Vegas?" Von Tillberg said.

"Yes," Bray answered. "Last weekend. For Wolf's MMA fight."

The slender little prick took a long drink of the water and just watching made Bray's throat feel dry, despite the moist environment.

Von Tillberg brought the bottle away from his lips. "And where are they now?"

Abraham, who looked as uncomfortable as Bray felt, glanced at him with an impatient look.

As if I could do anything to hurry this report up, Bray thought.

"McNamara's back in Arizona," he said. "Apparently on his way back to the border. Wolf was still in Las Vegas as of about an hour or so ago."

"And what was he doing there?" Von Tillberg asked. "Talking to a lawyer you said?"

Bray nodded and licked his lips. The rich man's head canted to the side and he cast down an imperious glance.

"That's right."

"What about?"

"That's unknown," Bray said. What did this little prick expect? That he and his team were going to break in and bug some lawyer's office.

Von Tillberg brought the bottle up to his mouth again and tipped it forward. His Adam's apple worked along his thin throat. The remaining liquid slowly disappeared, and then he crushed the plastic container and held it outward. Without a sound, the big bodyguard snared it and asked if he wanted another.

Von Tillberg's head shifted to the side once again as he waxed contemplatively, and then nodded. The black guy turned, rapped on the glass, and held up one finger. It looked as thick as a sausage to Bray. A shadow appeared on the other side of the frosted glass window and the outside bodyguard pushed open the door. An ever-so-slight current of fresh, air-conditioned air came trickling through the sliver of an opening.

"Mr. Von Tillberg wants another," the black bodyguard said. His words had a foreign twinge to them, but Bray couldn't quite place it. French maybe?

The second bodyguard accepted the crushed plastic bottle and the door closed once more.

The oppressive heat resumed.

"I hope he's not planning on initiating a lawsuit against my late uncle's estate," Von Tillberg said. "The government's still got all of his stateside assets tied up with their investigation."

Abraham glanced at Bray, as if expecting him to know the answer. Bray shrugged.

They sat in silence for several seconds and then the door popped open after a warning knock. The big, white security guard handed the black one a fresh bottle of water.

Bray noticed the label had some kind of foreign writing on it.

The door slammed shut again.

"Oh," Von Tillberg muttered accepting the bottle from the bodyguard. "I suppose I should have asked if you wanted any. But we're almost done here anyway." He twisted the top cap and it rotated with a distinctive click. After taking another long pull on the bottle, Von Tillberg leaned back against the titled wall.

Bray felt like he was getting a bit light-headed. He was glad the little rich prick was circling the field.

"I'm wondering what kind of case the FBI has," Von Tillberg said. "And how long it's going to linger."

"Traditionally," Abraham interjected, "the feds move at glacial speed."

Von Tillberg pursed his lips, like he'd been sucking on a lemon.

"As I mentioned before, financially, this whole matter is little more than a nuisance to me, but I don't want to take the chance that uncle left any trail that could be traced back to the family. Or to me, in particular. How can we make this go away?"

Abraham cleared his throat. "Well, you must keep in mind that your late uncle did allegedly kidnap McNamara's daughter and take her out of the country. And her husband's an FBI agent."

"But my uncle's now deceased," Von Tillberg said.

"Correct," Abraham said. "But there's still the matter of his... penchant for acquiring artifacts on the black market."

The rich man sighed and then took another drink from the new bottle.

"Which places me, as his primary beneficiary, in the spotlight and possibly a future subject of federal scrutiny."

Everyone was silent and Bray was glad it Abraham's turn on the hot seat.

"Which might somehow inadvertently lead them to look into my activities on the island," Von Tillberg said.

Abraham said nothing and Bray was surprised that the lawyer was for once keeping his trap shut. He did wonder, however, why Von Tillberg had summoned them both here just to rehash what they already knew.

"So," Von Tillberg continued. "I've come to a decision. It's time for us to become a bit more proactive."

"Meaning?" Abraham asked.

"Meaning," Von Tillberg said. "We take out the trash. The FBI won't have much of a case if their principal witnesses aren't around to testify, will they?"

"No," Abraham said. "But, we must be discreet."

Von Tillberg frowned. "And that's what I'm paying you for. You said McNamara was heading down to the border again, correct?"

Bray nodded. Another stern look from the bodyguard prodded him to give audible reply.

"Yes, sir."

The right corner of Von Tillberg's mouth twitched into something akin to a half-smile.

"And there was a possibility of Wolf joining him down there?"

He recalled conveying that Maureen had overheard a snippet of conversation along those lines during her masquerade at Best in the West.

"Possibly."

"Then our path seems like a simple one," Von Tillberg said. "Lure them both down to the border and take them out. Make it look like a cartel thing. After all, the border's a very dangerous place now. I'm sure my associate, Esteban Cortez would be most accommodating, if need be."

If need be, Bray thought. Things had suddenly shifted again, with him being cast in the role of arranging a hit, this time for some rich sociopath instead of an old, dying mafia don.

"Once that's done…" Von Tillberg held the frosty bottle against his forehead. "Arrange some sort of car accident for McNamara's daughter and her FBI husband." He held up the water bottle, took a small sip, and pursed his lips again. "See to it and report back to me when it's done. Discreetly, of course."

"Of course," Abraham responded.

Lap dog, Bray thought.

He felt a knot forming in his stomach. He'd just gone from arranging two murders to four, and one of them a federal agent. This was getting worse all the time. This security conscious sociopath was discarding people and consequences like a change of underwear.

And since he likes to tie up loose ends so much, Bray thought, *what's to stop him from deciding that me and Abraham are liabilities, too?*

"Now that that's settled…" Von Tillberg tossed the mostly full water bottle onto the floor and stood up.

"It's getting uncomfortably hot in here," he continued. His plastic clogs made a squeaking sound as his feet moved over the tiled section upon which Bray and Abraham sat. "As soon as things are finished up, I'll have you both as guests on the island."

He moved down to the floor and the bodyguard pushed open the door for him.

Bray and Abraham exchanged glances and then got up as well. The bodyguard followed Von Tillberg out of the steam room and let the door wing closed behind him, not offering to hold it for the other two.

I guess as the hired help, we don't rate, Bray thought.

He looked at the discarded water bottle which was lying on its side, discharging the contents onto the textured cement floor with slow undulations.

CHAPTER 9

INTERSTATE 8
MOHAWK, ARIZONA

Wolf was feeling the strain of the long road trip on the big Harley Road King, and he wasn't sure whether to attribute it to the residual aches and bruises from his most recent MMA fight, or to the fact that he hadn't been on a motorcycle in several years. The discomfort of the lack of a full backrest, having to keep his arms outstretched on the handlebars, the wind whipping around the windshield, and the constant tension of holding the accelerator with his right hand were all making him regret agreeing to assist Pike, who was right beside him on another big Harley, on this undercover foray.

"It'll be the simplest thing in the world," the big fed had told him. "All you gotta do is play yourself."

In actuality, Wolf wasn't sure exactly how much help he was going to be. Pike had set it all up, arranged everything as far as Wolf's phony ID's and driver's license—it didn't matter that his motorcycle classification has expired over eight years ago, and Pike had even gotten Wolf new biker duds, boots, and Harley all in the space of two days.

He probably had everything ready, Wolf thought.

And this brought up the persistent question in his mind about just how much influence the big federal agent really had over things. Pike seemed to know virtually everything about Wolf, down to his shoe size, and all about his pending case before the Military Court of Appeals. Leading up to last Monday, the Great Oz had all but assured Wolf that the case was going to be heard on that day, but it had somehow disappeared from the court docket. Oz had been mystified, but told Wolf to shrug it off. But up until that morning, the lawyer had been so certain the case would be heard, especially with the new, exculpatory evidence Wolf had recovered in Belize.

No such luck.

Wolf's hopes to clear his name had all evaporated like a rope of smoke.

And then Pike had come conveniently back into Wolf's life offering commiseration and new opportunities. The big fed was showing up with the regularity of a homing pigeon.

No, Pike was no pigeon. He was a feral alley cat, maybe, or moreover a marauding brown bear, pillaging through everybody's garbage. He had that ursine build to make the metaphor more appropriate. But this bear came bearing gifts: an assurance that he could and would get Wolf's appeal moved onto the fast track, with the hint of some official grease to push it on through with an accompanying exoneration and even the implied promise of reinstatement of all rank, privileges, and benefits. And all it was going to take was for Wolf to play himself to one of his old prison buddy's brother.

"An introduction, and then you're out," Pike had told him.

And he was getting paid, too. Not much, admittedly, but something. The main inducement was the promise of assistance, however.

How could I turn him down? Wolf asked himself. His lawyer was getting nowhere.

He'd agreed, yet the timing of it all kind of bothered Wolf.

From the onset, Pike always had known way too much. He was overly familiar with Wolf's prison time, his court martial, his appeal… And to top it off, Pike had playfully alluded to the case disappearing from the court docket.

Almost as if it had all been prearranged.

"There's nothing like a little inner-agency cooperation," the big fed had said when Wolf pressed him about his offer to "grease the wheels on the appeal."

Pike accelerated about six feet I front and motioned for Wolf to follow. They were coming up to an exit. Wolf acknowledged with a fractional nod and eased up on the accelerator just enough to let Pike take the lead as they exited the freeway and headed toward what Wolf assumed would be a gas stop. They paused at the stop sign only slightly and Wolf noticed that the van, which was being driven by Pike's partner, Teddy, was following them. When Pike had introduced them a couple of days ago after the run along Las Vegas Boulevard, Wolf understood why Pike needed a partner who would be believable to this biker group. Teddy, or Theodore T. Mitchell, looked more like a geek than a cop. Not only did he have an Ivy-league haircut, but he wore gray plastic framed glasses and had a rather slim build. His skin seemed a little thin for being in law enforcement, too.

"We're not police," Mitchell had said, his tone completely devoid of any mirth. "We're federal agents."

"So don't lie to him," Pike added flashing his infectious grin. "Or he'll charge you with Obstructing the Government. Or Conspiracy to Obstruct if you're even *thinking* about doing it."

Wolf didn't know if he was being serious or not, and he didn't want to ask. All he wanted to do was to get this over with.

Make the introduction and then I'm out, he told himself. That's what Pike had promised.

He'd told McNamara he'd be joining him down at the border shortly, not wanting to let the cat out of the bag that he was assisting Pike. That, too, was at the big federal agent's instruction.

"When you're U/C," Pike had said, "you've got to be all in. You got to live the role, just like it's real, because it is. You slip up, do something out of character, tell the wrong person what you're doing, and it can all come down like a house of cards."

Pike drove into a fast food burger joint and circled the lot twice before pulling into a parking space. Wolf pulled in next to him, and Mitchell parked in another area altogether. When he got out and ambled over Wolf saw the man was wearing a dark blue baseball cap and was dressed in a light blue short-sleeve shirt and tan Dockers. He wore a well-stuffed fanny pack which Wolf assumed contained his weapon. It was a Glock 21, as far as Wolf knew. Pike had his huge, six-inch Colt Anaconda revolver in a shoulder holster. He was dressed in total one-percenter biker garb—filthy blue jeans, a black T-shirt with the Harley Davidson insignia, and a black leather vest with rows of small motorcycle wing insignias lined up and down in columns. *Devil's Breed* was stitched across the back of it with large white letters outlined in red. Wolf knew each one of the smaller insignias had a special meaning, but just what these were, he didn't know, and didn't ask. In lieu of a helmet, he had a large black and white bandana tied over his head. When Wolf asked about the prudence of riding a motorcycle without a helmet, Pike had scoffed.

"No self-respecting one-percenter's gonna be seen riding with a fucking helmet on. It just ain't gonna happen."

The one-percenter designation meant "hard-corps biker" in motorcycle lingo. Wolf knew this from his prison time.

Pike had given Wolf a modified biker outfit to wear. It consisted of a Harley Davidson T-shirt, a beat up Levi jacket with the sleeves razor-bladed off, and another black bandana. Wolf rotated the jacket, looking it over.

"How come mine doesn't say Devil's Breed across the back?"

"Because you're just an apprentice," Pike said. "That way I don't have to make any excuses when it comes time to set you free."

"And when will that be?"

"As soon as possible. Ah, you can wear your old army boots, if you got 'em that is," Pike said.

Wolf didn't, and elected to hit the army surplus store for a new pair.

When they'd finished dressing, Pike had grunted an approval.

"Not bad, not bad," he said. "Of course, I'll be glad to take a piss on your jacket to break it in."

"Like hell," Wolf said.

Pike shrugged. "No choice. Like I told ya. Not only do you got to live the part, you gotta smell it, too."

"Just the same, I'll pass."

Pike shot him a wink. "Wise move."

There were a few other cars in the lot, but the restaurant seemed sparsely populated. After hitting the restroom, they ordered and the big fed motioned for Wolf to head outside and sit at one of the tables. No one else was out there and Wolf took one near the corner of the building. An L-shaped section of the drive-up and the signs obscured the table from view on three sides. Wolf took off his sunglasses and set them on the wire tabletop. Presently, Pike came out with the food and a tray holding their drinks. Wolf had opted for coffee while Pike had a large soft drink of some sort. Mitchell followed holding a paper bag and a bottle of water.

Pike sat down and set the food and tray on the table.

"Not bad," he said. "Good choice of location. Good cover. Must be your ranger training."

"I still think it's too risky," Mitchell chimed in. "What if someone sees us together?"

He'd now slipped on what appeared to be an old army BDU blouse and a baseball cap.

"Relax, Teddy," Pike said, poking a straw through the X in the top of his soft drink cap. "Were still far enough away that there ain't gonna be no Marauders around. And I wanted to make sure we're all on the same sheet of music."

"But what if somebody sees us?" Mitchell said, his tone huffy. "It jeopardizes my role as Control."

"Control?" Wolf said.

"It's just federal agent talk for surreptitious back-up," Pike said with a grin. "Secret squirrel stuff to you laymen."

Mitchell frowned. "It seems you haven't done a sufficient job of bringing your CI up to speed on protocol and procedures. I hope he's not going turn out to be a liability."

"Relax, Teddy," Pike said. "Believe me, this man can handle anything that's thrown at him."

Mitchell pursed his lips again. "This is still a violation of proper protocol."

Wolf was beginning to take a real dislike to Teddy.

Pike held up his big open palm. "Relax, like I told you. We're still far enough away that this quick meet isn't going to be a problem. Besides, there's that matter I wanted to address with Steve here."

That matter? Wolf wondered what he meant by that. He stared at Pike.

"Does the name Robert Bray mean anything to you?" the big fed asked.

It did, but Wolf held back, wanting to see what Pike and Control knew.

"Should it?" he said, choosing to remain coy.

"Now see here," Mitchell said. "Don't be flippant with us."

"Flippant?" Wolf said, turning toward the other man.

"Whoa," Pike said, leaning forward. "I just asked a simple question, that's all. Does it?"

Wolf mentally debated his options.

What the hell, he thought. *This guy knows everything anyway.*

"He's a private dick that was nosing around a few months ago," Wolf said. "Asking questions about the last little excursion Mac and I took south of the border."

"To Belize?" Pike asked.

Wolf jerked his head, giving it a quick mini-shake.

"If you already know the answer, why ask the question?"

"We'll be the judge of what we ask and don't ask," Mitchell said.

"You know, I've had just about enough shit from you." Wolf held up his hand, keeping his thumb and forefinger about a quarter inch apart. "I'm about this close to telling you both to shove it and pulling out of this whole thing."

Pike barked a quick laugh.

"Now you don't want to do that. How'd you get back to Phoenix? You're riding the G's motorcycle, remember?"

Wolf took a deep breath, realizing the big guy was right. Options were limited, and the promised rewards high. He sat in silence for a moment.

"Plus" Pike continued, "you got your appeal to think about."

Wolf frowned.

"And," Pike added, "Not to mention I saved your life back in North Carolina."

"You're sure getting a lot of mileage out of that one.' Wolf said.

Pike winked at him.

"Robert Bray investigation s out of New York," he said. "You said they were asking questions? What were they, and who'd they ask?"

"I never saw them personally," Wolf said. "Some guy came by Reno's gym in Phoenix. This was when I was still living in Vegas. Another one went to see Manny, the bail bondsman I used to work for, and another stopped by the FBI office."

Mitchell and Pike exchanged glances.

"Don't tell me you didn't already know that," Wolf said. "What about all that inner-agency cooperation you're always spouting off about?"

Both of the agents were silent for a moment.

"Let's just say," Mitchell said, "that the Bureau isn't

always forthcoming with information, even to other agencies within the government."

Pike flashed his grin again. "In other words, some of them are very tight-sphinctered assholes."

Wolf had to laugh at that one.

"So do you know why they're shadowing you?" Pike asked.

"According to Mac's son-in-law, they were supposedly investigating the death of a guy named Von Dien. We tangled with him in Belize."

"He's the rich asshole who had a penchant for stolen artifacts and the same one that set you up in Iraq." Pike made it sound like a statement rather than a question.

Wolf merely nodded.

"Well," the big fed continued. "They're still at it. Remember that chick that came out to Best in the West? The magazine reporter?"

"Yeah," Wolf said. "Tonya something."

"Tonya Knight," Pike said. "Well, she wasn't what she purported to be. I ran her plate that day and it came back to a rental. Guess whose name was on the rental form?"

"Bray Investigations?" Wolf asked.

Pike nodded. "That's who paid the bill. Her real name's Maureen Cistero. Sound familiar?"

Wolf shook his head.

"And I did a little more checking," Pike continued.

"That supposed magazine that she mentioned—Razor's Edge Tactical, or something, doesn't exist. It was all bullshit."

"Wolf felt his gut tightening. He'd known about the previous inquiries, but hadn't seen this recent stuff coming.

"And we had her tailing us on our run the other day, too," Pike said.

Wolf's brow furrowed. That did surprise him.

"In Vegas? You're kidding, right?"

Pike shook his head slowly indicating the negative. "Teddy picked her up on Las Vegas Boulevard tagging us. Or at least it was a female operative driving another rental car doing it."

"And the rental came back to…?" Wolf said.

Pike picked up his soft drink and sucked some of the liquid through the straw.

"You guessed it."

This was starting to bother Wolf even more. Despite the earlier inquires, he'd put it off to the insurance investigation story. He thought he'd been able to put all of that Von Dien business behind him.

"Anyway," Pike continued. "I just wanted bring you up to speed. Keep your eyes open when we're down there, and after we part company, too."

"You got that right," Wolf said.

"We can't afford any distractions." Pike sucked some more of his drink through the straw. "Now let's go over our cover story one more time."

They'd gone over it constantly for the past two days, but Wolf nodded.

"And remember, we're U/C, so you gotta *live* the part."

Now it was Wolf's turn to grin. He held up his hands and pointed to the ersatz biker outfit he was wearing.

"What do you think I have been doing?" he said. "And don't even *think* about pissing on my jacket."

***

THE PIERCE RANCH
SOUTH OF YUMA, ARIZONA

Alfredo Rivera was uncomfortable in the suit and tie, but felt it was needed to create the right impression. He was also getting a bit of unforeseen glee at the obvious discomfort Esteban Cortez Jr. was exhibiting being similarly dressed. The fat on the man's corpulent neck hung over the starched blue collar like the matching dollop that hung over his belt. And even with the air-conditioning cranked up on high, the wetness had crept through the dark blue material of the shirt in several places. *El hijo gordo* was not pleased that he had to dress up, but before they'd left Mexico his father had emphatically told his son to do everything that Rivera told him to do.

"Alfredo will show you the way," the older Cortez had said. "Follow his *instrucciones* and you will be all right. Remember, soon you will be in charge. Take this time to learn."

And so they went, passing through the customs once again using the expertly forged Mexican passports. It helped to have government officials on your payroll. Rivera made a mental note that he would have to reestablish those relationships once he took over. But the names of the corrupt officials were no secret, and bribe money was bribe money, no matter from whom it came.

He drove the rented Dodge Charger down the long driveway and toward the main gate. The sign hanging over the entrance specified *PIERCE RANCH*. The same as the last time, there was no gate guard, but as Rivera drove toward the house, which was also not very remarkable compared to the mansion of Cortez Sr. This one was two stories and made of wood and stucco. Not unlike a middle class home you might see in the neighborhoods around here, or even in some of the higher class sections of Mexico—nice, but unpretentious.

But still important, Rivera thought.

He drove slowly, taking in the sights, recalling any changes from the last time he was there. The same stunted trees surrounded by decorative rocks and the hardy desert flowers that grew in sporadic patches. Beyond the house and immediate area lay the immense fields where the lettuce and citrus plants grew. It was, as they say, the winter lettuce capitol of the world. And it was also the place where they would be bringing the herd of illegals, *los testarudos,* across under the cloak of darkness.

More people were present now, and not all of them the migratory workers or local farm workers. It was the winter picking season soon and it would be very easy to smuggle people across. One group of four men stood by a Jeep loading rifle magazines. AR-15's from the looks of them. A couple of the guns looked shop-worn, perhaps even of military grade M16's. The men loading them, three whites and one black, were not youngsters. Hardly that. But they had a hard, capable look. The look of old soldiers. The black man was bigger than the rest of them, perhaps close to 200 centimeters. Maybe 150 kilos, yet he did not appear to be the leader. That one was an older one, maybe even in his sixties, but in good shape. He moved with an assurance and his hawk-like eyes *were the first to affix on the arriving vehicle.*

Viejo, pero duro, he thought. *Old, but hard.*

"See those men over there?" he said to Cortez Jr.

El hijo gordo grunted that he did.

"Study their faces well," Rivera said. "We will most likely be seeing them again, if things do not go well with this meeting."

El hijo gordo snorted derisively. "*No problema. Son viejos.*"

"Do not underestimate them," Rivera said. "Or any of the other *americanos* you might see here. You had best remember that."

Cortez Jr. blew out a quick breath, obviously expressing distain.

You have much to learn, Rivera thought. *It is too bad that I will not be teaching you.*

With perhaps fifty or so feet to go on the winding driveway, he saw the front door opening and went on automatic alert. An attractive young woman, perhaps in her early-twenties with her hair pulled back into a blonde ponytail, came prancing out of the side door. She was wearing a tan blouse and blue jeans that conformed to her slender hips and legs. Waving toward the house, she ran to a red automobile parked next to the closed overhead garage door. It was a Corvette.

Rivera wondered if this rented Charger was faster. Perhaps he would get the chance to find out, but until then he placed such trivialities out of his mind.

It appeared that in the main house someone was home.

"That looks like the daughter," he said to Cortez Jr. "She is doing an internship at the hospital."

Cortez Jr. scrutinized her.

"*Es rubio*," he said. "I thought she was part *méx-*

icano?"

"Yes, but only a quarter."

"I'd like to fuck her in the ass," *el hijo gordo* said, flashing a lascivious grin. "And maybe I will. When do we take her?"

Rivera said nothing. His orders were to first try the bribe, and if that didn't work, then take the girl. He would need the help of Europa and his boys for that. But either way, he intended to remain professional—something this *chingado* did not understand, since he thought with his *pendajo*. He purposely slowed down until the girl had started the Corvette and zoomed past them going the opposite direction toward the main gate.

She glanced at them casually, a smile on her pretty face, as she sped past.

Muy bonita, he thought, thinking about what was in store for her.

With that he pulled to a stop on the circular stone driveway in front of the house and shifted the transmission into PARK.

Professional, he told himself.

Was it now time for him to become *El Tigre* once again?

No, he thought. *For now, it is better to remain Alfredo Rivera, businessman.*

Just as he and Cortez Jr. were getting out of the car one the men who'd been loading the rifle magazines, the old, tough looking one, strolled up.

Un hombre duro—An old tough guy.

"Hey there," the older man said. "Can I help you?"

Ah, Rivera thought. *Just as I suspected. Señor Pierce has added a new layer of security since my last time here.*

And this one had a pistol holstered on his right hip. No doubt he was told to be watching for the *méxicano* that looks like an *anglo* with red hair.

"I'm here to see Mr. Pierce," Rivera said, keeping his expression neutral and his English as unaccented as he could manage. He was fairly good at that, thanks to his American mother's teachings so long ago. He smiled.

"Is he expecting you?" The *hombre duro* asked.

"No, I am afraid that I did not take the time to call." Rivera kept his smile in place. "But I am sure he will want to see us. It is very important."

He had allowed a bit of the foreign tone tincture his words. At this point he saw no need for subterfuge. Obviously, Pierce had briefed his people well.

The *hombre duro* took a cell phone out of his pocket and said, "Let me see if he's available." He motioned to the group standing by the Jeep and they began meandering over, carrying their rifles. The front door suddenly swung open and Rolando Pierce stepped out onto the slab of cement and stared at them with a hard look on his face.

"*Señor* Pierce," Rivera said. "Nice to see you again."

"I can't say the same for me." Pierce's drawl was low and guttural. "And I thought I made it clear to you that I wasn't interested in any deals."

Rivera shrugged his shoulders. He was about to speak when Cortez Jr. muttered, "Do you know who I am?"

His tone was imbued with implied malice.

This fat idiota is going to ruin everything, Rivera thought.

Rivera issued the quick rebuke in Spanish: "*Cállate. No digas nada. Recuerda las instrucciones de tu padre.*"

Cortez Jr. closed his mouth at the admonishment concerning his father.

"I don't know what he told you," the *hombre duro* said, "but I expect it's sound advice. Now why don't you two get in this nice car of yours and hightail it back across the border before me and my friends here have to do a little leaning on you?"

Rivera's smile widened as he turned to glance at the *hombre duro*.

"Leaning on us?" Rivera arched his eyebrows and discreetly pointed to the gun on the other man's hip. "With one of those?"

"Mac," Pierce said. "I don't want no trouble."

"Nor do we, *señor*," Rivera said. He turned back to Mac, the *hombre duro*. "And, my friend, we did not scurry across the border. We are here on a visa."

"Whatever," the other man said. "But I ain't your friend and we don't want to see you here again."

Rivera told Cortez Jr. to get in the car and then opened the driver's door. Before he got in, he glanced first at Pierce and said, "I am sorry we could not reach any agreement." Then he turned to the one Pierce had called Mac. "And to you, *señor*, until we meet again. As you say in your country, have a good day."

The other man's face was impassive. If he had any fear, he certainly wasn't showing it.

Rivera slid in behind the wheel, put on his seatbelt, and started the engine. He was tempted to peel out, but instead shifted cautiously into gear and slowly drove away.

The one called Mac was already doing a quick jog to the Jeep.

He's going to follow us, Rivera thought, and with that he pressed down on the accelerator and increased his speed.

"Why did you let them talk to you like that?" Cortez Jr. spat. "They made fools of us."

Rivera glanced in the rearview mirror and saw the Pierce ranch fading from sight.

"Because it was part of the plan," he said. "This time we were here as businessmen, not *banditos*. And when you have a role to play, you must do the proper care."

El hijo gordo blew out another derisive snort.

"You should have let me continue to handle it," Cortez Jr. said. "I was doing fine."

Rivera shook his head. "Sometimes you must let your opponent think he has the upper hand."

"I do not like playing the fool," Cortez Jr. said, and took out a cigarette. He jammed it between his lips, flicked the lighter, and was enveloped in a wispy cloud of smoke.

Rivera merely smiled at the younger Cortez's frustration.

Soon he would realize that he'd been playing that role all along.

Viva al parte, he mentally added. Live the part.

***

ON I-8
NEAR DATELAND
SOUTHERN ARIZONA

Bray turned on his signal and glanced in the rearview mirror to make sure that Maureen, who was in the rental car following him, pulled over as well. He saw her slow down and head for the shoulder. Once they were stopped, he pressed the button on the burner phone and waited to see if Abraham would answer. Bray assumed that the lawyer was either in New York or Florida, but either way the time zone difference made it early afternoon out there. Abraham answered after about five rings.

"What's up?" he asked.

"Just checking in," Bray said. "We're tracking Wolf on the freeway heading south. He's with those two feds, as far as we can tell."

"As far as you can tell?" The irritation in Abraham's voice was obvious. "What's that supposed to mean?"

"We're keeping our distance. With the feds being involved, we can't afford to be spotted. We're, or should I say Bray Investigations, is probably already on their radar somewhere due to our inquiry a few months ago for our insurance death investigation."

"Any idea where they're going or what they're involved in?"

"No. Like I said, we're keeping way back. I'm using up a lot of favors tracking Wolf by his cell phone, but if I had to guess, he's doing something undercover with the feds."

"What about McNamara?"

"He's down in the Yuma area working for some rancher named Pierce. I've got Jack Powers on him. It appears as though him and his Best in the West buddies have lined up another border security job."

"Well, that should make it easier to take him out then," Abraham said. "Blame it on the cartels."

Just the thought of trying to engineer not one,

but two separate assassinations to fulfill a rich man's whimsy made Bray's stomach tighten.

"I told you before," he said. "I'm not a hit man. Nor are my people. I don't mind surveilling these jokers, but I'm not going to be pulling any triggers myself."

Bray heard Abraham's petulant sigh.

"I know, I know, but our employer made it very clear that if we can accomplish that, it would be very lucrative for us. You can set something up, can't you?' Abraham was talking fast now, and his tone sounded conspiratorial. Bray imagined that he was sitting somewhere ensconced in a corner, whispering into the phone. "You said you could. Remember the price he quoted us."

Bray remembered, all right. A cool million apiece, in addition to the substantial amount they'd been paid thus far. Was it any wonder that the lawyer had assured Von Tillberg in that Florida steam room that it would be no problem? Abraham had dollar signs swimming in front of his eyes.

Eyes… Bray also remembered the unconcerned look in the rich man's eyes as they all sat sweating in that steam room. He showed no visible concern about ordering the deaths of two men whom he'd never even met. There was no emotion at all, like he was ordering them to go step on a couple of bugs. Von Tillberg was a sociopath, all right, and that did concern Bray. The rich man was one cold son of a bitch.

"That was before I knew that Wolf was hanging with the feds," Bray said. "And don't forget that McNamara's son-in-law's an FBI agent."

"He said we could address that later. His main concern is eliminating the trail that Wolf and McNamara could provide to his late uncle's estate. Ending it sooner, rather than later. Once they're both out of the picture, it'll probably just fade away. Especially if we can blame it on the Mexicans."

"I told you, I'm not a hit man."

"Then find somebody who is. You know people, right?"

The lawyer was talking fantasies. In his youth Bray had fantasized about being a secret agent or hit man, but he had long since discarded that idea as foolish. Now here he was actually living that role. Life was funny sometimes… And deadly.

Abraham's voice interceded with the reverie.

"Are you there?"

"I'm here," Bray said. "And I've got a call coming in. I've got to go."

"A call? On this burner? From who?"

Bray really didn't have another call. He simply wanted to get away from the lawyer for a bit.

"It's from my tracking agency," he lied. "I'll get back to you when I have something more."

"All right," Abraham said. "And let's get something

set up, at least where McNamara's concerned."

Bray said he'd work on it and terminated the call.

He sat there idling on the shoulder as a couple of trucks whizzed past. Glancing in the rearview mirror he saw Maureen was still behind him.

He needed some time to think, to plan out his next moves. It would be better to keep the ball rolling as long as possible, unless some unexpected opportunity presented itself. It was a complex situation full of risks. Great risks. Yet, with great risks come great rewards... A million bucks, tax free, was ultimately very tempting. But one other factor kept dangling in the back of Bray's mind. If the rich sociopath was so obsessive about eliminating loose ends by capping people, why would he stop once the principals were eliminated? He'd made a suggestion that both Bray and Abraham could come to that island place of his... Would that be a trip from which they'd both return?

CHAPTER 10

HUFFINGTON INN HOTEL
YUMA, ARIZONA

It was late afternoon when Wolf and Pike finally pulled into Yuma and gassed up their motorcycles. Pike told him that he had the meet set up for later and they might as well check into their hotel and relax a bit. They got separate, but adjoining rooms on the second floor of the hotel. Wolf entered his room and quickly surveyed it. The room had a narrow bathroom adjacent to the door, a long waist-high dresser made of polished wood, a medium sized flatscreen television, one king-sized bed, a small desk, and a padded chair. Pretty much your standard hotel room. He dropped his backpack onto the bed and went to the window. The drapes were open providing a view of the parking lot. Peering outside, Wolf could see their two Harley's parked below in the front lot area. He also noticed that Mitchell, or "Control," was nowhere to be seen.

Was that a good thing, or a bad one?

A pounding on the connecting door jarred him.

"Lemme in," Pike bellowed.

Wolf went to the door and flipped the lock. The knob twisted and Pike entered carrying his backpack. He glanced around, smiled, and said, "Not quite what you were used to in Las Vegas, eh?"

"Oh, I don't know," Wolf said. "I had an apartment there that was about this size. Maybe smaller."

Pike smirked. "That reminds me of a joke. About this girl who asks her psychiatrist what a phallus symbol is, and when he shows her his, she says, 'Oh, it's like a prick, only smaller.'"

Wolf had to chuckle after hearing that one.

"I got us a meet with the Marauders for tonight," Pike said, holding up his cell phone.

"*Los Merodeadores en español,*" Wolf said.

Pike feigned a ludicrous expression of surprise and snapped his fingers. "Right. I forgot you speak that lingo, don't ya?" He grinned. "You know, it now looks like I might have to keep you working for me a little longer than I figured on."

"Marvelous." Wolf pointed toward the window. "I don't see Mitchell's van out there."

"And you won't, either," Pike said. "As far as you're concerned, he doesn't exist."

"That sounds like wishful thinking."

Pike canted his head. "Now don't be too hard on good old Teddy. He's our ace in the hole. He'll be keeping tabs on us the whole time, and hopefully, if we get in a jam, he'll call in the cavalry."

"And that's why he's called Control?"

"Exactly."

"Well, I hope he does a better job here than he did back in North Carolina," Wolf said. "As I recall, there was no cavalry."

Pike shrugged. "Teddy wasn't with me on that one, and remember, those were extraordinary circumstances. There was a hurricane winding its way up the coast, for Christ's sake. That messed things up as far as getting my backup in there fast, which was why I had to sorta deputize you. Besides, that one was just supposed to be a run-of-the-mill drop off like I'd done plenty of times before, building my case. Things just went bad, is all."

"Just run-of-the-mill huh?" Wolf said. "Just like this one is a run-of-the-mill drop introduction?"

"Yep."

"During which I'm supposed to do what again?"

The big fed took in a deep breath and exhaled.

"I told you, you're just there to add credibility. All you gotta do is be yourself. Ex-con and prison *amigo* of this punk, Europa's big brother."

"So he's going to check with Alejandro about me?"

"I fully expect him to."

"And when his brother confirms that I served time with him?"

"Then you'll be out of it," Pike said. "I'll have credibility with them, and you just hang out here for another day or so, and then take off and go back to Phoenix, or join your buddy down by the border, or wherever else you want to do."

"He's not that far away from here."

Pike grinned. "All the better. You'll be in the area in case I need you. Just like back home in North Carolina."

Wolf's mind flashed back to him and Paxton assisting the lone federal agent in the big shootout in the abandoned shopping mall.

His expression made the big fed laugh. He held up his open palms and added, "Now, now, I was only kidding. Ain't gonna be like that this time."

"Yeah," Wolf said. "Right. I'd still feel a lot better if I had a gun."

Pike shook his head. "You heard Teddy. Against the rules."

"The rules?"

"Yeah, you're a paid CI, not an official government agent. I give you a gun, I could get in a world shit. And I'm a rule follower."

"A rule follower? What about back in North Carolina?"

"That was different," Pike said. "Exigent circumstances. And thanks to your buddy, Paxton, being local law enforcement, I was able to keep your part in it pretty much out of my report." He grinned. "I'm kinda good at doing that."

"I'll bet. But I'd still feel better if I had a gun."

"What's the matter? You don't think the big snake and me can handle things if they go south?" He reached up and patted the concealed bulk of the huge Colt Anaconda hanging in the shoulder rig under his left arm.

"I never did place too much trust in reptiles, especially the big ones."

Pike emitted a sound that was somewhere between a grunt and a laugh.

"Careful," he said. "You'll hurt her feelings."

"Her? It's a female?"

Pike nodded. "Sure is, they're the meanest. And let's face it, after the way you let old Batton get the drop on you back then, and me having to step up and save your life, I'm not so sure I can trust you carrying a gun."

Wolf felt a sense of outrage. He'd acquitted himself fairly well in that instance, and he was getting real tired of Pike bringing it up.

"If I'm such a liability," Wolf said, "why are you even taking me along for the ride?"

"I told you. Credibility. And if I wouldn't have been there to save your life," Pike continued, "we wouldn't be sitting here now, would we?"

Wolf said nothing. Even though his part in this,

as a paid CI who was only there as window dressing according to Pike, Wolf had an uneasy feeling about it.

They sat in silence for several seconds and then Pike burst out laughing and clapped Wolf on the shoulder.

"Just busting your balls a little." Pike smirked. "And never let it be said that I let a fellow airborne trooper go naked."

He reached into his backpack and removed a folded rag. After setting it on the bed, he carefully unwrapped it and Wolf saw a small, stainless steel semi-automatic pistol. The gun itself was almost tiny and the grip was turquoise.

"Go ahead," Pike said. "Check it out."

Wolf reached down and picked it up, testing the heft of it in his hand. It was light and the chamber end of the slide was rounded and hammerless.

"It's a SCCY," Pike said. "Their CPX nine millimeter subcompact polymer pistol with a light-weight trigger pull. Also comes in a three-eighty, but I figured a big strapping boy like you would appreciate a little more bang for the buck."

"For the buck? You selling it to me?"

Pike laughed again. "That'd be against the law, considering you're a convicted felon."

Wolf felt the sting of those words, and Pike clapped him on the arm again.

"SCCY's all the rage lately for the concealed carry

crowd," he said. "All their firearms are made in the USA and are, according to their ads, designed to offer comfort and accuracy at an affordable price. This one's striker-fired. Nine millimeter Lugar rounds. Round capacity's ten and one."

Woolf hefted it again. "Nice and light."

Pike nodded. "Weighs 15 ounces."

Wolf gave him a sideways look.

"And you're letting me use it?"

Pike shook his head. "It's a drop."

"A what?"

"A drop-gun. Officially, I never seen it before. And if you have to use it, wipe it down and toss it, and walk away. You never seen it either. Got it?"

Wolf gave a quick nod as he pressed the button to release the magazine. He let it fall onto the bed and then grabbed the serrations to pull the slide back a quarter-inch or so to check the chamber. A flash of gold was visible. Racking the slide to the open, locked position, he let the expelled round fall onto the bed as well.

Pike chuckled.

"Just in case you didn't bring your latex gloves with you, pretty boy, know that it's real hard to get fingerprints off of expended brass. They come out so hot they burn away any residual latents."

"Good to know," Wolf said, but he intended on wiping the cartridge off anyway. He set the SCCY onto the bed.

"What?" Pike said. "You don't like it? I got a little three-eighty that'll fit in you back pocket."

He reached into the rear pocket of his blue jeans and pulled out a small leather square about the size of a wallet. As Pike rotated it, Wolf caught a glimpse of the shape of a gun.

"It's a Seecamp three-eighty." He pulled the tiny pistol from the leather holster. "Three and a quarter inches with a slide width of point seven-two-five. Carries six and one. Ain't she a dandy?"

"Another female I see."

"And another drop." Pike blew out a slow breath. "But I have to admit, it'd break my heart to lose this one. Took it off of the prettiest little Latina gang-banger you ever seen. And you'll never guess where she kept it." His grin broadened.

"I can imagine." Wolf pointed to the SCCY. "I'll stick with that one."

"Good choice." Pike slipped the Seecamp back into his pocket and dug into his backpack again. He came out with a small hard shell holster that looked like it was part polymer and part perforated padded neo-prene. "This is an Alien Gear holster. So comfortable, you'll forget you got it on. But don't."

Wolf grinned and accepted the holster. It looked flimsy, but beggars couldn't be choosers, could they?

"I know it don't look like much," Pike said, "but believe me, you're gonna love it."

Wolf slipped the SCCY inside and heard the faint

click of the lock around the trigger-guard.

"Hopefully, you won't need to use it," Pike said. "But like I said, if you do…"

"Drop it and walk away," Wolf said. "Is it okay if I run instead?"

"An Airborne Ranger running?" Pike twisted his face into a mocking frown. "You know better than that."

"All the way," Wolf said.

"Right on. Now getting back to what I was saying, the chances of you getting mixed up in any action are minimal. All you got to do is—"

"Come along to add credibility."

"Right. I been working this case for the longest time. If things wouldn't have gotten so messed up back East, and that stupid motherfucker wouldn't have splattered himself all over the back of that eighteen-wheeler, I wouldn't even be needing you at all."

"But you do." Wolf was getting tired of that same old song. He waited a few beats before adding, "So when did you decide on using my face card?"

Pike's lips twisted into a pucker as he considered the question.

"Well, I'm a man who likes to hedge his bets. So I do my homework. When I was researching your brother, I came across your file, read it, and…"

"You saw a good patsy you could pressure."

Pike's face took on a serious expression now.

"Actually, I saw a fellow ranger that, from the looks

of it, got shafted. And I meant what I said. You do this for me, and I'll do what I can to grease the wheels on your appeal."

"Inner-agency cooperation?"

Pike grinned. "You got it."

Wolf forced a grin, too, but in the back of his mind he wondered if that inner-agency cooperation had been responsible for getting his appeal knocked off the docket. But for the moment, he had little choice but to continue to march. It was his best chance at clearing his name and getting his life back on track. His lawyer's words echoed in his mind.

You gotta believe.

Yeah, he thought. *I do.*

***

EL PRIMOS'S RESTAURANTE
YUMA, ARIZONA

Rivera bit into the taco and assessed the taste. It wasn't half-bad, considering that the cook looked to be an *anglo*. What sense did it make to have a non-Mexican cook in a restaurant that promoted Mexican cuisine? But what sense did anything make in this stupid country? They had everything here, just laid it out for the taking, and the people didn't appreciate it. But at least the smells wafting from the kitchen area, which was behind a long open window separating it from the counter area and the rest of the restaurant, were reminiscent of home. The cushions on the booth in which they sat were comfortable, too. He took another bite and then drank some of the coffee. Across from him Cortez Jr. was stuffing his face. He'd ordered an enchilada, beans and rice, and a beer. A layer of sauce was mixed into the hairs of his mustache, and decorated his lower lip and chin. The man was a slob and Rivera couldn't wait to get rid of him.

But that would be a job for *El Tigre*. When the time came... And hopefully, it would be soon. He checked his watch, and then looked out the window. It would be fully dark soon. After a few more minutes, a gray van pulled up and parked next to the rental car. Europa and Julio, the one called *El Martillo*—the Hammer, got out.

A few moments later the door jingled as it opened and the two of them came in, almost strutting in their biker vests and heavy boots. They sauntered over and sat in the booth, with Europa sitting across from Rivera.

"How's the food?" Europa asked.

Rivera held his hand up, the palm facing downward toward the table, and waggled it.

"*Asi, asi.* But not bad, considering."

Europa smirked and whistled for the waitress.

A pretty Hispanic girl came over and smiled down

at him while she took out her pad and pencil. At least he assumed she was smiling, from the way her eyes looked. The lower portion of her face was covered by one of those stupid masks. His own mask as well as the one belonging to Cortez Jr., lay on the table. Europa and Julio removed theirs.

"Give me a couple of hard-shells," Europa said. "And some fries and a Coke."

"We only have Pepsi," the girl said. "Is that okay?"

From the pronunciation sound of her words, Rivera figured she'd been born here. She was cute, maybe seventeen years old.

"Whatever," Europa said.

She turned toward Julio.

"Gimme another one of these," Cortez Jr. broke in, thrusting his hand over his plate. He'd sprayed bit of partially chewed food across the table onto Rivera's plate. "And make it quick."

Rivera felt the burn starting.

Now is not the time, he told himself, and crammed the rest of his taco into his mouth.

After Julio had ordered the girl left. Rivera glanced around. There were a few other patrons in the place, but none of them close enough eavesdrop. He leaned forward a bit and looked at Europa.

"Well?"

"Piece of cake," Europa said. He just started to go into more detail when the waitress returned and set down waxy cardboard glasses with their drinks on the table. She laid a straw beside each one and Rivera noticed her staring at him. When he raised an eyebrow in her direction she blushed. Rivera found himself wondering what her smile looked like and if she had nice teeth.

She probably did, he figured. Just about everybody in this country did.

Good dentistry here, he thought. *And lots of pretty girls.*

He then turned his attention to the pressing matter that had brought them there—another pretty girl. As soon as the waitress had left, he glanced over at Europa, who was sucking on his straw.

"Did you check out the hospital?"

"You woulda been proud of me and my man, Hammer here, Alfredo," Europa said. "We found some old homeless dude and give him some free shit to swallow. A couple of minutes later, sure enough, the fucker was OD'ing and we loaded him into our van and drove him to the ER." Europa stopped talking and placed his lips around the straw. Some of the dark liquid rose up through the opaque translucence. "Me and Hammer carried the fucker inside, acting like it was a real emergency, or something, and then when they told us to put him in this room, he was gagging real bad." Europa grinned, obviously very pleased with the recollection. "So they started working on him right away, and one of them asked us if we knew what he'd took, but we said we just found him on the street, is all."

He paused to take another extended sip.

"How many of them saw your faces?" Rivera asked.

"Nobody." Europa's grin exposed an array of yellowish teeth.

"We wore masks," Julio added.

Rivera arched an eyebrow in acknowledgment. "*Muy bien.*"

"So's anyway," Europa continued. "We were inside the doors and we snuck off looking around and whenever anybody asked us what we were doing, we just said we was lost. Got the whole layout down good, and we also scored a couple of nurse's outfits out of a supply closet." His fingers tapped the mask lying on the table. "Got a bunch of these things, too. You gotta wear them down in Mexico?"

"We do what we please down in *México*," Rivera answered, using the Mexican pronunciation for his country of birth. "And did you see the girl?"

"Yeah. She was there, all right. It was kinda hard to pick her out because of the masks but they were all wearing name tags. We just looked for a bitch with a blond ponytail and spotted her right away."

"And what about the security?" Rivera asked. "And cameras?"

The waitress returned with their food and no

one spoke while she placed the plates onto the table. When she'd left, Europa picked up his hard-shell taco and brought it toward his open mouth.

"I asked you a question," Rivera said. *El Tigre* was close now, prowling and ready to come out… Ready to reach across the table and slap the shit out of this little fucking punk. But that would delay things, and he needed Europa and his crew on this side of the border.

For now, anyway.

Perhaps later, he thought, *when I've taken over.*

Europa seemed to sense Rivera's displeasure and answered before biting into the taco.

"I seen some security in the ER and the hallways, but they looked old and didn't have no guns, or nothing."

"Cameras?"

Europa had just finished biting off a substantial portion. He shrugged as he managed to shift the food to his cheeks.

"They got plenty of them ones on the ceilings," he said. "You know, they look like a bowl made of gray plastic."

"PTZ's," Julio said. "Pan-tilt-and-zooms."

Rivera glanced at him, impressed. Maybe this one called the Hammer wasn't not only strong, but smart as well.

"My old man had a job installing them," Julio said.

"I used to give him a hand sometimes."

"What about the parking lot?" Rivera asked him.

Julio nodded. "There's one on the building, by the entrance, and another couple in the parking lot."

"Then it will be best to take her when she leaves," Rivera said. "Tonight. We will have to find out what time she gets off."

"Midnight," Europa said. "We seen a schedule by the timecards."

Rivera acknowledged with a quick nod. Perhaps this one wasn't so worthless after all.

"But don't forget," Europa added. "We gotta meet that dude from the Breed tonight, too. That's at eight."

"I forget nothing," Rivera said.

To further exacerbate his irritation, Cortez Jr. didn't even appear to be listening. Instead, he was consuming his third enchilada with methodical gusto.

El Tigre wanted to reach across the table and grab the other man's fat throat.

And soon I will, he promised himself.

"Do you know what kind of car she drives?" Rivera asked.

Europa paused before taking another bite. "A red corvette, right? Ain't that what you said?"

Rivera nodded.

At least the punk had paid attention to that detail.

"All right," Rivera said. "We will take her tonight,

when she gets off work."

"And how will we do that?" Cortez Jr. asked, exposing a collection of half-masticated meat and cooked dough as he opened his mouth.

"Simple," Rivera said, half turning and placing a hand on Julio's shoulder. "We have a hammer. All we will need is a nail. A nail in her tire."

Europa grinned. Apparently he understood, or at least pretended that he did.

Julio smirked, too, and Rivera began to feel more confident with his plan. These two were competent, and malleable. They would do. Cortez Jr. had a befuddled expression on his corpulent face, though, and Rivera smiled benignly as he looked across the table at him.

He was *El Tigre* now... The big cat patiently watching from the bushes for the fat cow to meander closer.

And then...

CHAPTER 11

HUFFINGTON INN HOTEL
YUMA, ARIZONA

As they walked across the hotel parking lot toward their two parked Harley's, the evening air had cooled things off some, not that it had been what Wolf would call unseasonably hot during the day. He also noticed that it was totally dark now, but the ambient lighting from various sources was illuminating the immediate area to a certain degree.

Good sniper weather, he thought, trying to slip his mindset back into a combat-ready mode.

"So what did your buddy, McNamara have to say?" Pike asked.

Wolf reflected back on Mac's call earlier. Pike had been in his adjacent room and the adjoining door between them had been closed. Either Wolf had been talking louder than he'd thought, or Pike had exceptional hearing abilities.

Or could he have the room bugged?

Or maybe, Wolf thought, *it was Control.*

Wolf decided he was being paranoid, and regardless, Mac hadn't really said anything of note. He'd just mentioned that the employer, Rolando Pierce, seemed like a squared away fellow who was fed up with the bullshit of an unending stream of illegals marching across the border, leaving a trail of garbage, and wrecking his damn crops—citrus trees and lettuce plants. And it was now the picking season. Mac and Buck and Joe were doing mostly night patrolling around the perimeter and chasing people down. So far, it had been pretty routine.

"He's working security for a guy named Pierce," Wolf said. "Down this way. Says it's a pretty nice gig. The pay's good, and he says there's room for me once I'm finished up here."

"Well, let's get to it then." The big fed paused and looked at him. "Steve, I want you to know that I appreciate what you're doing, just like I appreciated you stepping up and helping me back East. And when this is over, I fully intend to help you with that appeal process."

"When this is over?" Wolf smiled. "Why do I get the feeling that you've just moved your promise of interagency cooperation into the twilight zone?"

Pike laughed.

"I love that old show. Watch it all the time on the nostalgia channel."

They were at their bikes now and Pike swung his right leg over the seat. Wolf did the same.

"You never answered my question," Wolf said.

"What question was that?"

Wolf frowned. "Never mind."

Pike depressed the clutch, inserted the key, and turned it. The big engine came to life with its customary percussive roar. After gunning the accelerator a couple of times, Pike shut the motorcycle off.

"Look, I wasn't bullshitting you," he said. "It's just I can't give you a solid time and date as to when I'll be able to help you. We been working this operation for a long time. It takes a while to set everything up. But you'll be out of it soon, and then I'll do what I can to help you out. You got my word on that."

Wolf looked at the other man. He seemed sincere. And he was airborne. That had to count for something.

"How far?" Wolf asked.

Pike grinned. "All the way, brother."

***

Bray held the night-vision goggle binoculars up to his eyes and watched the two men who were across the four lane street and perhaps one hundred yards or so away. Wolf and the fed were dawdling in the hotel parking lot. They were both on their Harleys, but hadn't taken off yet. The glow given off by the street and hotel lights hurt Bray's eyes. He brought the device down to his lap and blinked.

"Dammit," he said. "There's too much glare from those lights."

Maureen, who was using regular binoculars, emitted a musical chuckle. "I can see just fine."

They were both in the same car now, but her rental was parked right beside his.

"Great," he said. "Tell me what you can see."

"Wolf's still next to each other," she said. "It looks like they're getting ready to go somewhere... I wonder if they're going out drinking?"

Bray was rapidly blinking to try and clear his vision. He thrust his hand toward her.

"Let me see those."

She handed over the binoculars. "Want me to get out one of my disguises and follow them into the bar?"

"No." Bray adjusted the focus to sharpen the image. Bright dots still lingered in his field of vision. "I'm still not convinced that I should have let you get that close as Tonya Knight last week. We're not dealing with idiots here."

"Will you stop? I told you, all they were looking at was my boobs."

He couldn't resist casting a quick glance at them

himself. They were exquisite.

But, back to business.

"Let's get in separate cars and see where they go," he said. "Keep in touch by cell phone. I need to check in with Powers, too. And don't let them see you following. If you think they do, turn off and let me pick it up."

"Roger that," she said. "But don't worry. Chances are that they won't have a clue.

I sincerely hope not, Bray thought.

His vision was still not back to normal. He continued to blink and handed her back the binoculars.

She held them up to her eyes, adjusted the setting of the focus, and continued to survey their quarry. Then she gasped.

"Hey." Her voice was imbued with excitement, and he saw her lips curl into a smile.

"What?" Bray asked.

"Looks like they got company."

***

The distinctive roar of the two Harleys reverberated in the night air as the two new bikers pulled into the hotel parking lot and were heading right for Wolf and Pike. Wolf turned toward them and Pike angled the wheel of his motorcycle and slammed down the kickstand. He swung his leg back over the seat as the two pulled up. They stopped in back of the parked Harleys. Both of them looked fairly young—maybe late teens, early twenties, and most likely of Mexican descent. They each wore dirty Levi jackets—"colors" with red bandanas wrapped around their heads. And both had exaggerated sneers on their faces in an obvious effort to try and enhance that ultra-tough look. Their Levi jackets showed the customary, motorcycle gang filthiness and had the sleeves whacked off. They were decorated with a red script sewn into the lapels on both sides. The one on the left read *The Marauders,* while the opposite lapel had the same word only in Spanish— *Los Merodeadores.* Below the scripts on each were smatterings of the same motorcycle wing insignias that were on Pike's vest. His was much more extensive, though. Despite one of them having some impressive biceps and triceps development, compared to the big fed, these two looked like small boys trying to play tough guys. Wolf doubted whether they were actually full one-percenters, or just wannabes.

"You Pike?" the muscular one asked.

"Who wants to know?" Pike replied. His expression was neutral, yet menacing at the same time.

The muscle-boy frowned and then spat on the ground between them. It landed next to Pike's motorcycle. He'd done his best to make it look casual, but it was obvious posturing.

Pike looked at the splash of spittle and then back up to muscle-boy.

"You better pray that none of that got on my hog," Pike said, keeping his voice low and guttural.

"Or what?"

Muscle-boy's smile seemed a bit shaky, but he knew how things went. He'd responded with bravado, just the way he should.

Wolf knew that Pike had, too. He hoped this didn't escalate to an exchange of blows, or with both of them pulling down their pants to see who was the bigger man. But Wolf had little doubt who would prevail. The kid had some overdeveloped musculature, but Pike had football-sized arms and made the young Marauder look like a little boy trying to play in a man's league.

Pike smiled, glanced over at Wolf, then reached out with incredible speed and grabbed the young biker, lifting him completely off his bike. Whirling, Pike tossed muscle-boy over onto the grassy lawn in front of the hotel and then gave the now vacant Harley a kick with his foot. The motorcycle tipped in the opposite direction, the frame striking the rear fender of the second wannabe biker, causing him to wobble and then fall over.

"You fucker," muscle-boy shouted as he sprang to his feet and rushed toward Pike.

Pike sidestepped and drove his fist into muscle-boy's gut. The younger man doubled over holding his abdomen. Pike was on top of him in a moment, twisting the other man's arms behind his back. The second wannabe biker jumped up and started to reach inside his waistband. Wolf jumped over the fallen motorcycles and delivered an MMA Superman punch. The blow struck on wannabe number two on the jaw and he went down like a collapsing pup-tent. Satisfied this one was down for the count, Wolf shot a quick glance toward Pike, who now had muscle-boy in a full nelson.

"Get that one's gun," Pike said, leaning back so that the squirming muscle-boy's kicking feet were completely off the ground. "Now if you don't want me to break your fucking neck, asshole, you'd best settle down and quit trying to pretend you're a bad ass."

Wolf did a quick pat-down of the still unconscious second wannabe and found a blue steel, snub-nose Smith and Wesson thirty-eight caliber revolver tucked into the left side of the biker's waistband. There was a switchblade knife in his right front pants pocket. After pocketing both items, Wolf stepped over to the fallen bikes and checked the saddlebags. Pike was still holding muscle-boy, but the man had stopped squirming.

"Lemme go." His voice was barely above a whisper,

and transformed into a grunt as Pike exerted more pressure.

"In due time," he said. "Steve, see what he was reaching for in the left side of his pants, will ya?"

Wolf stepped over and pulled a Glock 43 from a pancake holster looped to the man's thick belt. He continued checking muscle-boy's pockets and found another switchblade.

"Put that shit in my saddlebag," Pike said.

When Wolf had done that, Pike leaned back again, lifting muscle-boy off the ground once again.

"You gonna be good, junior?" Pike asked.

Muscle-boy grunted an asset along with a few profanities.

Pike lowered him to the ground and then shoved him away. Muscle-boy whirled to face him, fists clenched.

"You don't really want to do that," Pike said. "Now take us to see your boss."

Muscle-boy's lips compressed. He glanced down at this partner, who was still out but starting to twitch a little.

Wolf reached into the saddlebag on his bike and pulled out a plastic water bottle.

"Here." He tossed it to muscle-boy. "Pour this on his face and that should bring him around."

Muscle-boy caught the bottle with an adroitness

that told Wolf that the muscular kid might have been more formidable had he not been caught off guard. But he'd been defeated now and he knew it. He turned and twisted off the cap, pouring the water on the supine biker's face. The second wannabe sputtered back to consciousness and sat up, his eyes dazed and unfocused.

"Want me to check his eyes for a concussion?" Wolf asked.

"Hell no," Pike said. "Looks straight enough to ride to me."

"I'm all right," the sitting man said, pausing to give his head a quick shake.

Muscle-boy helped him to his feet.

"Okay." Pike clapped his hands together. "Now that we got that settled, take us to your leader."

"What about our fucking guns?" muscle-boy asked. His eyes flashed with obvious hatred.

Pike's going to have to watch this one, Wolf thought. *Especially once he doesn't have me watching his six.*

"Never mind about them." Pike smiled. "Just be glad we didn't shove them where the sun don't shine. Come on. Let's go."

Wolf moved his right elbow against his side and felt the pistol there. Pike was right. The holster was comfortable, but it couldn't match the comfort of knowing the gun was there, too.

He remembered Pike's prediction that in all likelihood the gun wouldn't be needed, but after this initial confrontation, Wolf wondered how accurate that would be.

***

THE GAP
NEAR THE MORELOS DAM
YUMA, ARIZONA

Rivera accepted the night-vision binocular goggles that Europa had given him and peered through them looking across the expanse of field. The Morelos Dam lay perhaps a hundred yards away. The water of the Colorado River looked placid and still, appearing like a base of black satin while the surrounding area was populated with the variety of shrubs along with the dam's superstructure. It was all clear in variations of green illumination. Although he couldn't see it at the moment, Rivera knew that not too far away was the adjacent border of Pierce's property. The man had been fortunate to be close to the waterway so that the underground wells could be tapped and used to augment his planting wells during the growing season. The water was plentiful then. Now, it was the winter and things were dry, but it was also their harvest time. The snow in the mountains had yet to melt, sending nature's nectar running downward to feed the river and streams. It was the cycle of things, the cycle of life.

And of death as well, when that became necessary.

He then adjusted his view to survey the break in the border wall fencing. The river was shallow this time of year and it would be no problem for Martín, Paco, and Fernando to lead the group across after they had first released the runners—the decoy herd of young men whose job it was to run and hide, tying up the efforts of the border patrol and local authorities. Then the mules would be led across the river bearing within them the wrapped condoms full of the drugs that would yield so much money. This night would pass before that happened, but they were close now. He made a mental note to call Martín and find out if they were on schedule with the journey and the forced swallowings. The number in this group of mules was extensive: thirty-five, and the decoys over fifty—a massive amount of product was to be carried across. The Griggas brothers would be happy, Cortez Sr. would be happy, and *El Tigre* will have established himself as the new number one man. Hopefully, none of the condoms would break, and no field surgery would be required. He wanted everything to go smoothly this time, especially since this would be the first time meeting with these new Devil's Breed members.

He lowered the binoculars and turned to Europa.

"What time will they be here?"

"Soon," Europa said. "I got Hammer and Carlos going over to their hotel and bringing them here. Shouldn't be too much longer."

"I should hope not. Did you forget we have to grab the girl tonight?"

"I didn't forget nothing. I got two guys watching the hospital parking lot." Europa's upper lips curled up in what he apparently thought was a sly grin. "She don't get off till midnight, so we got plenty of time."

There is never enough time, Rivera thought. This is something this *pendajo pequeno* has to learn.

"Tell them to be mindful of any cameras," he said.

Europa's face wrinkled. "I already did. They got a twenty-two in the van to take it out before they deflate her tire."

Rivera nodded.

Europa's cell phone buzzed with an incoming text. He looked at it and then to Rivera.

"They're on the way now. You want to go over to the town to meet them, or what?"

"You have met with them before?" Rivera asked. "You know them?"

"Not these guys. I only talked to the one on the phone a few times. Pike's his name. He told me the other guy I met with before got killed."

Rivera considered this. "Such is life," he said. "But

just make sure you check out these new ones. We can afford no mistakes."

"He said on the phone that he was bringing somebody along that knows my brother."

"A new connection," he said. "We must be careful. Confirm it."

Europa pursed his lips and rolled his eyes.

"I know." His tone had a flippancy to it that made Rivera's irritation level rise a bit. Perhaps it was time for *El Tigre* to rise up and teach this *pendajo pequeno* a thing or two about judgment and maintaining respect. He glanced around and saw Cortez Jr. sitting in the SUV smoking a cigarette again. The *hijo gordo* had shown little interest in learning the family business.

"Come on," Rivera said. "Let's go meet the Devil's Breed."

***

REMOTE DESERT HIGHWAY
THE OUTSKIRTS OF YUMA

"I don't like this at all," Maureen said as they traveled along the darkened roadway. "We need to turn on the lights. What if we hit something?"

"Just shut up and let me concentrate on driving," Bray said. He regretted snapping at her after he'd done it, but the pressure was getting to him. Although there was some moonlight it was still hard to see, and there were no lights this far out. Luckily the road was fairly straight, except for an occasional banked curve. The red taillights of the four motorcycles about half a mile ahead of them appeared like a quartet of red dots. "There's nothing out here to hit, and I'm going slow enough that—"

Just then his right front wheel slipped off the pavement and the car bounced.

Maureen screamed and Bray swore as he swerved back onto the roadway, hoping the flash of his brake lights would go undetected. He took his foot off the accelerator and let the vehicle slow down.

"It just goes to show how much we need to put a GPS tracker on those damn motorcycles," Maureen said.

Bray agreed, but said nothing. He studied the rearview mirror for a few seconds, looked forward, and then checked the mirror again.

It showed nothing but blackness, but he could have sworn he'd seen a flash of red a moment ago when he'd hit his own brakes. He kept glancing in the mirror as he drove, but saw nothing else.

After about a quarter mile more the brake-lights of the motorcycles flashed and all four of them turned onto a side road.

"They're turning," Maureen said.

Bray already knew this but he said nothing. Instead, he tried to scan the area up ahead as he slowed down some more and then pulled completely off the road.

"Give me those night-vision binoculars," he said.

She handed them to him and he flipped the activation switch and adjusted the long-range focus knob.

Wolf and the others were on what appeared to be a lonely stretch of road leading into total darkness.

Had they gone off the road completely?

Bray exhaled, trying to figure out his next move. He lowered the binoculars and compressed his lips. Following them down an isolated side road would be risky... Real risky. They might have seen the flash of his brake lights in their mirrors before. What if they'd intentionally turned off to wait for him to see if he was following?

It wasn't worth the risk. He looked in the side view mirror, saw it was clear, and did a U-turn.

"We going back to town?" Maureen asked.

"Yeah. It's not worth getting made at this point in the game. Wolf and the fed are getting tied up with those low-lifes, and from the looks of it, they're probably trying to set something up. Some kind of a sting operation, most likely."

"Drugs?"

"Probably." Bray flipped his headlights on and began driving back towards town. They'd gone perhaps a hundred-and-fifty yards when the headlights washed over a black van pulled onto the shoulder of the road. A flicker of movement was visible for an instant behind the wheel, and then it appeared to be just an empty seat. But the shoulder-belt strap was extended, at an odd angle and it was apparent that somebody wearing it was crouching down in an effort not to be seen.

Federal backup, Bray thought, and wondered if he and Maureen had been spotted.

"Shit," he said.

"Think that guy was following us?" Maureen asked.

Bray accelerated to put distance between them and the black van.

"Keep an eye on it," he said.

Maureen turned in the seat and grabbed the binoculars. The roadway was fairly straight and after a minute or so she said, "It looks like he's taking off… Going in the same direction as Wolf went."

Good, Bray thought. It had to be their back-up and he's not going to leave his partners to tail us.

But then again, there was a good chance he wouldn't need to. He'd been following them all along, and no doubt had a fix on their plate and vehicle type.

"Get Powers on the phone," Bray said.

"Powers?" Maureen said. "But I thought—"

Bray held up his hand. "He's not too far from here. I'm pulling him from McNamara and bringing him here to assist us."

***

LAST GASP GULCH GHOST TOWN
UNINCORPORATED YUMA COUNTY, ARIZONA

After they'd turned off the lonely stretch of highway, Wolf and Pike followed muscle-boy and his partner down the stretch of a deserted dirt roadway. Wolf mulled over their situation and wondered if they were being led into a trap. If they were, it was probably going to be a one-way ticket to oblivion. Their only chance would be to fire back and move out on their motorcycles as fast as they could. There were no lights out this far, but the moon was nearly full.

The cloud of dust from the cycles ahead of them stirred up a torrent and made it hard to breathe. Wolf could feel a layer of grit seeping into his mouth. He ran his tongue over his front teeth. Then, up ahead, somewhat illuminated by their headlights, he saw what appeared to be the remnants of an upright structure of some sort. It looked like a set of pillars about thirty feet apart. As they got closer he saw they weren't pillars, but remnants of an old wall that had disintegrated leaving only the solitary twin support beams standing perpendicular to the earth. The roadway widened into a main street of sorts, with dilapidated structures on both sides. They looked to be a combination of upright wooden beams and deteriorated walls, some having lopsided remnants of ancient bricks and mortar, while others had sections of wooden planks that had once formed buildings. Now it looked like bombed out section of Syria or Yemen. More crumbling structures lined the street farther down, some in better condition, and others in worse. An occasional fragment of a well-constructed brick wall still stood upright and a few old buildings were actually intact. The majority of the structures looked to be just this side of collapsing.

Up ahead Wolf caught sight of a group of perhaps ten more motorcycles, a van, and a dark colored Dodge Charger. A group of men stood next to the vehicles.

This is it, Wolf thought. *Either it goes well, or we get our tickets punched.*

He instinctively dropped his left elbow against his side momentarily to feel the reassurance of the holstered pistol and reflected that Pike had been right about one thing. This was the most comfortable holster he'd ever worn.

They came to a stop and muscle-boy and his partner shut off their machines and slowly got off of their bikes. Muscle-boy glanced back at Pike and Wolf, his expression sour looking.

He's probably dreading telling his boss they lost their guns, Wolf thought.

The pair walked up to a diminutive man with his hair piled up in some kind of bulb on the top of his head and another guy in a black T-shirt who looked to be fair skinned with what appeared to be reddish hair. This struck Wolf as odd for someone in a Latino or Mexican motorcycle gang.

Maybe the diversity craze had affected them. too, he thought, trying to bolster himself with humor.

It didn't work.

The others looked typically Hispanic, especially a heavyset guy with longish hair and scrawny goatee. He was smoking a cigarette. Wolf tried to scan the group to see what kind of weapons they might have, but only saw a few handguns visible, tucked into waistbands or worn openly in shoulder rigs. At first none of them appeared to have any long guns, but that quickly changed as a quartet stepped out from behind a fragmented building with rifles. AK-47's from the looks of them. Wolf wondered if they were actual AK's or the cheaper, Chinese SKS version.

SKS's most likely, he thought. Everything was

made in China nowadays.

Regardless, he and Pike were way outgunned, and Pike had roughed up and denigrated the pair who'd been sent to escort them to here. Poking the beast with a stick was never a wise thing to do when you were going into the lion's den without sufficient forces behind you, but according to Pike projecting bravado was an essential part of the game.

"Just like Star Trek and the Klingons," Pike had said.

Wolf told him that he never watched that show.

"Too bad," Pike said. "You could learn a lot."

Wolf continued to assess the over-stacked odds against them.

But we've got Control, he thought, wanting to shake his head.

Mitchell.

Wolf's confidence ebbed some more at that thought.

Pike motioned for him to stop and Wolf pulled up alongside of him. The big fed kept his engine running. He leaned over so Wolf could hear him above the thrumming of the pistons.

"The skinny little shit's Enrique Europa," he said in a low voice. "You prison buddy's little brother."

Wolf recalled Pike's earlier briefing about the players with whom they might come into contact.

"The red headed guy's Alfredo Rivera," Pike continued. "I'm real surprised to see him here. They call him *El Tigre*."

Wolf remembered Pike showing him a grainy surveillance photo that resembled this man. The photo, however, did little to depict the man's formidable build now that Wolf had seen him up close. He was easily six-one or so, and looked to be a lean two hundred pounds plus of muscle.

"Remember," Pike said. "Play it just like we rehearsed it."

"I know," Wolf said. "Live the part."

"Right," Pike said. "Let me do the talking. Or most of it, anyway."

He shut off his Harley and Wolf did the same.

Pike strode up to Europa and the other man.

Up close Wolf could tell that this *El Tigre* character did in fact have reddish hair. He looked like an oversized Canelo Alvarez, but definitely a heavyweight version. Wolf also remembered Pike mentioning that this guy was "one bad-ass dude."

"Hey, Enrique," Pike said, holding his hand out with his arm upright at a forty-five degree angle for a "brother handshake."

"You Pike?" the diminutive biker asked.

"You're damn right I am."

Europa cast a sideways glance toward *El Tigre*, and

then shook Pike's hand.

"What happened to Keller?" Europa asked.

"Like I told you on the phone," Pike said. "The stupid fucker ended up as road-kill after plastering himself onto the rear of a semi." He shook his head. "Damn waste of a good bike, too. Totaled."

"Who's this?" Europa asked, looking toward Wolf.

He didn't know whether to offer his hand or just keep standing there. He decided on the latter.

Follow Pike's lead, he thought. And live the part.

He felt himself unconsciously reverting back to his prison days, the constant wariness, feeling vulnerable, yet always projecting bravado… Being ready for anything that came, and a promise to go down fighting.

Live the part.

"My buddy, Steve Wolf," Pike said. "He's in an apprentice position right now with the Breed, but we're testing him out for the organization, or at least the transportation part of it. He's still got a ways to go before he's fully accepted."

Europa eyed Wolf closely.

"He's okay," Pike said. "Served time with your brother."

That made Europa's eyebrows rise a little.

"You the one that knows my brother?"

Wolf nodded. "Alejandro, right?"

"Yeah." Europa's eyes narrowed slightly in a squint. "You got some Latino blood in you?"

"Indian," Wolf said. "But I speak a little Spanish."

"*¿Cuántos años estuviste en cárcel?*" the one called *El Tigre* asked.

The man's Spanish showed the accent and proficiency of a native speaker.

"*Cinco,*" Wolf replied. It had actually only been four years and three months, due to him getting credit for his stockade time.

El Tigre gave him a quick once-over, and then held out his hand toward Pike. They shook and then he offered the handshake to Wolf. He complied and as he did so felt the power of the other man's grip.

Pike's assessment had been right—this guy was no creampuff.

"*¿Es usted de México?*" Wolf asked.

El Tigre smirked. "*Sí,* but I don't look it, *no?*" He released his grip and held his extended fingers toward himself. "Canelo."

Wolf chuckled.

"Who's this *hombre?*" Pike asked, pointing to the heavyset guy next to *El Tigre.*

The red-headed man quickly raised his hand and shook his head.

"He is of no importance."

"What do you mean?" the heavyset man asked,

frowning. "I am in charge here. I am Esteban Cortez Junior, son of my father, Esteban Cortez, Sr."

It was Pike's turn to raise his eyebrows.

"The big man's son, huh?" he said. "Glad to meet you."

Pike didn't bother to extend his hand, and Cortez Jr. made no move to extend his either. After a few moments of awkward silence, Pike spoke again.

"We might as well get down to business. When do we expect the shipment to come in?"

Europa started to say something but *El Tigre* grabbed him by the upper arm.

"Soon," the red-headed man said. "But not tonight."

Pike arched an eyebrow. "When then?"

"We will let you know," *El Tigre* said. But first, we must verify you are who you say you are."

Wolf reflected that the man's English was very good. He'd apparently grown up as a native speaker.

"Aw, come on," Pike said. "I been in phone contact with you all for how long now? Three weeks or so? Plus, I brought along Wolf here because he knows your brother. Saved his bacon, too, I heard."

Wolf was hoping they wouldn't ask for details.

Europa started to speak again, but *El Tigre* tightened on the smaller man's arm causing him to wince.

Pike canted his head and heaved a heavy sigh.

"Well, I can't fault a cautious man," he said. "Especially with all we got at stake."

El Tigre released Europa's arm and the smaller man's face wrinkled slightly. He reached into his pocket and the movement made Wolf instinctively bring his hand back closer to the SCCY. But Europa only pulled out a plastic baggie full of white powder.

"Wanna do some coke with us?"

Wolf felt his uneasiness grow. He wondered if they were being set up for some kind of test. Doing drugs with these morons would be the last thing he wanted to do. And how would Pike handle this?

Pike shook his head and smiled. "I'd prefer to keep this purely a business arrangement."

"What?" Europa's head tilted to the side and a current of irritation rippled in his tone as his eyes bounced back and forth between Pike and Wolf. "You too good to party with us? What kind of biker are you?"

"Business," Pike repeated.

"Or is it something else?" *El Tigre* asked.

Pike flashed an easy grin.

"Like I said. Strictly business." He turned and looked at muscle-boy and his buddy. "And I'm not too fond of the company thus far."

Europa's brow furrowed. "What you mean by that?"

"Ask your little friends who escorted us out here,"

Pike said.

Europa turned and glanced at muscle-boy, who said nothing.

"We'll take our leave of you all," Pike said, "and go see if we can get ourselves laid tonight." He tapped Wolf's shoulder and turned back toward his Harley. "Let's go, Steve."

Wolf partially turned, and then said to Europa, "Give Alejandro my regards."

They both got onto their motorcycles, started them up.

Muscle-boy ran forward and whispered something to Europa, who then yelled for them to stop.

Pike gave him a questioning look, and then grinned.

"Lemme guess," he said, slamming down the kickstand and getting off his bike. "Your little buddies want their toys back, right?"

Europa said nothing, glanced at *El Tigre*, and then gave a quick nod.

Pike made a show of opening his saddlebag and removing each of the confiscated weapons. He dropped the magazine on the Glock first, then racked back the slide to eject the round in the chamber. Next he let the slide thrust forward, pointed the gun at the ground, and pulled the trigger. After the resounding click, he brought the Glock up and gripped it with both hands. He depressed the slide lock, slid the slide off of the receiver, and tossed the gun to the side. He then grabbed the snub-nose revolver, flipped open the cylinder, and pushed the ejection rod back expelling the shells. He threw that gun away, too.

"Them things needed a good cleaning anyway," he said.

After closing the saddlebag, he swung his leg back over the seat and resettled himself on the Harley.

"I'm kind of partial to knives," he added, speaking loud enough so that his voice could be heard over the percussive motor. "So I think I'll hold onto them. See ya when I see ya."

After using the toe of his boot to engage first gear, he cocked his head toward Wolf and released the clutch, sending the big motorcycle's wheels spinning down the dirt road toward the highway.

Wolf depressed the clutch, kicked his transmission up into gear, and followed.

I'm glad that's over with, he thought. *For now anyway.*

***

El Tigre watched as Julio and the other once scrambled around picking up the discarded gun parts and bullets like chickens scrounging for feed in the barnyard dirt. Cortez Jr. stepped over and spat on the ground between him and the other two men.

"*Mierda*," he said. "He made fools of both of your men. This is the best you got?"

Europa's scowl was deep. He didn't reply.

"I would have expected no less," Rivera said. "We don't deal with *conchas*."

El hijo gordo blew out a heavy, derisive breath and then walked off, lighting another cigarette. After watching the fat piece of shit meander away, *El Tigre* turned back to Europa.

"That big asshole," Europa muttered.

El Tigre laughed and wondered to whom Europa was referring—to Pike or *el hijo gordo*?

"Never mind," he said. "I like this one, Pike. He is *muy fuerte*. Very strong. I think this association will be a good one. *If* they check out."

The one called Wolf was impressive as well, but in a different way. He did not display the bravado of Pike, but had a confident look about him... That of a man who could handle himself well. One who has little or no fear. And *El Tigre* had the strange feeling that he'd seen him somewhere before, but where?

Regardless, Wolf bothered him slightly more now.

"But, as I told you," *El Tigre* said, "verify that the other one is who he says he is."

"I'll call my brother," Europa said. "But it'll have to wait until tonight or tomorrow morning. He keeps his cell phone turned off until certain times when nobody'll see him use it."

El Tigre nodded.

"Understandable." He glanced at his watch. "And we have another matter to attend to tonight."

"Right," Europa said, taking out his phone. "The girl. I'll check with my guys."

"Do it on the way," *El Tigre* said. "We need to get moving. We don't want to miss her if she happens to leave work early."

***

OUTSKIRTS OF TOWN
YUMA, ARIZONA

Pike was leading Wolf, and the van was trailing both of them. The big fed gave a quick wave, pointing to the right, and steered down a side street, then abruptly turned left, pulling into a one-story brick building that looked like it was vacant. Wolf followed and caught a glimpse of the van's headlight shining over him as it followed suit. Pulling up to Pike, Wolf shut off his motor and dismounted. Pike was already standing next to his silent motorcycle. The van driver, whom Wolf knew was Mitchell, pulled up behind both of them and shut off the headlights. He opened the door and slid out of the driver's seat.

"Well," Pike said. "That went about as well as could be expected."

"Where exactly did you go?" Mitchell asked. "I had to hang back a ways."

"I'm glad you did," Pike said. "There's a couple of real big fish there."

Mitchell stared at him. "Who?"

"We got Alfredo Rivera and Esteban Cortez's son."

Mitchell emitted a low whistle.

"There's an old ghost town off the main road," Pike continued. "Looks like they got a temporary HQ set up there. Rivera was coy about when they're bringing the next shipment across."

Mitchell pursed his lips and nodded. "So then their probably point of egress will be the Morelos Dam, as we assumed."

"Probably." Pike grinned. "But you know how I feel about the word assume."

Mitchell jerked his head in exasperation. "You and your jokes."

"Makes the time go by faster," Pike shot back.

"They're going to check on Mr. Wolf?" Mitchell asked.

"Yep," Pike said. He winked at Wolf. "See? I told you all you had to do was act naturally and be yourself."

Wolf nodded in acknowledgment, but he was thinking it wasn't over till it was over.

"What's the next step?" he asked.

"We lay low the rest of tonight," Pike said. "They might be watching. Maybe I'll see if I can call us in a couple of hookers to make it look good."

Wolf shook his head.

"Relax, boy scout," Pike said. "You don't have to indulge if you don't want to. Me and Mitchell here will service the ladies."

"Now see here," Mitchell mumbled. "That's against regulations. I don't—"

Pike made a derisive, farting sound with his mouth in reply, then emitted a hardy laugh.

"Okay, I'll take 'em all in my room," he said. "After all, I am a man of Epicurean appetites."

Epicurean?

That reference surprised Wolf. Evidently, Special Agent Pike's down home, good old boy, uneducated persona was part of his elaborate act.

"There's something else you should know," Mitchell said. "Both of you."

Wolf and Pike both stared at him.

Pausing until he seemed certain he had their undivided attention, Mitchell then spoke.

"Mr. Bray and his female associate followed you from your little donnybrook at the hotel," he said. "And I'm not sure that was such a good idea, Special Agent Pike."

Pike dismissed him with a wave.

"I wonder what those fuckers are after?" he said. "Any ideas, Steve?"

Wolf shook his head.

Pike mulled things over for several seconds, and then said, "I'll make a few phone calls up the chain of command about that. You mentioned the FBI was looking at them?"

Wolf nodded in assent.

"Maybe the boys at the Bureau can give us a heads-up." Pike took in a deep breath and turned back to Wolf. "Or maybe they won't. Anyway, your part in things is pretty much over with. Once they verify who you are, it'll establish my credibility. After that, we can part company and I can take it from here."

"Alone?" Wolf felt the uneasiness he'd felt before growing again. "Is that wise? Going in without back-up?"

"He's got back-up." Mitchell scowled. "Me."

Before Wolf could say anything, Pike clicked his tongue loudly.

"I only needed you and your ex-con status and association with Europa's brother to put the finishing touches on my cover. And Teddy's right. I'd rather not put a civilian at risk any more than I have to. Even a CI."

"Not to mention those private eyes following you," Mitchell said. "Why, they could blow the whole thing with their surveillance.

It was Wolf's turn to frown.

"Just like back in North Carolina, huh?" he said.

Pike flashed a half-grin. "That was different. Like I said, hell, there was a damn hurricane that night."

Wolf kept silent, but his thoughts were roiling:

Yeah, but you might be walking into another hurricane of sorts, Pike.

CHAPTER 12

HUFFINGTON INN HOTEL
YUMA, ARIZONA

Wolf woke up at his customary six am hour but didn't feel very rested. The night before was a blur, and not a very pleasant one at that. After splitting company with Mitchell, he and Pike rolled back into town where Pike insisted on hitting what he knew to be a biker's bar. The big fed spent lavishly, buying rounds for the house and convincing Wolf to down a couple of boiler-makers with him. Wolf agreed, but skipped the shot glasses and just nursed his stein of beer. Pike continued to be the big spender, and drinker. When they finally left about an hour or so later, to "meet some ladies of the evening," as Pike loudly put it, the night air had cooled things off substantially. As they hopped on their bikes and started them up, Wolf asked Pike if he was okay to drive.

The simpering, drunken grin that had been plastered over the big fed's face disappeared in an instant and took on a serious cast.

"You think I'm an amateur at this or something?" he asked in a low voice. "I'm only as drunk as I wanna be."

Before Wolf could reply, Pike slapped him on the arm and laughed.

"Like I been saying, look the part, live the part."

As Wolf had lain alone in his bed back at the hotel, listening to the sounds of feminine voices and frolic that came through the adjoining door, Wolf figured Pike was going the extra yard to do just that. The sleep had followed had been fraught with anxiety dreams and old nightmares. More than once he awoke in a cold sweat and peered around, thinking he was somewhere back in the sandbox or worse yet, at Leavenworth.

Now the promise of some morning sunlight was filtering through the window. He got up and walked over to it. The two Harleys sat down below, right where they'd left them. On the street beyond, traffic seemed light, but steady. Wolf slipped on his pants, a T-shirt, and his army boots and decided to go for a run. The prison dreams had left him feeling locked in, claustrophobic. That was one of the things that had bothered him the most when he was inside—the restrictions on his movement. Being confined in a small cell and forced to share intimate space with another man had been the worst part of it. Even though he'd gotten along with his cell mates, the strain was always there. Had he not gotten out when he did, had Mac not come to pick him up and give him a new start, he wondered where he would have ended up.

He'd gotten a call from McNamara the night before, too, asking him where he was and how things were going.

"Actually, I'm not too far from where you are," Wolf had told him. "We're in Yuma."

"Outstanding," Mac said. "This gig's turning out to be a real sweet deal. Pay's good and so far we ain't had to do much. Just stand around and look tough."

"You're good at that."

McNamara laughed. "Yeah, maybe. But I already told this guy, Pierce that I got another man coming. That's you, right?"

"As soon as I get this other matter finished up," Wolf said.

"How much longer that gonna be?"

"Hard to say," Wolf answered. "But if I had to guess, I don't think it'll be too much longer."

"That's good," Mac said. "We can sure use you. We had to kick out some bad looking hombres today. Might be connected to some human trafficking."

"Okay," Wolf said, wondering it was the same the

group he and Pike were infiltrating. "Watch your-selves."

"Shit," Mac said. "I just gave them one of my mean looks and they scurried out of here with their tales between their legs."

Mac had told him to keep in touch.

Wolf said he would and that he would see him soon. Now he wondered if his prediction would turn out to be accurate.

He finished lacing up his second boot and stood. As he started toward the door, he paused.

Live the part, he thought, and went back to the bed.

He'd slept with the pistol under his pillow, just to reduce the anxiety. The hard lump had most like-ly had the opposite effect, given the assortment to nightmares, but they never stopped coming anyway. Maybe if he could clear his name, get a sense of clo-sure or triumph, the dreams would cease.

He clipped the perforated, padded neoprene part of the holster inside his pants so it fitted against his skin, while the hard shell polymer shell was against the inside of his pants. Next he slipped the SCCY into place. Wolf stepped over to the mirror and checked his image.

No good, he thought, as the handle of the gun angled outward from under his shirt. He needed something more substantial, something bulkier. He went to the adjoining door, opened the one on his side, and pounded on Pike's.

There was no response, so Wolf pounded again.

Wolf heard movement, and then the sound of the bolt being drawn back.

The door popped open and the muzzle of the Anaconda presented itself.

Wolf stepped out of the line of fire.

"I hope I didn't wake you up." He glanced toward the rumbled bed. "You alone."

Pike nodded, lowered the gun, and swung the door open.

"What the hell time is it?" he asked.

"Six-fifteen."

Pike stared at him, and then arched an eyebrow.

"What the fuck you want?"

"I figured I'd go for a run," Wolf said. "Can I borrow one of your sweat shirts so no cop sees my gun?"

Pike Groaned and staggered back toward the bed. Several packages of magnum condoms littered the floor around the bed. He motioned toward a bag rolled up on a chair. "Take your pick."

"Looks like you had quite a night," he said.

Pike flopped down in a sitting position on the bed and set the Anaconda on the nightstand beside him.

"Like I said," he muttered. "Live the part.

At least living the part included having safe sex, Wolf thought.

Wolf sorted through the garments in the bag and

withdrew a solid black sweat shirt with the sleeves cut off.

"This one okay?" he asked.

Pike grunted again and flopped back down on the bed.

Wolf slipped the oversized sweat shirt on and headed back toward the adjoining door.

"Hey," Pike called out. "Give me a couple of minutes and I'll go with you."

Wolf chuckled.

"I figured you got all the exercise you needed last night."

"Looks can be deceiving," Pike said. "Because you never know who's watching. Besides, we're in phase two, and we got things to talk about.

"Your call," Wolf said, wondering if this run would turn out any better than the one a few days ago in Las Vegas.

***

AIR B AND B
YUMA, ARIZONA

Rivera looked at the girl slumbering in the chair next to his bed. The ropes had secured her in a sitting position and she'd spent most of the night sobbing and crying. He estimated that she'd finally fallen asleep in the early morning hours. In sleep she'd looked angelic, almost virginal, although he doubted that she was. Any young woman her age, her early twenties, could not be so. But it was appropriate that she was a nurse. Nurses were supposed to be angels, caring for the sick. Rivera was glad that he'd kept her in his room, away from the pawing hands of Europa's boys, and especially *el hijo gordo*, who'd looked at her with undisguised lust. Now that was less of a concern because her attractiveness had become somewhat tarnished. Not only was her face tear-streaked making her makeup a mess, but she had urinated on herself as well. The light green pants of her nurse's garb was stained with a ring of wetness at her crotch.

Such is life, he told himself, and fortuitous for her.

The other *idiotas* had been warned that she was not to be touched. At least not at this point. She was a bargaining chip, and anything that lessened her value, her worth, at this juncture would undermine the deal to come.

He picked up her phone and turned it on.

It was locked and he held the screen in front of her face. The phone unlocked and made a chiming sound. With this, she awakened, her eyes filled with fear once again. They were blue eyes. Very blue. The color of a summer sky.

Rivera smiled down at her keeping his expression as benign as he could.

"I imagine you are most uncomfortable," he said.

She said nothing at first. A pair of tears rolled down her face, then finally, "Why are you doing this?"

Her voice sounded garbled, cracked.

Rivera reached over, grabbed the open bottle of water from the dresser, and held it to her lips. She resisted, keeping her mouth tightly closed and the water dribbled down her chin, but he made soft, cooing sounds to her.

"Drink, drink," he said, his voice a plaintive whisper. "We need to call your father. Then I will let you go to the bathroom and freshen up."

Her lips parted slightly and she drank some more.

"Good, good," he said. When he set the bottle down, he looked at the phone. A flood of text messages had appeared after the text he'd sent on her phone last night.

Dad I'm going out with some friends. Late night. Don't wait up.

Ok we won't. be careful honey.

These were followed by another series, time-stamped this morning:

Honey where are you?

Are you still out with friend? Who?

Call me

Are you ok?

Sandy call us. Now please

Where are you?

This last one had come in only about half an hour ago.

He held the phone down in front of her face to show her the litany of text messages and watched her blue eyes travel back and forth.

"As you can see," he said, "your parents are very worried about you. I take it you do not stay out all night very often."

She shook her head slightly.

Good, he thought. *I have opened a line of communication.*

"We will call your father shortly. But understand that you must do exactly as I tell you."

Her mouth drew into a tight line.

"Why are you doing this to me?"

Her voice sounded fragile, brittle.

He made a tsking sound and shook his head, already punching in the button to initial the phone call.

"Make sure to tell them that we have not hurt you."

It rang only once before a nervous female voice answered.

"Sandy. Where are you?"

"Mrs. Pierce," Rivera said. "May I speak to your husband please?"

"What? Who're you? This is my daughter's phone."

"Your husband. Put him on please."

"Where's my daughter?"

"Your husband."

He heard her gasping breaths and a faint call: "Rob. Come here."

After a few more moments of muffled sound, a

male voice came on the line. Rivera recognized it as Roberto Pierce.

"Who is this? Where's my daughter?"

"She is here," Rivera said. "I will let you speak to her."

He held the phone down by her face.

"Tell your father you are all right."

"Dad, dad," she screamed. "They're holding me here. I'm all tied up. I don't know—"

Rivera whipped the phone away from her mouth. After a few seconds he could hear Pierce's voice again asking the standard questions.

"Sandy? Sandy? Are you all right? Did they hurt you?"

The last words came out with a bit of a stammer. Pierce wanted to know, but also, he did not. Rivera brought the phone to his mouth and spoke in a clear voice.

"Your daughter is our guest," he said. "She will not be harmed if you do what I say."

A torrent of threats mixed with profanity followed. Rivera allowed Pierce to bluster, and then cut in.

"Mr. Pierce, please. I want to—"

"I don't give a fuck what you want, you son of a bitch. You'd better release her right now. And you'd better not hurt her. Understand? If you do, I'll—"

But this time Rivera had reached out and gathered a fold of flesh on the girl's shoulder between his thumb and forefinger. He'd only exerted a modicum of pressure when she screamed. It was a loud shriek and he kept rolling her flesh between his digits, tightening his grip until the scream degenerated into a hiccupping guttural moan.

When her father's cries on the other end of the line stopped, Rivera released his hold on her. She thrust back in the chair as best she could and began sobbing. He brought the phone up again and spoke in the same clear, methodical tone.

"As I said, Mr. Pierce, we have no need to hurt your daughter as long as you cooperate."

He paused, waiting.

After a few seconds Pierce replied.

"Tell me what you want. Just promise me you won't hurt her."

Rivera waited a few beats, and then said, "Let's establish the ground rules. First, if you call the police, if we get any suspicion that they've been called, you will never see her again. Do you understand?"

He waited until Pierce agreed.

"Good," Rivera continued. "Second, you will fire all of the security personnel that you have recently hired."

"You... you..." Pierce said suddenly. "You're that son of a bitch that was here yesterday, aren't you?"

Rivera made no acknowledgment of that. He proceeded to speak in the same calm tone.

"Don't interrupt me again. And remember that we have eyes on you now. We have people all over. You'll never know who they are, and they are reporting everything— all your moves to me. If you do not do everything that I say, it will be your daughter who suffers the consequences."

"I'll—" Pierce's voice now sounded as brittle as his daughter's had. "I'll do anything you say. Just please, don't hurt her."

The sound of the fear in the man's voice made *El Tigre* smile as he looked down at the girl. Everything was going according to the plan.

***

THE JEDSTONE HOTEL
YUMA, ARIZONA

Bray's cell phone jangled rousing him from his slumber. Maureen was in the bed next to him lightly snoring. He grabbed his phone and glanced at the screen.

It was Powers.

Bray pressed the button to answer it.

"You ain't gonna fucking believe it," Powers said.

"Try me."

"They're out jogging."

This surprised Bray, but not a lot. He knew from the past surveillances that Wolf usually did a run early every morning. But the fed being with him… That was something new. It also gave him an idea.

"Where they at now?" he asked. "Are away from the hotel?"

"Yeah, they've gone a couple of blocks. I'm giving them plenty of lead time."

"You're in your car?"

"Shit yeah," Powers said. "You don't think I'm stupid enough to be out running, do ya?"

"Any sign of their back-up guy? He's driving a black van."

"Not that I seen."

Bray considered the options and made the decision. This was probably the one chance they had where Wolf or the fed wouldn't be possibly looking out of the hotel window.

"Okay," he said. "Break off your tail and go back to the hotel. If you're sure no one's around, especially that other guy, then slip a tracker onto Wolf's motorcycle."

"Ah, okay." Powers sounded dubious.

"What's wrong?"

"Nothing. It's just that trying to figure out a secure place to stick it, where it won't get bounced off, can be kind of tricky with a Harley. I mean them things vibrate so much."

"Just get it done," Bray said. "And don't let anybody see you."

"Okay, but—"

"No buts," Bray said. "Just do it."

"Hey, I been on this damn graveyard surveillance

for hours already." Powers tone had a nauseating whine. "How about sending Maureen out to help me? At least be a lookout, or something."

Bray was getting out of bed as he spoke. The tiled floor felt cold under his bare feet.

"I'll be your fucking lookout. Now do it."

He hung up and yanked open the blinds at the window. The view across the street was clear and unobstructed, except for the pillars and canopy of the other hotel. He couldn't see the motorcycles. They must have parked on the other side of the canopy last night. But his view of the rest of the lot and the street was clear. He grabbed the binoculars off the heating and cooling unit adjacent to the window and peered out.

There was no sign of any joggers.

Just do it, Powers, he thought. *And pray that they don't come back and see you.*

***

"Oooh," Pike said. "Hold on. I gotta stop for a sec."

Wolf slowed down as Pike's feet slapped the pavement in an ever deescalating pace. He came to a stop, leaned over, and placed his hands on his knees.

"How did I let you talk me into this?" he said between gasps.

"You talked yourself into it. Remember?"

"Yeah, yeah," Pike said. He took in a few more deep

breaths and straightened up. "Look, Steve, if all goes well, your part in all this should be over with today. I wanted to tell you that."

"Good to know," Wolf said. "But are you sure?"

Pike shrugged, took in a couple deep breaths, and motioned for them to start running again.

They took off at a slow pace.

"As sure as I can be," Pike said, "Under the circumstances. If all goes well, pipsqueak Europa will call big brother, who's bound to remember you since you saved him from being gang-banged, right?"

"Let's hope he does."

"And that should cement my creds as well. We should hear from him this morning, and if it's good, we'll meet up with them. Then I'll send you back on some kind of bullshit errand and find out about the set-up for the crossing tonight."

"You gonna bust them then?"

"Nah, that ain't how it works. The idea is to let them bring their mules across and get the dope. They'll give it to me, and I'll see that it's supposedly transferred to the appropriate people back East. They'll think the thing's going through to Batton's bunch via the Devil's Breed, but actually the agency's taken over the whole damn thing. We build our case, collect our evidence, let 'em do it a few more times, and then get the warrants to take 'em all down. Including old El Cortez down in Mexico. If we can find a squared away bunch of police or Mexican marines to do the job south of the border."

"Sounds pretty elaborate," Wolf said. He was gradually increasing the pace now, but monitoring Pike's condition as they ran. "You sure you can handle this on your own, after I go?"

"Piece of cake. It's what I do."

"All by yourself?"

"I ain't all by myself. I got Mitchell."

"Control," Wolf said.

"You got it."

"That doesn't sound like much of a back-up."

Pike was breathing harder now and Wolf slowed the pace again.

"Hey," Pike said. "You know this ain't my first rodeo. It'll be fine. And I've got it set for you to make a Lone Ranger exit."

"A what?"

"Don't you watch the nostalgia channel, *kemosabe*?" Pike snorted. "The Lone Ranger and his faithful Indian companion always slip away at the end of each episode without anybody noticing."

Wolf did remember the show, but he had his doubts about this. But now he was almost out of the equation. It was what Pike wanted and maybe it was for the best. After all, Pike was the big time federal agent and Wolf was just an ex-con with a DD who could get sent back to the joint if he got caught carrying an illegal drop gun in the event the shit hit the fan down the road.

Yeah, a Lone Ranger Exit sounded like the best course of action. Only he wasn't the Lone Ranger, and he was a poor excuse for Tonto.

Tonto, he thought. It meant stupid in Spanish. But all things considered, playing the Lone Ranger's partner wasn't such a bad gig for an Indian.

"And when can I expect you to grease the wheels for my appeal to be put back on the docket?"

Pike was breathing better now, and managed a sly grin.

"Believe me," he said. "It's already in the works. I always deliver on my promises.'

Wolf considered this and decided he had little choice but to put his faith in what his partner said.

"Hey," Pike said. "Slow down a little bit, would you?"

"How much?" Wolf said, and then added with a smile, "Or should I say how far?"

Pike smiled, too, and shouted, "All the way."

Yeah, right, Wolf thought. *Airborne troopers all the way.*

CHAPTER 13

AIR B AND B
YUMA, ARIZONA

Rivera stood in the open doorway of the master bedroom's bath and watched as the girl washed herself in the shower. He'd allowed her to pull the translucent curtain while she showered, but told her she could not close the door. To emphasize that fact, he'd stood there watching as she undressed and then while she washed her underwear and pants in the sink and use a hair dryer to drive out the wetness. Her body was slender and well-formed and very white. The sight aroused him, but he also felt something else. An almost foreign tinge of pity. The girl had cried, but she had not complained. She had spirit.

The water from the shower continued to rain down on her behind the plastic barrier.

A pounding on the bedroom door intruded on the eroticism of the scene.

"Hey, Alfredo. You in there?"

It was Europa. Rivera had allowed him and a couple of his cohorts to spend the night in the rented home along with Cortez Jr. He'd listened to them smoking marijuana and drinking until the wee hours. It hadn't been until after the noises had ceased that *El Tigre* had allowed himself to grab a bit of sleep, lest they try and sneak into the bedroom.

But that had not happened.

"What do you want?" Rivera said through the door.

"Open up. I gotta talk to you."

Rivera hesitated and debated whether to tell the *pedazo de imbécil* to go fuck himself. But having him shout whatever it was he had to say through the door might alert the girl to something he did not want her to hear at this moment. He stepped away from the door jamb, went to the bedroom door, unlocked it, and opened it a crack.

"What?" he asked.

Europa's head bobbled as he tried to get a glimpse inside the bedroom.

"Did you fuck her?" he asked in a whisper.

Rivera ignored the salacious question and repeated, "What do you want?"

Europa's face twitch with a frown of disappointment. "My brother called. I asked him about that guy, Wolf, and Alejandro says Wolf's the real deal," Europa paused, as if he had accomplished something.

Rivera said nothing.

"Served time and was real stand-up con," Europa continued. "Helped my brother out a couple of times. And he's one bad dude. Was the heavyweight boxing champion in the prison, and did a lot of ass-kicking on the side, too. Does MMA fighting now."

Rivera listened and then, like a light being turned on in a dark room, illuminating the contents, it suddenly came back to him.

Steve Wolf, "The Ranger." An MMA fighter. He'd seen a couple of the man's last matches streaming down in Mexico. Not only was Wolf good, but he was a champion. And he had military experience as well.

This brought another question. Why would a fighter of his position and stature want to get involved in drug trafficking with a motorcycle gang like this Devil's Breed? Did this make sense? Perhaps he had a drug problem himself? Or maybe the money to be made fighting was not as great as people thought?

Many more questions, only a few answers. But according to the last text message he'd received from Martín, the crossing was running ahead of schedule. They would arrive tonight, first sending *el tropel*, the flood of young men, who had paid to cross in first to be the diversion, and then bring the thirty-five *mojados* carrying the product. They would be then taken to the ghost town and relieved of the stuffed condoms. One of the Griggas brothers would be there, as well as these two, Pike and Wolf. Everything needed to be set to go off without any hitches or problems.

He heard the water stop in the shower.

"*Muy bien,*" he said to Europa. "I will be out shortly. Call Pike back and set up a meeting at the restaurant same as yesterday."

He saw Europa trying to look around him and into the bedroom, evidently trying to steal a glance at the girl.

El Tigre reached out and slapped the smaller man on the cheek. Europa stiffened, but said nothing.

"I want two of your best men to guard her here at the house," *El Tigre* said. "I will tie her to the chair once again and make sure they know that she is not to be touched. *¿Comprende?*"

Europa's face flushed as he nodded and *El Tigre* once again saw the flash of fear and respect in the other man's eyes.

Good, he thought. *He knows his place well.*

***

THE JEDSTONE HOTEL
YUMA, ARIZONA

Bray's anxiety continued to grow as he stared out of the hotel window with the binoculars. He'd seen Powers pull into the other hotel parking lot, get out, and then remove a cigarette as he strolled toward the front entrance. The idiot's head was bobbling around like fishing buoy.

Could the stupid son of a bitch make himself any more conspicuous?

He took another drag on the cigarette and tapped he ash away. Bray knew that there was an ashtray stand at that location, so that added some appearance of legitimacy to Powers being there. As long as Wolf and the fed didn't cut their run short and find him lurking around their bikes... But then again, a lot of motorcycle enthusiasts liked to check out other rider's machines.

Then Powers took another look around, dug in his pants pocket, and quickly disappeared from sight.

Bray swore and hoped for the best as he switched his view from the parking lot to the street down which Wolf had run.

The seconds ticked by with a frustrating reticence. Then he suddenly caught sight of the two runners. They were heading back toward the hotel, perhaps only a hundred yards or so away.

"Shit," Bray muttered.

"What's wrong?" Maureen asked from the bed, her voice still groggy with sleep.

"They're on the way back."

"Who?"

Then Bray realized she'd still been asleep when he'd told Powers to plant the tracker. He picked up his phone and hit the button to initiate a call to Powers's cell.

"That fucking Jack," he said. "He's trying to put a tracker on Wolf's cycle and they're coming back now."

Maureen got out of the bed and walked over to him. He could feel the heat from her naked body as she stood close to him.

"It'll probably be okay," she said. "Jack's good."

"The horse's ass," Bray said and swore again.

The phone kept ringing until it went to voice mail.

Bray scanned the parking lot again.

No sign of him.

He switched back to the oncoming runners on the street. They were narrowing the gap, getting closer and closer, but at least neither of them was doing an all-out run. If they'd seen Powers tampering with one of their motorcycles they most certainly would be sprinting by now.

He switched back to the parking lot area and saw Powers walking briskly toward his rental car.

Looking back to Wolf and the fed, Bray saw they had increased their pace substantially.

"Dammit!" he yelled. "They must have seen him."

Powers got into his car very matter-of-factly, slammed the door, and started it up

Wolf and the fed continued to run fast, sprinting now.

Bray watched Powers shift into gear, back out, and

pull into the drive way.

Wolf and the fed were approaching Powers's position, going all-out now, but instead of zeroing in on the car, they stayed on the street and went right past the front entrance of the hotel. Powers pulled out after they'd passed and drove off in the opposite direction.

Bray let out a burst of air, relived. He then felt Maureen press her body against his and run her tongue over his neck below his ear.

"See," she said. "I told you it would turn out all right."

Bray's phone buzzed and he saw it was Powers.

"Did they see you?" he asked without saying hello.

"Almost," Powers answered, "but I got away clean."

"You get the tracker installed?"

"Yep. Put them onto the frame, underneath the saddlebags."

Saddlebags?

Bray felt like somebody had just shoved an ice sickle up his ass.

"You only did Wolf's bike, right?"

Powers did not reply immediately, then, "Well, no. I didn't know which one of them was which, so I did them both."

"You fucking idiot," Bray said. "That guy with him is a fed."

"Well… That's what you get for keeping me in the

dark about everything while you and her take all the easy stuff."

Bray was furious. The last thing he was that federal agent finding the tracker and tracing it back to him.

But for now, there was little he could do about it.

"Just get your ass back here," he told Powers. "And make sure you take a roundabout way so no one sees you."

He terminated the call before the other man could respond.

I hope things don't turn to shit, he thought.

***

EL PRIMO'S RESTAURANTE
YUMA, ARIZONA

Wolf and Pike sat across the table from Europa and Rivera. The red-headed man regarded Wolf with a renewed curiosity, even though he spoke primarily to Pike.

"Everything is set for tonight, my friend," Rivera said. "Only a few hours from now. The plan is pure artistry. I am anxious for you to see it in action."

"Me, too." Pike grinned and glanced around. The four of them were practically alone in the restaurant, except for the three of Europa's motorcycle brethren who sat at another table and a man and a woman in a booth a few yards away. They were really into each other. "But why don't you give me a little rundown about what I can expect."

Rivera sat in silence for several seconds, and then smiled.

"Of course," he said. "You should also know that one of the money men will be there tonight also, although he will not arrive for several hours after our little extraction exercise."

"One of the Griggas brothers?" Pike asked.

Rivera raised an eyebrow. "Very good, *Señor.* You have done your homework."

"I try," Pike said.

Wolf was feeling more and more uncomfortable. On the way over Pike had told him to just stand by and listen. "Let me do all the talking."

Wolf was good with that.

Rivera moved the plates out of the way and flipped over one of the paper place mats. He took out a pen and began drawing a crude sketch on the paper. Suddenly, he stopped and looked at Wolf.

"I have seen you fight," Rivera said. "On the television."

The statement surprised Wolf, and peripherally he noticed Pike stiffen momentarily.

Wolf struggled for a reply. Things had been going smoothly and he didn't want to do anything that might upset the applecart.

Best to keep silent, he thought.

"Yeah," Pike said. "He's damn good, too, ain't he?"

Rivera switched his gaze to the big fed.

"He is." His eyes remained on Pike, staring intently, and then went back to Wolf. "You are a champion, are you not?"

Wolf shrugged. "Right fight at the right time, I guess."

"At one time," Rivera said, "I was training for the Olympic Boxing Team of *México*."

Was this what it was all about? Was this guy a wannabe fighter, or something.

"I figured you for a fighter," Wolf said. "You look to be in pretty good shape."

"*Gracias*. It is kind of you to say so."

Wolf felt a bit of relief. It appeared that this *El Tigre* fellow was only searching for a compliment. Or was he?

"So why is it then," Rivera asked quickly, "that a man such as yourself, a fighter of the professional class, wishes to become associated with our business?"

When he said, "our business," he waved his hand toward Pike and then back toward himself.

"Hey," Pike said, insinuating himself into the conversation. "It's a free country, ain't it?"

"And nobody gets paid enough to get beat up on a regular basis," Wolf added, hoping that would settle it.

Rivera tilted his head.

"The money is not good?"

Wolf did his best to muster an acknowledging smile.

"It's good," he said. "For the time being. But I'm an ex-con with a dishonorable discharge. Nobody's gonna be hiring me once I hang up my gloves, and if you saw my last fight, you'll know that I ended up on the receiving end of a lot of punishment. You can't stay on top forever. I'd much rather be in a position where I don't have to worry about some up and comer trying to take my head off."

"Always a danger," Rivera said. "But only if they succeed."

"Still, always a danger," Wolf repeated.

Rivera lowered his gaze momentarily, as if the words resonated with him, and then he looked up and smiled.

"Perhaps someday we will spar," he said, held Wolf's gaze for a good five seconds and then looked back to Pike and tapped the paper.

Wolf felt a surge of relief that he had passed whatever test or doubts Rivera might have had about him.

"It is our plan to establish this as a new location for our crossings," Rivera said. He drew another pair of parallel lines on the place mat. "And soon, we hope to start construction of a new underground tunnel in this area."

"Smart," Pike said, giving an appreciative nod.

"Once that has been completed, we will no longer have to worry about land crossings and crowd diversions."

"Diversions?" Pike asked.

Rivera nodded and drew a circular spiral on the paper.

"A diversion of many men to run across first, diverting the authorities from our real purpose. The mules."

Pike grinned again. "I like the sound of that."

He lowered his voice to a whisper. "Then my team will bring—"

Europa's cell phone jangled with sudden and untimely intrusion, and he picked it up from the table top. After looking at the screen he muttered, "It's Hammer," and answered it.

Rivera was obviously irritated by the interruption, but Europa's face creased immediately.

"Now?" he said. "Oh shit."

Covering the phone, he turned to Rivera and smacked him on the arm. "Your buddy, Esteban is putting the moves on your girl. Real bad."

Rivera's mouth immediately drew into a thin line and he rapidly slid out of the booth, crumpling the place mat as he got up.

"Forgive me," he said. "But we must go."

"But what about the plan?" Pike said.

"I will call you later."

He motioned for Europa and his pals to come with him and hurriedly left.

Once they had gone Pike snorted.

"Sounds like good old El Tigre's got some woman problems."

"It does," Wolf answered. "And he mentioned Esteban. That the son of…"

He intentionally didn't finish the sentence. The woman, who'd been in the other booth, sauntered by apparently on the way to the ladies' room.

Wolf didn't see her face, but watched the sway of her hips and internally noted that she had a very nice figure.

"Yeah," Pike said. "I agree. Very nice."

Did he just read my mind? Wolf thought, then smirked.

"But getting back to what you were saying, it is the prodigal son," Pike said. "Come on, let's get the hell out of here. We look too much like a n old couple sitting here like this."

They'd been sitting on the same side due to the prior conversation. Wolf smirked again and pushed out of the booth.

"Forget it," he said. "You're not my type."

"I should hope not," Pike grunted. "But you never can tell."

At least he didn't make any jokes about my prison time, Wolf thought.

As they walked to the counter, Pike pulled out a roll of currency and paid the tab, asking for a receipt. He then stripped off a few more bills and presented the waitress with a hefty tip. The girl's eyes widened appreciatively.

Outside they walked to their motorcycles, noting that the Dodge Charger and the group of motorcycles were gone.

"What do we do now?" Wolf asked.

"We go back to the hotel and wait for them to call." Pike smirked. "Hurry up and wait, just like in the army."

Hurry up and wait, Wolf thought. *The story of my life lately.*

***

AIR B AND B
YUMA, ARIZONA

As soon as the Charger had screeched to a jerking stop in front of the rented residence, Rivera slammed it into PARK and was doing a quick walk up to the front door. He knew he'd made a mistake leaving *el pendajo gordo* here instead of forcing him to come with to the restaurant, but the *hijo de puta* had refused to get out of bed, claiming to be sick. Now Rivera controlled his urge to run up the walkway lest one of the neighbors see him and find it suspicious. The last thing he wanted at this point was a visit from the police.

The door was opened one of Europa's boys as he arrived.

"*¿Donde está?*" His tone was guttural.

The *idiota* in front of him looked perplexed. Another Chicano who didn't speak Spanish.

"Where is he?" Rivera repeated.

The young hoodlum jerked his thumb toward the bedroom. The door was closed.

"Sounded like he was beating her," he said.

"And you did nothing?" Rivera said as he moved across the living room with four charging steps. He'd reached the door before the other one could answer.

The door was locked.

Rivera stepped back, raised his foot, and kicked the door, which hurled inward sending the doorknob mechanism flying.

Cortez Jr. was kneeling on the bed, his pants down under his fat bare ass. The girl was sprawled out almost underneath him. He glanced back, his lips twisting into a snarl.

"*¿Qué coña?*"

"*Corta, puta madre.*"

Rivera, now *El Tigre*, stormed inside, glaring at Cortez Jr., who was now messing with his pants. Was he pulling them up after finishing?

Sandra Pierce lay on the bed, her jaw gaping, her face a bloody mess. She appeared to be unconscious.

"*Chingado,*" *El Tigre* said. His expression told it all.

"*Qué te jodas,*" Cortez Jr. muttered.

"I gave orders that she not be touched."

"So what? She is nothing," Cortez Jr. said. "Take her if you want. She is yours."

El Tigre saw that the girl's underpants were still on. But her pretty face...

He stepped over to her and placed his finger under her jaw, checking for a pulse. It was rapid, but strong.

Good. She was still alive.

He turned back to Cortez Jr.

"I gave strict orders that she not be touched," *El Tigre* said. "I gave her father my word she would not be hurt."

Cortez Jr. blew out a burst of air. "I do not care. *Su palabra es mierda.*"

He spat on the floor.

El Tigre felt the burn of anger. "She is of less value now."

"*Coma mierda.*" Cortez Jr. was managing to button his pants now, his fingers working under the dollop of fat hanging from his abdomen. "I didn't even get to do nothing anyway."

"You beat her."

"So what. She's a *puta.*"

"We are trying to build a tunnel under her father's

property," *El Tigre* said. "You have made negotiations for that task more difficult."

The two ersatz guards stood at the doorway now, watching, but they both backed away as Europa and the minions who had flanked him at the restaurant approached.

"Man," Europa said. "She looks like shit."

Cortez Jr. laughed.

El Tigre stepped over and backhanded the sloppy, fat *hijo de puta*. He staggered for three steps, then caught the dresser and steadied himself. A then, needle-like stream of blood crept from his lip and disappeared into his scrawny beard.

"You dare to hit me, *hijo de puta?*" he said. "When my father hears about this, *estarás muerto.*"

El Tigre considered this and thought it was no doubt true—he would be dead. He thought about the situation, his master plan, and the prudence of delivering another blow, a killing blow, but he did not.

The time was close, but not right.

Esta hijo de una puta gorda was going die on this foreign soil. That was certain, but not quite yet.

The only thing I must figure out, El Tigre thought, *is who I am going to blame for his murder.*

"Pack up everything," he said. "We are leaving. Now."

CHAPTER 14

PARKING LOT OF THE HUFFINGTON INN HOTEL
YUMA, ARIZONA

The wait had turned into hours, but finally it had come. Now, as the early onset of the darkness of winter descended, Wolf and Pike made their way across the parking lot to the two waiting motorcycles. When they got there, Pike stopped, stretched, and turned toward him.

"You know, it's a damn shame we're not going to be working together anymore," he said. "I got a feeling you'd get me into pretty decent shape."

Wolf smirked. "You're in good shape. Let me know if you want me to fix you up in an MMA match."

Pike barked out a quick laugh.

"I ain't that stupid." All signs of mirth vanished as he then assumed a contemplative look. "And, this is where we part company."

"What?"

Pike's head rocked with a fractional nodding motion. "I think I'll leave you out of it from here on out. Don't need you."

"Come on, Pike. You can't do this alone. It's too dangerous."

The big fed shook his head. "Doesn't make sense to involve you anymore. You've done your part—more than your part. And at a certain point, having a civilian in the mix can cause more problems than it's worth."

"But you'll need a back-up."

"I've got back-up. Control."

"Mitchell? Come on."

"Believe it or not, he's pretty good at keeping tabs on things. Plus, there's that matter of those jokers that been tailing you." Pike paused. "The last thing I need is for them to follow us out there to that old ghost town."

Wolf instinctively glanced around. He saw no one, but knew that didn't mean they weren't out there.

"You think that's where the thing's going down?"

Pike swung his leg over the seat of his Harley, balanced the bike, and slipped the key in the ignition.

"That's a pretty good assumption," he said. "Although I never assume."

He started the big motorcycle and revved the motor a few times.

"You're out of it as of now, Steve. Hopefully for good." He extended his open palm toward Wolf. "Once again, thanks, brother."

Wolf shook his hand.

"And," Pike said. "Don't worry. I ain't forgetting about that promise I made you. That appeal's as good as on the docket again."

His voice was barely audible over the thrumming of the engine. The single, large headlight illuminated the area in front of them.

It had gotten totally dark so quickly, but Wolf was thinking of being trapped in another type of darkness.

As good as on the docket again, Wolf thought. *Does that mean you had it taken off the first time?*

He wanted to ask Pike that, but decided against it. It would serve no good purpose at this point.

"Wait a minute." He gestured toward his motor-cycle. "What am I supposed to do with this thing?"

"You can ride it back up to Phoenix tomorrow, if you would you would be so kind. I'll tell Control to contact you about where you can drop it." The back of his boot knocked the kickstand up in place and he used his feet to walk the motorcycle backwards a few feet.

"What'll you tell *El Tigre* about my absence?"

"I'll think of something. He just thinks you're an

apprentice anyway." His grin was wide, and then he winked. "See you around, trooper."

Pike kicked it up into gear and started to leave, but Wolf's hand shot out and smacked Pike's massive right biceps.

"Hey," he said. "I almost forgot. What about the SCCY?"

Pike depressed the clutch and the brake.

"Keep it," he said. "Consider it a gift. Just remember, don't try to register it, and if you happen to use it to shoot somebody..."

"I know," Wolf said. "Wipe it and drop it."

Pike nodded. "And don't look back."

He winked and popped the clutch sending the huge motorcycle surging forward and in another instant he was out of the lot and going down the street.

Wolf's cell phone rang and he saw it was McNamara. He answered it immediately.

"Glad you called," he said.

"Don't be too glad," McNamara said. "Things ain't good. Can you get away for a quick meet without causing any suspicion?"

"Sure. Where and when?"

"How about now? Out by the Morelos Dam? Know where it's at?"

Wolf recalled seeing a sign advertising it yesterday. Pike was going that way, too.

"I think so."

"Good," Mac said. "See you there."

Wolf took one more look around as he wondered what Mac had going. There was an undercurrent of tension in his voice.

I hope everything's all right with him, Wolf thought as he straddled his motorcycle.

After starting the motor, he sat for a moment enjoying the experience of feeling the percussive vibrations of the hefty machine under him and the accompanying feeling of precision and power.

***

THE JEDSTONE HOTEL
YUMA, ARIZONA

Bray watched through the binoculars as Wolf's motorcycle pulled out of the hotel parking lot and went in the same direction as the other one.

He raised the cell phone to his mouth and said, "They're both leaving. You got 'em yet?"

"This damn laptop wasn't booting up," Powers said.

Seconds ticked by, with the clock moving in slow motion.

Finally, Powers's voice came back through the phone.

"Okay, got 'em. And it looks like they're both heading west."

"All right." Bray motioned for Maureen to unplug their laptop from the charger. "Stay on them. We're going down to our car and we'll follow."

"Gotcha."

"Where do you think they're going now?" Maureen asked. She was stuffing the laptop into the carrying case.

"I wish I knew," Bray said. "It would make things easier to plan out."

Hopefully, the two of them would stay together, although the fed had left earlier than Wolf had. If stupid Powers would have been ready with his laptop, they might have been able to distinguish which tracking signal came from Wolf's motorcycle. As it was, they'd have to trail them both, and if they split up...

But he'd cross that bridge when he came to it.

The thoughts of the million dollar bounty kept dancing in his head.

***

LAST GASP GULCH GHOST TOWN
UNINCORPORATED YUMA COUNTY, ARIZONA

Rivera was ensconced behind the remnants of a broken wall on the second story of a partially demolished brick building as he watched and waited.

It was now fully dark and Martín should have sent the diversionary runners across the dam by now. Once they had been detected, then the rest of them, *los testarudos* carrying the product, could be brought across. The big American, Pike, had asked a bunch of questions about when Griggas would arrive, and had also seemed extremely interested in Cortez Jr. The *hijo de puta* had a swollen lip where Rivera's blow had landed, and he remained sullen and angry.

It's a certainty that he will try to convince his father to kill me as soon as we are back in México, he thought.

Which was why Cortez Jr. would not be making the trip.

He looked through the night vision binoculars once again, and checked the progress of Europa's team that was checking out the SUV parked about a hundred yards away on the highway. He'd seen it perhaps fifteen minutes ago, not long after Pike had arrived. Was it *la policía*, or could the big man have something up his sleeve? Somebody watching, maybe waiting to interfere?

He watched as the trio of motorcycles descended on the lone vehicle. Their approach had been dark and from the rear. Now the scene a few hundred yards away became immersed in too much illumination. Rivera closed his eyes and switched off the night-vision feature and went with just the standard ocular enhancer.

The Marauders, as they were called, danced around the vehicle pointing their weapons at the occupants. Young punks with guns. A dangerous combination. One of the guns flashed with sudden brightness. Rivera heard some noises close by and turned. Pike was scaling the ladder to the roof.

"What you got?" Pike asked. The big man had moved up next to him as silently as a wraith.

"A car out on the highway. Somebody watching us."

"Want me to go check it out?" Pike asked.

Rivera shook his head. "Not necessary. I already got some of Europa's men on it. I told him to have a couple of roving patrols moving up and down the highway."

He hesitated to call them "men," but they would have to do. At least for tonight.

"So what did they find?" Pike asked.

Rivera studied the scene and saw the gang extracting two people from the SUV.

"You gonna tell me what's going on out there, or what?" Pike said. His voice was full of tension.

Still, Rivera didn't answer. Instead, he took out his cell phone, called Europa, and told him to bring in the two gapers and their vehicle.

"Who they got?" Pike asked.

"Here" he said, handing the binoculars to Pike.

"Have a look for yourself."

Pike took the binoculars and lifted them to his eyes.

Rivera thought the big man looked worried.

Real worried.

***

UNINCORPORATED YUMA COUNTY

The five of them stood in a semicircle between Mc-Namara's Escalade and Buck's Jeep. Wolf's motorcycle was parked off to the side. Buck passed out the paper cups and then poured some coffee into each from the big cardboard container. They were on a side road about twenty-five yards off the main highway on a flat expanse that was not readily visible due to a slight elevation adjacent to the main roadway.

But that worked both ways, and Wolf was uneasy about the location since they had no lookouts.

He said nothing as Buck poured some of the coffee into his cup.

"It'd be a shame to let this hot half-gallon of java go to waste," he said.

Wolf declined the bag of creamer and sugar packets that Ron offered him. Joe reached in and grabbed three sugars.

McNamara shook his head at the offerings, sipped

from his cup, and then spit it out.

"Hell's belles," he said. "I've tasted horse piss that was better than this."

"What do you think I used to warm it up?" Buck said with a laugh.

McNamara smirked and turned to Wolf.

"What do you think, Steve?" Mac asked. "Is something up, or what?"

Wolf drank some of the brew from his cup, and was surprised by the bitterness. He almost had to agree with Mac's assessment.

"You said he seemed real nervous," Wolf said. "And so did his wife. You think he's being threatened?"

McNamara shrugged. "That'd be my guess. It doesn't make sense him hiring us one day and then firing us the next." His head tilted back slightly and he squinted. "Come to think of it, he's got a real pretty daughter living at home. She's a nursing student. Drives a red Corvette... I don't remember seeing her, or it today."

"Me neither," Buck said.

"You think this could be tied into that thing your friend was working on?" McNamara asked.

Wolf had wondered about that. He knew that Pike was dealing with some pretty rough customers. Threats, extortion, even kidnapping would be right up their alley.

"I don't know," he said. "But it's a distinct possibility."

"Can you call and ask him?" McNamara said.

Wolf shook his head.

"Not tonight. He's working an undercover operation, and it took him a long time to get it all set up. Besides, if Pierce's daughter was kidnapped, it's a matter for the police, not us."

"Yeah," McNamara said. "You're right, but it hits close to home."

Wolf nodded, recalling that Mac's daughter, Kasey, had once been kidnapped.

"I wish I had a chopper to a fly-over," Ron said. "Preferably one equipped with thermal imaging."

"Look," Wolf said. "Why don't we all go back to the hotel and we can sort this out tomorrow?"

"Or," Buck said, "we could stick around here for a bit and see if we can grab some more illegals sneaking across the border."

"Shit, man," Joe said. "You forgetting how much trouble we got in down in Texas trying to play policeman?"

"It's border patrol, not police down this way," Ron said. "But Joe's got a point. Working security on private property's one thing. Going out looking for trouble's another."

"Well," Buck said, holding his coffee cup in one hand and then subtly pointing with his other. "It don't look like we'll have much of a choice."

Wolf rotated his head slightly so that he could peer in the direction Buck was pointing without being obvious."

Three men dressed in dark clothes were crouching next to a patch of mesquite staring at them. Suddenly, they all started running.

"Hot damn," Buck said. "Let's get in the buggy and track them down."

Joe was already moving toward the Jeep. Buck was alongside of him.

Mac smirked at Wolf.

"You gonna sit this one out?"

Wolf took a deep breath and shook his head.

"I got this," he said. "I'll get that one."

He took off at a sprint after the fleeing man and wondered how Pike was doing.

***

LAST GASP GULCH GHOST TOWN
UNINCORPORATED YUMA COUNTY, ARIZONA

Bray felt the trickle of blood pouring down from his nose and ruptured lips. The rough, gravelly dirt tore into his knees. His hands were tied behind him with extra-strength zip-locks. They hadn't bought his story that they were just a couple of lovers making out under the velvet sky. Not when they had a laptop and all that surveillance equipment.

Everything that they needed, except a gun.

Maureen screamed as one of the bikers squeezed her left breast. The red-headed guy they'd seen yesterday with Wolf and the other guy, the big fed in the restaurant stood about three feet in front of him. The big fed was saying that he could take care of them for him.

What the hell did he mean by that?

He's a federal officer, Bray thought. *He's not supposed to let them do this to us. Is he crooked?*

Unless…

Then it dawned on him. He must be on an undercover op.

"Let me take the two of them outta here," the big fed was saying. "I'll call my buddy and he'll find a nice spot in the desert here to plant 'em."

"We can plant them right here," the red-headed guy said. He reached into his waistband and removed a big Glock.

Maureen screamed again.

The red head walked over and pointed the muzzle of the gun at Bray's forehead.

"I'm sick of your bullshit," the red head said. "Now you tell the truth or you die. Why were you watching us?"

He's probably going to kill me anyway, Bray thought. *I need to buy some time so I can escape.*

But how?

Bray felt the muzzle jab his forehead. "Why were you watching us? Last chance, *pendajo*."

The hard steel felt cold against his skin, and Bray felt a surge of warmth engulf his groin.

Shit, he'd pissed himself.

But no one appeared to have noticed. Or cared.

"Or maybe I should let the boys here gang rape your girlfriend while you watch."

Bray said nothing.

"Or maybe I just cut her throat." The red headed man stepped over and caressed Maureen's face. "How about you, *Señorita.* You got something you want to tell me?"

She shook her head violently. "Don't touch me. Rob, do something."

The red headed man smiled.

"Aiee, she has spirit. I'll bet she is hot in bed, no? Maybe I try her out myself."

Bray shook his head. "Do what you want to her," he said. "But listen, I got information that's of value to you."

"What is it?"

Bray hesitated, debating what to say.

The red head smacked the side of his face. His fist felt like a club.

"Why were you watching us?"

"Okay, wait," he said. "We weren't watching you.

We were watching someone else."

Bray took in a deep breath. He had to tell.

"Steve Wolf," he said. "We were watching him."

"Wolf?"

"He's bullshitting," the big fed said.

"No," Bray said. "I'm not."

The red headed guy smacked him again.

This time Bray saw stars flash in front of his eyes, and then almost collapsed under a swarm of black dots.

"Please," he gasped. "Please don't kill me. I got something to trade."

"Trade?" The red head laughed. "Like what?"

"You promise to let me go if I tell you?"

The red headed man smiled. "Don't waste my time."

Bray felt another nudge from the muzzle of the gun.

"Come on," the red head said. "And it better be good."

"It is."

Bray's mind raced. He had one chance to stay alive, and he decided to go for it.

"You've got a Judas among you." He spoke quickly and blurted the next part out. "That guy behind you. He's an undercover cop."

The big fed's face twisted into a scowl.

"That's bullshit!" he shouted.

The red head turned and glanced at him.

"A cop?" He arched an eyebrow and smiled. "Are you a cop, Pike?"

"Rivera, you know better than that," Pike said. "He's fucking lying."

"I'm not," Bray said. "His partner's Steve Wolf and he's in on it, too."

Rivera lowered the gun. "How do you know all this?"

Bray felt a surge of relief as he saw that black hole of the barrel recede.

"I know a lot more than that," he said. "And I can help you find him right now. I got a man watching him. I know his location."

"This is fucking crazy," Pike said, reaching his right hand inside his leather vest.

The red headed guy jumped in the air and did some kind of pivoting flying kick that collided with Pike's temple. The big fed's head jerked to the side and he went down like a house imploding. One of the other bikers scrambled over to him and kicked him in the back. Pike moaned, barely conscious. The biker reached inside the fed's vest and pulled out a huge revolver.

Rivera placed the gun into his waistband and turned back to Bray.

Bray felt a surge of relief, but it was short-lived.

Rivera reached into his pants pocket and pulled

out a wicked looking knife, which he flipped open with his thumb.

"Now, *amigo*, you will tell *El Tigre* all of it, and if you lie, *la garra del tigre*—the talon of the tiger will punish you."

"I won't lie to you," Bray said, his bladder going into spasms again.

"That is good," Rivera said. "If you tell me the truth, I am going to let you live."

Thank God, Bray thought.

"But first," Rivera said, "where is this other one? The one called Wolf?"

CHAPTER 15

UNINCORPORATED YUMA COUNTY
ARIZONA

Wolf finished pulling the heavy-duty plastic zip-lock around the man's wrists and turned to Buck and the others.

"Okay," Wolf said. "We got 'em. Now the question is, what are we gonna do with them?"

"Turn 'em over to the Border Patrol, I guess," Buck said.

McNamara snorted. "And what'll they do? Just give 'em a notice to appear in six months and release them? Or maybe they'll put 'em on one of those midnight flights to Pittsburg or Miami."

"Miami," the one illegal said with a smile. He pronounced it me-ah-me. "*Quiero ir allí.*"

Wolf started to translate but McNamara cut him

off.

"I get the damn gist," he said, shaking his head. "Maybe it's better that Pierce did fire us. We're just beating our heads against the wall thinking we're making a difference down here."

"But the money was good," Joe said. "And it was fun while it lasted."

"Especially when they rented that chopper for me to do air surveillance," Ron added.

"Hey," McNamara said. "Vehicle approaching. You three spread out and stay out of sight."

Wolf glanced and saw a black van approaching. He told the three illegals in Spanish to face the Escalade and get down on their knees.

The three compiled without protest.

Wolf glanced back at approaching van, still unable to ascertain much about the driver or if it had any occupants. He thought about the SCCY and automatically bumped it with his elbow to reassure himself that it was still there. It was, and that brought a new set of concerns. If the approaching van were the authorities, and they did a routine pat down of him and Mac, Wolf would be an ex-con with a gun. Trying to pass it off to Mac or simply toss it under the cars was too risky.

Nothing to do but hope for the best, he thought, and bumped the pistol with his elbow again. He wasn't even sure if Pike could get him out of this one.

The van's driver flipped on the brights and it blinded Wolf momentarily, causing him to blink and look away. He heard the driver's door open and thought about taking cover or maybe drawing his pistol. Then he heard someone call him by name.

"Mr. Wolf, I need to talk to you."

If the familiarity of the voice weren't enough, the "Mr. Wolf" salutation sealed it.

Mitchell stepped out of the van as both Wolf and McNamara backpedaled out of the projected illumination of the headlights. Mitchell was wearing the same outfit, the baseball cap, the blue T-shirt, and the tan Dockers, as he had before.

"It's okay," Wolf said in a voice loud enough to alert the others. "It's Pike's partner."

"Well, cut them damn lights then," McNamara yelled. "You got us lit up like a Christmas tree."

"The lights stay on," Mitchell said, and then to Wolf: "Have you heard from Pike?"

"No," Wolf said. "We parted company at the hotel. Why?"

The special agent's mouth compressed into a straight line.

"He missed his hourly check in," Mitchell said. "He was supposed to text me."

"Not good," Wolf said. "I wanted to go with him,

but he cut me loose at the hotel."

"I know," Mitchell said. "I agreed at the time, but now I'm a bit worried."

Wolf considered the options and then said, "I can go in and see what's up. As far as they know, my ex-con creds were confirmed."

Mitchell gave his head a minute shake, frowned, and then pointed to the three men kneeling by the Cadillac.

"Who are they?"

"Illegals," McNamara said. "We apprehended them."

"You what?" Mitchell's tone was ripe with outrage. "You have no authority to do that."

"I got plenty of authority, buster," Mac shot back. "It's called a citizen's arrest."

Before Mitchell could respond, Wolf interceded.

"Look, let's quit splitting hairs here. Your partner could be in trouble. He said there were some real heavyweights involved in this."

"Yes," Mitchell said, still eying the three kneeling men. "This has all the earmarks of a section seven-twelve alpha."

"A what?" Wolf asked.

"Security breech," Mitchell replied. "He's never missed a check-in before."

"Then let's do something," Wolf said. "What does

your SOP say?"

"The book says I should wait, but my gut's telling me something's really wrong. They brought in the people who were watching you as well. At gunpoint."

Wolf was confused. "Are you talking about that Bray guy?"

Mitchell nodded. "They captured them about twenty-five minutes ago. A man and a woman. I think they were the same ones who were watching you at the restaurant."

"Watching me at the restaurant?" Wolf said. "Why didn't you tell me?"

"I told Pike. That's all I had to do."

Wolf felt like slugging the man, but didn't.

"Captured them?" he asked. "What do you mean?"

"They took them at gunpoint, and their Lexus R-three-fifty, into the ghost town."

"And you saw this?" Wolf asked.

Mitchell cocked his head back toward his van. "I have the latest in night-vision and telescopic technology."

"Well then use some of it to check on Pike," Wolf said.

Mitchell again shook his head fractionally.

"I'll have to call our supervisor for instructions. "If he feels it necessary, we should be able to mobilize a force."

"What about the Yuma SWAT Team?" Wolf asked. "They're closer."

Mitchell shook his head, his mouth pursed into a pucker of disdain. "We don't like to involve the locals. It's a possibility, but a remote one. Besides, I've been listening to the police band. Their units are tied up with that flood of illegals that's already running loose. Who knows how long it would take them to mobilize, even they *were* to assist us."

Great, Wolf thought. *Pike's life is on the line and this idiot is worried about some jurisdictional crap.* "How soon can you get your SWAT team here them?"

"A federal team?" Mitchell's puckered lips drew back into a thin one. "Soon. But it may take more than an hour or an hour and a half. I'll have to my supervisor contact the Bureau to see if they have a team they can gather."

"You call that soon?" McNamara said. "Sounds like a damn merry-go-round."

"If Pike's in trouble, he may not have an hour," Wolf said.

Mitchell's mouth puckered again. "Listen, you don't' understand the way things work. I have to go through proper channels."

"Believe me, I know all about those proper channels," Wolf said. He recalled his last time in Iraq, and then some. "They're about as efficiently as our orderly withdrawal from Afghanistan back in August. Usually way too little, and way too late."

"Nevertheless, I'm duty bound—"

"Duty bound shit," McNamara said. "We've got a team right here. Let us go in and get them out. Covert op."

"Absolutely not," Mitchell said. "Some amateurs mudding around can only gum up the works. I forbid it. I absolutely forbid it."

"Amateurs?" McNamara said. "Who the hell do you think you're talking to?"

Wolf put his hand on Mac's arm. It was rigid.

"Mac, assemble the team," Wolf said. "We're going in now."

"Like hell," Mitchell said. "No way."

"Hell's gonna be your next stop if you try to stop us." Mac said.

Mitchell's eyes darted from McNamara to Wolf, and then back to Mac. "I'm warning you—"

McNamara glanced beyond them, "Warn us later. We got more company, and it looks like they're coming in hot."

All three of them turned and watched the rapid approach of two vehicles, both Lexus SUV's. Once again, the darkness obscured the visibility of any occupants through the windshield, but from the speed of approach, it was evident that this was something of a hostile nature.

Buck's voice boomed from beyond in the darkness: "Hostiles inbound. Two vehicles from the highway. High rate of speed."

McNamara and Wolf immediately ran for the cover of the vehicles.

***

Bray strained to see through the windshield of the Lexus as it sped over the uneven ground toward the slight hill. It hit a rut of some sort and bounced, sending all the occupants except him bouncing up against the roof. He was secured by the seatbelt, thank God, but his tied hands were secured behind his back and his legs were bound at the knees and ankles. The three biker idiots squealed with glee and laughed.

It was a fucking game to them, and they were armed to the teeth.

So were the other three in Powers's SUV. He'd hated to betray Powers, talking him into an unsuspecting but uneventful surrender. If there had been a chance that the idiot might have been alert enough, and skilled enough to figure it out beforehand, Bray might have gambled on him. But Powers fell right into being captured before Bray could even entertain the fantasy of a rescue. Now they were both captives, with Maureen still back at the ghost town as a hostage. He'd seen another white girl there, too. She looked like she'd been worked over some, and Bray wondered about her.

Hell, he wondered about all of them, and what was to become of them once Wolf had been captured and brought back to Rivera.

I've got nothing left to bargain with, Bray thought, and the prospects of that scared him.

The Lexus' front end jerked upward, Bray saw a flash of darkened sky, and them it slammed down onto solid ground again and the headlights illuminated three vehicles in front of them. Four, actually, counting Wolf's motorcycle.

"Let's get 'em," one of the bikers yelled. He was a muscle-bound ox, and he was holding a bad-ass PSA-15. It looked like an undersized AR-15 and mean as hell.

The Lexus bottomed out as it bounced over another big rut and Bray felt his wet pants racking over the skin of his thighs.

This is going to be bad, he thought.

***

Wolf yelled for Mitchell to take cover, but the gawky fed just stood there like the perpetual deer in the headlights. Only these headlights most likely had something lethal in mind. Wolf drew out the SCCY and ran to the other side of Mac's Escalade as the first Lexus skidded to a stop, its rear end lurching sideways. One of the bikers jumped out of the passenger side brandishing a sawed-off shotgun. Another followed from the rear passenger side. This one was armed, too, but with a semi-automatic pistol. The driver got out as the other SUV came to an abrupt stop about ten feet away.

Mitchell had his gun out now, holding it down by his leg with his right hand. His left arm was extended and he was holding a badge case.

"Federal agent," he yelled out.

The fool, Wolf thought, and a split second later muzzle flashes burst from the biker's guns and the sound of a torrent of gunshot echoed in the night.

Mitchell grabbed his chest, twisted, and fell.

Wolf aimed at the closest adversary and squeezed off two rounds. The biker holding the sawed-off jerked slightly, then curled forward. His cohort quickly looked at his collapsing partner momentarily, and that gave Wolf enough time for target acquisition.

He fired again, and then again, losing count of how many rounds he'd squeezed off.

The second man fell.

More gunshots sounded, some louder than the others, and Wolf knew that Buck, Joe and, Ron must have opened up with their AR-15's from three different positions. Despite the onset of audio exclusion, Wolf could distinguish the piercing sounds of rounds penetrating the metal bodies of the vehicles, although whose cars were getting hit, he couldn't tell.

Probably all of them, he thought.

Two more biker adversaries fell. That left two more, as far as he knew. He scanned the area and saw one of them pop up, aim over the hood of the sideways Lexus, and let off a quick series of what sounded like AR-15 rounds. A green streak shot through the night from the other side and the adversary stiffened and fell.

A tracer round? Wolf thought, and then figured that Mac had probably given a few out to the boys. Remnants from his many wars.

The last biker reappeared, firing what appeared to be a mini-AR-15 with one hand as he worked his way to the driver's door of the first Lexus and opened it up. He turned and fired the gun inside the cab, striking someone there, then slid into the driver's seat and held his gun in his left hand, pointing it through the open space between the frame and the door. More rounds spat outward leaving a trail of hot, expended brass sailing outward. The vehicle lurched into reverse mode as he continued to fire. Wolf started to take aim, but suddenly Mac was there, out in the open off to the right, holding his Glock in a combat-ready

Weaver stance.

A series of rounds exploded from Mac's gun, looking like bursts of yellowish fire from the muzzle against the black velvet sky.

A close-knit grouping of holes spider-webbed the windshield of the Lexus

The man behind the wheel of the reversing SUV sagged out of sight, the mini-gun tumbling from his slack fingers. The vehicle continued to drive backwards for several feet, then slowed and stopped as it came upon the angled incline of the terrain. The driver plunged out.

All firing ceased and Wolf signaled to Mac to move forward to help clear the vehicles and check the assailants.

They moved forward quickly, kicking weapons away from the prone bodies and doing cursory checks for any signs of life. Find none, the closed in on the first vehicle. Its only occupant was a white guy who was trussed up like a captured animal.

"Don't hurt me," the man said.

He was leaning over and after Wolf checked the bonds securing him, both he and Mac left him there and moved to the second SUV, the one that had been traveling backwards. Wolf came to the fallen driver, who now lay on the ground a few feet from the open driver's door. Wolf kicked the mini-rifle away from the body. He saw that it was muscle-boy from before, and that he'd been firing a PSA-15, one of those pistol-sized AR-15's with a collapsible stock. Stooping without kneeling, Wolf thrust the finger of his left hand against the fallen man's open eye.

No reaction.

Mac was already at the second SUV. After checking the man in the rear passenger seat, he shut off the engine and looked at Wolf.

"This one's dead," he said. "Looks like a hostage. All tied up like the other one. That guy shot him as he got in the truck."

Wolf signaled an all clear and Buck, Joe, and Ron all came out from their covert positions.

"Nothing like a nice little fire fight in the evening to get the blood pumping," Buck said.

"Who were these fuckers?" Joe asked.

"Bikers," Wolf said. "They were part of the gang my partner, Pike, is working on."

He started to walk back to the tied-up man in the other SUV, but Ron called out.

"Casualty," he said.

Wolf glanced over and saw Ron kneeling by Mitchell, who was lying on his side. He told Buck and Joe to see about the guy who was tied up, and ran over to the fallen agent.

Blood was coursing from a wound in Mitchell's

right side. He was unconscious.

"I got compression bandage in my kit," Mac said, and ran to his Escalade.

Wolf pressed down on Mitchell's wound and spoke to him.

"Agent Mitchell, stay with me," Wolf shouted. "You're gonna be all right."

Mitchell didn't respond.

Ron had his finger on the man's carotid.

"Weak," he said.

Mac returned with the compression bandage and they ripped up Mitchell's shirt.

"Looks like a through and through," Mac said, applying the bandage. "Probably ruptured his intestines. We got to get him to a hospital fast."

They loaded him into the van, putting his wound-side down.

"As soon as you get him there, call in the cops," Wolf said.

Ron nodded and slid into the driver's seat. The engine ground for a few turns and then started.

Buck whistled and waved his arm.

Wolf and Mac headed over to the SUV at a run.

"This one's alive and tied up," Buck said.

"Who are you?" Wolf said. He saw the man's face was bruised and bloody and he smelled like fresh urine.

Mac took out his mini flashlight and shone it on the man's face.

Buck took out his knife and started to cut the zip-locks securing the man's hands.

"Thank you for saving me," the man said.

Buck cut the man's hands loose.

Mac was still shining the light shining on the bound man's face and it looked familiar to Wolf. He'd seen this guy before, but where?

A rumpled bag lay on the floor by the man's feet, and a black wig was partially out of it.

Then Mitchell's statement about the people following Wolf came back to him. They'd been driving a Lexus SUV. He grabbed the bag and emptied the contents. A woman's wig with long black hair fell out, along with a pair of oversized glasses, and a lot of makeup. A picture was starting to come together.

Buck was working his knife over the zip-lock securing the man's knees.

"Hold on, Buck," Wolf said. "What's your name?"

The man hesitated, his jaw quivering. He made no reply.

"It's Bray, isn't it?" Wolf said.

The man still refused to answer.

"Bray?" McNamara said. "The son of a bitch that's been following us."

Wolf nodded.

McNamara placed his hand on Buck's arm and gently pulled him away. Mac then insinuated himself about an inch from Bray's face and grabbed the other man's jaw in his powerful fingers.

"Okay, asshole," McNamara said, his voice heavy with implied menace. "You got one chance to talk or I'm gonna make you wish you were never born."

Bray's breathing was shallow and rapid now. It looked like he'd already been taken to the brink and was now broken. Tears streamed down his face as he spoke.

"All right," he said. "I'll talk, just don't hurt me, okay?"

***

LAST GASP GULCH GHOST TOWN
UNINCORPORATED YUMA COUNTY, ARIZONA

The sounds of the gunshots had ceased, but Rivera couldn't shake the uneasy feeling. Perhaps fifteen minutes had passed. Should he send somebody to check on them, or go himself?

No, he thought. *El Tigre* is in command, and my place is here. Still, the lure of combat, the taste of danger caressed his face like the hands of a siren.

Things were getting more fucked up by the minute. He was watching as Martín, Paco, and Fernando herded the thirty-five *testarudos* into the big trailer truck. The product could be extracted later. The best course of action would be to get them out of here for now, away from this area. Soon it would be swarming with police and Border Patrol and he couldn't afford to get caught. Europa approached him.

"Griggas is here," the slender man said. "He wants to know what's going on."

"Tell him I'll talk to him in a bit," Rivera said. "Have you heard from your men yet? I heard gunshots."

"Yeah," Europa said. "They texted me. Everything's cool. They had to shoot a couple of them, but they're bringing Wolf back now."

"Good," Rivera said. His head swiveled from side to side. "Shit, where's Esteban?"

Europa shrugged. "Maybe he's trying his luck with that chick again." He smirked. "Want me to go look for him?"

"No," Rivera said. "I will find him. Bring Wolf to the place where we have Pike and the women."

"Europa smirked. "Whaddya wanna bet you'll find Esteban there?"

I am counting on that, Rivera thought.

***

It was risky, but it was their only chance. From what Bray had told them, *El Tigre* had three hostages: Pike, a young woman in hospital scrubs, and Bray's operative, Maureen. He was also expecting a group of illegals, internally carrying loads of drugs, and some kind of big payoff. Then he was going to take off back to Mexico.

Wolf and Mac left Bray tied up in the SUV and walked out of earshot.

"This sounds pretty bad," McNamara said. "Maybe we should back off and hope that Mitchell can send a react-team."

Wolf debated the situation in his mind. He knew what Mac was suggesting was the most sensible thing, but if *El Tigre* took the hostages back across the border, it was the end for them, and it wouldn't be a pleasant one for Pike.

He shook his head. "Mitchell's down for the count. I gotta go in. I've got to try to get them out."

"You sure?"

Wolf nodded. "I've got to. Pike saved my life back in North Carolina. I owe it to him to try."

Mac clicked his tongue. "We're way outnumbered and outgunned. Won't be a milk run, that's for sure, but I'm ready. I imagine Buck and Joe are, too."

"I can't expect you guys to go with. You guys have done enough."

"We ain't done shit yet," Buck said, inserting himself into the conversation. "Besides, I'm in the mood to kick ass and take no names."

"Me, too," Joe said, his dark face shiny with sweat.

"Let's roll."

Wolf looked to each of them.

"Band of brothers," he said, recalling the line from *Henry the V.*

***

After securing the three illegals to the floor shackles in Mac's Escalade, Wolf told them in Spanish that the police were on the way and to tell them what they'd seen as far as the shootout.

"*Ahora son testigos importantes*," he said. "*Pueden solicitar asilo político.*"

The one who'd expressed interest in going to Miami grinned. "*Gracias, señor.*"

Whether they'd be deported or not, Wolf didn't know, but at least they could corroborate what happened when the police got there.

Then Wolf called in the location of the shootout on Joe's cell phone, giving a quick summary and telling them to send the troops. The dispatcher demanded that he stay on the line until the units arrived, but Wolf refused.

"Sorry, ma'am, no can do," Wolf said. "My partner's a federal agent and he's in danger. Send the troops now."

He then set the phone down, leaving the connection open, so the police could use their telemetry to zero on it. Hopefully, they'd get there sooner and not later.

Joe had been less than happy about the prospects of leaving his phone, but Mac clapped him on the shoulder and said, "Combat loss, brother."

Wolf considered taking Pike's advice and wiping and dropping the SCCY, but decided to keep it with him for the time being. He had only four rounds left. You could never have too much ammunition in a fire fight, and Mac offered to give him a Beretta 92F from the go-bag in the Escalade, but Wolf declined. He was sure, judging from the amount of firepower the dead bikers had, that the rest of them would be well armed. Mac and the others would need all the firepower they could muster. Buck suggested taking some of their dead adversary's weapons, but Wolf nixed that idea as well. There would be too much confusion when it came time to sort out who shot who. The authorities would most likely lock them all up while sorted things out and tested everything. Having their fingerprints or DNA on a weapon that was used in a homicide was a definite no-no. Wolf thought about his experience in Iraq, the court martial, the prison time… He didn't want to face the prospect of going through all that again, much less get Mac and the others in trouble. This was his fight, and he knew he had to try. No other choice… He owed it to Pike. The man had, as he'd said so many times, saved Wolf's life. He just hoped his decision about leaving the guns wouldn't come back to haunt him.

"All right," Wolf said to Mac, who was driving Bray's Lexus. "Slow down and let me out up there."

"Steve's getting out," Mac said into his phone. "Get ready."

Get ready. One of the first jump commands on the plane.

Stand up, hook up, shuffle to the door, Wolf told himself. How many times had he done that in training and in ops?

Too many to count.

He opened the door of the Lexus and anticipated the stealthiest way to exit. The vehicle had a running board so as Mac slowed down, Wolf slipped out, shut the door behind him, and stood on the rail.

"Please," Bray said from behind him. "Let me out here. Don't take me back in there."

"Shut up and stay down," Mac said to him. "You'll be all right."

Wolf could hear Bray sobbing from his place on the floor in back.

"All right," he said. "Slow it down a little bit."

"Nice and easy," Mac said.

"I'll call you when I have Pike and the girl." With that, Wolf jumped off the running board, did a few rapid stutter-steps, and then dashed to the cover area between two decrepit buildings. He had the night vision-goggles on up on his head and he flipped them down now. Mitchell hadn't been lying when he'd told them he had the latest in surveillance tech gadgets.

The green-tinted world came to life in front of Wolf as he ran to the corner of one of the dilapidated structures.

Now, he thought. *To find the hostages before the fun begins.*

***

Rivera was heading toward the building where they'd stashed Pike and the two women certain that Cortez Jr. would be there, the fat *hijo de puta*. Things were moving fast and it was time to improvise. Then, he heard Griggas call to him.

"Rivera," Griggas yelled. "What the hell's going on?"

Rivera turned and saw the lanky anglo moving toward him in the middle of the dusty street. He had his two bodyguards with him and one was carrying the usual leather briefcase. It had to be full of cash.

It would make a nice nest egg to start over with, Rivera thought. *Since I am going to be on my own.*

He waited.

Griggas got closer, within about three feet. He was huffing and puffing.

"What the hell's going on?" he asked. "Where's the stuff?"

Rivera considered his answer carefully, and then decided on a course of action.

"We have not extracted it yet. It took longer than

expected to make the crossing. I have instructed my men to lock up the mules in the long truck. We will move them to a new location and then get the product for you."

"All right," Griggas said. "But what else is happening? I heard some gun shots down the highway."

"Unfortunately," Rivera said. "We have been compromised. We have captured a DEA agent who infiltrated your network."

"What?" Griggas said. "Who?"

"He goes by the name Pike. *¿Lo conoces?*"

"What?"

"You know him?"

Griggas shook his head. "I don't think so. Where's he at?"

"Over here," Rivera said. "Come with me, but we must hurry."

As the three of them fell into step behind him, *El Tigre* smiled and reached into his pocket for the *la garra del tigre*—the talon of the tiger.

***

Wolf crept between the remnants of two old buildings. The one on his left had practically collapsed but the one on his right seemed structurally sound. Perhaps fifty yards away on what had once probably been called the main street he saw a semi tractor-trailer. A group of the bikers and three other men had pushed what appeared to be a bunch of illegals inside and were securing the trailer's back doors.

He flipped up the goggles and rubbed the fingers of his left hand in the dirt. After gathering a handful, he smeared it over his sweat-covered cheekbones, and chin to offset the possibility of providing a distinct a target. The goggles covered his forehead.

As he gazed out through the break between the structures, he saw something that gave him hope. A dozen motorcycles were parked along the street, along with a Dodge charger and a Corvette. Wolf couldn't tell the color in the darkness, but it could be red. He remembered that Mac had said the Pierce girl had a red Corvette. He had to be getting close.

Four men were walking down the street from the direction of the trailer-truck. One of them was *El Tigre*. The other three he didn't know. The guy in the middle was thin and the other two were tall, burly, and armed. One of the good-sized ones carried a briefcase. They appeared to be heading toward an adjacent structure—another full-sized brick building that had a faded sign above the entrance. The letters could barely be discerned, but spelled out *BANK*.

Must be a payoff, he thought. An appropriate place for that.

And a fortuitous one, if he could get the drop on them, capture *El Tigre*, and then force him to tell where Pike was. And the Pierce girl, too, if they had her. Bray had also said they were holding his female associate.

Ms. Tonya Knight, Wolf reflected with a degree of irony.

He was tired of being played for a fool by these assholes. Once he had Pike and the others safely extricated, he'd have a little talk with Mr. Bray... Find out who was behind this new surveillance. He'd thought all of that was over when they'd put old Von Dien down for the count. A quick memory of the rich man's helicopter exploding into a fireball and plunging out of sight flashed in his mind's eye. How was all this connected?

The voices of the four men grew louder.

"They are in there," *El Tigre* said. He gestured toward the bank building.

Paydirt, Wolf thought. *That has to be it.*

He straightened ups and ran back down the passageway to the rear of the brick building.

It was time for him to make his own withdrawal.

He stopped and held his phone to his mouth and whispered into it, "Mac, I think I'm close. Start the diversion."

"Roger that."

***

Gunshots will be too noticeable, *El Tigre* thought as he pointed to the entranceway.

The front doors were gone, but in their place was

a make-shift wooden barrier of dilapidated plywood.

"In there," Rivera said, pausing to grab the plywood and move it off to the side.

"Do you have a flashlight?" he asked Griggas.

"Of course not," the other man said.

"Then use mine." Rivera handed him a mini-mag. "There is debris in there. You might trip."

"Are they in there?" Griggas asked.

"But of course," Rivera said, and stood back, holding his left arm with implied magnanimity, gesturing out for the three to enter first.

Then *El Tigre* reached in his pocket and withdrew the tiger's talon, flipping it open while he still held it down by his thigh. The sound of gunshots would be too noticeable, and the talon would be quiet and efficient.

It was time to make his move.

But just as they started to go inside, a loud crash came from the other end of the street, down by the semi. All three of them stopped and Griggas said, "What was that?"

"Looks like a car crashed into the semi," one of his bodyguards said.

"Shit," Griggas muttered. "Hank, go down there and see what's what."

The bodyguard who was not carrying the briefcase turned.

"And get the car," Griggas yelled after him.

"Wait. My men can handle it," *El Tigre* said. "Whatever it is."

He had lost the element of surprise, his edge.

Suddenly the sounds of gunshots—rifle rounds, ripped through the night air.

"Sure they can," Griggas said, his tone laden with sarcasm. "In the meantime, I'm getting out of here."

"Not yet," *El Tigre* said. "It is too dangerous."

Griggas ignored him, turned and started to walk away. The second bodyguard, the one with the briefcase turned to follow.

More gunshots erupted, and *El Tigre* flipped the talon closed, jammed it back into his pocket, and withdrew the long-barreled revolver he'd taken from Pike.

A few more gunshots won't matter now, he thought.

***

Wolf had pulled three of the planks off the rear entrance to the bank building and peered inside, flipping the night-vision goggles down. The room was capacious and empty, except for piles of detritus strewn in various places on the floor. He ducked under the sole remaining plank and entered, feeling dismay that he hadn't found the hostages.

Three gun shots reverberated in the night from outside the building, followed by several more. These sounded way too close. It couldn't be the fire fight that Mac, Buck, and Joe had initiated. That was farther down the street by near the semi. He continued forward a few steps and heard something.

It was a gasp, followed by sobbing.

"No, no, leave me alone, you animal."

It was a woman's voice.

Wolf heard a solid thump, like a body being thrown to the floor.

Turning, he looked into an adjacent room and saw a body lying on the old wooden floor... A woman. She was naked. He looked closer and the lines of her body became more distinct. Her figure was voluptuous.

Tonya Knight, Wolf thought.

He pulled out the SCCY, intent on taking out whoever was in there threatening her. More shots echoed from right outside. Torn between checking on the hostages and taking a look at the ongoing firefight in the street, he decided on the former.

Take out the immediate threat, he thought.

If Pike was alive, he could free him and have him take the women out the back way. Wolf entered the room with caution, advancing with the small pistol held at combat ready, swiveling his head from side to side. He gazed to his left and saw two more figures lying on the floor, their arms tightly bound behind their backs. One was Pike, the other another female, this one fully clothed in some sort of hospital scrubs.

It had to be Pierce's daughter.

What was her name? Mac had told him.

He started to rotate back when a flicker of movement flashed to his right and he turned. The image of a green-tinctured form—a large, flabby man was suddenly visible inside the visor. He was naked from the waist down and holding a two-by-four like a club.

Wolf whirled and fired a round. The flabby man jerked and an inky blackness beginning to blossom on the front of the shirt stretched over his big gut. He grimaced, raised the board again, and lumbered forward.

Wolf fired again, this time double tapping center mass. The man still kept advancing and Wolf fired what he knew was his last round into the center of the wide forehead.

The advancing adversary dropped like he'd been pole-axed.

Wolf's ears were ringing. He pivoted just in time to feel the slice of a blade slit through the uppermost part of his right shoulder. The green image of *El Tigre*, holding some kind of hooked knife appeared in the night-vision goggles. Wolf threw the now-empty SCCY at the man and it hit him in the face. He stumbled backwards, his arms flailing as he tried to keep his balance, but failed, tripping over one of the piles of loose garbage. He was wearing night-vision goggles as well. Wolf turned and grabbed the board that the other adversary had used. After picking it up, he turned and saw *El Tigre* on his feet, advancing. His mouth, visible under the projecting lenses, twisted into a smile.

"You cannot escape," he said. "And did I not tell you before that we would one day spar?"

Wolf said nothing. He stepped back into the room with the hostages. His feet made crunching sounds on the littered surface, but the move made it necessary for his opponent to come through the narrow aperture. It would limit his movement, which was a small advantage. Wolf hoped *El Tigre* didn't have a gun.

But if he did, he would have already used it, he told himself.

His move would also confine him to a smaller space, but both of their movements would be limited. He was fighting a man with a knife.

Not good.

But instead of advancing, *El Tigre* stepped back and kicked at the garbage pile that had caused him to trip before.

He beckoned Wolf to come to him, and that's when Wolf saw the spreading dark stain on his adversary's left side.

Blood?

The gunshots before, the close ones… Maybe he'd been shot.

Wolf moved forward, using the board like a combat rifle, thrusting it outward.

El Tigre danced back, careful to maintain his footing this time. He swatted the end of the board away, and swung the blade in an arc. Wolf pulled back just in time, and swung the board in a downward motion. He felt it connect with something.

A leg, perhaps?

El Tigre grunted and lurched forward, swinging the hooked blade back and forth. Wolf felt it tear into the underside of his left forearm. He grabbed at the other man's right wrist, seizing it with both hands. *El Tigre* smashed his left fist into Wolf's temple, and the goggles went flying. Everything reverted to the pervasive darkness right before a burst of white light flashed inside Wolf's head. He managed to maintain his grip on the other man's wrist as they both fell to the floor. Particles of dust filled Wolf's nose and mouth. His eyes stung with grit, too. The two of them rolled over, kneeing each other. *El Tigre* pounded the right side of Wolf's face with blow after blow. He tasted blood mixed with the filth inside his mouth.

Ground game, he thought. *Concentrate on the knife. They're only arm punches.*

Another one collided with his cheekbone and Wolf felt lightheaded again.

Slowly, he managed to twist the other man's clenched hand upward. The punches stopped as *El Tigre* brought his left hand onto Wolf's, trying to pry the grip loose. They struggled together like ungainly lovers on the floor, until Wolf managed to gain the uppermost position and then pushed down with all of his strength. He felt the cluster of hands connect with something.

The other man's neck?

With a surge of strength, Wolf raked the blade to his left, encountering a substantial cutting resistance, and then nothing.

El Tigre made a gasping sound and Wolf felt a sudden river of warmth engulf his fists. The hands gripping Wolf's went slack, then fell away. Wolf stayed where he was until he felt the choking breaths of his adversary finally cease.

The gunshots continued to echo down the street and then stopped.

No time to be a slacker, he thought, and rolled off. His hand brushed something and it was the discarded pair of night-vision goggles. Wolf slipped them back on and looked at *El Tigre*. He lay on his back his open, vacant eyes stared up at the ceiling. The wound across his throat was a jagged line.

Wolf felt his pockets for his cell phone but couldn't find it. Frantically, he scanned the room, and then he saw it. Crawling over to pick it up, he pressed the button to call Mac.

After hearing McNamara's quick response, Wolf said, "Sit-rep."

"It's all over but the crying," McNamara said. "We told the punks they were surrounded, keep on firing, took out a couple of bad-ass Mexicanos, and the rest of them gave up quicker than the Saddam Hussein's army. We got 'em laid out by the truck."

Wolf breathed a sigh of relief.

"Any sign of the hostages?"

"I found them," he said. "Let me check to see if they're okay."

"Okay," McNamara said. "Where you at exactly?"

Wolf told him.

"Okay, I'll work my way down there in a bit. The cavalry's on its way. And if you're near a window, take look-see."

Wolf managed to stand and staggered into the room to the three hostages. He checked each one, finding them all conscious and alive.

"I'm here to help you," he said, searching for the right words to reassure them. "It's over now. Don't worry."

The Pierce girl let out a cry of relief that segued

into a hiccupping series of sobs.

Pike groaned, and Wolf saw that the big fed had been badly beaten, but he still managed to deliver one of his usual quips.

"What the hell took you so long, airborne?"

Wolf wanted to laugh, but his face hurt too much. He used the hooked knife to cut him loose. The Pierce girl was next. She said her face was bruised, but she was all right. He went to Maureen, or Ms. Knight, who made no effort to cover herself either above or below after Wolf freed her hands. Instead, she affected a playmate-like pose and laughed.

"I know you've got those goggles on," she said. "So tell me, how do I look in green? Like the She Hulk?"

Wolf told her she looked good and that he'd try to find her clothes.

This is one tough chick, he thought.

After helping them outside, the coolness of the night air revived all of them. Three bodies lay in the street in twisted, unnatural positions. Wolf went to check them and saw they were all dead. A leather briefcase sat upright off to the side. Wolf didn't touch it. He flipped up the goggles and let his eyes get used to the natural conditions. There was a three-quarter moon and the sky was lit with a velvety darkness. In the distance Wolf could see a caravan of oscillating red and blue lights winding its way along the twisted ribbon of highway toward them.

"The cavalry's here," Wolf said, then added, "The police. You're safe."

The Pierce girl's sobbing had ceased, at least for the moment and Wolf was thankful for that. He felt Pike tug on his arm.

"Hey, brother," the big fed said. "Don't forget. Wipe it and drop."

Wolf chuckled.

"Already done," he said.

***

The artificial glow from the various vehicular headlights and the portable floodlights the police had set up brightened the dilapidated area like an artificial sunrise. A female paramedic from one of the ambulances was applying a butterfly bandage to the jagged cut on Pike's right eyebrow. She'd just finished bandaged his ribs.

Mac, Buck, and Joe stood off to one side. Sandra Pierce was chatting on a cell phone to her parents. She waved at Mac and nodded her head emphatically.

"For a kid who's been through the wringer," Wolf said, "she seems to be doing okay."

"Time will tell," McNamara said. "But her father's already offered to hire us all as body guards for his family."

"And the money's good," Buck said. "Real good."

"Good," Joe said with a wide grin. "I'll need it to buy a new cell phone."

Maureen was apparently the least injured of the three of hostages. She was leaning on the side of the ambulance smoking a cigarette. Bray stood beside her.

He and I are going to have that long talk, Wolf thought. *Soon.*

And if that didn't work, he knew Special Agent Franker, not to mention Pike, would apply the necessary leverage.

"See?" Buck said. "I told you the cavalry would get here."

"Cavalry hell," Joe said. "The *infantry*."

Wolf managed to flash a tired smile, but he knew they were both worried. They'd all put themselves on the line for him.

We few, we happy few, we band of brothers…

He felt honored to stand beside such men. But at what price?

"Well, whatever you want to call them," he said. "With all these dead bodies and illegals, don't be surprised if we're the ones who end up in custody tonight. And just me saying thanks doesn't seem very adequate."

None of the four of them spoke for several seconds, and then Mac said, "Aw, shit. Sometimes you gotta do what you gotta do, and to hell with the consequences. I look over there at that little gal talking to her daddy and I know we did the right thing."

"Damn straight," Buck added. "I ain't had so much fun since my first Christmas in Fallujah."

"Mac," Joe said. "You think you can get your buddy Manny to post bond for us?"

"You ain't gonna have to worry none about that," Pike said, staggering over to them using a long piece of wood as a makeshift cane. He reached out and placed a hand on Joe's shoulder to steady himself. They were about the same height. "If I can borrow one of your cell phones, I'll make the call and keep us all footloose and fancy free."

"Sounds like a plan," Mac said, handing his over.

Pike started to punch in a number, stopped, and winced.

"By the way, those two are both under arrest." Pike pointed to Bray and Maureen. "Obstructing, conspiracy, and attempted murder."

Neither of them reacted, but Bray placed his hand on her shoulder. She brushed it away with an emphatic push.

"You know," Pike said, continuing to glare at Bray. "He was the one that dimed me out to *El Tigre* and caused all this. Sold his girlfriend there down the river, too."

"Bullshit," Bray said. "I'm the real victim here. And

I don't want to say nothing until I call my lawyer."

Maureen glared at him.

"You know," Pike said. "If I wasn't feeling so damn poorly, I'd punch that son of a bitch right in the nose."

"Allow me," Wolf said.

He stepped over toward Bray and told him to put up his hands.

"Don't you touch me," Bray said. "I'll have you arrested… I'll sue your ass. I'll—" He stopped and tears ran down his cheeks.

Wolf hesitated, not because of the threat, but hitting this creep, who was covered with his own excrement, seemed like something a bully would do.

Bray's breathing was rapid.

"Careful, Steve," Mac said. "He might piss himself again."

Suddenly Maureen pivoted, and drove her right fist into Bray's groin.

He grimaced, made a gurgling sound, and then sank to his knees holding the front of his stained Dockers. A couple of uniformed officers rushed forward to separate them.

Maureen then jumped back and held up her hands.

"Hey, that asshole deserved it," she said, flashing an alluring smile. "He don't know how to treat a lady."

"I agree, *Ms. Knight*," Wolf said, using the inflection to emphasize the irony. "But let's get one thing straight. You ain't no lady."

"That's for sure," Pike said and continued to dial. "But I got a feeling, if she cooperates, I can talk to the judge and he'll go real easy on her."

He winked.

Maureen clasped her teeth over her lower lip for a moment, gazed his way, and then smiled once again.

"Sounds like a plan," she said.

When Pike had finished dialing, he lifted the phone to his ear and waited a few seconds. Someone answered on the other end. Pike rattled off his name and a bunch of what sounded like coded numbers, waited, then looked over all of them and held up his thumb.

"I need five get out of jail free cards," he said into the phone. "Well, better make that six. We got a lot of dead bodies to account for. I'm probably gonna need one, too. And, boss, we need to get to work on that other thing I told you about, too."

He listened some more and then said, "Yeah, I'm sure." He looked straight at Wolf and winked. "He's a good dude. And, hell, the guy saved my life. Mitchell's, too. He's a real hero. Won the silver star. And... he's airborne."

All the way, Wolf thought. *Maybe this isn't going to turn out so bad after all.*

A LOOK AT BOOK SEVEN: DEVIL'S RECKONING

It's just like they say... the real trouble is only just beginning.

Ex-army ranger Steve Wolf is hoping to clear his name for a war crime he didn't commit. But when a mysterious fixture in his life resurfaces with a dire warning for him and his mentor, Big Jim McNamara, he discovers that his past has once again come back to haunt him. Wolf is being stalked by powerfully corrupt foes—plural.

With a vicious drug lord's bounty on his head and another powerful enemy dispatching a pair of resourceful agents to ensure his demise, Wolf struggles to prepare himself for a once-in-a-lifetime shot at the coveted MMA heavyweight championship of the world—a dream achievement and his only chance at paying the outrageous legal fees he's racked up trying to clear his name.

When bodies start dropping and Wolf finds himself stalked by ruthless predators hellbent on having him in their sights, he must battle the odds in a desperate fight for survival. But in a deadly game of winner takes all, are the only stakes truly life or death?

COMING NOVEMBER 2022

ABOUT THE AUTHOR

Michael A. Black is the author of 36 books and over 100 short stories and articles. A decorated police officer in the south suburbs of Chicago, he worked for over thirty-two years in various capacities including patrol supervisor, SWAT team leader, investigations, and tactical operations before retiring in April of 2011.

A long time practitioner of the martial arts, Black holds a black belt in Tae Kwon Do from Ki Ka Won Academy in Seoul, Korea. He has a Bachelor of Arts degree in English from Northern Illinois University and a Master of Fine Arts in Fiction Writing from Columbia College, Chicago. In 2010 he was awarded the Cook County Medal of Merit by Cook County Sheriff Tom Dart. Black wrote his first short story in the sixth grade and credits his then teacher for instilling within him the determination to keep writing when she told him never to try writing again.

Black has since been published in several genres including mystery, thriller, sci-fi, westerns, police procedurals, mainstream, pulp fiction, horror, and historical fiction. His Ron Shade series, featuring the Chicago-based kickboxing private eye, has won several awards, as has his police procedural series featuring Frank Leal and Olivia Hart. He also wrote two novels with television star Richard Belzer, I Am Not a Cop and I Am Not a Psychic. Black writes under numerous pseudonyms and pens The Executioner series under the name Don Pendleton. His Executioner novel, Fatal Prescription, won the Best Original Novel Scribe Award given by the International Media Tie-In Writers Association in 2018.

His current books are Blood Trails, a cutting edge police procedural in the tradition of the late Michael Crichton, and Legends of the West, which features a fictionalized account of the legendary and real life lawman, Bass Reeves. His newest Executioner novels are Dying Art, Stealth Assassins, and Cold Fury, all of which were nominees and finalists for Best Novel Scribe Awards. He is very active in animal rescue and animal welfare issues and has several cats.

Made in United States
North Haven, CT
22 October 2022